The Crystal Crown

DAN PAYNE

DEDICATION

For Emily

CHAPTERS

Desert and Blade

The Nullarbor desert shimmered with heat and thirst, but inside the car the summer sun paled next to the roiling force of her anger.

Throughout the long Australian summer afternoon white-hot fury had curdled into something resembling hate. But while anger makes us hasty, hatred is a slower emotion, taking its time to broil and grow. She felt no remorse for her actions, but she'd had plenty of time during the sweltering drive to regret not planning them better.

Jess McTiernan let the car roll to a stop beside the roadhouse. With a concentrated effort she released her white-knuckled grip on the steering wheel.

Outside the car the endless desert stretched to the horizon, a barren plain of red dust and sand and scrub brush, scorched flat and bare by eternal hot winds and remorseless sun. The horizon seemed flat enough to rule lines. Above, the sky was a crystalline blue unbroken by even a wisp of cloud. The worst extremes of the day were past, the sun lowering towards the horizon, but it was still a good forty degrees in the direct glare. The land was a dozen shades of red; even the scrub brush had an orange hue.

If there was ever a place that deserved the name "sunburnt land" this was surely it.

Jess sat for a moment in the car, reluctant to face the oppressive heat, but after eight hours of driving the tightly coiled springs of her legs desperately needed to unwind. The air conditioner in the old Taurus had fought valiantly, but now, with the engine off, the Australian summer would have its revenge. Already angry waves of heat beat through the windows. Jess took a final deep breath of lukewarm air, smelling the chemical taint of the air conditioner, before she cracked the door and stepped out into the baking afternoon.

The Yallara roadhouse sat on the plain like a wart on skin. The main structure was a long, low building, a cluster of adjoining buildings welded together and stranded in a sea of desert. A kiosk and shop anchored the complex, darkened with all the windows sheltered by canvas sails; attached was the restaurant and bar. A low garage stood open and barren to the right, a faded sign still readable and claiming, optimistically, "Service"; attached was a wire and timber pen for goats or camels, now mercifully unoccupied in the afternoon heat. The roadhouse was completed by two dusty petrol bowsers under an inadequate tin roof.

With the gentle hot breeze stirring up zephyrs of red dust, the place felt abandoned. She could only hope appearances were deceiving, as Yallara was the only source of petrol, food and water in reach. More than a hundred kilometres due west to the next roadhouse, and the needle on the fuel gauge was already nudging empty.

Jess stretched, her back popping as a man exited the kiosk and crossed the open space to the meagre shelter of the pumps. His eyes shaded from the actinic glare by a wide-brimmed, threadbare cotton hat, dressed in loose khaki shorts and shirt, he moved with an easy, energy-saving slouch evolved through years of heat and labour. If his beard was a little longer and a bit whiter than she remembered, if his arms, always tough, were slightly wirier, he was still the man she remembered from her many crossings. She pasted a false smile on her face and felt the makeup by her mouth crack. "Hi, Bruce."

"G'day," he responded. Several years at least since her last visit, but he seemed to remember her. "Jess, right? Still driving this old bastard. I thought it was just about done last time you came by."

"Not quite," said Jess. "Her pipes are so old the rubber's turned into chalk but she just keeps going."

They're common as shit in the States, had been her mechanic's professional opinion on the Taurus, but they were rare as hen's teeth here in Australia. Only eight thousand were ever imported, which she had considered a part of its charm. When the mechanic went on to explain that any parts would need to be shipped in, and replacing one pipe meant replacing all of them, and replacing the pipes meant replacing the engine, she had decided to sleep on it. Three years on, and she was still sleeping on it.

"So long as she doesn't die out on the road," Bruce said. "It's a long walk to the nearest servo. Full tank?"

"I'd better pick up a jerry as well," Jess said. She had left Melbourne in too much of a hurry to plan. "I don't have an empty."

"Just you today?" Bruce asked, as he busied himself with the pumps.

"Just me," Jess agreed. She didn't volunteer any more information and Bruce didn't ask. After a moment of uncomfortable silence, he jerked his head towards the buildings.

"Why don't you head on in? The air's on inside. Give Dot a yell, she'll make sure you can freshen up."

Jess needed no further encouragement. The hot air was dry but her thin shirt was starting to cling with sweat. When she stepped into the blessed cool of the kiosk she needed a moment to pull the material away from her skin.

The place hadn't changed. The same 60s-era formica counter, supporting the same honest-to-God cash register, the same visitor book Jess remembered from countless crossings. A quarter of the pages still blank. Decades-old brochures in a rack on the wall, souvenir knick-knacks on shelves that tourists would buy once and forever regret. Standing in pride of place was a rack of Australian Outback collector spoons and car bumper stickers reading "I survived the Nullarbor", and a chrome tree from which dangled a dozen plush kangaroos, each labelled "Made in China".

At Jess's call Bruce's wife, the indefatigable Dorothy, pushed through the bead curtain that separated the restaurant and bar from the shop front.

She bustled in with a cheerful greeting, familiar as if Jess had been here yesterday. "Hey-ho. Good to see you again. Here for the night or just passing?"

If Bruce was starting to show his years, Dot hadn't changed a bit: that leathery face had always looked ancient. "Can't stop today, Dot," Jess said with a smile. "Could do with some water and maybe a sandwich."

"We'll rustle something up. "

"How's business keeping?" Jess asked, as Dorothy shuffled to the ancient refrigerator rattling behind the counter.

"Well enough," said Dorothy. "There was a nice young couple stayed over last night, and we had a fair amount of through traffic yesterday. And there's always the rigs."

"Mindajee seems to have closed. A good thing you're still going."

"It's a crying shame. They were planning renovations, but the whole place was built out of asbestos, forced them to close. They're supposed to rebuild and re-open but they've been saying that for a year now."

Jess bought a half litre of cold spring water, grimacing as she counted out coins. Everything here cost at least twice city prices. Worth it to keep Bruce and Dot afloat. "Nundroo still open?"

"Last I heard."

Seven hundred kilometres side to side. While a full tank of petrol might get you across the Nullarbor, plenty of folks still tried the journey unprepared. Without Yallara, there'd be a lot more dead city people.

"You're sure you don't want to stay the night?" Dot placed the beaded bottle of water on the counter. "It'll be night soon, and you shouldn't drive the plain in the dark. Damned easy to run into a roo, and that'd kill your car, and maybe you."

Jess smiled. "I'll drive slow."

"Well, it's your choice," said Dot. "So where's your young man today?"

"He's back in Melbourne." She didn't want to talk about Mark or even think about him. But it was too late, his face had swum back into her mind, unbidden and unwelcome.

Dorothy peered short-sightedly at Jess and nodded. "Like that, is it."

Jess had done her best with her makeup, but the bruise had darkened and there was only so much foundation could do; it would pass scrutiny from a distance, but it couldn't hide the marks at close range. Her flash of anger at the intrusion fled just as rapidly. She could hardly blame the old woman for being observant, and Dot was respectful enough to say nothing more about it.

II

"Does your pay-phone still work?" Jess asked. She'd turned her out-of-reception mobile off hours ago.

"From time to time. Should be working today, the wind's turned northerly. Give it a try." Dot pointed to the back corner of the kiosk, where the battered burnt-orange phone sat on a plinth.

"Thanks," said Jess. Under the phone was a shelf on which sat an ancient Yellow Pages directory, which she ignored. It took her a minute to rummage together enough coins to make the call. She dialled the number from memory.

She listened to the ringing at the other end and fended off second thoughts. *This is a mistake.* She'd come this far on steely determination, but she wasn't sure she was ready to face arguments. The urge to put the handset down was becoming unbearable when, on the fourth ring, her call was answered.

"You've got Rebecca." The line was good and she might have been in the next room, rather than a thousand kilometres distant.

Jess took a deep breath. "Hi, Bec. It's Jess."

5

Bec sounded surprised. "How could I mistake that sexy husky voice? Thanks for brightening up my afternoon."

"Actually, what you're hearing is dust," said Jess. "But thanks."

"So what's up? I love you dearly, but Sunday afternoon's not my thing. Something couldn't wait for tomorrow? Wait, I know, you just couldn't bear to be without me."

This was as good an opening as any. Once she'd started the words came in a rush. "I won't be in the office tomorrow. I just... I wanted to let you know, before you found out from someone else. Before you heard rumours. I'm going home. I'm going back to Perth."

"Wow," said Bec. A momentary pause. "That was unexpected. Are you okay? What's happened?"

"It's Mark. We just... I had to get out. I know it's sudden, but I couldn't stay."

"Fighting again? Look, I appreciate you've put up with a lot of his shit," said Bec. "He's never driven you away before. What's he done this time?"

Jess opened her mouth to respond and realised she had no words ready.

She'd really tried with Mark. Ignored his growing disrespect and his anger. She'd forgiven his occasional affairs and his regular flings. She'd endured his belittling, his shouting, his threats. And for years she watched the man she married slowly turn into a stranger; someone she not only did not like, but more importantly did not understand.

She should have known better than to confront him, stumbling into the house in the early hours of Saturday, stinking of cigarettes and alcohol and perfume. But she was tired and angry, she'd been waiting for him almost ten hours, she'd had at least a couple of drinks herself, and her normal inhibitions had failed her. But her own angry questions had unleashed such an unexpected wellspring of rage and violence in him that it had terrified her.

It might still have been salvageable. Holes in plaster can be repaired,

6

raised voices fade and harsh words can be forgiven. But that was before he turned his violence against her. When he hit her, before slamming the den door in her face, she didn't wait. Within an hour she was packed, and within two she was gone.

The decision to return to her parents in Perth had been a long time coming but once made it felt inevitable. Thirty-six hours ago, and of her many regrets since, none of them were about leaving. The punch was the final straw, but it capped a mountain that seemed to have taken years to build, stone by stone.

But how to explain? Where to start? Jess didn't have the energy to put years of frustration into words. She was so damn tired.

"I don't want to talk about it," she said. "I won't change my mind and I'm not coming back. Not... not yet."

"I just want to be sure you're okay," said Bec. "What should I tell people?"

"Whatever you like. Someone will have to pick up my accounts." Jess paused for a moment, forced her mind to focus. "I've left a message for Rick. My resignation."

"He's not going to be happy," said Bec.

A smile played at the corner of Jess' mouth, there and then gone. "I expect he'll go ape-shit mental," said Jess. "He'll cope."

"Where are you now?" Bec asked. "Perth's a long drive."

"I'm on the road," said Jess. "Doesn't matter where. If Mark calls you, don't tell him where I'm going. He'll figure it out on his own but I don't want him following me."

"He may be my cousin, but apart from when he's been with you we barely speak. I like you a lot more than I like him. I won't say a word. But listen. You don't have to do this. Don't let him scare you away."

"He's not," said Jess, wondering if she was lying. "I'm just... going home."

"Perth isn't home," said Bec. "Not for you. Not any longer. You belong here. Come back, we'll find somewhere safe and private for you to stay. I've a spare room you can use for a few days until we get you sorted. I can talk to Rick, explain things. I'm sure we can smooth this over."

Jess blinked away tears. "I love you, you know that? Thanks. I just... I need some space."

"Just don't disappear on us. If you need time off, Rick'll be good for it. If not, I'll have a word with him, then he'll definitely be good for it. I know you — after a few days in Perth you'll be itching to come back. That whole damn city closes at eight, and you've never been a morning person. Seriously, what's in Perth that's worth going back for?"

"My parents are in Perth."

"Like you've talked to them more than three times in the last two years," said Bec. "I'm not giving up on you. I won't rest until you're back with your real family."

"I'll think about it," said Jess. "I'll call you."

"You better. I don't want to have to come across the country and hunt you down. And you know I will."

Jess gently placed the handset back on its cradle and stood for a moment. Rubbed at her eyes to wipe away the dust that was making them hot. Then she turned back to the front of the shop.

III

Dot was still behind the counter, busying herself with a ledger, but Jess was certain she'd heard every word. Jess swallowed against the dryness in her throat. "I'll take another couple of bottles. Still have a long way to go tonight."

The door to the kiosk banged open, admitting a blast of hot air and the smell of sand. Bruce had his hat off and was scratching at his forehead. "Dot? You got my binoculars there? Think I saw something out north.

Can't quite make it out."

The binoculars were tucked away under the counter, and Dorothy brought them around to her husband, accompanying him back to the door. Jess found herself tagging along. After the cool and dim interior, the brilliant sun outside threatened to blind her and fresh sweat beaded on her neck and back.

Bruce raised the glasses and peered towards the horizon. "That's not right," he said. "Not right at all." He handed the binoculars to Dorothy. "People out there, on foot. Don't know how they got out there by themselves, but they're at least a klick away. We can't let them walk. I'm going to grab the Jeep and bring them in."

"I'll call the docs," Dorothy said.

"Hold off. Let's at least get 'em under cover and get some water into them first." To Jess, he added, "Flying doctor service is free but it don't seem fair to call them out afore we know what's going on." He smiled affectionately at his wife. "You grab some cloths, get some water ready. I won't be more'n a few minutes."

"Mind if I tag along?" said Jess. "You might need a hand."

"I'd thank you for that," said Bruce. "Let's just grab the wheels. Dot, you get yourself back inside afore you give yourself sunstroke."

"I can look after myself very well, thank you," snapped Dorothy. "Think I'll head back inside out of this sun before I burn," she added, turning on her heel with dignity.

The Jeep was parked around the back of the buildings, covered with a dust sheet to protect the olive-green paint from sun glare. Jess helped Bruce pull the tarpaulin off. The Jeep was a classic model, open topped with a canvas cover rolled up in the back. The metal was hot to the touch. As they started off across the plain Jess found that the seats lacked belts; she braced herself with the roll cage as they bumped across the desert.

Out here the plain was empty apart from occasional scrub grass dotting the ground, but between the patches of grass were soft sand depressions which gave the Jeep a jolting vibration. Even at a moderate speed the hot wind felt refreshing.

The figures quickly resolved themselves as they approached. Too short to be adults, young and slim. Two exhausted children, clinging to each other and stumbling through the sand. Bruce brought the Jeep to a halt as they drew up alongside, and before the vehicle had stopped rolling Jess jumped out and ran to the youths.

Just children, a girl and a boy. The girl was no more than sixteen, lithe but still gangly. The boy was even younger, but it was he who supported the girl, one bony shoulder under her arm.

Jess approached the pair. "Let me help." She lifted the girl's other arm over her shoulder and took her weight; she was a paper doll, weighing even less than Jess expected. The boy tried to keep hold, glaring at Jess, but the girl slipped away from his arm. Relieved of his burden, the boy reeled and would have fallen, but by then Bruce was there to support him.

Together Jess and Bruce wrestled the children into the back of the Jeep. The children did not resist, although the boy's scowl never relented. Once reunited in the vehicle, he clung to his companion. The girl managed to whisper a rasping *thank you*, until Jess shushed her. "Don't speak. We have water and shade just a couple of minutes away."

Bruce set a dangerous speed across the uneven ground, the four occupants of the Jeep jostling from side to side. As they drove Jess examined their passengers. Both were coated in red dust, and both were the worse for wear; their faces were flushed, and while the boy's skin was slick with sweat, the girl's face was dry. Jess's first aid training was many years and another life ago and she struggled to recall what she'd learned. *Dry skin - sunstroke?*

The girl was too weak to do more than loll in the seat, and while the boy was trying to help her it was clear he wasn't much better off. Under the dust, he wore long sleeves and pants; a dark grey colour that must have absorbed the heat, but at least protected his skin from the scorching sun. The girl's clothing was less appropriate. It may have originally been a formal dress, now more bone-tan than white; the sleeves a translucent lace that would not have protected the skin of her arms. Volumes of billowing silk swirled around the girl's ankles. The kind of dress a girl would wear two or three times in her life, better suited to a ballroom than hiking through a hot desert. The train was ragged, and it appeared that they had tried to tear the fabric. The dress was probably awkward to walk in but it was unclear their efforts would have improved matters.

The Jeep pulled up to the lengthening shade of the buildings in a cloud of dust. Lifting the girl over the side of the tray almost proved beyond Jess. Somehow Jess managed to get the girl's feet under her, and once she was upright the going was easier.

Dot had already pulled a couple of sun-loungers into the kiosk, making the cluttered space even more crowded than it had been. The boy and the girl flopped bonelessly into the recliners. The girl's eyes fluttered closed. Jess knelt in alarm, but the girl's breath was strong and regular. The boy glared at the three of them in turn, and his hand waved weakly in the direction of his companion before falling back to his side.

"Christ," said Dot. She had bottles of water ready; the boy was able to hold one and take desperate swallows of the precious fluid. Jess had to trickle water slowly into the girl's mouth at first, but she quickly responded, her eyes opening and her throat working. Jess helped her until she was able to hold the bottle herself, then turned her attention to the girl's clothing.

Treatment for heatstroke is simple: provide fluids and bring the body temperature down as quickly as possible. A cool environment, a sponge bath — even an ice bath, if necessary, but that would require a bathtub. First step: loosen clothing.

Bruce was already assisting the boy to remove his long-sleeved top, revealing a singlet underneath. Lots of layers; he must have suffered in the heat.

The girl was going to be harder to deal with. The bodice was tight and topped with a high collar, laced behind her neck. Jess brushed aside the girl's shoulder-length chestnut hair and drew a hissing breath in surprise.

The girl had two small wounds at the base of her skull, fresh, the scabs still a dark red. The back of her neck was crusted with dried blood, but they weren't bleeding now. They weren't what was going to kill the girl first.

The collar was a futile cause. Sweat, blood and dust had caked the laces, making them swell and merge, and Jess couldn't tell where one lace began and another ended. "Dot, do you have scissors or a knife handy?"

Bruce looked up. The boy was sitting up in the lounger, drinking slowly but steadily from the bottle of water, his arms bare; colour was already starting to come back into his face. "Dot, keys," Bruce said.

Dot ducked around behind the counter and pulled a key ring out from under it, tossing it across to her husband in a jangle of metal.

Leaving the boy to look after himself for a moment, Bruce crossed to a glass-fronted cabinet near the door. A fine layer of dust coated the glass; merchandise an outback store was expected to stock, but few would ever buy. Camping gear, akubra hats, ropes, magnetic compasses, water bottles — and, in leather sheaths, a selection of bowie knives. Bruce opened the cabinet, retrieved a knife and brought it across to Jess.

"Any more folk out there?" Bruce returned to the boy's lounger. "Are you kids alone? How'd you get out there?"

The boy stared at him but made no sign that he had even understood the question. It was the girl who answered, her voice little above a whisper. "There is nobody else. We are alone." Her words were clearly pronounced but slightly accented. A foreigner with a prestigious school education.

The boy said something then; a long string of syllables, but not any language Jess knew. He stared at Jess, who was trying to get the knife under the laces of the girl's collar, and his hostility was palpable.

"You must forgive my brother," the girl said. "He knows no English." She looked across at the boy, then replied to him, a few short unrecognisable words, Jess assumed in the same language.

Under the sharp blade the laces at the girl's collar parted smoothly, and

12

Jess was able to put the knife aside and pull the edges of the collar apart. It surprised her when the dress split down the back, but after an initial hesitation she kept going; there was some kind of shift underneath. The girl did not object, weakly raising her arms to aid in its removal.

"I'm Jess, that gentleman is called Bruce and the lady is Dorothy. What's your name?"

"I am Vi," said the girl, pronouncing 'vee'. "And my... brother is named Aran."

Jess noticed the fractional pause, but let it slide. There were far more pressing questions. "What were you doing out there? Where are your parents? Is there someone we can call for you?"

"No. There is nobody to call. My mother..." Vi paused for a moment. "My mother is out of contact. Thank you for your help. We will refresh ourselves and be on our way."

"No you won't," said Bruce. "Not on foot, not out here. How the hell did you get out here in the first place?"

"There's a hundred kilometres of desert between here and the next source of water," Jess added. "You're lucky we saw you when we did, you could easily have died out there."

Bruce rose to his feet and crossed to the counter where his wife still stood. "Would have died, we hadn't seen you."

"We need to know how you got out here," Jess continued. "Like Bruce said, you can't walk from here. You'll need transport. Did someone bring you out into the desert? Are they still nearby?"

"I... cannot talk about it," said Vi. "All I may say is that we are alone. We can look after ourselves."

"Nope," said Bruce from the counter. "Not good enough. If I let you walk away from here you'll be dead inside a day. I'm not having that on my conscience." He nodded to Dorothy. "Reckon you're right. I don't like this at all. Make the call."

Dorothy nodded and started towards the rear of the kiosk as Bruce grabbed another bottle of water from the fridge.

"We should get you something to eat," said Jess. "How long has it been since you last ate?"

"We have nothing to trade." Vi stared across the kiosk at Dot as she neared the phone. "What is she doing?"

"Don't worry," said Bruce. "Just relax, little lady."

The boy said something, a stream of sharp syllables. Jess didn't recognise a word but she could hear the anger clearly enough.

Vi's eyes fixed on Dot with distress. "That is a communications device. Who will she call?"

"We're going to find someone who can help you," said Bruce. "They'll take good care of you. Don't worry, they won't hurt you."

"Please, call nobody." Vi locked wide eyes on Jess. "Just let us—"

"It's alright. We're trying to help you."

"No, please." Vi raised her voice. "Please, stop!" Her voice broke as she shouted, and "stop" came out in a strangled croak. If Dot heard, she didn't heed the request, her hand reaching for the telephone.

Aran tried to struggle to his feet, but Bruce ducked to his side and put a hand on his chest to keep him down. "Just hold on, son. You're not ready to get up yet." The boy yelled at him, thrashing his arms, but he was yet too weak to push against the older man.

Vi grabbed at Jess' arm, her hand feverishly warm on Jess' bare skin. "Make her stop," she begged.

The desperation in the girl's voice was too compelling to ignore. Jess closed her eyes for a second before standing and turning. "Dot, hold on a moment."

Dot paused, still clutching the handset, and peered at Jess from under lowered eyebrows.

"Are you in some kind of trouble?" Jess watched the girl's face for reaction. "Nobody's going to hurt you."

"Please, no messages," Vi said. "We cannot attract attention."

"If somebody's hurt you, we need to tell the police. They can protect you. You should see a doctor, too."

"No. No police. No doctors."

"But why not?" A thought occurred. "Have you... done something? Are you running away? You can tell us. We won't stop helping you."

"This is stupid," said Bruce. "These kids need help. How'd they get out here by themselves? Look how she was dressed!"

Jess couldn't disagree. "You're in the middle of a desert. You don't have family or friends nearby. You were on foot, but you can't walk out of here."

Vi stared around the kiosk. "We do need your help. We must get away from here, as far away as possible. As quickly as possible. There may be others coming. They cannot be allowed to find us. Are you able to provide us transport?"

"Wait... others? Are they the ones who did that to your neck?"

"There is no time to explain," said the girl. "Will you help us?"

No police, she said. They could insist, it wasn't as if the children could stop them. But for what purpose? The police would just take the children back to town — Port Augusta to the east or Eucla to the west, depending who attended. Jess was going that way already, she would pass through Eucla on her way to Perth. She could drop the children off at the local cop-shop when they arrived. The girl would have time to calm down by then.

Never mind the logic, Jess *wanted* to help them. Something had happened to her and her "brother"; they, like Jess, were retreating from

15

abusers. Fate brought them together and cast them onto the same path.

"I'll help them," she told Bruce and Dot. Turning to Vi, she nodded. "That's my car outside. I'll drive you to the next town and then we'll see."

Vi's thanks seemed like genuine relief.

Bruce was less sanguine. "Are you sure? We don't know anything about these kids. We don't know what brought them out here... or *who*."

"They're *kids*," Jess replied. "We know they're in trouble. They're going to town one way or another, with me or in the back of a divvy-van. I'm headed there anyway."

By now Aran had struggled to his feet, declining Bruce's offered assistance. Unsteadily at first, but with steps firming rapidly, he crossed the kiosk to his sister. He reached out a hand to tug at Vi's arm. Perhaps weakened by his exposure to the sun, he seemed unable to lift his sister's weight out of the lounger.

Jess took pity on him. "Here, let me," she said, reaching to assist. But a second later her fingers were tingling, her skin stinging, and it took a moment for her mind to catch up with his lightning-fast reaction. The boy had slapped aside her hand before she'd even seen him move.

Vi glared at her brother. "Please forgive Aran. He can be overprotective." She said something to him, words of reassurance, and he nodded. His reluctance was obvious as he allowed Jess to take over getting the girl to her feet.

"You're going to drive them?" Bruce sounded doubtful, but Jess nodded. "We'll call ahead to Eucla and let 'em know to expect you. You're stocked up and ready to go. Two full jerries in the back."

Vi smiled her thanks at Jess, who carefully released her hold to allow her to stand unsupported. The girl wobbled on her feet and Jess stayed ready to catch her, but she shook off the assistance, muttering something in her own unrecognisable language. By the time Jess looked up, Aran had dodged around the lounger and was now standing next to her, and in his hand was the big bowie knife.

16

The boy hefted the knife, resting it on his palm as if checking its balance, and smiled as if satisfied with whatever he had found. He turned his head towards Bruce and Dot and took a firm grip on the knife; a killing grip.

Suddenly Jess knew what he was intending. He lurched into motion, stalking across the kiosk towards Dot at the phone, and for a moment Jess didn't know what to say. "You're kidding me. What do you think you're doing?"

Aran ignored her as he approached Dot, the knife steady in his hands.

"I am sorry," Vi said. "I must ask you to cooperate. If you do not resist, you will be unharmed."

"No, wait, what are —"

The knife flashed.

Dot blinked and stared at the phone's handset, its wire now severed and dangling free. The boy turned to her, his lack of English no impediment as he gestured with the knife.

"All right, young man," Dot said, shuffling in the direction indicated, towards Bruce at the counter. "Don't get upset. I'm doing it."

"There's no need for this," Jess said urgently. "We're trying to help you."

"There is no choice. I am very sorry," the girl said, "but they will call for help as soon as we leave. "

"Of course they will. You need help."

Vi shook her head. "We cannot afford attention."

"You don't have to hurt anyone! We're on your side."

"We have no wish to hurt you."

17

"Listen," said Jess, improvising desperately. "Okay, you don't want official attention. I understand. You've turned up in the middle of nowhere, with no explanation. Half an hour more in that sun and you wouldn't have made it. But okay, no police."

"We have no time to explain," the girl said. "Aran will not hurt them, if they cooperate. We only need to restrain them."

"You can't tie someone up out here. It's not safe."

"We must. Aran will not hurt them unless they force him to." Vi didn't sound upset — merely resigned to an unpleasant task. *Children don't act like this,* Jess thought, but it was followed by another: *How exactly would you know how children act?*

"Just leave them alone. They'll promise not to call anyone. *Won't you,* Bruce?"

"Guess we can promise that," he said. "If you leave Dot alone."

Vi nodded. "I would like to trust you. We are not ungrateful for your help. But there is more at stake than you know." She called some rapid commands, then turned to Bruce. "Cooperate with Aran. Please do not resist him. He *will* hurt you if he must." She turned back to Jess. "Now, help me to your... your car. We must be away from this place."

Dot and Bruce clung to each other behind the counter as Aran crossed to the glass-fronted cabinet. The boy used the hilt of the knife to smash the glass, razor shards splashing out across the linoleum like surf. He retrieved a coil of rope from the cabinet and tugged at it to test its strength.

Vi stood at the door of the kiosk and raised her eyebrows at Jess. "When we are gone, they will be out of danger. But we must leave now, for your own sake. And theirs."

Was that a threat? The words sounded so, but it didn't feel like one. The girl's face was serious, her cheeks white, her eyes wide, but without malice.

18

Seemingly satisfied, Aran started across the floor towards the counter. The knife was in his waistband, both hands occupied with coils of rope. Jess wasn't fooled: she'd already seen how fast the boy could move.

"You won't hurt them?"

The girl nodded. "You have my word. They will be unharmed — if we can leave here immediately. If we do not, I make no promises."

Did she mean the "others"? They were still hypothetical, a vague threat. The boy with the knife was right here. Better he use the rope than the blade.

"Okay. I'm coming." Reluctantly Jess moved towards the door. The last thing she saw, as it swung closed behind her and she stepped into the sweltering heat of the outside, was Bruce, staring in mute accusation in her direction. Then the closing door shut out his eyes.

Vi was still weak and unsteady on her feet. Jess had to help her into the Taurus. After half an hour in the sun the big car was an oven, but Jess found that her concern for the girl's well-being was rapidly declining. *He will hurt you if he must*, she had said, as if she were discussing the weather.

They sat and waited for Aran to join them, uncomfortable minutes in the broiling car. It didn't take long for Jess to relent and turn on the engine. The wash of warm air from the fan was still a welcome relief from the cruelty of the summer heat.

Finally the boy emerged from the roadhouse and approached the car. On his back was a bulging rucksack; he had taken the time to rummage through the shop for supplies. The bag wasn't fully zipped closed and Jess glimpsed water bottles. He paused at the rear passenger door for a moment, before lifting the handle and climbing into the vehicle. Jess wondered about the girl's uncertainty at the word *car*. Could it be possible that neither of them had encountered a car before?

Who the hell are these children?

Vi had not objected to being placed in the front passenger's side seat.

Now she commanded Jess: "Let us go. Which direction were you heading?"

"West," said Jess, nodding towards the road, shimmering in the afternoon.

"Then let us keep going west. Drive. Now. Please."

Jess drove. As the roadhouse dwindled behind them, Jess watched in the rearview mirror. She hoped that Bruce and Dot were okay. If Vi had been true to her word and told Aran to leave them unharmed, then every passing kilometre made them safer. She suspected the true danger was here in the car with her. She was acutely aware of Aran coldly staring at her from the rear.

She hadn't missed seeing, as the boy climbed into the rear seat, that he still had the bowie knife clipped to his waistband.

Six Hours Earlier

I

Somewhere to the north a fire was alight, plumes of black smoke billowing into the dusk air. It seemed large, silhouetting the closer high-rise buildings of the business district, and Vi expected it was just getting started. It must be somewhere in the densely built residential zones. The power had been out in the city for weeks, and the fire would burn unchecked. Just last week a similar fire had burned through the west quarter, razing hundreds of buildings, running free until it met the river. Blind luck that the wind had been low that day and the fire did not jump the water.

There were no longer any fire services in the city; those who were born to the Corps had fled the city long since, and those few civilians remaining were unwilling to fight fires. The besieging army had no skills, resources or intent to preserve the city's outer regions. Of the defenders, the Imperial Guard could not help either. Even had the fire not been outside the Barrier that protected the inner city, the Guard were too few and too heavily committed for such duties. So the fire would burn until it ran out of fuel to consume. Standing atop the Imperial palace, Vi wondered how much of the city would be left to rule by the time this was all over.

Over the past few weeks she had adopted this little nook as her own. She'd had her guards bring up a chair from an inner room; unasked, they'd also erected a shade-sail. She suspected her mother's hand in that. The balmy autumn hardly warranted the shelter and it was unlikely the guards would have taken that initiative on their own. They were here out of duty, not any love for her; she had failed to ever convince them to join her under the shelter and they barely talked to her, responding to questions in monosyllables, until she had stopped asking.

Her nook sat in a semicircle overhang at the front of the palace. Directly below the overhang was the balcony where the Empress would traditionally stand to wave to the crowds in the square below. Many a time Vi had waited in the antechamber behind that balcony while the Empress presented herself to the masses.

There was nothing magical about it, the Empress once told her, but the people liked to see her. They would travel for days or weeks to be here, and they would return to tell their friends and families that they had stood in Imperial Square, and it was just as splendid as they had heard. People came to Capital Island, travelling halfway around the planet just to gaze upon their Empress, their ruler.

Ruler — now there was an irony. *Chief administrator would be more accurate,* the Empress once told Vi. *We have more layers of government than decisions that need making.* It had proven true: Harke and his rebellion had decimated the top layers of government without greatly affecting the daily life of the common people.

The reach of the Empire had constricted to a circle of the city a couple of kilometres wide. Outside of Capital Island the world went on uncaring; the rebellion, which had sprung up all at once in seemingly a hundred Regions, had ignored cities and states and focussed instead, with single-minded intent, upon the capital. To millions of people outside of the conflict, the coup against the government had no effect upon their lives. Many might not even be aware there was a war. There would be no rescue from that quarter.

The square below was empty now. Large enough for half an army to marshal, it stood bare and lonely, an echo of the empty city. The height of the palace gave her a vantage from which Vi could see much of the central district of the city. Once a thriving metropolis, brimming with people —— hundreds of thousands in dense inner-city living. Now the city was practically deserted.

In the early days of the siege she had been permitted to walk those streets, accompanied by just a small entourage of guards and servants. One afternoon of walking through windswept streets and into empty apartments had robbed her of further desire to explore. Early in the siege, shortly after the riots, the invaders had provided their ultimatum: free passage for all who wished to leave. All besides the nobles. A magnanimous gesture from the rebels, and the population of the city had shrunk overnight to a sliver. It had been counterproductive for the rebellion; the siege could never have lasted this long with the city full. The city would have run out of food long since.

Not all the civilians had left, of course. Following the emptying of the city had come the looters. Most of the Imperial Guard had remained to protect the nobility, as was their duty, but there were too few of those. Barely enough to guard the palace and man the Barrier, and none to spare for guarding deserted buildings. Now the empty shells down in the streets held nothing of value except memories. One afternoon amongst that desolation was all that Vi had wanted and she had no interest in it now.

Her tutors had long since left the city, as had a large part of the palace staff, vanishing overnight without so much as a note. Even the nobles had noticed the disappearance, the sudden decline in the level of service they received. Without its hundreds of servants the palace now was cold and barren, a place of drafts and ghosts. There was nothing there in which she wanted to invest her time.

Of all the depredations of war, she had never anticipated boredom.

Vi fished her pad out of her bag. Settling the writing interface around her ear, she adjusted the contact onto the data point on her temple and pulled up her diary, the words swimming into resolution. The city was lonely now but her journal remained to her, a more faithful companion than her peers. She turned to her most recent page and waited for words to come to her. Instead, her mind provided her with faces.

They were all gone now. Adair, Hertja and Kabnia had headed for the Regions with their families early in the hostilities, smuggled out before the rebels had the island surrounded. Their choice had cost them any possibility of accession to the throne, but it seemed now that they were the wiser ones. It seemed unlikely there would be a throne after this rebellion was done.

Alysa was gone too. One day she had simply not been found; along with her guards and her dearest possessions, she was nowhere in the palace. Her parents were still here but they swore that they did not know where their daughter was, if she was hidden within the inner city or had attempted escape.

They are lying, of course, the Empress had told Vi, *but it's not worth making an issue of. When you sit the throne, you must note all things, and remember all things, but you have the luxury of choosing upon which things you will act.* Empress Jede had given such a long, strange look at Vi then that she'd started to wonder if she'd done something wrong herself.

Majan and Lirra were gone too. They had vanished separately but in identical circumstances. Each family simply disappeared overnight. Word around the palace was that they had spoken unwisely, claiming sympathy for the cause of the rebels. But if they had been punished for some misdemeanour, nobody would tell Vi anything about their fate. They had joined the long and growing list of people who were not seen again, about whom it was not polite to speak. There had been too many disappearances over the past month for Vi to pass off as mere departures. And she had repeatedly been advised that there was now no way out of the city; the rebels controlled all the access points and would surely intercept any of the nobility who sought to escape.

Keren was gone.

Prissi was gone.

Tyra was gone, Tyra with her glossy hair and her haughty refusal to accept that the war was lost.

Plump Jera was not gone, but might as well have been; for the past weeks, her parents, the Lord and Lady Jateth and Zafa, had confined themselves and their daughter to their rooms, and the servants who brought them their regular meals were the only people to lay eyes on them since.

It seemed that everyone Vi had ever cared about, everyone she had grown up with, had left her or been taken away. They were her rivals for accession to the Crown, competitors and enemies, but they had also been her friends. And now she was alone, the only remaining contender to a throne that would surely fall, and for the first time ever she wished she had been born into any class but the nobility.

She couldn't concentrate, the data interface struggling to produce more than random gibberish. Reluctantly she unhooked the interface, swiped the notepad to a blank page and unshipped the stylus. Sketching required less direct attention.

The desolation of the northern cityscape, with its column of black smoke rising, was an apt subject for her mood. For a while she lost herself in a world of light, shade and perspective, the tapping of the stylus on the pad punctuating her thoughts; and the faces of her friends receded from her mind.

II

She wasn't sure how much time had passed before a vague sense of unease penetrated her concentration; some change in the atmosphere so slight as to be almost imperceptible.

The expanse of the palace roof was bare of threat. Her two omnipresent guards were sitting together against the access cubicle, speaking in low voices; they showed no signs of having noticed anything out of the ordinary. Vi turned her attention outwards, to the city.

There was a subtle difference to the cityscape. She ran her gaze across the rooftops, along the empty streets, trying to put her finger on the change. She had spent many long hours on the roof over the past month, and the city was laid out beneath her as always, but when she realised the alteration it hit her with a shock of ice. Out beyond the inner city, where the ring of razed earth marked the groundfall of the Barrier, smoke swirled through the avenues, the dots of distant people milling. The faint blue shimmer of the Barrier... was gone.

The sun was almost below the horizon now and long shadows scarred the cityscape, but she could clearly see the outer ring. The energy haze was no longer blurring the streets beyond.

The Barrier was down.

The inner city stood undefended.

Vi bolted to her feet, the bottom dropping out of her stomach. Behind her the chair toppled, unnoticed. The pad dropped from her nerveless fingers.

As she stared, swinging her gaze in an arc around the city where the Barrier had stood, the tenor of the sounds on the breeze changed. Sounds of discfire, screams and violence. Movement, too: from a point far to the east, hidden from view by buildings that still stood, a point of light arced into the sky. The rebel artillery emplacements, so long silent, were coming back to life.

Behind her, her guards had sprung into action upon hearing her chair tip over. Now they were receiving urgent orders, barked through their earpieces. Moving as one they swept towards Vi and took her by the arms. Gently but firmly they turned her around and started pulling her across the rooftop. "We have to go, my lady," said the one on the left, the one with the moustache. "The Barrier's fallen. They'll be targeting the palace."

"Wait. My things!" She tried to struggle, but the guards had been selected for strength and speed, and she was being carried more than escorted. She caught a last glimpse of her pad and her bag still sitting at the edge of the roof. And then they were inside the cubicle and the door was closing behind them.

Inside the access cube was an exit point for a gravity tube, but as she stared the guards swept her past it without hesitation. "Power could go any time," explained the second guard. "It's a long way down." Beyond the grav tube was the top of a staircase, spiralling down and out of sight. Vi baulked at the steep descent, but the guards gave her no pause. The first guard took point, the other behind her, and Vi had no choice but to descend in the tight space between.

She was unaccustomed to stairs. They were marble, with a polished black handrail, and the walls were decorated with small but tasteful abstract paintings, but it was still a set of stairs and not proper for a noble.

They descended a couple of complete turns before Vi found her voice. "How long will it take the rebels to get here?"

"To reach the palace? Maybe an hour," said the second guard, behind her. "But they'll have the place half levelled by then." As if to illustrate his words, the stairs shuddered as the palace suffered its first direct strike from the artillery. Vi had seen the fortifications on the outer ring of the palace, had walked past them a thousand times, but it had never occurred to her before that the palace itself could become a target for bombardment.

The stairs seemed endless. It seemed forever they had been turning in circles; it didn't take long before Vi needed to use the handrail to combat her dizziness. The constant shuddering of artillery strikes did not help. The stairwell was filling with a fine white dust; stone powder hung in the air as the building groaned under the assault. She soon lost count of the landings they passed, each with doors leading to another level of the palace, each ignored as they passed.

"Where are you taking me?" Vi asked. She was sure they had now descended deeper into the palace than she'd ever been. The bowels of the palace were for the working classes, and hearsay would have it that they were full of kitchens, and laundries, and sewers, all manner of places that a lady should never go. Still the staircase continued down, unchanging in marble, the closed doors betraying nothing.

"The Empress is waiting for you in the Gate chamber," said the first guard, breathless from the pace.

Gate chamber? What's that? She had no capacity for questions; she needed to concentrate on her footing or she'd lose her balance, and she feared that once she started falling there would be nothing to catch her. The ground seemed a mere fantasy.

Another landing came into view. The door here stood open with more guards in attendance. Her guardians steered her unceremoniously through the door, and the new guards fell in behind.

A maze of corridors followed. There were more guards down here, resplendent in blue dress uniforms. All were armed, but for now their flingers stayed holstered at their hips, their swords safely strapped to their backs. Vi was steered from one corner to another, through doorways, into halls with many doors, until she had quite given up trying to keep track of even which direction they were facing.

Abruptly their circuitous route ended; before them stood an imposing set of metal doors. Beyond, a straight corridor stretched into the distance, sloping gradually downwards. The guards again pressed her into motion. They followed the straight corridor for what might have been hours, or it might only have been a few minutes.

Eventually the corridor ended in another set of metal doors. Yet another soldier opened these. Vi stepped inside and stumbled to a halt, agape.

There is a palace... inside the palace.

III

The chamber was a cavernous room, longer than the throne room many floors above, but narrower; made narrower still by its contents. Both walls were lined with magnetos. Large-scale versions of the generators found in any powered machine, these were many times larger than even the ones powering the Capitol building itself. Each steel sphere stood taller than a man, couched in metallic coils the thickness of her thigh, and the magnetos lined the walls on each side of a central aisle. There must have been two dozen in all. What could possibly use that much power? Cables snaked from the rear of each magneto and joined ceiling conduits running the length of the chamber. Vi followed the cables with her eyes until they came to rest on the unassuming machinery at the far end of the chamber. Two tall pillars of electronics flanked a raised, bare platform. Vi stared at it in trepidation. A single magneto the size of a man's fist could kill him; she couldn't imagine what the effects of this much power would be.

The space in the centre of the chamber was thronged with people. Technicians bustled from sphere to sphere, or adjusted settings on a myriad of control consoles. Imperial guards dotted the chamber, with more guarding the door they had just entered by. Another small cluster standing to one side drew her eyes. She knew many of those in this group. Several of the remaining nobles were there, led by the imposing figure of Lord Garth, whose corpulent frame had always put her in mind of any two of the other Councillors stitched together.

Vi and the other girls of the court had never felt comfortable with Lord Garth; he always seemed to be staring acquisitively at them, as if he was measuring their value. She was used to being judged against her peers, but some of the girls had been known to wonder aloud whether Garth was weighing them against his greed for his son, the puffy Lord Kelus, or for himself.

He wasn't leering now. His eyes were wide and his cheeks bloodlessly pale, the veins standing out on his temples. He was standing with his face inches away from the Lady Priyal, his voice raised. The statuesque lady seemed undaunted by his anger. At her back a gaggle of other lords lent her support as she responded to Garth's shouts with studied calm.

To the side of the group the Master of Services hovered. Like a scared bird in the palace gardens — a slightly plump bird, not sleek and graceful. A pigeon, perhaps. Jarem had always seemed timid, twitchy. A room like this was his natural environment, but it should be empty. Perhaps daunted by the company of the High Councillors, he seemed to be trying to become a part of the machinery that surrounded him.

At the rear of the group Lord Gabe towered head-and-shoulders over the rest of them. The Captain of the Imperial Guard was sparkling in his dress uniform, a solid wall of metal on his chest.

Lord Captain Gabe, the Empress's eternal protector. The one man who was always around, always with a smile, a kind word and a treat. With Gabe in sight even the shuddering of the palace seemed to settle, he brought such a sense of solidity to the air.

Gabe locked eyes on Vi and nodded. Then his head ducked out of view as he bent and murmured to someone else in the group. The little gathering shuffled and opened a gap to allow a slim woman to emerge from the core.

Her guards had stepped away, leaving Vi alone at the doorway. *You are a lady of the court. They owe you respect.* She squared her shoulders and stepped forward to meet the oncoming woman, the Empress.

Who opened her arms wide and swept her into a hug. Vi was so shocked she didn't think to bring her own arms up, standing instead like a mannequin. She couldn't remember the last time her mother had displayed such an obvious affection in public.

Jede had never looked less like a ruler than she did now. She was coated in plaster dust, turning her clothes a pale ochre. She was not in her usual finery; roused at short notice from her chambers, she had not taken time to change from her plain pants and blouse. Her hair hung loose, and her hands were empty; no staff of office. Even in the gravest emergency the Empress never stepped out of her chambers without being properly attired.

"Thank the Crown. I feared the worst," Jede said. "You might have been killed."

"I was on the roof," said Vi. "My pad's still up there. Somebody has to go get it."

Jede shook her head, but it was Gabe who answered. "No chance. The roof's gone. Anything up there is rubble by now."

The Empress agreed. "I'm sorry. Even if anyone could get up there, there's no time. We have to get you out of the city while the opportunity lasts." The Empress disengaged from Vi and held her at arm's length, staring intently into her face. "Listen to me. The siege is over. Harke has won. The Barrier's down, and they'll hold the palace before dawn."

"You said that Beryn would break the siege," Vi protested. "You said we just had to hold out."

"Too late for that," said Gabe. "Another week, two, and Beryn might have been able to get through. If the Barrier had held, we might have lasted. But the army's still too far. Last I heard they were caught on Jeryth, and even if they've managed to get across the straits they're still at least a week away. Meanwhile the Barrier's down and the rebels will soon have the city."

Empress Jede continued. "Harke must have known that he didn't have long. He doesn't have enough forces to fight an army at his rear and still maintain the siege. No coincidence that the Barrier has come down now. He's always been good at fostering traitors." Her voice was sour. "Now he'll be hoping to capture the nobles."

"I thought he was killing the nobles when he got his hands on them," said Vi, confused.

"Bugger the nobles," said Gabe. "I don't think he cares about them. It's you he wants, you and your mother. With the Empress and her daughter in hand, they don't think Beryn would dare try to retake the capital. And they need you if they're going to convince the people that the Crown must end."

"That can't happen," said Jede. "I can't *allow* that to happen. We still have enough of the Council here to make this official."

Lord Garth protested, his words robbed of gravitas by his high-pitched voice. "We can't do this. It's a breach of protocol." He shook a pudgy finger at the Empress, perhaps not aware of how ridiculous that looked. "You don't have my agreement here."

"Your protest is already noted," said Lord Fenwyth. The Imperial Archivist was unshaven and unkempt, white hair billowing about his head in wisps, but he still clutched his pad; he would have seemed more naked to be seen without that than without his clothes. "And as I have already pointed out, your concurrence is not required in this. The statutes are clear. The conditions are met; you agreed that yourselves. The Council must witness but the decision belongs to the Empress alone."

"Decision? What decision?" asked Vi.

Jede stared at her. "The only decision left to us. It's the only way to save the Crown. As the only eligible daughter of noble birth present, there are no other claimants. My lords and ladies, do you concur that the lady Vi is the only claimant to the rule of the Empire?"

It was the Lady Priyal who answered for them, her words echoing through the sudden roar of blood in Vi's ears. "We do so concur."

Priyal was echoed by the other Lords, some with clear reluctance. Not surprising that Lord Wickham seemed particularly unhappy about it; he had high hopes for his daughter Maije, and her grades had been good enough to lend that ambition weight, but she was not here.

The only claimant. How much effort had been required to ensure none of the other girls were here now? Vi stared at her mother.

"Then under law," continued Jede, "and as we are in a declared state of emergency, I invoke Transition. The lady Vi will become Empress."

"I don't *want* to be the Empress," protested Vi. "*You're* the Empress. I'm not even first in the Lessons."

"Listen to me," said Jede. "The Barrier is down. Harke and his army of traitors will be here soon. We must all be gone from the palace before then. Some of the Council will take shelter in the city, but it would be foolish to think they will escape discovery. Harke will have his men going door to door until we're found. There's a ship at the docks with a loyal captain. I'll try to escape that way, but the chances are slim."

An understatement: the docks were outside of the outer ring of the city, which meant that Jede would need to fight or sneak through Harke's cordon. "That's not —"

"We'll probably be caught; they may even take me alive. I don't know what will happen to me, but the Crown must continue. I will *not* be the last Empress.

"I wish there were another way — but there is no choice left. I pass the Crown to you."

"That's impossible!" cried Vi. Being Empress was for life; that was an understood fact.

"Whilst passing the Crown is traditionally done on a deathbed," said Lord Fenwyth, "there is nothing that says it *must* be. Abdication whilst in good health is not without precedent."

Vi had never been the dux of her class but had always been a decent student. She knew the line of Empresses by heart. "I've never heard of—"

Jede interrupted her. "My darling, there are some truths we don't include in the Lessons. Some of our darker histories are known only to a few. We ensure that they are not *entirely* forgotten." She tapped her temple. "They are safe here — just another reason that we must preserve the Crown. Fenwyth? Is all prepared?"

"It is, my lady," said the Archivist. "We're ready."

"Let's get it done, then," said Jede. "Vi, the Crown is more than mere title or position. It is history itself. It must not be lost, so I give it to you. The Crown, and with it the title of Empress. You will be the rightful ruler now. Whatever happens here — whatever damage Harke may cause — you must keep the Empire alive. Protect the Crown. It's all that matters, more than me, more than you."

"My lady," murmured Gabe.

Jede ignored him. "I hoped to avoid this. If I could spare you I would. I thought one of the others...... no matter now. It cannot be helped. You *will* be Empress."

"Spare me?" This was absurd enough she had to protest. "Mother, since I was born you've prepared me to rule. Why, if you don't want me to succeed you?"

The Empress shook her head. "Because it was expected of me! Every noble daughter aspires to the throne. If you knew what it involved you'd never go near it, but it's *expected*. It comes down to tradition and duty. Always duty." Jede reached out and caught hold of her daughter, held her close. "Being Empress, it's the least powerful job in the world." Raising

33

her voice, she continued over Vi's objection. "*Least* powerful, yes. If power is measured in choice, the ability to make decisions for yourself... In twenty years as Empress, I have never made a decision on my own behalf. I have never had a choice where the correct path was unclear. Not once. Not even today."

"My lady," said Gabe again, more insistently. "They've crossed the square." The rebels would be entering the palace above. Every moment that passed now would make it harder for Jede to get out of the building.

"My dearest," said Jede, "we're out of time. We should have had years together, time to teach you what you should know. But you're strong; you'll come to understand it all soon enough. There is so much more that you don't know. There's no time. For now, I can only tell you that there is one other way out of the city, one avenue for escape that Harke cannot close. It's a one-way trip, but if I can, I'll find a way to bring you back. As soon as I can."

"The Gate," Vi guessed. "This is the Gate Chamber. Where is it a gate to?"

"Another world," said the Master of Services. Vi had almost forgotten the little man's presence. "Not as civilised as here. They don't follow the Crown." Jarem's eyes were bright, his cheeks flushed. "Warlike and monstrous. But it *is* possible to survive there."

"Jarem has been studying this other world for years," said Jede. "If I could send him with you, I would."

"It's not possible," said Jarem; "Too much mass. We're at the edge of tolerance already. We would have to wait for the magnetos to spin up to full power again, and that could take half an hour."

"Too long," said Gabe. "This is already taking more time than we can spare. We must move."

Jede guided Vi across the chamber to an open space in which stood two chairs, carved from white marble, placed back to back. Ragged shards of stone at their bases showed that they had been moved here specially for this moment. The Empress pushed her into the chair and brushed back her hair, her hands lingering on her daughter's scalp. There was a sense of finality to the caress. One last human touch.

Fenwyth had come with them. The old man beckoned to his team of archivists who had been standing by. One approached, lifting the lid of the ornate carved chest he carried. He passed its contents to Fenwyth: a complex contraption, all needles and blades and glittering chrome. Vi stared at it in horror.

"I regret we don't have time to do this neatly," the Chief Archivist said, "but at least it won't hurt." He hesitated. "Empress, I must be certain that this is your choice. You *know* what the consequences will be. Once I begin, I cannot stop. So I have to ask, *is this your intent*? Do you accept this action?"

"The Council agreed. We *all* agreed. So do it," said Jede. "Do it quickly."

IV

Lord Garth had been staring, the veins at his temples throbbing. Now he stepped forward. "You can't do this," he said. "This is a mistake."

Before he had moved three steps, Gabe had drawn his flinger and had the weapon levelled at the fat Lord's chest. "Stay there," he said, calmly enough. "This is not your decision, and it is being done within the boundaries of law."

"It's not right," said Garth. "She's too weak. She's not ready for this."

With a flurry of movement Jede was out of her chair and had Garth by the throat. Her fury gave her strength as she drove him backwards, the fat man's feet tottering under him, until they fetched up at one of the magnetos. The giant sphere *boomed* hollowly as the Lord's skull bounced off it.

Jede kept her voice steady and cold. "That's my daughter. I'd advise you be more careful with your insults. She's stronger than you think, and she will be Empress. But if you belittle her again in my presence, it's not her wrath you'll need to face."

Garth looked around himself, searching for allies, but even the few nobles who probably agreed with him weren't coming forward. Lord Garth's shoulders slumped as Jede let him go. Turning, he fixed Vi with a glare. "You're going to lose yourself, *girl*," he snarled. "You're not ready." Raising his voice, he proclaimed to the chamber as a whole: "She's not ready!" They were his parting words as he stalked out of the chamber, bearing as much dignity as his waddling gait would allow.

Slowly, Jede moved back to the chair behind Vi. When she moved out of her daughter's line of sight, the room felt somehow smaller.

"Don't be afraid," said the Empress, behind her. "I was not much older than you when I was Crowned. It's not as bad as it looks."

"Every Empress for the last thousand years has done this," muttered Fenwyth, behind her. His words were reassuring even if the aged quaver in his voice was not. "I myself passed the Crown to your mother. Most Empresses do not receive the benefit of hands-on experience."

There were noises behind Vi, a combination of mechanical whines and horrid liquid sounds. She stared around herself desperately, seeking distraction. But her eyes fell upon the platform at the end of the chamber and the power conduits running to it, enough energy to crack the world concentrated on that ominous space, and that only increased her fear.

It seemed to take forever, but it was only a minute later when Fenwyth murmured to Jede, "It is done." More clicks and rattles followed. Vi tried to turn to see, but a hand fell on her shoulder and gently held her. Moments later she felt hands on her scalp; Fenwyth and his assistant were settling the chrome contraption onto her head. It fit neatly enough, its arms cradling her skull and caressing the nape of her neck. She felt a momentary sense of cold on her skin before it went numb.

She had read enough about Transition that she knew what was being done; but even in the lessons which described its history and legacy, details were vague. Her head rocked forwards as she felt pressure behind her, but the hands held her in place in the chair.

Jede stepped back into view. The Empress was holding a pad of cloth to the back of her neck with one hand, as she kneeled in front of Vi's chair. With her other hand she reached out and grasped Vi's knee. "This will only take a moment, and then the world will open up for you. It's a wonderful gift as well as a curse," she said. "Remember yourself and you'll find it amazing."

The claws of the device were digging into her scalp. More clicks and rattles, a high-pitched whine behind her and her head wobbled as the pressure on her skull shifted. She was in a room with enough power to light a country. Around her stood dozens of people, and they all seemed to be staring at her. It was all too much; she felt tears coming to her eyes. She had always imagined herself becoming Empress, but it was too soon; Garth was right. She was not ready.

Of course she wasn't ready, ascending to the throne at the age of eight. As Bella, she learned, she grew in the role. She became one of the greatest Empresses in history. She has done this before, and she will do it again.

Her eyes widened at that thought. That memory was not her own. Someone else's experience, emerging from her own mind. And lined up behind it were others, a dizzying succession of visions — she barely had time to recognise each image before the next was pressing on her mind's eye. A score of times she had done this before — received the Crown under the surgeon's knife. And before that, when the Crown was still something the Empress would wear. In her mind she was passing the Crown to her successor, and she was receiving the Crown a hundred times; in her bedchamber, in the throne room, in the countryside, in a surgical bay. She was old, and young, and younger still.

Vi struggled to make sense of the images, but they kept coming, flooding her senses with sights and sounds and smells she had never experienced.

She cried out in panic, and for a second the world settled around her at the noise. Only a moment, then it whirled away again. The Gate Chamber stood before her, empty in one moment and thronged with dozens of people in the next. She stood before the platform, and before her, kneeling, was a man, and was a woman, and was a man again. They were bound in ropes, and they stood free. Around her the spheres stood cold and silent, and brilliant with fire and light.

She remembered a secret gate concealed behind one of the magnetos in this chamber, leading to a passage that led out into the inner city; but even as her eyes were flickering in that direction, she remembered it being collapsed and walled up again a century later.

She remembered the Palace — standing outside as it was under construction, standing over workstations as technicians designed extra wings or floors, walking its wide corridors, seated in the old throne room and the new.

Around her people were talking, moving. Memories or reality? The rush of images, of voices, of thoughts not her own, left her reeling. A voice — her mother? — saying "This will pass soon." Was that real or was she remembering another? Hands under her armpits helped her to her feet and drew her forwards; her balance kept her feet under her, walking a habit beyond the reach of memory, but her mind was not present.

She stood before armies and sent them to war; she stood in front of thousands gathered in the square below and waved to them, and they loved her; she stood at the head of the High Council chamber and endured the frustrated shouts of the Lords. Faces flooded her vision — hundreds of them, each face bearing a name and a lifetime of experiences.

Around her the magnetos were spinning into life, a crescendo in decibels and light, but she had seen that a hundred times before. A young lad was ushered towards her — Aran, she recognised, and could sense that *this* experience, at least, was her own. Aran was rubbing at his bicep: a tight leather band encircled the arm. *A Guard? He's just a boy!* That thought was followed by another: *Not Aran, I want Keres, he's so beautiful.*

Aran came forwards, shepherded by his father. Captain Gabe called across to a soldier. "Corporal? Your weapon. Now!"

"They can't take a flinger," Jarem protested.

38

"I'm not interested in protecting our technology." Empress Jede turned to face the technician. "We're well beyond that now."

Jarem shook his head. "It's too heavy. I can barely get the two of them through. I've pushed the coils as high as they'll go, we can't afford more mass. They'll exit the Bridge in deep space."

Gabe held the weapon in his hand as if weighing it. Reluctantly he passed it back to the corporal. "How much more can they carry?"

"A hundred grams. Two hundred at most."

"Fine." Moving rapidly, Gabe detached the earpiece from his headset, then accepted another from the corporal. Touched the two nubs of metal together so they momentarily glowed blue. Then he handed them to the boy. "These are paired."

Vi's attention was slipping, as her mind whirled away again. When Jede stepped up to her and wrapped her in her arms and kissed her cheeks, she was a hundred other mothers. Jede was saying something but Vi couldn't hear, her mind awhirl in thoughts of birth, and sex, and death.

But when she was ushered up onto the platform, this was new; in a thousand years of memories, she had never experienced this, never stood here. The hands supporting her withdrew and she fell, her knees bruising on the platform.

Focus, girl.

The stranger's voice in her head roused her. With an effort, Vi raised her eyes, blinking furiously to focus on the room. The pressure of the memories was building up, threatening to overwhelm her again; yet for a moment she was herself.

Her mother stood before the platform. Tears ran down her cheeks and a trickle of blood traced a line over her collarbone. "Remember who you are," said Jede. "And this: find Hareth Rede. *Hareth Rede*. He will help you. Remember!"

Gabe was there too, standing beside Jede, a hand on her elbow. "Keep her safe," he said, and it took a moment for Vi to realise this was directed to Aran. His son, she thought dully, of course it would be Aran. Dutiful Aran, always struggling so hard to excel, but never attaining the heights of the natural talent with which Keres had been blessed. Keres was not here.

Jede held out a hand. Vi stretched out to meet her but she was too far away to reach. "I love you," Jede said. "We'll bring you back soon. I promise. We'll bring you back!"

The roar of the magnetos reached a crescendo, and the chamber filled with fierce light as the spheres blazed. The world was stretching, blurring, and her mother's face distorted and melted into featureless colour. The Gate Chamber too, and with it Jarem, feverishly working controls; Fenwyth, the chrome device still dangling from his fingers and dripping red; Lady Priyal and even Lord Gabe, all standing and watching and dissolving.

And then the world was gone, and for a time there was only blackness.

V

The Gate Chamber stood dark, still and silent. For a time. Sealed, and sealed again, the biometric locks closed, the magnetos cold and dead.

Then, light. The darkness was breached, the inner doors sliding open. Silhouetted against the bright corridor without, a tall figure stood and surveyed the darkened room.

"Are you here?" His voice echoed through the chamber.

Waiting in silence would not make him go away. "I'm here." Jarem, until recently the chief technician for the Imperial palace, came to his feet. His knees creaked, stiff after so long immobile.

"Pretty sombre in here," said the tall figure in the doorway. "Is that on purpose? I got your signal."

"They told me to turn it all off," said Jarem. "I was ordered to disable the Gate; to dismantle what I could, smash what I had to, make it irreparable."

The tall man's voice was gentle. "And did you?"

"No. I did not. I... I couldn't."

"I'm glad," said the man. "Can we have some light in here? I can't see a thing."

"Of course." Jarem operated controls on the nearby console. Slowly the room brightened, the light bars on the ceiling and walls coming to life. Jarem watched as the figure in the doorway became visible. He had never met the man face to face, but he recognised him immediately. Who else could it be?

Harke had never been a handsome man, his brow and cheeks too heavy, his nose and lips too pronounced; but even with that in mind he was not currently at his best. His face was dark with grime and smoke, and his tactical armour was sprayed with dried blood. His shock of blond hair, the trait most consistently described by eyewitnesses, was dishevelled and matted. A bandage covered a shallow wound on one cheek.

Despite this he seemed full of good humour as he strode into the chamber. Behind him came a gaggle of men, dressed in the patchwork of urban camouflage jackets and coats that passed for a uniform amongst the rebels. They dispersed into the chamber, goggling like tourists.

"Is it over?" asked Jarem.

Harke shrugged. "We hold the palace and most of the inner city. We haven't yet captured the Empress but that's just a matter of time." His face clouded with sudden anger, as fleeting as it was foreboding, before he replaced it deliberately with a hooked grin. "I should say, *former* Empress. Abdicating, to her daughter. A child Empress. Such an interesting idea. Who would have seen that coming?"

"I couldn't prevent it," said Jarem. "There were guards and nobles and... lots of guards. And they were very insistent. I wouldn't have been able to persuade them."

"Relax, my friend," said Harke, crossing the final distance between them and taking Jarem's hand in his own. "I couldn't ask any more of you. I won't forget your contribution."

Jarem marvelled at the feel of Harke's hand; not soft and smooth like the hand of a noble, his hands were calloused and rough from years working at manual labour. According to rumour Harke spent his early decades cycling through trades, seeking a guild to call his own. He could have chosen anything, Freemen of any talent could always find a home. Nothing he tried could satisfy him. Until he set his sights on the one class to which he could never aspire. Until he had conceived his notion to change the world.

Jarem pulled his hand out of Harke's grasp. "The Empress is gone. Out of reach. You don't have to worry about her. It's a one-way journey; she won't be resisting your new world order."

"*Our* new world." Harke frowned. "Is that a note of regret I hear? You don't know me, but you should understand. I can't abide unhappiness. If you're feeling tired and unsure I just won't be able to keep you around." His voice was matter-of-fact but Jarem didn't miss the veiled threat.

Harke waved behind him, and Jarem assumed he meant the palace and the city, rather than the troops scattered across the chamber. He went on more gently. "Think about what we've achieved. The Barrier is down without a shot fired. The Capital has fallen quickly. There's an army on its way and if we were still outside the Barrier when they arrived, whether they prevailed or I, thousands more would have died. Instead, I'd be surprised if there were more than a hundred dead, and that includes twenty of mine. You've saved countless lives. That's a pretty good outcome for your part of pressing a few buttons."

Jarem had heard accounts of Harke's tendency to grandstand, but this was the first time he'd seen it in action.

"More than that. You're witnessing the beginning of a new era. An age where your destiny doesn't have to be set by the accident of your birth.

Where every man and woman can make their own choices and find their own destiny."

Jarem flinched. An inspirational idea, until you're standing before a man with blood across his face. "I've been working with these people all my life."

"You've been working *for* them," said Harke. "Not with them."

"It will take me some time to get used to them not being here, I guess."

"You'll have time," Harke said. "When you're ready, there may even be room at the Council table for you, if you're tired of being a tinkerer. But first things first. Let's see this fascinating Gateway of yours."

Jarem had no interest in being on the Council. He was an engineer, it was all he knew how to be. He was a *good* engineer — but now was not the time to argue.

He led the way into the chamber, Harke at his side. When they stood in front of the platform, Harke put his hands on his hips and frowned. "So. Tell me about this other world, this destination. What do we know about it?"

"We know enough," said Jarem. "The people there call that world 'Australia'." The name was thick and awkward upon his tongue. "We send drones whenever we get a chance. It's slow: we only get a tiny batch of data back each opening. We've made some progress on the language."

"You're serious about this." Harke ran his fingers over the sphere of the nearest magneto. "It ought to be fiction, but it's real. Another world. And it's been kept secret for hundreds of years. I wouldn't have credited it."

"It had to be secret," said Jarem. "If it ever became public knowledge, it would be... revolutionary. Just imagine. People would clamour to know more, to go through and explore. There would be talk of diplomacy, of trade."

"You said it's a one-way journey."

Jarem nodded. "It's a pulse — an energy bubble. By the time it reaches its destination, it's closing at this end. Even if you could enter the bridge at the other end, there's no way to get out on this side."

"That makes the idea of trade a bit difficult, don't you think?"

Jarem paused. "We could build a device. A reflector. Something to keep the Gate open for two-way travel."

"But we haven't pursued that option. Why not? Why have we not sought to investigate that other world?"

"Because it would mean the end of ours," said Jarem. "The world on the other side is nothing like ours. The warrior clans there are not interested in diplomacy and certainly not in trade. Power there is earned by the force of arms. You'd like it there."

The look Harke gave him could have liquefied nitrogen. "Careful."

Jarem went on, carefully. "We can't allow the people on the other side to become aware of us. Every time we send someone through the gate, we risk its discovery, and that could be *very bad.*"

"So they have no idea we exist." There was a note of delight in Harke's voice. "I can see potential in that."

"I don't think you understand," said Jarem. "There's no potential. No benefit to us. How many people do you think there are in the whole world? All people, everywhere?"

"I understand that global population is approaching one thousand million," said Harke. "So I have heard."

"Over there our best estimate is that they have about *ten times* that number. Here, we have maybe five million fighting men and women, and that's including the various militia. We think that Australia has closer to *fifty million.*" Jarem gestured with his hands. "They outnumber us ten to one. That's not the worst of it. They have advanced technology. Some of their weapons, they scare me. Weapons that can lay waste to an entire city in a matter of moments.

"They have millions of trained and experienced soldiers. They're savages, with terrible engines of war. If there was ever a conflict between our world and theirs, we wouldn't just lose. We'd be obliterated before we even picked up our weapons."

Harke was staring at him wide-eyed. "It sounds like quite a risk. But I'm not known for avoiding risks." He rubbed his chin. "So this child Empress went through to this violent place. With what support?"

"A guard in training," said Jarem. "Just a boy. The Gate can't handle any more than about a hundred kilograms at a time. After that the magnetos need to spin up again; there's at least twenty minutes between departure windows. And there just wasn't time to send anyone else."

"The Empress, and just a boy to guard her," said Harke thoughtfully. His face lit up with a wide smile; it almost made him look pleasant. "Excellent." He slapped the pillar to the side of the platform, the noise ringing through the chamber. "Fire it up."

Roadkill

I

The road stretched ahead, an arrow-straight ribbon of fake water in the late afternoon sun. The air conditioning had brought the temperature inside the car down to an almost pleasant warmth. Exhausted and wrung out, the susurrus of the tyres on the bitumen could have dragged Jess into sleep, but it was impossible to relax with the boy's angry stare burning a hole on her back.

Aran had perched in the centre of the rear seat, and his eyes in the mirror never wavered. Jess wondered if she should ask him to put his seatbelt on, and then she wondered if he would know what a seatbelt was.

The girl had taken the front passenger seat. The sun was lowering towards the horizon and directly ahead of them, and Vi was squinting. Jess didn't have a spare set of sunglasses and wasn't about to share her own.

Jess glanced sidelong at the girl. There was a slight resemblance between the two children: the same olive complexion, similarly sharp cheekbones. But where the boy's hair was almost jet black, the girl's was much lighter; in the orange dusk glow it almost looked red. Their expressions also separated them. Aran glowered in sullen anger, while Vi peered ahead, exuding calm.

Children, the pair of them. A girl of sixteen, at most, and a boy who might not even have reached his teens. It was like being kidnapped by Wednesday and Pugsley. It should have been laughable, but there was nothing amusing about the knife.

Driving in silence wouldn't answer any of her burning questions. If the girl wasn't going to volunteer information, it was up to Jess to fish. "I offered to help you. You didn't need to threaten them."

"I did not want them harmed," Vi replied. "I had them restrained for their own protection. They will be well."

"Maybe things are different wherever you came from —" *Somewhere in the middle of a barren desert.* "But if you don't want someone hurt, the best way is generally not to hurt them."

Vi smiled for the first time since leaving the roadhouse behind. "I understand that subtlety. Aran is less nuanced."

Jess paused. "He's not really your brother, is he?"

"No," answered Vi without hesitation. "He is a guard in training, sworn to protect and serve me. Do not underestimate him. Guard training begins very young."

"So why do you need guarding?" Jess asked. "Why are you afraid of the police?" She paused, hesitant of the next question, the possible ramifications. "Have you... have you done something that would make them look for you?"

"It is complicated," said Vi. "The people following me are not your police."

"They are now," said Jess. "You know they'll be looking for you."

In the back seat, Aran said something. Vi listened, looking over her shoulder, then turned back to Jess. "Aran thinks I should not talk to you. I disagree. You must understand why we are running. Also you deserve some answers."

"Well, thanks very much." Jess paused to frame her next question.

"This is a very long road," Vi said. "How far is the next settlement?"

"This is the Nullarbor desert. In front of us is another three hundred kilometres of nothing. Eventually we'll reach Eucla on the WA border. There's a customs station there, not much else."

"Tell me about this *customs station*," said Vi. "We are not... local... and we need to know what to expect. Will we need to pay the warlord for passage? Will we require papers of identity?"

"No papers." Jess raised her eyebrows. "And we don't really go in for warlords."

Vi tilted her head. "It seems I have been misinformed. Have your clans made peace?"

"What the hell? This is Australia, not bloody Kosovo!"

Vi was no longer listening. She turned to face the rear and engaged in a low-voiced discussion with Aran.

Jess concentrated furiously on the road ahead, her cheeks hot. She expected children to be ignorant, but this was well beyond ignorance.

Eventually Vi turned back. "This border crossing. What should we expect?"

Once again Jess found herself answering without stopping to think. "There's an inspection station just outside the town where they check for fruit and vegetables. There'll be government officials who'll inspect the car and luggage. If your friend back there stole some fruit when he filled that backpack, eat it or chuck it out the window before we arrive."

Vi nodded. "And will your police have had the opportunity to call ahead? Will these government officials you speak of be looking for us?"

Jess hadn't actually thought about it before now. "Of course they will. This is the main highway across the desert. They'll be keeping watch on both ends. Bruce knows this car, they'll be ready for it."

"In that case we must go a different way."

"It doesn't matter," Jess said. "We won't get that far. Eucla's our last stop. I'm dropping you off at the police station. They can look after you there."

"I cannot allow that," Vi said.

48

"Are you going to have your sidekick stab me in the back, then?" Jess tensed her shoulders in anticipation.

"I hope not. I understand I have some time to convince you."

"So long as you understand I'm not running from the police." Jess shook her head. "I've never been a fugitive from justice. I'm not exactly an expert at eluding capture by the authorities. It's never been a big part of my life."

Vi smiled. "I am no expert either." She turned again in her seat to look into the rear. "Fortunately," she added, "Aran is."

II

A prime mover with its trailer fully-loaded with three hundred head of sheep weighs about 23 tons. A lot of momentum. Ivan Brecac's truck was a good hundred metres eastward down the road before it shuddered to a halt, with a squeal of pneumatic brakes and a cacophony of disturbed livestock.

Ivan scratched his scalp for a moment, considering. Instinct made him apply the brakes, but instinct can be mistaken. He had been driving trucks for the better part of twenty years, at least half of that in constant crossings of the country's interior. The Nullarbor was no stranger to him. But something about the roadhouse had caught his eye.

Jumping down from the cab, he walked around the truck, automatically scanning the tractor, bed and tyres. All seemed okay after the sudden stop, so he turned into the sunset and shaded his eyes as he stared back at the roadhouse.

No lights.

Full dusk had fallen, the sun a sliver of red above the horizon, and the front of the roadhouse was in shadow. Ivan had driven this road a hundred times, and every roadhouse along the way should be lit up like a Christmas tree, visible in the desert night for miles around. Not Yallara.

No lights, and he could just about make out the thing that had caught his eye. The front door of the shop hung open and swayed in the hot breeze.

It didn't take him long to jog the distance. He neared the door to the shop and slowed. There was a Jeep sitting on the tarmac close to the front door. Sand piling up around its tyres, it had been motionless for a while. The front door of the roadhouse was ajar, enough to create a bubble of cooler air at the front of the building. No sounds from inside.

Ivan crouched low and checked around the corner of the building. No other vehicles. Back at the unfastened door he listened for long moments. Instincts honed in hostile environments told him that any attackers were long gone, but instinct can be mistaken.

Finally satisfied, Ivan pushed the front door open and eased himself inside. Immediately, movement caught his eye: the jerky movements of a person in restraints. Carefully, he pushed through the bead curtain that separated the kiosk from the restaurant and surveyed the scene.

Nearly twenty years driving, almost half of that in war-torn Iraq and Afghanistan. There wasn't much that could still surprise Ivan Brecac. But he'd never come across an elderly man and woman trussed up like turkeys, back-to-back, gagged with strips of tablecloth. They must have had a hundred and fifty years between them, but somebody had tied them tight enough to hurt.

The old man was trying to say something through his makeshift gag. Ivan ignored him and swept the room quickly but thoroughly with his eyes. No other occupants visible in the restaurant. He glided past the tables to the kitchen doorway and peered inside. Even in the semi-darkness it was clear the kitchen was empty.

The place appeared to be deserted apart from the tied couple. He crossed back to them. "I'm here to help." He reached to remove the man's gag. "Whoever did this... are they still here?"

The old man swallowed a couple of times to wet his throat. "No, they went a while ago. Bloody ungrateful kids. I should have left them to fry."

"What kids are those?" Ivan worked at untying the uncooperative knots behind the woman's head.

"I have no idea who they were, but we pulled them out of the sun and saved their arses, and in return they threatened us, tied us up and robbed us."

The woman needed help to get back on her feet. "We need to call the police," she said, her voice scratchy. "That poor girl. I hope she's alright."

"That girl was working with them," said her husband. "She ought to be arrested too."

"I don't think so." In response to Ivan's blank stare, she added: "There was a girl stopped here, passing through heading west. The children took her and her car."

"Did they hurt you? Did they steal much?"

"No, they didn't hurt us," said the woman.

"Don't know how much they took yet. There's not a lot here for them to steal," added the old man. "I don't know who they were, or what they were doing all the way out here, but I do know I'm calling the police. The phone's dead. You have a C-B? The range on mine is pissweak."

"In the truck," said Ivan. "I'll keep trying until I raise someone and get them to relay. And I'll stop at Nundroo for a phone."

"Much obliged. Name's Bruce, by the way, and I haven't thanked you yet for getting us out of those ropes, so thank you."

"Ivan," said Ivan, shaking hands. "I saw your lights were off and had to check it out."

"We're very glad you did," said Dot. "Speaking of, I'll get the lights now." The building was getting very dark now, but the gloom was dispelled as Dot flicked switches and overhead fluorescents came to brilliant life. "It's not every day we get mugged out here, but life goes on."

Bruce excused himself to duck into an outlying building in search of his radio set, and Ivan tailed along with Dot as she walked through the complex, turning on lights as she went. It was full dark outside by the time Ivan had satisfied himself that there were no intruders left in the roadhouse. Bruce had returned to the shop and was doing a stock-take to see how much they'd lost.

"They left all the money in the till," Bruce said. "Don't even know how to rob someone properly."

"I've three hundred head of sheep out in the truck, and they're due in Adelaide by tomorrow morning," Ivan said. "I need to get back on the road. You're sure you're alright?"

"We'll be fine now," said Bruce. "Thanks again for your help. If you can get word to the police we'd appreciate it."

"No problem," said Ivan. With the short range of CB radio and the vast empty stretches of desert, it might be quite a few hours before the word could reach the rest of civilisation. Ivan scribbled his name and contact details into the guest book on the counter. "In case they want to talk to me."

Dot handed him a Red Bull. "On the house. Drop by on your way back through and we'll make sure to thank you properly."

"I might at that," said Ivan.

III

Ivan jogged back down the road to his truck, shaking his head. Kids with knives. What next? They couldn't be locals — obviously, and not just because they were in the middle of nowhere. It took a big city or a fanatic to corrupt a kid. Nothing unusual about corrupting kids: over in the 'Ghan, the jihadists had not been above strapping teenagers into explosive vests and sending them into checkpoints in search of a shortcut to paradise. But he wouldn't have expected to find this kind of behaviour this far out bush. No, they had to be city kids, slumming it in the outback, but this was a long way to come.

His truck loomed ahead, a darker shape against the faint grey of the highway. The livestock had mostly gone to sleep by now; as he walked past the boxes one lone sheep gave a forlorn mewl before falling silent. He'd lost a good half an hour, but he'd been making good time. Should still make the deadline.

He stepped up onto the footplate and swung the cab door open.

There was a figure in the driver's seat, a man-shaped darkness with a glint of teeth. No child. This was a full-size adult and Ivan got the indefinite sense that he was male. More importantly, it was pointing a hand at him, and in the hand was something that could only be a weapon.

"We need to borrow your vehicle," said the dark figure. "Sorry."

Bugger that. The weapon was just about within reach. The man in the driver's seat had the advantage of height, but Ivan had training and surprise on his side. He tensed his muscles.

The stranger's eyes, barely visible in the night, were looking beyond his shoulder. Ivan turned his head carefully and followed the gaze.

There was a second man on the road below, another of the oddly shaped pistols in hand. Something strange about the silhouette of the man below, and it took Ivan a moment to recognise it.

A sword. That guy's got a bloody sword strapped to his back.

A combatant in front of and above him, and another below and behind, both armed. He was exposed and balanced precariously and held no weapons. *Tactical situation: not good.* Ivan let his muscles relax. *Not now.*

"We will not keep you long," continued the small man in the cab. "Two hours and we will be done, and then we can all go home."

Ivan nodded slowly. He would cooperate. He would give these men no trouble. He would follow their instructions, and when the chance arrived he would take their weapons from them and break their legs, tie them in one of the sheep pens and drive them to the police. Corporal Brecac didn't appreciate people pointing guns at him.

He smiled. "What do you need me to do?"

IV

In addition to bottles of water, packets of crinkle-cut chips and a loaf of bread — and, indeed, half a dozen pieces of withered fruit — Aran had taken a map from the kiosk. Now it was spread over the rear hatch of the big station wagon. Aran might not have understood English, but he proved a quick study with translations from Vi and Jess.

The merest fraction of the blood-red sun was above the horizon, and the day's heat was rapidly leaching from the air. Last night was frigid, and this morning's dawn had brought a light frost. That had been further east, back in Port Augusta, and it was likely to get even colder this far west.

She had rummaged through the plastic bin liners that held all her worldly goods in the back of the car until she had found a t-shirt, jumper and track pants for Vi to cover her bare legs and arms. The jumper was way too large for the girl and she had needed to roll up the ankles of the pants; in the oversized clothing she looked even younger than she had in the white dress.

Aran asked a question. The language had a rough feel to it and gave the impression of something eastern European — Serbian, maybe.

"What is south of the highway?" Vi translated Aran's question. The map was large-scale and below the line of the highway the map was awash with blank white. The girl's finger was pointing to a small text note on the coast. Jess peered closely in the dim light.

"Koonalda homestead," she replied. "Caves, I think. The coast isn't far from here, and it's mostly cliffs along the south. Limestone caves all the way along — the plain is riddled with them."

"Aran says we could hide out in the caves for some time," Vi relayed. "Are they large enough to enter?"

54

"They go for miles," said Jess. "But you'd be naïve to think that the police didn't have them mapped out and know where to look. Besides, a lot of them are full of water and dangerous."

She waited whilst Vi and Aran argued softly. Eventually Vi turned back to her. "Not the caves. We may need to avoid capture for a long time... perhaps months, or longer. The roads are patrolled and they will be watching at each end. If we leave the road? Can we travel across the desert?"

This was not going according to plan and she had no intention of driving the children off-road. A couple of hours to Eucla, that's all she needed. She pretended to take the question seriously. "Before we reach any towns, we'll come across cattle stations. Fences. I don't know what they make the fences out of... probably just wire. We'd be able to get through them. I'd be more concerned about the car. It's not made for off-road."

Vi translated for Aran and nodded at his response. "Cutting fences will leave a trail. Once we reach more populated areas, Aran can help us blend in. We must go where there are more people."

"What will you do there? Say you do make it to Perth. Do you know anyone there? Do you have anywhere to go?"

Vi shook her head. "We will manage."

They had threatened her, effectively kidnapped her; but they were still children. "And what then? What kind of life will you have? *He* can't speak English. You won't be able to work. You can't get government handouts if they don't know who you are. And it's not pleasant living on the streets." *Particularly not for a girl who wears that kind of dress.* "Let me take you to the authorities. Tell them who you are. If you're refugees, Australia has a legal responsibility to look after you. They won't send you back." She wasn't sure if that was true but it was believable.

"Refugees," Vi mused softly. "I suppose we are, of a sort."

"*Tek'gra co savass,*" said Aran sharply.

Vi's head snapped around. "Lights. He sees lights."

In the darkness the lights were clearly visible, further down the highway but approaching. A large vehicle — probably a cattle train. "It'll be a freight truck," Jess said. "They're always travelling along the highway, day and night."

"I do not like us being beside the road. We need to get moving again."

Without argument Aran folded the map and took it with him into the back seat of the car. Jess took a couple of moments to resettle her belongings and close up the hatch; by the time she was settling in the driver's seat Vi was agitated. "Let us go."

"*Et jev co*", said Aran as the car started moving. Slowly the heavy car came up to speed, the dotted yellow centre line becoming solid in the headlights.

"Turn the lights off," said Vi. "We are too bright."

"That's *really* not a good idea," Jess protested. Experimentally she flicked the lights off, and the road ahead blinked into invisibility. She edged off the accelerator, shook her head and turned the lights back on. "We shouldn't be driving at all at this time of night. We can't drive without lights. The desert might look empty, but it's not. Kangaroos, wombats, foxes, even camels. If we hit something, it's not just inconvenient. If we break the car, we could die of heatstroke before anyone came to our rescue."

"We must leave the road," said Vi, stubbornly, "and we need the lights off. We will be seen."

"We've already been seen," argued Jess. "If we can see the truck, he can see us. He doesn't care about us, but you can bet he'll remember us if we leave the road and drive off into the middle of nowhere. He might even stop to see if we're OK. Then you'd just have someone else to threaten." She flinched as something hit the windscreen — just an insect, leaving behind a smear. They were driving way too fast. "We have to slow down. Just let him pass. He'll have no reason to remember another car on the road."

Vi twisted in her seat, staring out the back of the car. The truck was gaining on them rapidly, growing steadily clearer. The square shape of the cab was now visible, outlined in argent lights. The girl seemed to weigh up its proximity and speed and come to a decision. "You are right. He has seen us. But drive faster."

Jess tried to ignore her, but there was something about the oncoming truck that seemed off. The lights were dimming and brightening, and it took Jess a moment to recognise that the driver was flashing his high-beams.

The girl's apprehension was contagious and Jess gave the car more speed before she had thought about it. Soon she had the Taurus near the speed limit, the needle resting just below 110, but the truck was still visibly gaining on them. She felt the first cold tendrils of doubt coiling. "Who did you say was chasing you?"

The truck was close enough now that they could hear its engine even over the whine of the straining Taurus engine, and now it was joined by a louder noise: the truck's airhorn. One long blast, then two shorter ones, then it fell silent.

"I did not *know* we would be followed. But if our pursuers are in that vehicle, they will not be satisfied with *chasing*. So *drive faster!*"

Unbidden, Jess' foot drove the accelerator to the floor. The car leapt like the fish that had inspired its design. The engine complained, the ride becoming rougher. "Okay," said Jess, wrestling with the wheel to keep the car straight, "now you really need to explain to me what this is all about. Are they going to try to ram us? Shoot us?"

Vi paused, choosing her words. "There is a war. We are not here to fight; we came to escape from the fighting."

"Child soldiers." That might explain a few things — like Aran's comfort with the knife. But who the hell in this region was using child soldiers?

She was hardly aware she'd spoken aloud until Vi shook her head. "We are not soldiers. We came here to escape capture. There was always a chance they would not let me go easily."

A warning light on the dashboard blinked into orange. Jess tried to ignore it. "If you're not soldiers, what do they want with you?"

The girl's eyes were bright in the dark interior of the car. "They may have instructions to return me alive. I am sure they will kill anyone with me. I suggest we stay ahead of them and avoid finding out."

"This is ridiculous," Jess protested. "It's just a driver, taking his stock across to Perth. He'll drive right by us."

"If you are certain of that," said Vi, "then slow down and let him."

Jess wasn't certain of it at all. All the talk of soldiers and wars and killing was getting to her. "There's no way we're going to outrun them," she told the girl. "There's nowhere to go."

Aran was jabbering in the back, and Jess found it very distracting. Vi shook her head, turned back to Jess. "Just try to stay in front," she said. "Perhaps they will drive by, as you said. Or perhaps they will try not to harm me."

He's just a trucker, Jess told herself. *He's got a load of timber or DVD players or canned emu meat bound for Perth.* It hardly mattered; the truck was bearing down on them and they would find out soon enough.

On the dash, the 'engine overheating' light turned from orange to red.

V

The truck's engine was the roar of a wild beast; not in tortured pain, but finally let off its leash. The truck ate up the bitumen before it, tyres thrumming; the sheep on the tray were awake and frightened, but barely audible through the rush of the slipstream.

The man in the passenger seat wasn't taking his eyes off Ivan. The man held his strange, stubby gun back, close to his chest, out of reach of an easy lunge. Wrestling with the wheel took all his attention and he had none to spare for escaping his captors, but they were taking no chances.

The other man was taller and far fitter. With his body-builder physique and his bald head, he reminded Ivan of that wrestler who'd gone into the movies. The big man had taken one glance at the sleeper cabin behind the truck's seats, considered folding himself into the cramped space, and shaken his head. Now he rode outside the cab, clinging to the driver's door, standing on the spacious foot-plate. The separation of the window's glass gave Ivan a false sense of safety, but the guy was also armed with another of those strange pistols, and in all likelihood the window would be no safety at all.

Ahead of them the car was rapidly getting closer. Hurtling down the highway in a vehicle with the weight of a small train, armed hostiles to either side. Ivan felt an exhilaration he'd missed for years.

He was buggered if he was going to let himself get killed, but it was starting to look like that might be what it would take not to kill the driver of the Ford.

"That's them," said the passenger. He was holding some kind of tablet computer in his left hand. His glances at the tablet were not long enough for Ivan to take advantage of his distraction. "We need to stop them. Block them in, run them off the road, whatever you can."

"Block them in with what?" Out here there were no fences, no curbs, nothing but the road and the desert. Ahead of them the car was losing ground; even at top speed it was no match for his rig.

"Ram them, if you think it will help," said the passenger. Ivan could make out the man's eyes, white all around; he looked more scared than angry.

The world had shrunk to a motion blur of sand and darkness; the car and the truck seemed to be the only things real. The Ford was close enough now that he could peer down from the cab and see through the windows. There was a woman at the wheel. The truck blundered on through tendrils of mist in the cold night, until Ivan started; it was far too dry out here for mist. That was *steam*, escaping from the vehicle now just metres in front of them. The Ford was on the verge of breaking down.

Ivan brought the truck up to the rear of the station wagon, nudged the corner of his bull-bar into the rear of the car.

A mistake. The Ford was a heavy car, and the collision robbed momentum. The rig was too back-heavy, and the road was slick: in addition to steam, the car was spilling oil. The cab nudged left, the tyres slipping under the sideways force.

Ivan backed off the accelerator. He was once riding shotgun in a truck that jack-knifed while carrying cattle; that had been a godawful mess and cost the company a shitload of money. Not while *he* was behind the wheel. Ivan feathered the brakes and the accelerator until he had the truck back under control.

The big Ford had swerved under the impact but stayed on the road. The interruption had allowed their quarry to gain some ground. Ivan had to shout at his passenger to make himself heard. "I don't know if I can stop them safely!"

"Do I look like I care about safe?" In addition to being scared the passenger now looked nauseous. Ivan stole a glance to his right; somehow the giant had managed to hold on and was still with them.

Ivan pulled the truck back up to the Ford, which was slowing now. This time he swung out to the car's left, the truck's left wheels crossing onto the dirt shoulder, and slowly edged up beside the Ford. "Push them off!" ordered the passenger, his eyes bright with excitement.

Glancing out the window, Ivan could see right into the passenger seat of the wagon. There was a young girl in the seat, staring directly at him. She was about the age of his niece.

Suddenly this wasn't exciting any longer. He was trying to run a young family off the road.

And the giant, outside his window and close enough to the car he could have reached out and touched its roof, was levelling his pistol at the girl from near point-blank range.

Not fair, not fair at all. "You got it," he growled, and wrenched the wheel to the right.

The manoeuvre took the bald man by surprise, throwing him back against the cab. The truck barrelled into the car and the cab rocked wildly. The Ford went into a spin, tyres squealing on the road, and disappeared behind them. The bald man outside the cab lost hold of his gun and had to grab hold of the roof with both hands to avoid being thrown. The weapon clattered against the chassis and then went under the cab and was gone.

Ivan stepped on the airbrakes. Behind them, the Ford was unmoving, still somehow on the road but facing back east, black smoke pouring from under the bonnet. "They're stopped," Ivan grunted as he wrestled the truck back into submission.

"Good," said his passenger, as the truck came to a halt. "Now you must come with us. We still require your vehicle."

The giant jumped down from the cab, reaching to unsheath his sword. A big man with a long blade, but he was much less of a threat without his gun. One-on-one, Ivan was sure he could take him.

He only needed to wait for his moment.

VI

This was what happened.

The moment the car stopped moving, Aran was out the back door like an eel and ducking off the road. He stumbled, his head spinning. No training could have prepared him for the kind of pinwheeling the car had just put them through. It only took a few strides before he regained his balance and was steady on his feet, dashing across the hardpan.

The night was ink, the moon the merest sliver overhead. Less helpful was the terrain, which was still stubbornly flat and featureless. No contours to hide in, distance and darkness his only friends. The big truck was coming to a halt ahead. Far ahead; it took a long time to stop and it was not close.

That gave him a moment to get some range, find a scrub brush to break his silhouette. Not too far; he needed to stay close enough and wait for his moment.

This was what *always* happened. Every time an Empress ignored the advice of her Captain, it was the warrior left to pick up the pieces. The insurrection under Uki, the Empress putting herself at risk for the sake of a few petty baubles against Captain Arrol's counsel. Empress Ramia, whose Captain Tolo sacrificed himself to win back her Crown after she'd lost it. Captain Wirren, who saved his Empress from being lost in an avalanche at the cost of his own legs. Some day Aran's own name would be remembered in that list. But first he needed to kill these men.

The vehicle — the *car* — had died during that last spin along the road. Smoke was pouring from the front, a column of darker black against the night. The Empress had stumbled out of the front seat, falling to her knees in the road, the local woman by her shoulder and supporting her. That should have been Aran's place, but he couldn't be in two places at once.

Besides, he had more useful skills. If the Empress was so intent on throwing in her lot with this woman *Jess*, let her provide the comforting hand. It was time for Aran to prove his value in other ways.

The Empress didn't respect his advice, his skills, that much was crystal clear. Not knowing the language, the people in this strange place, was a handicap. He knew only what she deigned to tell him, and she'd told him nothing.

This is what happened. Now it was up to him to get her out of it.

The assailants from the truck approached. Even at this distance he recognised the lead of the three approaching men: the technician from the gate chamber, the one controlling the mechanisms. Harem? No, Jarem. Had the High Council relented? Were they trying to bring the Empress back so soon?

Was the war over already?

No. Even if Beryn had managed to reach the capital, it would take him time to fight through Harke's forces. More time still to reopen the Bridge. And then there was the attack by the truck: proof of malice. And the moment when the other man had levelled his weapon at the Empress through the window, there could be no doubt remaining after that. These were enemies. Jarem was working with the enemy.

Behind Jarem was the bearded, tattooed man who had been driving the truck, his hands behind his head. The big soldier was bringing up the rear. Instead of his flinger the soldier held his sword, low and angled to rest the tip of its blade against tattoo-man's shoulders.

Lost his flinger. Interesting.

That made tattoo-man a non-combatant. Leaving just two for Aran to handle. He could do that. He'd handled worse odds before.

Keres and his fellows had never dared approach him singly. Aran's body remained stubbornly thin and ungainly; his tutors kept at a more than respectable distance, avoiding any suggestion of favouritism for Captain Gabe's only son; his peers had shunned and taunted him. For all of that, they at least had respected him. *Because* of these handicaps. They forced him to train harder than anyone else, to improve himself. To become better than them, just to survive.

Because they respected him, they came at him in packs. The second time he left six of his peers bloodied on the floor was the last time they tried.

He could handle two enemies, and one of them a civilian.

He crouched low on the packed dirt, behind a patchy shrub a short distance from the road. Drillmaster Warren's voice ringing in his head: *Camouflage is all about shape and movement. Don't worry about colours and textures. If you can break the silhouette, if you can remain still, there's a good chance that your enemy won't see you.*

Of course, if he's looking for you it's a different question.

Aran crouched behind the shrub, broke his silhouette and remained still. In the desert night, sounds travelled on the crystalline air; he could hear the conversation clearly.

"Praise the Crown," said the technician. "My lady, I was afraid you might have been injured."

"Master Jarem," said Vi. "I am astonished to see you here."

"I've been sent to bring you back. You won't be harmed. You'll be safe."

"Funny way you have of keeping me *safe*," said Vi, nodding towards the still-smoking car. "Your man was about to shoot me."

"Captain Aesk wouldn't have harmed you," Jarem assured her. "You're not hurt, are you?"

"I'm fine," said Vi. "You're telling me the war is over? Harke is vanquished? Did Beryn arrive sooner than expected?"

Jarem shrugged. "The war *is* over. *Emperor* Harke wishes you returned to him safely. It's time to rejoin your mother."

Vi bit back a laugh. "'Emperor' Harke. I see. He sent two people, and one of them was you?"

"Two of us." Jarem shrugged. "Two of you. And yet, here we are." He gestured with his weapon. "But we're not alone. There's a squad gathering back at the Bridge. You should know: Utara is here."

Aran's blood ran cold at the name. Utara. The Butcher of Brank, famous for his ruthless efficiency as much as his sadistic enjoyment of the spoils of war.

"Utara," said Vi, her voice colder than the chill night air. "I thought Harke wanted me alive."

"He does. That won't stop Utara from having his fun with you. I'll tell you something, Harke may be dangerous, but it's Utara who really scares me." He held out an imploring hand. "My lady, please come back with me now. Come peacefully, I can ensure you're unharmed. Be glad that you didn't make him have to come and find you. If you fall into his hands, I might not be able to protect you. If you come with me now, I promise you'll be well treated."

"You sound almost like you care," said Vi, anger seeping through the fright in her voice. "But then, I guess you've had a lot of practice at sounding sincere. How long have you been working with Harke? My mother trusted you. For twenty years you've had unrivalled authority. What did Harke promise that turned you? Power? You already had that. Wealth?"

"It doesn't matter," Jarem said. "I didn't do it for the reward."

"Tell me what you want," Vi insisted. "I am Empress now. If it's in my power, I'll grant it."

"No, you won't. You could, but you won't. It would go against everything the Crown stands for. Three hundred years of tradition. Even the Empress isn't going to change that. But Harke will."

The native woman, Jess, stared blankly. She couldn't hope to understand the rapid-fire dialogue: she didn't know the language. Aran didn't understand either, and he had no such excuse.

Vi evidently understood what Jarem's meaning. "The Guilds will revolt."

"Harke doesn't care about the Guilds. They wouldn't have him."

"So he has payback in mind?"

"He's going to disband the Tiers. If the Guilds have to disappear as well, I don't think he'll be unhappy." Jarem shrugged, the flinger in his hand wavering to the side, and Aran tensed, but the moment passed too quickly. "I've been offered a place on the High Council, wealth and privilege. I don't want any of it."

The Empress had lowered her voice and Aran had to strain to hear it. "Perhaps you had reasons for what you did. But why are you here now? There's no way home for either of us."

"I'm the Gatemaster. I'll get us back."

Aran's sudden intake of breath was far too loud. *A way home*. Until this

65

moment Aran had been trying not to think of the likelihood they would be trapped here forever.

"So you've found us. What happens next?"

"You come back with us. I can start building the reflector straight away. We can be home in three days."

"The gate's in the middle of the desert," said Vi. "Two hours in that sun almost killed me. You plan to stay out in the open for three days?"

"There's a building," said Jarem. "Shelter, shade and water."

"There are civilians in that building," Vi said softly. "You know what Utara will do to them."

"There's no choice. You said it yourself. We can't survive without shelter."

"You'll draw attention," Vi insisted. "Are you ready for that?"

"That's Utara's problem, not mine." There was an uncomfortable hitch in his voice. "You're my problem. I'll make sure you're not mistreated. Whatever else happens, I won't let Utara get his hands on you."

"Are you expecting gratitude? What about my friend?" Vi glanced across at Jess, whose eyes were fixed on the weapon in Jarem's hand.

"She's a civilian?"

"This isn't a combat area," said Vi. "They're *all* civilians. She doesn't know anything important. You should let her go."

"You know we have to kill her," said the soldier. The first time he'd spoken. "Lord Harke said as much; we can't leave witnesses. I'll do it."

Jarem shook his head. "I'm not going to be responsible for that. We'll head back. Utara can decide."

Aran tightened his lips. A quick death here might be preferable to what Utara would do to the woman.

Vi turned to say a few words to the woman in the strange language they used here. Jarem lowered his flinger and relaxed, and Aran saw his chance... possibly his *only* chance.

VII

The sand was almost silent under his feet as he broke cover and ran towards them. They were all facing away from him now: the guard with the sword, the tattooed man and Jarem were all facing Vi and the woman at the car, and the two women were not looking in his direction. *Don't look, don't turn.* Aran lifted the knife and closed in on the soldier. One strike to disable him, then on to kill Jarem before he knew what was happening, before he could bring the gun to bear. He would get only one chance at this; he had to be perfect. He was light on his feet. He was fast and deadly. He was the most dangerous person in this desert. This was his moment.

At the last moment, as he was closing the last few steps towards the road, the bald guard must have heard something. He started to turn and Aran's knife, intended for his lower spine, went instead into his back just above his buttocks.

The bald soldier roared in surprise and pain and lurched away, and Aran lost hold of the knife, the weapon spinning to the ground. The man swung to face him, the sword whistling around with him, and Aran knew that he was lost. But the wound to the soldier's side unbalanced him; his foot went out from under him, he stumbled, and the strike missed. The sword hissed as it passed Aran's ear and bit into the dirt.

The Drillmaster's voice in his head: *You don't need your own weapon to kill an enemy. Control the enemy's weapon, and you control the fight.*

He'd lost the surprise, a far more valuable weapon than the knife. He still had his training. He couldn't let the big man take the initiative again; he wouldn't get another reprieve. Aran shouted, hating his shrill voice, and launched himself at the big man, wrestling for the sword.

The bald man had size and strength on his side, but Aran let his muscle memory take over as he came into close contact. He was trained for this. Combat moves, drilled for countless hours, came to him now without pausing for thought. He ducked under a wild left-handed punch —barely needed to duck at all, the man was swinging too high. With the edge of his left hand he blocked the man's upswing, instead pushing the sword aside and down. Used his right fist to strike at the inside of the man's elbow, a strike that should have made the man's arm explode with pain. He got a hand under the soldier's thumb on the hilt of the sword, *levered*, and the man's hand came open, the sword swinging away in Aran's left hand. His heart leapt in exultation as he started the spin that would take him away from the captain, giving him the space to use the man's own sword against him.

And then the world exploded into white and red as the guard's other fist crashed into his face. He felt himself spin, pitching to the ground, sand driving into his cheek. The world spun around him and slowly settled. Aran found himself on his back, his head a blaze of pain, flat in the dirt. He still held the sword in his off hand, but he didn't have the strength to lift his head, let alone the arm.

It wasn't fair; that strike hadn't been in the training. He'd seen the fist coming but lacked a practiced technique to avoid the blow. Now he was done. It was over. He felt tears welling in his eyes and his cheeks burned with the shame of it. He didn't want to die crying.

Moments later he was still alive. He forced himself to sit up and blinked. Everything was blurred and his left eye wouldn't open. It took a moment to make sense of what he was seeing.

The bald guard was on his knees on the road, his hands above his head. Jarem was next to him, also kneeling. The tattooed man was facing them, and in *his* hand was the flinger.

Then Vi was at Aran's side, helping him to his feet, keeping him from touching his face. "Leave it be," she said, "you're hurt."

The woman, Jess, came to him too with a bottle of water and rags, and she reached out to bathe his face. The mere touch almost made him fade out again, and he pushed away from her. The world swung around him, but he held his feet until it steadied. When he was confident to move, he forced himself to approach the men on their knees.

"You cut me," said the bald soldier. "You're going to regret that, *boy*." Blood was running down the back of his right leg and pooling around his knee in the sand, but he showed no indication that it hurt him.

Jarem eyed the sword, still swinging loose in Aran's hand, and tried to smile. The technician's lip was split, blood trickling down his chin; obviously he didn't give up the gun easily. "I was wondering where you'd gone. Are you going to kill us now?"

"I should," Aran growled. The words came out slurred; his lips had swollen. "You're a traitor." He stopped in front of them, glanced back at Vi. *Give me permission*, he asked with his eyes.

Vi shook her head. "I don't..." She paused, straightened her shoulders, turned to face Jarem. "I've known you all my life. I can't —I'm going to let you go. Both of you." She glanced at Aran but wouldn't meet his eyes, quickly looking away again. "I won't make that offer a second time. Go back to your Emperor. Go be a Lord, or live a life of quiet and solitude, I don't care. Just make sure I never see you again."

"Utara will come after you," said Jarem. "By the time this is all over, you'll have reason to appreciate seeing me again."

"Go," Vi said, her voice strangled. Like there was another voice inside her trying to get out.

Aran waited for that word. His hand, wrapped white-knuckled around the sword hilt, burned with the desire to end them, despite the Empress's command. But Vi turned away, and the moment was past.

He stepped forward. Jarem winced but Aran slipped past him. He bent towards the big soldier, close enough to smell the man's sour breath. A moment later he stepped away, dangling the sword's scabbard from his left hand. He looped the scabbard over his shoulder and moved to Jarem's side. The technician held himself rigidly still while Aran unfastened the holster from his belt.

Only after Aran had moved away did Jarem respond, nodding at the Empress. "A very practical young man. It will be a shame when Utara takes his fingers."

"I can cut you if I want," Aran told him. He remembered something his father had once said to him and repeated it verbatim. "The Empress gives the orders, but her guards are the ones who have to make it all work, and sometimes that means making our own rules."

"Go," said Vi. "It's a long walk back to the Gate. You'd best get started. It gets hot during the day." She turned her head to address both the native woman and the tattooed man, speaking in their native language. Aran watched as the tattooed man stepped away from his captives and allowed them to struggle to their feet. The man kept the flinger aimed until they were well away down the road, the big man limping.

Only when their receding forms were well distant did Aran finally allow Jess to help him with his battered face. Cold water on a cloth soothed the worst of the ache, but his left eye was nearly swollen shut and would need some time to heal.

He sat against the residual warmth of the smoking vehicle's tyres and closed his eyes, trying to calm his pounding headache, holding the cloth to his face. Indecipherable discussion wheeled around, the local language harsh gibberish to his ears. The tattooed man seemed to be arguing for something, but Vi and the woman talked him around. Eventually the conversation ceased and for a few moments there was blissful silence.

A gentle touch on the shoulder roused him. "Ivan has agreed to help us," the Empress said. "It's time to go."

The tattooed driver had turned the enormous vehicle around to face east, and now he brought the transport to a rolling halt on the road beside the dead *car*.

"Ivan will take us east. We don't have to go through the customs station, and their authorities will not be looking for this vehicle. Ivan will take us as far as the next major town."

"East. That's where Utara and his squad are gathering," said Aran. "They'll think we're still heading west."

Vi tilted her head. "Even if they see us coming, perhaps they won't be able to stop us in the truck."

"I hope they do," said Aran fiercely. "I'll kill them. We should have killed them already. You should have let me."

"Next time." The Empress's voice was faint. "I won't hold you back." She shook her head. "We won't get any warning the next time they find us. At least you've got a flinger now."

Aran smiled; his battered lips gave a sudden flare of pain but he ignored it.

All his life, he'd been outclassed. Keres had always been fitter and faster and stronger, better looking and better liked. Perhaps Keres might have done better in that fight against the soldier, might not have been so easily knocked out. But Keres had never been able to beat Aran at sleight of hand, and he'd never beaten him in a game of wits.

Aran held his prize up for her to see. "That's not all I have."

He let Jarem's data pad, the pad with the schematics and data for the gateway to home, dangle from his fingers, and smiled in spite of the pain from his battered face.

Connecting Flights

Red and blue light washed over dark hillocks of sand in stark, otherworldly beauty. Razor shadows sliced across the front of the roadhouse. Jeffrey Lang unfolded himself from the cruiser, placed his hands on his hips and rolled his shoulders. Five hours speeding through the empty night. He ought to have been aggrieved, but instead the outback terrain energised him. He loved this country.

On the wrong side of two in the morning the roadhouse was in darkness. The owners had evidently retired for the night. They were the sensible ones. "A bit of a drive", Sergeant Young had said, and the malicious glint in his eyes should have given Jeff warning. He'd been at Augusta long enough to understand what *a bit of a drive* meant.

Still, he was here now. A quick finger-check confirmed that his holster was unbuttoned, pistol ready to hand, but he wouldn't need it. Armed robbery, Sergeant Young had said, but he'd neglected to add that it took hours for the report to reach the station. This case was stone cold.

No obvious signs of disturbance around the entrance to the Yallara roadhouse. The front door was sealed tight and all the windows seemed intact. He had to knock for almost a minute before he got a response.

"Didn't expect you tonight," grumbled the old man as he ran his eye from Jeff's boots to his head. "Christ. You're a townie."

"Been in Augusta eighteen months," Jeff said.

"Is that right?"

Jeff sighed. No point fighting it. It took a long time for some guys to lose their new-city smell. Some people didn't become a part of country until they were buried in it. Jeff let it pass and moved onto his reason for being here. "We take armed robbery seriously. They tied you up. That's aggravated burglary and false imprisonment."

"Yeah, well, that was hours ago," said the old man. "And we've got an early morning tomorrow. Just like every morning."

They sat in the diner, a single overhead globe casting a pool of orange light over the table, as the old man introduced himself. Jeff earned no favours when he insisted Bruce's wife get up to give her side of the story. He took notes as they told him of the woman in the Ford with her bruises. The mysterious appearance of the children in the desert. The unexpected threat of violence. "Been running this place for twenty years," Bruce complained. "Never been mugged before."

Jeff had half expected to hear about townies, maybe shaggy teens in a stolen car. Nothing in the report had hinted at kids being involved. And as for this woman... "Tell me about the woman in the car."

"That girl's been through here a dozen times in the last five or eight years," said Dot. "She's never given us any trouble, and she's always had the same car. Seemed a nice young lady, friendly, polite. I can't believe she's responsible."

"Maybe." Her frequent passage was a pattern, but being unaccompanied was a deviation. Bruises on her face. There was something more to this, a mystery waiting to be uncovered. He loved this feeling.

Bruce described the woman's car: a Ford Taurus, teal green.

"Wait. A Taurus? That's a big station wagon, isn't it?"

"That's about right."

Interesting. "There's been a report of an abandoned vehicle." About thirty kilometres west. "They might be on foot."

It was Bruce's turn to look doubtful. "Out here? Not if they know what's good for them."

73

"If they're on foot, they won't get far," said Jeff.

He had Bruce and Dot show him through the kiosk. They pointed out the broken cabinets, the empty spaces where the boy had stolen food and water. Jeff examined the page of the address book with the truck driver's details and wondered that they had not heard from this 'Mr Brecac'.

"How much did they take?" Jeff asked, tapping the lever on the register to eject the cash drawer.

"They weren't interested in the till," Dorothy said. "Never even looked at it."

"That's odd, don't you think?"

"Wouldn't know. Never been robbed before," Bruce said. The old man was holding out a bundle of white fabric.

Jeff raised an eyebrow. "What's this?"

"The girl's dress. She left it behind. Don't know if you can use it?"

"Sure. It's evidence." Jeff accepted the offering with care. The dress crumpled as he pushed it into an evidence satchel. That dress held possibilities. *Doctor Ferguson.* Suddenly Jeff was anxious to get moving. "I should let you get some sleep. I've got a bit of a drive ahead anyway."

"Don't be silly," Dot said. "It's late. Take one of the rooms, get a start early tomorrow when it's light."

He fully intended to get an early start but he didn't want to do it two hours from the station. "Thanks, but no." He tried to keep the impatience out of his voice. "If we find the woman, the children, we may need you for a formal identification. You're not going anywhere?"

"Our travelling days are done, son," said Bruce.

He stowed the bagged dress securely into a compartment in the cruiser and allowed himself the thrill of a vision. An image of slender hands peeling the bag open. Long fingers, graceful movements. Doctor Adele Ferguson had amazing hands.

One small bundle of fabric. No need to send it to the big labs in Adelaide; not when they had a local consultant capable of handling smaller jobs. Doctor Adele Ferguson, part time microbiology lecturer, part-time pathologist and the woman Jeff planned to marry. Not that she knew it yet.

That bundle of white cloth might have held a myriad of clues, data to make sense of the Yallara roadhouse robbery. Just as likely, it was a dead end. If it gave him the opportunity to interact with Doctor Ferguson, it hardly mattered. Jeff Lang would take advantage of any excuse.

He thought it entirely possible that he loved Adele Ferguson.

II

Beyond the plate glass of the floor-to-ceiling window, his city was in ruins.

Even now engineers were turning their attention to the city's infrastructure. He had too few of them, his army predominantly made up of uneducated labourers. That would change. When things were a little more settled he would draft in experts to rebuild the city. For now, he'd directed his best people to concentrate on repairing the generators for the Barrier. If Beryn ever crossed the straits with his forces he would find himself confronted with the same defences that had held Harke at bay for so long.

His hands were shaking. Harke frowned, staring at the tremors. He clasped his hands together, wrung them, shook them from the wrists. Hours of stress and adrenaline, finally souring into fatigue. He reached blindly behind himself for the swivel chair. He fell into it and told himself it was a graceful lowering.

There was nobody else in the room to impress. For the first time in hours he had a moment to himself. He closed his eyes, breathed deep and enjoyed the sensation of falling, just for a moment. No longer. He didn't dare rest, for fear that his exhaustion would pull him down into sleep.

There was still too much to do. Too many people to placate.

It had already started. Today had been a never-ending procession of his generals, each one demanding he fulfil on the instant the pledges he had made to them, undertakings he had made in advance of this day.

Without his generals, without the men they brought to his cause, he might still have been a worker in a far-flung province. A baker. Perhaps a guard in one of the labour camps. He certainly would not have been in the Imperial Palace, seated at the heart of power. He owed them, and they had not been slow in reminding him.

Tomorrow would be worse.

They were already lining up: the artisans who had provided him material support, well-behaved citizens who surreptitiously provided him money and supplies and weapons, the Regional controllers who turned a blind eye to his armies' passage. All of them would be expecting his boon, and he wasn't yet able to grant it. They all seemed to think the war was over. Didn't they realise the real fight was just beginning?

Harke drummed his fingers on the broad wooden expanse of the curved data desk. Old wood, carved at great peril from a native tree in the forests; none of the plantations produced wood of this stature. He'd fallen in love with the desk, and by extension the office it sat in, the moment he set eyes on it, and claimed it for his own. The appeal had soured throughout the afternoon as he couldn't work out how to operate the thing. A control prompt on the embedded screen mocked him relentlessly, daring him to have another go. *You'd think that after almost thirty different professions I would have learned to operate a data terminal by now.*

He was at least capable of bringing up a video call. The screen resolved into Joteun's jowly face, his morose expression a fitting match for Harke's mood.

"I need to see Jadda," Harke said. "And do you think we can find someone to cover this damn window?" The city, with its rubble and its smoking ashes, was beginning to depress him.

The palace staffer arrived first. The man was of indeterminate age — not old, but certainly not young — and he operated the controls on the table screen with deference. As the windows darkened to opaque, the man never looked Harke in the eyes.

"You're not in trouble," Harke said. "You're just doing your job."

The servant glanced up from the screen, then back down. It wasn't fear in his eyes. Harke diagnosed a deep-grained self-loathing. The man had been a serf under the old regime. Now here he was: still a serf, just for new masters.

Harke sighed. *I did all this for you.* No point in saying it. Here he was, conquering hero, victor and ruler, but never a liberator: he had won a city full of people who wanted to be ruled.

Thankfully Jadda was not long arriving. As always immaculate in a tunic with razor creases, wire-framed glasses hanging around his neck. Next to him Harke felt underdressed.

"Tell me you have good news," Harke pleaded.

The technician had been with him almost since the beginning, long enough to have his irritating deference beaten out of him. "What do you want to hear? We've repaired the comm-links."

Harke had already known that; he nodded impatiently.

Jadda went on. "We sent the communiques as requested. The news is out — you can be sure that the Regions are aware."

"Aware. And have they responded?"

Jadda shuffled his feet awkwardly. "There has been no response. As yet."

"Not from *any* of them? We're sure the messages are being received?"

"Oh yes," said Jadda. "The link works on the basis of paired magnetic field fluctuations. When the link is established there's a..." He became aware of Harke's blank and disapproving stare. "There's a detectable attenuation..." He changed tack. "The messages are being received and decoded at the other end."

"And they're not answering," said Harke.

He shouldn't have been so disappointed. When he had first embarked upon this grand insanity, he had been possessed of a vision of the populace rising up to join his glorious crusade for freedom. He should have known better. He *had* known better, but he'd ruthlessly squashed that doubt, just as he'd spent the better part of his lifetime squashing all doubts and fears.

"Keep trying them," he said. "Let me know as soon as any of them respond. *If* any do." Any response at all would be good. The inland sea that ringed Capital Island had eight Regions sharing its coastline. He would prefer that they openly declare their position, join their own troops to support Beryn's, rather than this deliberate inattention. Instead, they ignored him.

He'd decapitated the Empire. Acknowledging him would be simple courtesy. How long could life go on in the regions without the support of the Capital, the High Council and the Council of Lords?

Outside of the covered window, he could almost imagine that he could see the entire breadth of his domain. He'd set out to win a world, and he'd won a ruined city. He had a few thousand troops at his command. Perhaps ten thousand civilians, their declared loyalty suspect at best. The people had not flocked to him in their thousands at first. They hadn't gravitated to his cause as he had started to win battles. And they still refused to heed him now he was victorious. His engineers had repaired the communications links out of the capital as a matter of priority, but the Low Councils of the surrounding Regions weren't even taking his calls.

And then there was the Empress and her stupid, brilliant inspiration to entrust the heritage of a thousand rulers to her girl-child and send her into a world of war and barbarism. His plans had absolutely depended upon capturing the Crown. Instead the Empress had found a way to thwart him, his prize slipping out of his grasp even as his fist tightened.

Maybe he *did* have something to be disappointed about after all.

What was done, was done. If it could be achieved, Utara would bring her back. The most ruthless of his generals, the most violent, the most dependable. The child Empress's escape had at least given him a reason to get Utara out of his hair. He should be grateful for small mercies. Harke had no illusions about the man's enduring value; he would surely have become more of a liability than an asset once the fighting was done.

Even on a different planet, Utara felt like a threat.

III

The front of the palace still held its shape but great holes had been smashed in the marble, as if God had flicked chova-nuts at a castle of sand. Harke shook his head as he descended the steps to the square. He'd done enough time as an apprentice stoneworker to see that it would be no easy job to patch the walls to match the original facing.

When the siege first began, the mag-lev trains had been halted for fear of a power interruption. With the siege over, Harke's technicians had restored power to the system, but there were no drivers. His destination was only a short distance from the palace, so he walked.

He had ordered his men to set up temporary prisons for the nobles. The string of hotels in the second ring of the city centre had seemed ideal. From the outside The Grand Hotel didn't live up to its name: an unassuming frontage of glass and concrete, all grey and silver. Just like every other hotel in the city. But the doors opened onto an ornate wide foyer, aged wood and polished glass. The scrollers guild had been enhancing the interior for decades, and the railings, bannisters and reception desk were carved into ornate loops of wood with inlaid ebony.

A dozen soldiers lounged around the foyer, clustered in twos and threes or resting booted feet on scattered furniture. Despite their ease they were alert, their measuring gazes locking onto him as he strode through the double glass doors.

The squad's captain approached him.

"Good afternoon, captain," Harke said. "I trust all is in order?"

"Not a peep out of any of them," said the captain. "They're all behaving. We haven't needed to be too rough."

Harke scratched for the captain's name; within moments, it came to him. Erdinis: originally a sewer worker, with no love of the noble classes. Harke nodded. "And *she* has no access to the other levels? I want her isolated."

"As you ordered, sir. She has the whole top floor to herself."

"Excellent. Let's go see her."

The platform in the grav-tube was unsteady underfoot and Harke frowned, but Erdinis reassured him: "There's a flutter in the impellers but it's nothing to worry about."

Easy for him to say. Harke fretted until the platform had lifted them the eight levels to the penthouse: his year as an electrician apprentice had left him with no illusions about the reliability of electronics.

Another guard was stationed outside the penthouse. The man had taken possession of an Imperial Guard jacket and wore it with every evidence of pride. He crashed to attention as Harke approached; this one at least had been trained in the army. The lights in the penthouse were up high, the window shutters firmly closed. They would stay that way until the occupant of the suite had entirely lost track of time. This would be her little world, for as long as Harke needed it to be.

They found the Lady Jede in the main lounge of the suite, seated in a deep armchair and staring at the vid screen. There was no signal, of course. The screen was awash with meaningless static. Another guard stood just outside the open door to the room, looking bored. Harke didn't bother knocking before he entered.

Someone had found Jede fresh fatigues, comfortable but not elegant. The right half of her face was blue and swollen: an injury caused by the building collapsing during her capture.

Harke placed himself between the Lady's chair and the screen. "I trust that you're being treated well?"

"Well enough," said Jede. "I know you, don't I?"

"You know me," agreed Harke. "We met, briefly, when my men brought you back to the palace. You were hurt and there was a lot going on so I won't blame you if you don't remember."

"Vague," said Jede. "I don't remember how I got here."

"My men brought you here after my doctors had finished looking at you. You've put me to a lot of trouble, you know."

"Rumour had it that the rebels were killing every noble they got their hands on," Jede said. "And I *am* still a noble."

"My people did kill a few," Harke admitted. "I only really wanted you." Which wasn't true. He needed the Crown. The Empress without her Crown was useless to him. "In any case, here you are, safely in my care. I'm sorry for your injuries. I gave orders you were to be taken unharmed."

"It doesn't matter," said Jede. "Do what you like to me. Your glorious leader has failed. I beat him."

"My leader? I thought we were clear. I am General Harke."

She choked down something that might have been a giggle. "Hope he's happy now. He thought he won. Ha! He's won nothing. I beat him. Tell your General. That monster. Hope he's happy."

"My lady, *I* am Harke. I'm not a monster."

Jede glanced at him, shook her head dismissively. Her eyes wandered off without sign of recognition. "No. He's no technician. He's *ab-vesht*."

By choice, he almost said. He could have had a place in one of the Guilds if he'd wanted it, but that would have meant settling.

But right now he was wearing a technical corps uniform. Desperate to lose his blood-stained battle tunic he'd changed into the first set of clothes he could find to fit him. "These are not my clothes."

Jede perched on the edge of her chair, looking around the room in little, jerky movements. Like a scared bird. "So tired. Where am I?" Her eyes caught his and she attempted a brittle smile. "I know you, don't I?"

Harke glanced sidelong at Erdinis. "She's not medicated? Head injuries?"

The captain shook his head. "Doctors said no. She's been like this since she was brought in. The doctor said it might be something to do with the removal of the Crown."

"Just when I thought my day couldn't get any worse," said Harke.

IV

The next hotel was further out from the city centre and far less ornate inside. He didn't know these guards by name and wasted no time on introductions. An anonymous sergeant saw him up to a single-room billet on the fourth floor. The guard followed him inside and stood just beside the door, one hand on his flinger, but this prisoner wasn't going to make any sudden moves.

The man inside had been offered neither fresh clothing nor food, but on looking at him Harke doubted that would do him harm; the man was enormous. A few days' deprivation might be good for his health.

Harke pasted a false smile on his face. "Do you know who I am?"

"I know, my lord," said the noble. "Emperor Harke."

"It's a little late to be acknowledging me now."

"I, my name is Lord Garth," the fat man stammered.

Harke held up a finger to stop him. "I don't care who you are."

"No reason you should," agreed the fat man quickly. "I'm not important. I have no real power or responsibilities."

"What am I to do with you then?" asked Harke. "I have all these Lords and no Council of Lords to put them in. You can see I've got a bit of a problem."

"I come from Ataraio. I'll go home. You'll never see me again."

Harke had never heard the name. Some far-flung province, probably. But if the fat Lord thought he was going to retire to a comfortable life in the country he was sadly mistaken.

"I don't think so. I don't care for nobles, but some of my men positively *loathe* you all. I believe in giving the people what they want. They'll want to see you punished."

"No, my Lord!" Garth all but squealed. "I would have supported you! There were always guards. I'm on your side!"

Harke ignored him. "I could let my soldiers hang you, I suppose. But I hate to kill people who could become productive members of society. So I'm going to offer you a choice. How old are you?"

The question seemed to take Garth by surprise, and it took a moment for him to answer tentatively, "Forty-five?"

"That's not old," said Harke. "So. I can have you sent out and executed right now. My men would enjoy that and it would be over quickly for you. Or choice number two: twenty-five years as a menial. There's a lot of work to be done. We need people right now for the cleanup, but that shouldn't take more than a month or two. After that, you might expect lighter duties. That will be up to your skills. A talented man can go far in the lower professions."

A menial. Harke kept his face immobile to prevent his distaste showing. Old structures like *menials* and *nobles* and *crafters* — they had no place in his new world. No need to tell Lord Garth that, not while the threat was still effective.

The man's face had drained of colour. "My... my lord," Garth whispered, shaken. "Twenty-five... I *can't*. Please!"

Harke shrugged. "Twenty-five years, you'll be getting on a bit, I admit, but you'll still have some years left to you, and you'll be free to choose your own path. *Not* as a noble, of course, I don't think we'll be needing the nobility by then. But if you work hard, you might save up a bit to retire on. A nice little hovel somewhere."

The fat man fell to his knees. His cheeks glistened with tears. "My emperor! My lord! I can't do menial labour. I won't survive. I don't deserve this!"

Deserve? That was almost worth calling in the guards for a summary beheading right now, but Harke clenched his jaw and let the rage subside.

When it was safe to talk, he continued. "You've had forty-five years of privilege. You didn't earn it. It was given you due to an accident of birth. Forty-five years as a parasite on the labour of others, who could never aspire to your place. Men worth *ten* of you. Look at you! Have you ever denied yourself anything? You talk to me of *deserve*? I ought to just shoot you here and now, that's what you deserve!"

Garth was spoiling the carpet.

Gently, gently. He took a deep breath to calm himself. After a moment, calmer: "I'm offering you a choice. Make something of your life or lose it."

Garth stared at the floor, broken. He mumbled an inaudible response.

"Speak up. I don't have all day."

"I want to live." Garth's whisper could barely be heard.

Harke nodded. "Then that's sorted. If at any time you wish to change your mind, just tell your supervisor and we'll have you put down the same day. Guard? Can you please ensure that this man is given some more appropriate quarters? I'll leave him in your hands now."

As he left the hotel behind him, the waning day seemed to glow brighter. Nothing like the satisfaction of a job well done. And his forces still held at least another dozen Lords and Ladies. He would ration them out. One a day would give him something to look forward to.

The Beginning and Ending of Dreams

I

Once before Jess had packed her life into bags and driven them across the Australian interior. Back then, nine years ago, she had possessed little of lasting value. Whatever she could not fit into her suitcases she had abandoned without regrets: second-hand furniture chosen less for its aesthetics than for its ability to fit into the two cramped rooms she rented in her parents' house; an extensive collection of My Little Pony toys she hadn't touched in years; a bicycle slowly maturing into a jangle of spikes and rust always hungry for stockings and sweaters.

That summer, leaving her childhood home, she had carried with her everything she valued. In her bags, and on her person, had been her true treasures. The earrings she had worn on that trip were the ones that Mark bought her after their first meeting; a summer dress in her bags she had worn on their first date, outside of the conference where they had met; the sweater he had given her one night caught in the rain. So many of her mementos from Mark, and so few her own. A cheap plastic trophy won in an art show, a series of show programs for university plays in which she had acted, her testamur from the University proving that she was fully qualified and prepared to step out into the real world. Back then, it had seemed enough.

Driving into the east across one long day and night and another day, Eurythmics blasting from the stereo, they had chatted and laughed and celebrated and planned a new life together. Mark had been in high spirits: he was coming home with a new possession. Jess had carried with her all the possessions for which she cared.

Those clothes were lost to history now, all so threadbare or stained or eighties that she would never wear them again. The garbage bags in the

85

back of the Taurus were full of newer clothes, a few paperbacks, some photographs. Little enough to show for her second life.

Once again she travelled across the desert with no clear idea of what awaited, but this time she left behind more than stifling expectations and threadbare furniture. Back in Melbourne remained *her* house — paid for largely by Mark but planned and designed and decorated and maintained by her own hands and care. Behind her lay her bright career. The ashes of her marriage and her hopes for a family. Against this loss, her anger was little consolation. Anger is not about letting go; it's about holding onto things we cannot keep.

The Taurus was dead. Another casualty of violence. Something had jarred loose inside the engine when the truck sideswiped them.

Something had jarred loose inside her, too. Her understanding of the world had to be mistaken. There could be no explanation for the two men in the desert with their unfamiliar guns and their swords and their strange, brackish language.

The driver of the truck, Ivan, was full of apologies — for the car, for the terror he'd put them through - but Jess didn't blame him. He'd been on the wrong end of a sword. Ivan's actions, at least, she could understand. Unlike the men who had forced him. Jess had watched them during their conversations with Vi, both before and after the boy made his move, and she saw nothing in them she recognised.

Vi had not sounded like a child, during those discussions. None had been in any language Jess could understand, but the girl had held herself as someone in authority, someone used to giving commands. For all that the shorter assailant held the gun, there had been a deference in his voice. Vi had accepted that deference as if it belonged to her.

And then there was Aran.

The boy's face was a mess, his cheek and lips swelling around his smile. His right arm was stained dark brown with the blood that had sheeted from the big soldier after he stabbed him. The soldier had been a Goliath, Aran his David. The boy had been a shadow, flickering away from the sword, twisting and leaping like a shaolin master until he took the man's weapon away from him. But for the soldier's final wild swing, that fight would have ended differently. Jess had no doubt Aran would have killed him with his own sword.

Don't underestimate him, Vi had said, and now Jess had an inkling of why.

Leaning to the right in the passenger seat of Ivan's cab, Jess watched as her car diminished in the side mirror. Most of her belongings still sat in garbage bags in the rear; she kept only three small bags, light enough to carry. If the world ever made sense again she might eventually be able to reclaim the rest.

Vi and Aran rode in the sleeper compartment behind the seats, their knees hunched to their chests; they talked together in low voices, but Jess couldn't make out a word over the throaty rasp of the truck's engine. Jess would have liked to talk with Ivan; she had a serious need to unpack the insanity of the last few hours with someone sane. Instead she held herself still and watched as the dot of her car vanished into the night darkness.

Vi had told her, before they climbed up into the cab: "Do not tell him any more than you must. It is safest for him, and for us, the less that he knows." Ivan was already putting himself at risk by helping them. Jess didn't want to endanger him further.

They were driving east. Ivan's cargo was due in Adelaide, and his offer of passage did not extend to sacrificing his contract. Vi had gratefully accepted his offer to transport them; for Jess there was little choice but to accompany them. Staying with her dead car in the desert had been an option, but not a good one.

The Yallara roadhouse was in view again, looming dark in the night beside the road, when Vi leaned forward, between the seats. She kept her voice low. "I am sorry. I never intended to put you at risk."

"That's my life, back there. In the car." Her own voice sounded flat and defeated. "There's nothing left."

Vi was quiet for a moment. "I keep a journal. I write in it every day. It knows things that I have never told another person. I left it behind to come here. I left behind my friends, my family. Everyone I have ever known and everything I have ever owned is so far away I cannot even conceive it. I understand about loss. At least when this is over you can go back to your life."

Jess snorted in bitter amusement. "My life," she said. "Right." Her life had already ended.

"What do you do? How did you come to be in the middle of the desert?"

"I was going home. Back to my parents in Perth. I'm a building draftsperson... I draw building plans. I'm hoping... I *was* hoping... to find a new job."

"After Aran and I reach your city, you can return to that. You do not need to protect us."

"You'll go to the police? Those men attacked you."

"We cannot."

"If you don't go to them, they'll come to you. Aran stabbed..." Jess swallowed. "I've never seen anyone stabbed before."

"Our home used to be peaceful," Vi said softly. "Then the war came. I have seen more than enough violence. I hate it." The girl screwed her eyes shut for a moment, as if to blot out memories, before she continued. "That man was a soldier, experienced at killing. Before he was... interrupted... he was arguing that they should kill you as a witness. Ivan, also."

Ivan overheard this. "He might have tried. He wouldn't be the first."

Vi raised an eyebrow. "The captain would have killed you easily."

"You said he was arguing," said Jess. "The other man didn't agree?"

"The other man," said Vi, her voice going cold, "was a trusted official until he betrayed us. But he was not immediately agreeing to kill you." She brought a hand forward, passing a weighty object to Jess. "I want you to keep this. Aran has the sword, and I doubt that you would be any good with that."

Jess turned the handgun over in her hands. It was heavy, from the feel of it almost solid metal. The grip fit comfortably into her palm, but it didn't have the familiar shape of a pistol. "I've used rifles, but I've never fired a handgun," said Jess. Then it occurred to her that it might be safest all around if Aran were not equipped with a firearm. "OK, I'll keep it. How does it work?"

Vi arched an eyebrow. "I am not a soldier."

"Why a sword?" Jess asked distractedly. "Why do you even need it if you have this?"

"A flinger is effective at range, but not good in close quarters." With that, Vi withdrew into the rear.

Jess looked back at the gun — the flinger. Apart from the familiar shape of the grip, a firing stud where the trigger should be, it didn't really resemble a pistol at all. Instead of a cylindrical barrel, it had a flat rectangular shaft, looking like nothing so much as a hip flask. Atop this sat a circular canister, no more than ten centimetres in diameter, and maybe three centimetres deep.

"Careful," said Ivan. He reached with his left hand to train the weapon away from him. "Not sure how that works, but a gun's a gun and I don't like them pointed at me."

"Sorry," said Jess. It was too dark to inspect it closely and she was too tired to be safe. She slotted it back into its custom-fitted holster and laid it at her feet.

She rested her head on the side window and closed her eyes. The seat was just the right side of firm. The cab smelled slightly of cigarettes but the faint scent was not unpleasant.

She must have dozed part of the way, lulled by exhaustion, but the truck was not a smooth ride nor quiet. Each time she came close to sleep, her head would crack painfully against the window or she would imagine she caught sight of movement in the darkness outside the truck, and jerk awake again. Slowly the night drained away, the black leaching into a pre-dawn pale grey. Her head ached from the continued bumping. Rather than try to settle again, she turned in her seat to face Ivan. "Why are you helping us?"

For a moment she wasn't sure he was going to answer her, or if he'd even heard. She was about to try again when Ivan responded. "You seem like a good person to me."

"Thanks," said Jess, but Ivan was continuing.

"The girl seems OK too. But that kid - that boy. He's bad news. You need to keep an eye on him." Ivan glanced at her sidelong to make sure she was taking him seriously. "I know his type. I know an angry fanatic when I see one. I don't know what kind of stuff you're caught up in, but you watch him."

"Don't worry," Jess said, "I'm watching him. Believe me."

The truck was slowing. Behind the cabin, the livestock were starting to stir with the ambient light of the dawn. "Port Augusta's just ahead," Ivan said. "I'll let you out here. I can't stop; I'm already behind schedule."

Jess wondered about asking if he would take them further, but Ivan was shaking his head as if he could read the question in her eyes. "I've done as much as I can for you. I promised that old man and his wife that I'd contact the police. I'll give you a couple more hours to lose yourself, but then I've got to make good."

"You saw Bruce and Dot? Are they okay? Did Aran hurt them?"

"They're fine. Bruce is fucking ropeable... sorry." Ivan had the good grace to blush. "I mean, he's damned angry. But they're not hurt. Your friend back there stole some stuff, but I think it's more a matter of pride."

"He's not a friend," Jess said automatically.

"The cops will want to talk to me," Ivan went on. "If they don't ask, I never met you or those kids. But I'm not going to lie to them, and soon as they look at the truck they're going to ask about the marks, so no promises. After that, they'll be swarming here like flies. If I were you, I'd stay on the move. Or..." He paused, giving her a measuring glance. "If you stay put for more than a few hours, they'll catch up with you. I'm not sure if you want that."

Jess glanced over her shoulder into the sleeper cabin. Her eyes met Vi's, shining brightly in the dark. Beside her, Aran dozed against the window. Vi shook her head.

"I don't think we're going to let that happen," said Jess honestly.

The sun wasn't yet over the horizon when Jess, Vi and Aran gathered at the roadside, Jess' bags at their feet, and watched Ivan's truck rumble up to speed away from them. In front of them were the outskirts of Port Augusta. Sometime during the night the flat scrub desert had given way to a thin scattering of trees, eucalyptus lining both sides of the highway. Ivan had dropped them beside an open expanse of watered green; it took Jess a moment to recognise it as a golf course. *Civilisation.* On the right of the highway, a rural suburb of dark houses stretched; in the pre-dawn gloom, a few were coming to life with internal lights. The highway continued on in front of them, curving gently; Jess watched with some regret as the tail-lights of Ivan's truck disappeared around the bend.

Aran spoke, his words indistinct through swollen lips.

"We need another car," Vi translated.

"*Car*", Aran said firmly.

Jess raised her eyebrows. Obviously they'd been putting the drive to good use. "Good for you," she said. "But no." She shook her head. "I'm not driving anywhere. I need sleep. He needs rest, to heal. Besides, there's no way to get another car. We have to stop."

"We cannot stop," said Vi. "The police will be looking for us, even if Utara does not catch up to us."

"We don't have a choice," said Jess. There seemed to be a delay in her hearing; she felt herself saying the words, but it took a moment for her brain to register that they'd been said. "I've been awake since early Friday morning. I'm so tired I can barely stand up. I'm not getting behind a wheel like this."

"We must keep moving," Vi said stubbornly. "Ivan said that we had hours, at most."

Jess turned to face the girl directly and found herself staggering slightly. "Here's the deal. Even *if* I was somehow able to get another vehicle, *if* we knew where we going, I'd run us off the road before we got ten kilometres down the road. Can you drive a car? Can Aran? Go on if you like, but you'll have to do it without me." Jess was too tired to feel angry; her defiance was born out of sheer stubbornness.

"Very well," said Vi reluctantly. "We will stop. But only for a few hours."

"*Car*", said Aran.

II

Somebody had put a panel of gauze between Jess and the world, and everything was coming at her from a distance. Thirty-six hours ago she had stopped here, in Port Augusta, trying in vain to get some sleep after the long drive from Melbourne. It felt like thirty-six years.

An idea occurred to her. Perhaps she never left. Perhaps she was still asleep, dreaming all of this: the girl who claimed to be a refugee but wore the clothes of a princess, the boy with a fetish for knives, the men trying to run them off the road, even the roadhouse itself. When Mark slammed the door to the den in her face, it was the end of the life she'd known. Now in a dream she had lost everything she had: her mind making sense of her losing everything she was.

She screwed her eyes closed, counted a slow five, then had to force them open again against the lead weights holding them down. Nothing had changed. She was mildly disappointed to find that she was still standing by the side of the highway, garbage bags of clothes at her feet, the children staring at her expectantly, and the strange, stubby gun in a holster at her waist.

Not a dream. Damn.

"Let's go," she growled, hefting her bags and starting after Ivan's vanished brake lights. She didn't wait to see if Vi and Aran were following her.

They made a peculiar group, walking on the wide verge beside the highway. The bags of clothes and belongings weren't heavy but Vi and Aran both struggled under their burdens. In the half-light of the morning Aran's bruised face looked dark and misshapen, and the cream-coloured jumper Jess had lent to Vi fell well below her waist and made her appear stunted. The pommel of the sword standing above Aran's shoulder completed the tableau. "We've got to get off the street," Jess said. "You can't go walking around with a sword on your back. People notice that kind of thing."

Ivan had left them less than a kilometre from the end of the Eyre highway, where it met another great highway, the Stuart, this one travelling north to south. Near the intersection a wide expanse of flat greenery sat behind a high wire fence, a tower sign looming over them. It was unlit but the morning was bright enough to read its words: Crossroads Holiday Park. That would do. As they walked around the fence, Jess took stock; the park held a combination of empty lots for caravans or tents, and bungalow-style cabins. The cabins looked incredibly tempting.

"Wait here." Jess left them at the corner of a bungalow just inside the gateway to the park, sheltered under a great gum tree. The darker shade ought to obscure them well enough for a few minutes. Jess headed in alone to the park's office building.

Even before she reached the steps up to the front verandah of the building, Jess could see she was out of luck. The place was locked up and dark. The sign on the door proclaimed opening hours of eight in the morning to six in the evening; a glance at her watch showed her that it was slightly after five. She closed her eyes again and took a deep breath. She wasn't sure how much longer she could go on, but they couldn't stand in the open for hours waiting.

When she returned, Vi was standing alone under the gum, the bags of

Jess' belongings at her feet. Of Aran there was no sign. "Where is he?" Jess asked.

"He is mapping escape routes," explained Vi. "He insisted."

"Well, he's wasting his time. We can't stay here," said Jess. "The office doesn't open for hours; we can't hire a cabin. There's bound to be a hotel or motor inn before too long. Maybe one will be open."

Aran returned, materialising out of the shadows like a ghost; if Jess had been more alert she might have been startled. Vi shot rapid-fire words at him. Aran shook his head, speaking in clipped sentences; while she couldn't understand the language, it was clear that he disagreed. After a moment, he darted away, deeper into the park.

Vi lifted a bag. "Come with me," she said, and somehow Jess found the energy to move her legs.

Aran led them deeper into the park, to a cabin in the far corner. This cabin appeared less well maintained than some; grime and cobwebs marred the windows and the grass verge was ragged. Aran skirted around the front of the building. By the time Jess caught up with him, he had lifted a window and cleared enough space to squirm inside.

Jess instinctively recoiled. "I'm not breaking and entering. We'll find a place where I can rent a room."

"It is nearly daylight," said Vi. "We will attract too much attention, you said it yourself. And you can barely walk. We will rest here; it does not appear to be visited frequently."

Aran, on the inside of the open window, said something else, and Vi nodded. "Aran has mapped the approaches. It can be defended."

"We're in enough trouble already," mourned Jess, but Vi was adamant.

"Get inside," she said. "You need sleep."

Jess clambered through the window without too much difficulty. She found herself in a lounge area, which was dusty but still comfortably furnished. Off to the side was a bedroom and she staggered in that direction. The bed — two singles pushed together — seemed to sparkle in invitation.

It was no good. She was spent; she couldn't go another step. If the police caught them now, if the people chasing Vi and Aran caught up with them here, they'd have to rely on Aran to save them, because Jess was past being able to do anything practical. She dropped her bag, uncaring if something broke, and stumbled towards the bed.

Vi had followed her inside. She flipped at a light switch, with no effect. "No power. Perhaps that is why the place is so run-down," she said. "We will move again soon. Aran will keep watch and wake us if anyone approaches. Rest now."

Jess had already stopped listening. She bent to remove a shoe. Felt herself overbalancing, but she couldn't find the energy to catch herself, and the bed was right there. And falling onto the bed she plunged into a sea of black velvet, and was gone.

III

The knocking at the door was like a pounding of war drums from hell. Mark McTiernan flung open the door, ready to tear strips off whichever neighbour or hawker had disturbed his morning. The hangover coiled inside his skull wasn't happy he was upright. The flare of morning sunlight as he opened the door sent spikes of agony through his temples, but as his vision cleared he saw the blue of police uniforms and his anger ran away like water, leaving disquiet in its wake.

"Good morning, officers. Can I help you?"

There were two of them: a tall, athletic young man with short-cropped brown hair, and an older, shorter officer who must have been a metre wide from shoulder to shoulder and appeared to be built entirely of muscle. From the outset it was the taller officer who did most of the talking. "Mr Mark McTiernan?"

Courteously both officers held up their identifications and kept them there long enough for Mark to read them. The tall one was Senior Constable Harvey, and the body builder went by the name of Johnson. Harvey went on. "Sorry to disturb you this morning, but we need a few minutes of your time. May we come inside?"

"I guess," said Mark, but before he'd even finished speaking the officers were pushing into the hallway. Mark closed the door and squeezed past them into the lounge.

He wished he'd taken the time to put on a shirt before opening the door. He was proud of his body, product of many long and expensive hours at the gym, but this was not the time. A shirt was draped over the couch in the lounge. It smelled of spilled beer and cigarette smoke and perfume, but he shrugged into it anyway.

Senior Constable Harvey accepted the offer of a lounge chair; Johnson declined, and prowled the perimeter of the room. Mark restrained himself from swivelling in the lounge to watch. It made him nervous. He was a wildebeest, and Johnson was the lion.

"Are you aware of your wife's whereabouts?" asked Harvey.

"Not entirely. Has something happened?"

Harvey raised his eyebrows. "We were hoping you could tell us. Is there any reason your wife would be in South Australia?"

Mark felt his face freeze. South Australia. Not a bluff, this time.

"Her parents live in Perth," he said, keeping his voice level. "She might be going to visit them."

"You don't know?" asked Johnson from behind him.

"She didn't have to ask for my permission. We don't always keep each other up to date on our movements."

Mark found his attention wandering as Harvey asked a series of background questions. He answered with perfunctory brevity. No, his wife didn't use drugs — she didn't even smoke. No, he wasn't aware she had any friends or colleagues with connections in crime. Yes, she owned a 1998 Ford Taurus.

Without any segue or warning Johnson asked another high-bounce question. "How is your relationship with your wife?"

He was unprepared for that and it flustered him. "All married couples have their ups and downs," he managed. "We're okay."

"It's just that there's no pictures of the two of you together," said Johnson. At that, Mark's head did snap around. Johnson was right; Jess had taken a couple of photographs off the wall, leaving slightly fainter gaps where they had been. The remaining photographs showed various other family members — exclusively on Mark's side. He hadn't even noticed the photos were gone.

Harvey was saying something about the car. "What?"

"The photos that are missing. We have them. We have a team going over your wife's car; when they're finished with it we'll let you know."

"Good," said Mark, for want of anything more appropriate.

"Interesting. You drive an Aston Martin," said Harvey suddenly. "I saw it outside. Nice car. Your wife's driving a 98 Ford?"

"It's her car," Mark said defensively. "We can't afford another new car."

Harvey glanced around the room and Mark winced. He could imagine what the policeman was seeing: the open-plan design, the furnishings — comfortable and good quality, the tasteful fittings. An air of careful interior design. Jess's handiwork. Mark had never had a lot of time for interior decorating.

Johnson was seeing it too. "Nice décor."

Harvey raised an eyebrow. "Maybe they shop second-hand."

"We're saving for a college fund," Mark said defensively.

"You don't have any kids," Harvey observed.

"Not yet." Even he could hear the edge of anger in his voice as he said it.

Johnson's circuit of the room had brought him back around in front of the lounge suite. "What do you do for a living?"

"I'm in advertising," said Mark. "Mostly television."

"Sounds well paid. And you're home at eight on a Monday morning?"

"I've taken the day off." There was a growing knot of cold in his stomach. "I'm not feeling well today."

"You don't look crash hot," agreed Harvey. "We won't take too much more of your time. We have to let you know, we have reason to believe that your wife has been caught up in an armed robbery in South Australia."

It took Mark a moment to process that. "Caught up? Is she OK?"

"It's a bit unclear at the moment. We're still trying to find her," said Johnson. "There are a couple of children involved, too. Does your wife have nieces? Nephews?"

"None I'm aware of. Her family's in Perth. We're not close."

"We're still trying to find out who these kids are," said Harvey. "If your wife calls, can you let us know?"

"Of course," Mark replied. "Thank you for letting me know. If there's anything I can do…"

"Don't worry," said Harvey. "If we have any more questions for you, we'll be sure to ask."

As Mark was showing them back to the front door, Johnson nodded at the wall in the entry hall. "You've got some nasty plaster damage there," he said. ""You should get that looked at before it gets any worse."

Mark was sure they knew more than they were saying. It made him feel absurdly guilty, and he knew he hadn't done anything to be guilty about. "You will let me know if you find Jess."

The two police paused on the doorstep. "We'll be in touch, Mr McTiernan," said Harvey politely. The two of them nodded, then took the few steps to the front fence without looking back, and were gone.

As he closed the front door against the bright morning, Mark reflected they hadn't answered his question.

IV

Gladys hated him.

It was the only explanation. You could depend on it: when Jeff pulled a late-night shift, he'd be scheduled at the station early the next morning. He didn't know what he'd done to piss off the roster sergeant but he was entirely resolved never to do it again.

After the long drive back from Yallara, he'd barely had time for a coffee and a shower before he had to head into the station. The only solution was to take the day on a go-slow — *country time*, as he called it. Not his normal style.

Port Augusta police station was modern, well-equipped, but smaller than it appeared from the outside. Somehow they'd squeezed ten desks and computers into the main room. The sergeant had his own tiny office, as did the captain they rarely saw. Jeff brought his coffee to his desk and cracked his knuckles as he waited for the computer to warm up. "Mrs McTiernan, let's see who you are."

It didn't take him long to see who Mrs McTiernan was. No criminal record. No huge outstanding debts. No bells to ring. By all accounts Jess McTiernan had been a model citizen until this weekend's events.

The roadhouse was far more fruitful for leads. "Mrs McTiernan," Jeff murmured. "Master criminal, you are not." One phone call was made from the roadhouse in the moments immediately before the incident.

That number led him to a Miss Rebecca Brici. Several more calls, and he had the woman's mobile number.

He got through to Ms Brici on the first try. It was still early in the morning and Ms Brici was cooperative. Jeff noted the details of Mrs McTiernan's workplace. The name of her husband. A quick call and he arranged for locals to pay him a visit.

Mark McTiernan's record was just as clean as his wife's. Maybe he wasn't husband of the year, but neither was he from a motorcycle gang. Still, he was in advertising, and creative types had a reputation for illicit substances... *Okay. Now you're reaching.*

Your husband gets violent, Jeff mused. *You skip town and head west.* The timeline Jeff was piecing together didn't have a lot of slack in it. She barely had time to reach the roadhouse from Melbourne before the events as Dot and Bruce had recounted them. By appearances she'd been just as surprised by the children's appearance. *So who the hell are the children?*

Someone else who didn't appreciate country time was Sergeant Mick Young. At four minutes past nine precisely Jeff was making his third coffee for the day when the doorway to the station's tiny kitchenette darkened. Mick Young was not a small man, and he leaned against the jamb to avoid squeezing into Jeff's personal space. "So. Let's hear it."

The memory of Mick departing the station for home, five minutes after assigning Jeff yesterday's outing, should have annoyed him. Jeff headed that off with a vision of Doctor Ferguson's face when she received his evidence package. "Not a big deal, Mick. No real injuries. The perps were kids. Also there was a woman who might be involved. They left their car abandoned on the road. Might have hitched a ride with a road train."

"A woman involved? Best call forensics. I'm not sure you know what those look like." The sergeant grinned fiercely. "Better get on it."

Incident report forms and evidence submissions and vehicular investigation requisitions brought him no closer to answers. Paperwork. Country time.

He was working on his fourth morning coffee when Captain Hartcher entered the station. With him was a visitor: a civilian, in a beige suit that matched his ash-blond hair. In eighteen months Jeff felt he'd met all thirteen thousand residents of Port Augusta. This guy didn't have the look of a local. The captain and his visitor disappeared into Hartcher's office. Moments later Mick Young stepped out of his own and through the doorway to join the captain.

Jeff caught the eye of the only other officer in the building. Pedro was even fresher than Jeff, spit-polished and eager to please. "What's that about? Who's the guy?"

Pedro shook his head. "No idea. Never seen him before."

Jeff shrugged. "Sure we'll find out soon enough."

He turned back to his paperwork. Even with his head down he could see the captain's office door and the unexpected conference wore at him, but as the minutes turned into an hour and nobody emerged it was clear *soon enough* might take a while.

At 11:43 his phone range. The number was one he recognised.

He'd been waiting for this call. He paused, took several deep breaths, cleared his throat. This had to go right. He had practiced this discussion, planned it in every detail. She would give him details about the dress, perhaps some evidence — trace elements that might eventually crack the case. Interesting, he would explain. Of vital importance to the investigation. He would like to discuss the evidence in detail. In his mind's eye, the candlelight dinner would start off talking shop but it certainly wouldn't end there.

He grinned as he brought the phone to his ear. *Think positively*, his mother had been fond of telling him, *and it will come to pass*. Life was like fishing, was his dad's advice: bait the hook, then just reel it in.

"Are you the silly bugger who's been stuffing me around?" Dr Adele Ferguson's voice was brewed in cold fury.

The candle-lit dinner in his mind blew away like smoke. "I'm... not certain what you mean. Dr Ferguson, this is Jeffrey Lang, *constable* Jeffrey Lang, at Port Augusta Police. I take it you received my evidence package?"

"I got it," she said. "I don't know what you think it *is*, but I got it. I take it that it's not some kind of a joke?"

"Perhaps you'd best tell me what you've found." He took refuge in procedure. "I sent you a crime scene package for evaluation. It's quite serious."

It was difficult to be certain over the phone line, but she sounded mollified. "Unusual, is what it is," she said. "Obviously, it's a dress. Quite a small dress, I think it would suit a short woman or a girl. But the fabric isn't familiar. The weave... I've never seen anything quite like it. Over fifty different kinds of particulate. I've identified about half of those, still working on the rest. There's blood on the collar: A-positive. That's about the most ordinary thing about it. If you want a forensics report on this," she continued, "you're going to have to wait. It's going to take me *days* to write all this up."

"I was hoping for a bit of basic information to start with," Jeff said. "I didn't see any labels on the dress. Any way to identify where it comes from?"

"Well, it's not local," said Dr Ferguson. "I'm going out on a limb to say it wasn't made in Australia either. Further than that, I couldn't say. I'll tell you one thing that's unusual. This dress is caked with marble dust."

"Marble? Where the hell do you get marble from?"

"From a stonemason?" Her voice sounded as confused as he felt. "From the amount of it I've found, I'd say the dress has spent some time in a masonry or a building site; somewhere marble's being used in construction. Look, there's a heap of other particles, hairs, plant materials I've found that might be useful. This might benefit from a bigger lab."

The bigger labs in Adelaide might be able to tell him more, but their services weren't cheap. Too expensive for a simple robbery and assault case. Jeff shook his head. "You're doing great, Doctor Ferguson. This is all... very helpful."

"Well, can you tell me anything, some background? I might be able to be more helpful with some context."

"I think," Jeff heard himself say, "it might be easier if we could meet. Can we discuss this over coffee?"

"Sure, that works," said Dr Ferguson. "I'm free the rest of today. Do you know the Flinders?"

"Of course."

"Meet you in the bar in half an hour?"

"Sounds great." Jeff's voice sounded a hundred miles distant in his own ears. "I'll bring the case file."

"You'd bloody well better. You've got me interested now. Tomorrow I'm back to teaching kids about soil erosion; until then I'm your intrepid assistant."

After she hung up, it took Jeff long moments to collect himself and remove the phone from his ear. Not exactly how he had envisaged it, but a definite success. Think positive. *Thank you, mum.*

Half an hour. Barely any time at all.

He collated forms and files in a ring binder. Snapped the rings together and folded the binder closed, and the captain's office door swung open. The captain and the man in beige exited, Mick following up the rear. The sergeant went directly back to his own office, while Hartcher brought the civilian to the door, ushered him out of the station.

Jeff pushed to his feet just in time for Captain Hartcher to stop by his desk. "Jim Maxwell got himself done over last night," he said. "They found his truck burnt out on the Eyre. There's a body in the driver's seat, and it's likely to be him. Jeff, you were on the highway last night — you didn't see anything?"

Jim was — or had been — harmless enough, doing a regular trade between Perth and Melbourne in his battered canvas-sided truck.

Occasionally he got pulled over for inspection, for appearances' sake, but every police officer between here and Kalgoorlie knew every inch of that truck. If old Jim had gotten himself mixed up in contraband all of a sudden, it was a break from thirty stubborn years hauling low-value tourist goods. Jeff shook his head. "Nope. Don't think I passed a soul in either direction."

"Likely he was on the road a bit later than you," the captain admitted. "Didn't hurt to ask." He rubbed his eyes before continuing. "Now, the robbery out at Yallara. You attended last night, yes?"

Jeff nodded towards the binder. "Just doing up the paperwork. A few interesting things have come up in the forensics. I'm about to go and get the results."

"Who're you using?"

"Adele Ferguson," Jeff said. "It's just some kids having a lark."

The captain frowned. "No, it looks like we might need to bring in the big guns. Find out what she's got, then wrap it up. Grab any evidence you gave her, bring it right back here and give it directly to me. I'll need all your notes. Then leave it alone; plenty of other stuff for you to be doing."

Jeff tried to keep the dismay out of his voice. "You're giving it to someone else? It's my case, Captain."

"If it were up to me, I'd let you run with it, but it's out of my hands. It's not our jurisdiction. Another agency — federal — just took it over. Wrap it up, leave it alone, move on."

Jeff glanced towards the doorway, but the man in beige was long gone. "Was that him? What makes a robbery in the middle of nowhere interesting to the feds? Which agency?"

"Nobody I'd ever heard of," said Hartcher. "But it's real enough. So get the forensics, leave 'em on my desk, and then get on the road; I think I saw your name on the roster for highway patrol this afternoon. I promise, the next interesting thing comes along, it's yours." The Captain clapped a hand on his shoulder. "Chalk it up to experience. Everyone has a case or two taken away from them in their career."

They were good words; encouraging words. There would be more cases. *Think positive* would bring him the success and rank he craved. But right now all he could think about was the conversation he was about to have with Doctor Ferguson, and the only positive had just walked out the door in a terrible beige suit.

Port Augusta

I

Jess woke like surfacing from a deep and still lake; slowly the light behind her eyelids brightened, noises, muffled at first, became clear, and after stillness she felt the buffeting of ocean currents.

Vi was shaking her awake, rocking her shoulders. "Wake up. We have to keep moving."

Jess forced herself upright. Her head was full of cotton wool wrapped around sharp edges; the headache was dull but insistent. "What time is it?" she asked, but Vi shook her head.

"I left you as long as I dare. Utara will be on the way."

Jess rubbed at eyes that felt like sandpaper. "We left him in the middle of the desert. And he'll be looking in the wrong direction."

"He will find transport." Vi sounded certain. "He found us once already. He will do so again. And we need also worry about your police."

"They won't find us in here." Unlikely that the police would search the empty cabins in all the local caravan grounds. *Unless someone saw us.* "They'll think we kept moving, so they'll be watching the roads."

Her spine creaked as she stretched. Two hours of sleep was not enough, not *nearly* enough, but the wobble in her ankles was gone and her mind was no longer lagging seconds behind her eyes.

In the unforgiving light of the morning, the cabin was more decrepit than it had seemed. What in the half-light of dawn and the haze of exhaustion had seemed like black satin was now revealed as dark-grey in shades of dust and mildew; mould and rat droppings lined the walls. The corners of the room were nests for spiders and there was a pervasive musty smell — essence of possum. Bright daylight crept past the edges of the drawn curtains, sketching lines on the ceiling and floor and causing glittering eddies of dust in the air.

Aran was sprawled with the loose-limbed splay of a teenager, taking up most of the couch in the main living space. Fast asleep, drool leaking from the corner of his mouth. The bruising on his face had spread and lightened, giving his face a lopsided appearance.

Asleep — and harmless. Jess thought about her mobile phone, turned off and buried somewhere in one of the garbage bags of her belongings. She could call the police, summon the kind of help these kids really needed, and not risk the boy sticking her the way he'd stabbed the big soldier in the desert —

The soldier. The chase. The truck. Ivan. The images cascaded into Jess's memory and she reached out a hand to support herself on the dining table. For a second she had forgotten the impossible events of the past hours.

Vi followed her gaze. "He needed the rest more than you did," she said. "I remember a daughter who fell off a roof. She slept sixteen hours a day for the next month."

Jess stared at her. "That can't be true," she said flatly. "If you've had children, then I'm Walt Disney."

The girl's eyes shifted away from hers. "I'm sorry. Of course I meant someone else." As if she were explaining, she added: "Sometimes inherited memories are like that. One can become lost, personal memories mixed with implanted ones."

Implanted. Jess mouthed the word, as the frustration and the mystification of the last day rose up like a volcanic force. Two quick steps brought Jess to the girl's side, and she grasped her by the shoulders and sat her down forcefully on the bed. "Enough! No more games. Time you gave me some bloody answers. Where are you headed? More to the point, *who the hell are you?*" Jess took a deep breath, taking a moment to calm her voice. She had been shouting, fists clenched at her sides, looming over the young girl like a vengeful goddess.

For a second Vi continued glaring up at her, but then her composure seemed to dissolve. Her impassive face of authority cracked, her lips working, tears welling in her eyes. "I am sorry," she managed to say, "I am sorry," but then her voice hitched and she had to jam her jaw shut. For a moment it seemed touch and go, as Jess stood in baffled sympathy, but something in Vi seemed to crack. Suddenly she was a young girl again, crying in earnest.

Against this, Jess had no defence. Anger and fear, confusion and stubborn denial, all fled; in their place welled protectiveness. She settled on the bed next to the girl and held her, feeling the slim body shudder. Vi accepted the embrace, her arms encircling Jess's waist with a feel of desperation.

Just as quickly as it had arrived, the moment passed. Vi withdrew from Jess' arms, rubbed a hand across her eyes, took a deep breath. The eyes she fixed steadily on Jess again seemed too old.

"I have been terrible to you. You have been caught up in events you did not seek, that you do not deserve. You have been — so kind." The girl stood again, straightening her borrowed clothes. "You are right. You deserve to be told. I will tell you what I can. Perhaps you will understand the importance of what I have dragged you into."

Jess stood as well. "I understand you're in a heap of trouble, and you're not making it any better by running. I still think your best option is to go to the police. Let them worry about these people chasing you... this 'Utara'. They'll protect you. They're trained for this kind of thing."

"No, they are not," said Vi. "You don't understand at all."

"So explain it to me," said Jess.

They left Aran asleep as they unpacked his stolen backpack onto the bare wooden table. As they talked, they made peanut butter sandwiches without butter, split the fruit into three piles and put aside the packets of crisps for later. Working with her hands, preparing meals for children, felt like an echo of a different life. A life she might have had, with different choices.

The sense of domestic bliss faded as Vi launched into her explanation. "Where Aran and I come from, there is a war. I already told you this."

"You did," agreed Jess. "I get it. You and Aran are refugees. But I never heard of anyone *pursuing* refugees to Australia. Why do they want you? What makes you special enough to chase into another country?"

"The answer is simple," Vi replied. "They pursue me because of my rank."

"Your rank? What are you, like some kind of a princess?"

The girl set down her butter knife and fixed her eyes on Jess. "My mother's name is Jede Corala. Until yesterday she was Empress, ruler of Zama, and the leader of my people. I am her only daughter."

Jess blinked, her hands pausing, sandwiches forgotten. "Right. Your mother was an Empress. Okay. So you're the heir to the throne? Where the hell is Zama?" As she asked it, she realised there were more pressing questions. "Never mind that. Even if you *are* the heir, it doesn't explain why soldiers are chasing you. Why would they even consider killing Australian civilians? We're not involved in your war — are we?"

"The position of Empress is not hereditary. It is won on merit." Vi took a deep breath. "The war of which I speak is a rebellion against the crown. The capital has fallen; all of the Council are dead or captured. In our last moments together, my mother abdicated the throne. To me.

"I have never sat in a Council meeting, I have never sat in the Empress' chair, and I have never held the staff of office. But my name is Vi Corala, and I am the rightful ruler of my people, and I am the last barrier that remains between the rebel Harke and total victory."

The words hung in the air for long moments, circulating with the dust. Jess couldn't keep the sarcasm out of her voice. "So should I be calling you *your highness*?"

"You don't believe me."

Jess was tempted to snap at her: *not a word of it*. But not five minutes ago this girl had been crying in her arms and the words felt too cruel. She forced her voice to gentleness. "I believe you've gone through... something terrible. Someone's hurt you. I saw the cuts on your neck... no, it's no use hiding them. Whoever did that to you, it's not your fault. You need to talk to the police; I promise they'll help you. You don't have to be afraid.

"I really do want to help you. What you're telling me... it doesn't make any sense. Maybe you think it's real, I don't know. But if you let me help you, we'll find out what's happened and we'll get you the help you need."

The girl's eyes were unwavering. "I am not delusional, and I am not lying. Every word I am saying is true." She frowned. "I cannot prove it to you. But consider the men who attacked us. They exist, and they really will kill you if they catch us."

"I can't deny their existence," Jess admitted. *A big man with a sword - a sword! - in the middle of the desert.* "I don't know who they were. I couldn't understand what you were saying to them. But when the police catch up with you, you'd better have a more believable story. There are no *empires* and *emperors* left. I've never heard of a 'Jade Corella' or whatever you say your mother's name is. And you haven't explained how you turned up in the middle of a bloody desert!"

"You cannot know..."

"Do you have any idea how ridiculous you sound?" Jess didn't let her finish. "Can't you see it's impossible, you're not thinking straight?"

"It only seems ridiculous," Vi said, "because you misunderstand. It is not surprising that you have never heard of my... my country. You could never have known the name of my mother, the Empress of Zama. Zama is not the name of a country. Zama is the name of my *world*."

III

Monday was supposed to be clear, hot and windy, and it had wasted no time in making good on its promise. As Jess led the two fugitives out of the cabin wind swirled around them, shaking the bushes and stinging their eyes with dust. This deep in the caravan park there were no other people visible, and Aran led them to the wire fence on the side of the park. Here a tree had fallen, its roots pushing the fenceline askew and leaving a gap at ground level just large enough to crawl through. Next to being chased by a truck full of sheep, defending old ladies from a teenager with a knife, and hitch-hiking with garbage bags of clothes on her back and a strange disc-gun at her waist, crawling under fences felt entirely reasonable.

They had repacked Aran's backpack. They had cut a hole in the bottom of one of the backpacks, and the sword could fit from corner to stretched corner with the bottom of the sheath poking out behind Aran's leg. At least now it wasn't strapped to his back like he was some kind of damned samurai.

Jess walked with her thoughts in a whirl of denial. What Vi had told her was flatly impossible; she couldn't believe it for a second. A teenage Empress of a planet fallen into civil war, suddenly transported to the middle of the Australian desert?

Ridiculous. And yet...

"Examine the weapon I gave you. See if it is similar to anything you know," Vi had recommended, and so she had. The device had bucked in her hand as she depressed the trigger, a low buzz like a ripcord the only noise as the razor-sharp disc raced down the shaft. The disc had flown fast and true and buried itself so deeply into the plaster of the wall that she couldn't get a grip on the edge to pull it back out.

Rebel soldiers, armed with swords and razor disc guns, chasing them through the night in a truck full of sheep. The concept was laughable.

But then there was their strange language. Aran's willingness to be violent and Vi's apparent acceptance of violence. She had no better explanation, no alternative theory to bring a semblance of meaning to the past hours. She resolved to leave it unresolved for now and focus instead on the coming day's events.

After the barren Nullarbor desert, the civilisation of Port Augusta was comforting. Across the street from the caravan park was the petrol station where she had stopped to refuel on her journey west, two days and a seeming lifetime ago. Here on the outskirts of the town the roadside was lined with cheap weatherboard houses, well-spaced and separated with wide lawns, fronted with identical low brick fences. Traffic on the road was sparse but constant. Nobody seemed to pay attention to them as they walked, but Jess was not fooled. This was a country town, and Jess was certain there were eyes behind every curtain tracking their passage.

They weren't going to get very far like this. Jess was fit enough and could walk for hours but Aran and Vi were both burdened by the bags they were carrying, and the girl was already struggling. "So what happens now? Do you have anywhere in particular you want to go? Anything you want to do?"

"I need to find someone," said Vi. "His name is Hareth Rede. I was told he could help me."

"Hareth Reed. Doesn't sound like a common kind of a name. There can't be too many like it."

Jess fished her mobile from her pocket and waited for the cheerful boot-up chimes. After the thousand-kilometre black spot of the desert, Port Augusta (population over 13,000) had decent coverage. She struggled for a moment with the phone's internet browser; she had always had trouble with the device's tiny touchscreen. "Okay. There's about a thousand people in Australia with the name of 'H Reed'. Another... nine hundred-odd who are 'H Read'. With an A. Have any idea how to find the specific one you're after?"

"He might be using a different name," said Vi. "I do not know how we will find him."

"Well, we can't stay here," said Jess. "The police will eventually get around to looking for you if they haven't already. Unless you have a better idea, we'll take a train to a capital city. That ought to give you a bit of breathing room." *And me some time to convince you.* "You could start making some phone calls. Then maybe we can get this whole business over with." *Maybe then I can go home. Wherever* home *is now.*

The world had changed in a weekend. Monday morning now. She should have finished her morning jog, had her first coffee of the day, been halfway to work. A day spent among friends, drafting building plans for clients, negotiating with local governments for permissions, these were the things she knew. Detailed, technical work and she was good at it.

Instead she was halfway across the country, walking on the roadside with a garbage bag of clothes slung over her back, a girl with delusions of grandeur on one side of her and a boy with a knife and a sword on the other.

Even in fresh clothes she felt begrimed. She needed a shower. She needed a proper night's rest; she found herself feeling nostalgic for her own bed.

One other thing she needed, above all else. She had never met the morning that could not be improved with coffee. Today she needed it more than most.

The little cafe stood in the middle of a strip of shops, set back from the road by a spacious parking lot. The sign on the door that advertised *Caffiato* coffee sat just below another that offered free wi-fi. It was perfect.

Inside, the cafe was compact and almost uncomfortably cool, the air-conditioner already running. Jess waited her turn in the queue while Vi and Aran claimed a table; apart from a mother with her toddler in one corner, there were no sit-down customers.

An overworked but bored assistant served her a large macchiato for herself and milkshakes for the children; they could pretend to be the King and Queen of Denmark for all she cared, she still wasn't buying coffee for Aran. He was already excitable enough.

Settling at the table, she claimed her belongings back from Vi. One possession she had been unwilling to leave behind in the car was her laptop, and she quickly fired it up and connected to the cafe's internet connection. Moments later she was browsing timetables.

"Trains are no good," she told her companions. "They come through here in the middle of the night, we'd be waiting all day. We can take a bus. They drive from here to Adelaide every couple of hours, and the best thing is that the terminal's only a short distance down the road."

"That's good," said Vi. "Is Adelaide very big?"

"Bigger than here. It's a main city. There will be lots of crowds around, plenty of places to get lost. If that's what you want to do. Do you even have a plan, an idea of what you're going to do with yourselves? You don't, do you?"

"I need to find Hareth Rede," Vi repeated. "I must stay free, and wait for my chance to go home. We have no other plans."

"Well, Hareth Rede isn't going to be easy to find, but I can't be looking after you forever," said Jess. "Once we get to a capital city, I'm done. You're on your own." All Jess needed was a little distance and then she could point the police in the right direction. Let them handle the boy.

The buzz of her phone against her thigh startled her. Feeling a strong disconnection from reality, she fished it out of her pocket and answered it by reflex before she even considered whether she should. "Jess McTiernan."

"Jess? It's Rick. I just got your note. Are you okay?"

"Rick." His big, friendly face swam in her mind's eye. He'd accepted her on recommendation, taken a risk in hiring her sight unseen. Vanishing overnight was hardly the best way to repay him. "I'm sorry. I'm okay but I'm not coming back."

"Is there something I can do? Is it a pay issue? Because we can talk about that."

"It's nothing to do with work. I love my job, and I have no complaints.

Well, maybe about Jerry," she added. *Everyone* complained about Jerry. She could almost hear Rick smile. "But I'm leaving Melbourne for good."

Rick was silent for a moment. "This is inconvenient," he said. "You know you're supposed to give a couple of weeks' notice."

"I know," said Jess, "but I couldn't stay. I'm sorry. I understand I won't get my leave."

"It's not about the money." Rick's voice over the phone was a mixture of concern and anger. "I can reassign your clients. Dunno who I'm going to give half of them to, but we'll manage. If you've got to go, I can't make you stay. But you've always got a position here, if you change your mind."

"Thanks," said Jess. "I'll remember that."

"Would you be interested in a little drafting work out of the office? You can still take the occasional job, yes?"

"I'd like that," said Jess.

"Great. I'll put together a contract for you and email it through."

"Thanks, Rick. It's been great," she said, and she meant it.

"Whatever you're going through," said Rick, "let me know if there's anything we can do. We'd love to see you back."

The click of the phone being put down was like a full stop on her old life.

The coffee wasn't great but it was hot and strong, and Jess could feel the caffeine coursing through her veins. Along with alertness, it brought a renewed sense of vigour. The new day surprised her with a curious sense of liberation: her responsibilities, her expectations, even her belongings were behind her. Unexpectedly she was enjoying herself. A part of her still wanted to be caught, wanted the police to put an end to this inexplicable drama and return her to a predictable life. But, she thought, not yet. Not yet. "All right," she said. "If we're going to keep running, let's do it properly." *Time for a new start. Let's get on with it.*

Vi wasn't prepared for this. Despite Jess's assurance, it was a long walk to the city centre and Vi found herself tiring quickly. Life in the palace, surrounded by servants and menials, luxuries like grav-lifts and flitters, had not accustomed her to exertion. The bag of clothes on her back was unwieldy, and no matter how she shifted it on her shoulder it wouldn't stay put. Walking was a constant struggle against the bag's attempts to escape. The first two times it slipped off her shoulder and slapped to the ground she hoisted it back up and continued without complaint, but the third time her aching shoulders and cramping fingers forced her to ask for a rest.

"Are you tired, *your highness*?" Jess asked, but at least she stopped walking.

They were in the middle of the long, curving road bridge, a span over glittering water that seemed to connect two halves of the town. Small pleasure boats dotted the inlet. Vi lowered the bag to rest at her feet, rested her hands on her hips and gazed at the boats with an unexpected feeling of loss.

Bimini stands at the prow and lets the wind stream her long hair out behind her. The sunlight turns the spray from the vessel's passage into a billion tiny diamonds, and the light mist dampens her summer dress. She feels like swimming. She's a good swimmer. For a moment she considers diving off the boat, holding her breath and seeing how deep she can go. Legend holds that Lake Lamean has an ancient, abandoned city on its bed, and she imagines swimming amongst underwater buildings, ancient granite towering over her on all sides.

Not her own thoughts. Someone else's memories. The water below was not Lake Lamean.

When she is Empress, nobody will prevent her from swimming, if she feels like it.

Bimini turns now to the old Empress, lounging under a sun-shade further back in the boat, and says, "When I'm Crowned, I'll have a boat.

The Royal Barge, I'll call it. I can hold High Council meetings in the middle of the lake."

Empress Uki smiles sadly. The Crystal Crown sparkles on her brow, a glittering tiara that the Empress is never without. Uki's response is gentle. "And you will find that Lord Kennit hates being on water, Lady Feston will fear the open spaces, and half of your other Councillors will spend the meetings retching their lunch. You would do better to keep your barge for your own pleasure. You will learn that a chance to get away privately is to be treasured."

Bimini watches as the old Empress eyes the low grasslands on the approaching shore, the wide and pristine beach, and frowns at the towers that mark the estate beyond. The estate is a place of peace and serenity, a fitting environment for a retiring Empress to enjoy the last years of her life. There's no reason for her to be unhappy. Bimini feels cross that this moment, her moment, is being spoiled.

Bimini has no conscious memory of making a decision, but now she is stepping up onto the railing, and without hesitation she launches herself into the air. For a moment she really is flying, curving gracefully through the air towards the water below. The Empress' guards will come into the water after her, but for this moment she is free.

But the water is further below than she had thought, the wide expanse misleading in its immediacy, and she hits the water awkwardly. The breath goes out of her lungs, her legs go numb, and she spins in the water. The lake is cold, colder than she had imagined. And suddenly she is in trouble, the water turning her light summer dress into freezing ropes binding her arms, the spray blinding her, crashing into her face and preventing her from breathing. A second later she goes under again, and thoughts of swimming amongst ruined buildings flee, replaced by fear. Already her breath is gone and she can't tell which way is up, as the passage of the boat tumbles her over end.

Frantically she kicks out her legs, strikes forward, hoping to arrest her spin and let her get her bearings. This gets her a bit of distance, clearing the wake of the boat, and she steadies; her arms are heavy, weighed down by the dress, but her legs are free and she is in control again. But *already she is too deep, and as she tries to see which direction to find the surface, her lungs are burning and protesting.*

Sunlight through the waves shows her the way, and she kicks for the surface. But her legs betray her, kicking out of sync, and she realises that she desperately needs air. Dark shadows, above, the silhouettes of the guards diving gracefully into the water, but they're too far, it's too late, and it's not fair how quickly a fleeting desire to swim turns into something fatal, as her willpower gives way and she takes a last, agonising breath. As her lungs fill with water, all thought of her accession to the title of Empress are fled, and she is again just a girl, drowning.

The memory snapped and Vi staggered, reaching out a hand to steady herself on the railing. She found that she had been holding her breath. Jess and Aran were staring at her. She took three deep breaths, then trusted herself to let go of the railing. "I am fine," she said. "Just... tired." But even when they got underway again, the feeling of panic, of death reaching out for her, remained, and it took her a long time before she regained her balance.

She was starting to get used to these flashes of memory. Each time it became easier to push the memories aside. But why did they always have to be the most traumatic, the most frightening of the memories, that came to her?

A little further on, a turnoff took them to the city centre. Jess seemed to have found a new source of energy and determination, and she pushed them ahead at a brisk pace. "We have a head start," Jess had said shortly after they left the café. "If you're concerned about this Utara finding us, let's not waste it."

Port Augusta was a picturesque town. The main stretch of the city centre was lined with trees and big orange-stone buildings. The trees were large and old and Vi flinched every time they passed one: wide and gnarled, each was large enough to host a family of barkers. The trees should have been under guard, behind fences, not standing out here in the open surrounded by unsuspecting passers-by.

The streets were host to a variety of little shops selling jewellery, housewares, lingerie. Vi felt her head was on a spring as she gazed wide-eyed from one shop window to another. Jewellery offensive in its ostentation and underwear scandalous in its cut prompted the same thought: *they wear that here?*

There, a large, multi-story building with a glaring red sign. Her memory of English was good but did not include the written form. They passed a tavern, bright and glittering and chattery with machines of flashing lights; a beauty salon.

It was the clothes stores that seemed to hold Jess's interest. "You can't come trailing through these stores with garbage bags on your back," Jess said firmly. "You're obvious enough already without looking like shoplifters." She made sure Vi and Aran were settled in plastic chairs outside an ice-cream parlour and bought them each a local pastry delicacy. Vi took note of the local currency, small pieces of dull bronze metal.

"Let me guess, you've never eaten a pie before," Jess said, handing out pastries. Then she had to show them how to eat the *pies* Australia-style, still wrapped in their paper bags and dripping with sauce. Vi took a tentative nibble from the crust, the bright red dressing flooding her mouth with unaccustomed richness so that it took her long moments to decide whether the experience was pleasant.

Jess shook her head. "I'll be right back. I need to pick up a few things. You don't look too badly out of place. Don't draw attention and nobody should bother you." She didn't seem entirely convinced, shooting backwards glances at them as she entered one of the nearby stores.

The day was warming, and the locals were coming out to get their shopping done before the heat drove them indoors. People swirled around them in a constant whirl of motion. Most seemed Jess's age, or older, but there were some youths: a small group of teenagers were gathered a bit further up the arcade. Several of them appeared to be engrossed with their own data pads. So there were some things in common between this world and her own.

Vi paid the youths scant regard; she was more concerned by the endless stream of adults. Every face reminded her of another, and another, and another again. For every passer-by, a hundred people she remembered but had never known. Gaits and smells and voices in a tide of *deja vu,* and memories swam at the edges of her vision. Here, a man who reminded her of a past enemy; *there*, a woman who might have been a Lady from a Council long past; *there again* a man who once loved her. The scent of roses in a woman's perfume tried to send her back to a long-ago garden and a forbidden tryst, and the sour, unwashed smell of an old man nearly lost her in an ancient Council meeting, adrenaline sheeting through her as she recalled voices raised in anger and threats of violence. Memories that were not her own circled her like vultures, and if she surrendered to them there might be no easy escape.

Desperate for distraction, she turned her attention across the table. Aran had pulled out Jarem's data pad and was fiddling with its controls.

"Is it working?"

"It's encrypted," the boy answered, frustration in his voice. "I need a password." He paused. "It has a data cube reader."

"That's not a lot of use unless we have data cubes."

"If *they* had a reader, they might have had cubes."

"Maybe they did," said Vi. "Without the reader, they're as useless as the reader is to us. And we're *not* going back to find out if they have some."

"I just think it's interesting," Aran said sullenly. For a moment he stared at the empty paper bag his pie had come in. The stains of tomato sauce looked like blood. "I don't like it here."

"It's very different from home," Vi allowed.

"It's horrible. It smells; I can barely breathe this air. I thought these people were meant to be advanced. There are so many *cars* — almost as if everyone has their own. I don't like them being so close."

Vi couldn't disagree. Vehicles on the ground, only metres away from where they sat; she felt like flinching every time one passed, belching fumes. "You'll get used to it."

"I don't want to get used to it," Aran said. "I want to go home."

"There's something you need to know," Vi said, taking a deep breath. "We're not the first people from Zama to come here."

Aran stared at her. "But they said we can't go back."

"They didn't think anyone could. But they sent people here anyway."

"People?" Aran looked around them, at the shoppers on all sides. "What kind of people?"

"The wrong kind of people," Vi said softly.

V

Dawn found Jarem trailing Utara and his men on the outskirts of the town, where the first sparse stands of trees began to break the monotony of empty flat plains and knee-high scrub brush. In the predawn gloom they had crept past outlying homesteads and sheds, crouched and single-file, camouflaged by their dark grey tunics. With the sky lightening Captain Aesk had directed them away from the highway and its growing traffic, across the fields. The captain claimed this was for the purpose of preserving their secrecy, but if they were really concerned about staying hidden, Jarem considered, then they shouldn't have burned the old man in his truck.

The war had come to Earth, and the old man had been its first casualty.

A simple trip, Harke had assured him. *In and out. You'll be back before you know it, and I'll reward you richly.*

The only reward Jarem wanted was an end to the killing.

One button. Lowering the protective Barrier, his one contribution. A quick and bloodless end to Harke's bloody rebellion. He had not signed up for more than that. *The war was supposed to be over!*

The squad hunkered in a dip in the landscape, a trench that might have been a riverbank in times of rain. Far enough from the road that passing traffic shouldn't spot them, but close enough to the first few houses of the town to need concealment. Here on the cusp of the residential suburbs, sheds and factories giving way to the houses, stands of gum had been planted as windbreaks. A few scraggly trees threw a mottled shadow across the riverbed in the morning sunlight. The sun was warm at their backs, a relief after the frigid night. A false comfort. Soon it would become too hot.

His body was a thousand aches. His face throbbed where the truck driver Ivan had hit him, but it was his legs that bothered him more; the long march, from the scene of their ignominious defeat to the squad gathering in the desert night, had taken its toll. By the end of that walk Captain Aesk had been leaning on his shoulder, his injured leg stiffened under him almost to uselessness.

Now Aesk rested at the end of the line, grey-faced with pain and exertion, so when Utara beckoned Jarem couldn't pretend he wanted the captain. Reluctantly he approached.

"Somewhere in that city, somewhere close," Utara said softly. The sensor drone told the tale: their quarry had come to a halt in the town, remaining stationary for hours when they might have instead been half a country away. The general held out a hand and clenched it to a fist as if he were grasping the town. "I feel like I could reach out and take them."

Jarem dared a glance at the General's face. His eyes fixed unblinking on the town ahead, he might have been making up his mind to simply march the men in. That would have been foolhardy for a man of Utara's reputation, but Jarem couldn't be sure how much that reputation was deserved. "Your men are in uniform. They'll draw attention, and the response will be quick and violent. We don't want to engage in hostilities. We'll be outgunned."

Utara's voice was dismissive. "So you say. I note that we haven't seen any sign of your promised checkpoints or patrols."

"The girl said it was a civilian area. We're behind the lines."

"If we're detected, it might take some time for them to marshal a response. But best not to risk that until we must. What do you recommend?"

The early-morning sun was already hot on his shoulders. "We should find cover. We need to get out of this sun."

"Cover," agreed Utara. He ticked off their needs on his fingers. "Somewhere to rest. Food. Civilian clothes, and transport." He waved a hand at the buildings in front of them. "We have some dwellings. Pick one."

This is not *what I had in mind.* "They'll be occupied! These are civilians. Innocents."

"Innocents die in war. *Pick one.*"

Jarem ran his eye along the residences in desperation. "That one," he said, pointing. The building was long and low, the window shades tattered with age, and the driveway standing empty at its side. It might be empty. *Please let it be empty.*

Utara shook his head. "I think not," he said. "There." The house he indicated was closer, more exposed, and Jarem could see why Utara would choose it. Two vehicles were parked in front of it, the four-wheeled transports they favoured here. "There's our base of operations."

"There's people inside."

"That's the point. We need food, clothing, transport. We won't find those in an empty house."

"We'll find another way. Don't hurt them," Jarem said, but Utara had already turned his attention elsewhere, starting off along the line. Jarem hesitated, but he hadn't been dismissed and angering Utara was not a risk he wanted to take. He followed the general in a low crouch.

He could feel the eyes of the squad upon him. One face blurred into another; he hadn't been able to learn all their names, although some of them were best recognised by their callsigns. The big man staring at him with hostile eyes and bristling hands and arms was The Bear. Jad the Younger, the junior of the squad by a long way, was idly taking apart and reassembling his flinger. A squat man with his hair in a tail gave Jarem a wink as he passed; his name was Renn or Rell, but Jarem didn't know if the wink was companionable or dismissive. None of these men had reason to respect him and he had no cause to feel safe around them.

Captain Aesk was at the far end of the line, crouched on one leg with the other extended straight out. The only obvious sign of his wound was the rent in his trousers and a trouser leg stiffened to black with blood. As Jarem drew within earshot Brec was packing away his tools. "It's still clean," the medic said. "It just needs time to heal."

Utara glanced at Aesk's leg, then back to the Captain's face. Beyond his pale face, if Aesk was in pain he wasn't showing it. "Captain, we need one of those houses. We need an assault. Are you up to it? Or should I talk to your men directly?"

"They won't take your orders," Aesk said. "*Rigge* is second in command, if I'm incapacitated. What's the target?"

"That house. There may be resistance. Quick and quiet. I want the vehicles. And we need somewhere to rest and plan for a time, so we can't afford alarms or noise."

"We can handle that," Aesk said. "My team's good."

"I have complete faith in your abilities."

"'Complete faith', my bones." The soldier next to where Jarem squatted muttered the curse under his breath. Deaf Illen, a big soldier with a shaggy beard he'd grown out to obscure the patchwork of scars that marred his cheek. The beard did little to hide the gaps in his teeth and nothing at all to cover the stub where his ear used to be. Harke's army was replete with men like this, men who had fallen through the gaps in the system, with little education and no prospects. Unguilded, like Harke himself.

Jarem flinched. "What?"

The scarred man shook his head. "Not your fault, little man. The Captain asked for more men, but *Lord* Utara wouldn't listen."

There hadn't been time to wait. When they reached the road on their initial scout, only to find Ivan's truck right in front of them, the driver had already been returning. No time to wait for more troops through the Gateway, and Utara hadn't anticipated the level of resistance.

A teenage Empress, protected only by a boy barely out of school and a civilian. The captain, with Jarem along for translation, should have been sufficient. Nobody's fault the attempt had gone awry. Certainly not Captain Aesk's failure, but Utara seemed to need someone to blame.

Injured or not, Aesk wasn't about to give up his command. With terse commands he directed his men into small teams, the squad moving with the fluid efficiency of long experience. This group had taken down fortresses and hardened enemy emplacements. They treated this civilian building like a stronghold, descending upon the building in three groups. Storming the house at front, rear and side, and it was less than a minute before the scene fell back into stillness, silence broken only by the gusting of the wind.

Jarem waited in the ditch while Utara counted seconds below his breath. Then the General nodded and clambered his way forward, approaching the house, and Jarem was left alone in the field. Jarem closed his eyes and shivered, then followed. What else was he going to do?

Captain Aesk met them in the entry hallway. "The house is secured. Six occupants, all subdued. We took no casualties. No communications got out." Several doorways opened onto the hall, and a low, huddled shape on the floor obstructed their path through the closest. Jarem glanced at it and shuddered; a flinger disc had opened the man's throat, a lake of blood flooding the hall. Utara nodded with approval; Jarem felt sick. "We took hostages," Aesk added. "A woman and two children."

Utara sighed. "Did I ask you take hostages, Captain? Never mind. Show me."

Jarem had no choice but to follow as Aesk drew them deeper into the building. At the end of a long hallway they stopped in a doorway. A child's bedroom.

The woman and children were under guard from two of Aesk's men. The woman was too old to be the mother to the two children, neither of them possibly any older than ten. All three looked terrified, intimidated into silence. Jarem couldn't bear the mute terror of the captives, his eyes flinching away from them, seeking the corners of the room, the walls; but everywhere he looked he saw smiling children in photographs, he saw pink ponies and model airplanes, and there was nowhere he could look that his eyes were not met with the lives of children.

This was too much for him, too much to ask. He turned to escape the sight, only to find his way blocked by soldiers, and they wouldn't let him through.

"Hold him," Utara said, and Jarem found himself turned to face into the room, the soldiers' hands iron on his arms. "You should be thanking me," Utara said. "The strong survive. I will make you strong. I'm not asking you to do it. But I *will* have you watch."

Held by the unyielding grasp of the soldiers, Jarem was left with no choice but to endure, and hope it would at least be over quickly... but of course, it wasn't.

VI

Jess stepped through the heavy double doors into the Flinders Hotel foyer and paused, overwhelmed with the sense of stepping into the past. The ornate architraves on walls of whitewashed stone, the faded oil landscapes on the walls, the heavy oak-framed doors leading off in three directions, struck her with inexorable nostalgia even though she'd never been here before. "I grew up in places like this."

The sense of history was marred by flashing lights through one of the doorways and the bored, uniformed guard standing in it. Jess shook her

126

head. They weren't here for the gaming room. She led the children through the second door, into the restaurant.

Monday mornings during school holidays. The clientele seemed to be comprised entirely of mothers, clustered at tables with a slight air of desperation as whirlwind children battled it out in the glassed-off ball pit. A heavy oaken bar took up a large part of the room, low tables scattered across the floor and cubicles lined along the exterior glass window, half-height dividers offering an illusion of privacy. Jess led the children towards one of the cubicles. "It's too early for lunch, but we need somewhere to talk."

The cubicle offered enough shelter to allow them to discreetly transfer Jess's belongings from the plastic bags into her newly-purchased backpacks. The bags were too small but Jess packed the fabric in tight until all that remained were a couple of bulky sweatshirts that Jess decided, reluctantly, she wouldn't miss too terribly.

There were more shopping bags and clothing now, the results of Jess's retail expedition, and she handed a bag across to Aran. She addressed Vi for translation duties. "There's a men's toilet over that way. Have Aran change into these. He'll blend in better, and they're clean. I had to guess his size, I don't have a lot of experience buying clothes for teenagers. There's a belt in there too if he needs it." The clothes had been expensive but she had unexpectedly found she enjoyed shopping for them.

Aran seemed reluctant to abandon them, departing the table with many backward glances. When he had gone, Jess handed a second bag across the table. "These are for you. We're going to have to do something about your hair as well, but one step at a time. You can make a start, there's a brush in the bag." Jess ran a hand through her own hair. A day of inattention, fleeing through desert and scrub, had not been kind to it.

While the children dressed Jess crossed to the bar. The girl behind the bar seemed too young to be legally allowed to drink at it. As she waited for the lemonades, Jess idly turned a vanity beer coaster over in her hands, staring at but not really seeing the words "Crossroads to the West", and examined her motives.

It wasn't too late yet to betray them. Turn them over into the hands of the police — Aran's threats notwithstanding, they were still just children. Jess could outmanoeuvre them. They might not know about CCTV, anti-theft sensors in shops, plainclothes detectives. Easy enough to bring this whole adventure to an end.

And yet she had bought them new clothes, other supplies she had still to reveal to them. A part of her seemed to wish to help them remain fugitives. She shook her head. *Make up your damn mind.*

"You're not from around here."

The speaker was a tall man who had come to stand beside her at the bar. She hadn't heard his approach and his interruption startled her, the coaster rolling across the bar and off the side as she shuffled slightly sideways to gain space. She ran her eyes over the man. Slim, well presented, a navy blue long-sleeved top complementing cream trousers. His hair was short but not cropped, traces of silver at the temples. He looked older than her, upper middle-aged, but very fit. He looked like money.

"Just passing through," Jess said cautiously. "Who's asking?"

The man smiled. "You look like you could use some conversation."

The girl finished with the lemonades and placed the bowl of chips on the counter beside a scattering of sauce sachets. Jess ignored them for the moment. "Thank you," she said, "but I'm really only here for a short time."

"Short conversations can be just as fulfilling as long ones."

"Maybe. But you don't look like the short conversation type." She shook her head. "Besides, what I really need now is to eat my chips and get back on the road."

The man shrugged. "Fair enough." He nodded at the three glasses of lemonade on the counter. "You must be thirsty."

Jess was starting to feel uncomfortable. The man didn't look like a policeman and he seemed unthreatening, but he was being too intrusive. "I think I'd like to go back to my table now. It was nice to meet you." She didn't ask his name, and she didn't offer her own.

"When you're ready for that long conversation, feel free to look me up." The man withdrew a card from his hip pocket and dropped it onto the bar. One side of the card was blank and he quickly scribbled something on it before flipping it over; he used one forefinger to push it closer to Jess. "You'll find me a very useful conversationalist."

She thought he was going to do more, maybe lurch at her with grasping hands, but instead he turned on a heel and headed for the exit, walking with an easy authority. Jess watched as he departed; thinking both *Very nice legs*, and *Definitely money*. She picked up the card and turned it over in her hands. The front side had a single mobile phone number printed in stark black on the white card; no name, no address, nothing else. Unusual. The scrawl he had left on the back of the card seemed meaningless, a jumble of loops and lines. Strange, but after the events of the past twenty-four hours, not inappropriate.

She returned to the booth in time to meet Aran, coming back from the men's room. Now in jeans and a printed t-shirt, the backpack he'd refused to leave at the table slung over a shoulder, he looked like any other teenager. The t-shirt was too big for him but baggy was in and he would definitely pass muster. He nodded to her grudgingly as he slid back into his seat. "Thank you," he said thickly, impeded both by his unfamiliarity with English and by his swollen lips. Evidently the sentiment was all the language he had yet been able to pick up and he didn't try communicating anything else. Jess handed him a lemonade and demonstrated by example that he ought to help with the chips.

Vi wasn't much longer returning. Jess had picked out chinos, a light top and a summer jacket for her, and her guesses at the girl's size appeared to have paid off. The new clothes changed her look, and she had brushed out her hair, leaving it loose. The changes brought her a good sixty percent of the way to a functional disguise. "You look good."

Vi accepted the other soft drink. "Thank you," she said again. "For everything. So what do we do next? We cannot stay here. Utara will not be far behind."

Jess had her answer ready. "We'll take a bus to Adelaide. We should arrive before dark, and we'll stay overnight in a hotel. We can start making phone calls to try to find your Harold Reed."

"Hareth," Vi corrected.

"After that, I don't know. The buses run every couple of hours, so we'll aim for the midday bus; it's still more than an hour from now, but there's nothing sooner."

"I do not know if we can wait that long. Either Utara or the police will find us soon."

"I have a couple of ideas that might help," said Jess. "The clothes are step one. When we're finished here I'll help you with step two."

Vi glanced down to pick up her glass, and her eyes came to rest on the card the man at the bar had given Jess, lying on the table neglected. She froze, her lemonade forgotten. "What is that?"

"Just some guy I met at the bar," said Jess, reaching for the card, but Vi was faster and grabbed it before Jess could pick it up.

"What 'guy'? Is he still here? Show me," she said. At the tone of command, Jess found her hand lifting to point, but the man hadn't hesitated when leaving the restaurant and was well out of sight.

"He's not here now. Why? Is something wrong?"

"This writing," Vi said. "It is in our language."

Jess looked again at the card, at the random loops and whorls the man had left. It didn't look like any kind of writing she knew. "It is? What does it say?"

Vi was looking past her shoulder, to the doorway they had entered by. "It says we should meet him outside."

The Fixer

I

It took Mark over an hour to find the phone number. In addition to taking from the walls every picture in which she appeared, Jess had also taken their shared address book. True, the book had been her idea and her work over the years, but he had relied on it. It annoyed him that she should be so inconsiderate.

Eventually he located an old mobile phone with numbers in its memory. He placed the call on the landline. It had been a long time, but the gravelly voice that answered brought back the image of a man run to dissipation, beer belly straining at the waistband of his slacks; a victim of too much salt and butter and oil in four decades of meals. Ian Cartwright had never liked Mark, had shown an almost instant antipathy the few times he and Jess visited his wife's family in Perth. The feeling was not mutual; Mark felt little but pity for the man.

"It's Mark," he told the phone.

"Yeah? What do you want?" Cartwright sounded even grumpier than usual.

"I'm calling about Jess," said Mark, undeterred.

"Police already called. You got anything to add?"

"I think she might be coming in your direction. Has she called you?"

"Haven't spoken to her in ages. Don't think she cares for us much these days. Not rich enough, I s'pose."

"Well, if she comes by, can you get her to call me? I've been trying to get through but she's out of mobile range."

Mark could practically feel the old man's disdain. "Seems to me she'll call you if she wants to call you. Don't see why she'd come by here, anyways. Is it true you beat her?"

The question was so unexpected that Mark answered without thought. "We had an argument," he said. "I didn't mean to hurt her." Four extra words hung unspoken in the air: *it was her fault*. He jammed his jaw closed; Jess might be the man's daughter, but she was Mark's *wife*, damn it, and he had no right asking. Perhaps more importantly, how had he known? The police must have said something, and Mark wondered bleakly what conclusions the cops were drawing.

"Few years ago I'd have strapped the shotgun on the bike and come east, I heard that," said Cartwright. "Guess you're lucky I'm getting older. She might not want anything more to do with us, but she's still my girl."

"Who you talking to, Ian?" interrupted another voice before Mark could respond. Moments later came the clunk of a phone changing hands. "Mark? How nice to hear from you."

Where Ian Cartwright was broad and slow, Barbara was an inexhaustible dynamo of energy. Purveyor of too much salt and butter and oil in everything she ever cooked, she was the very model of a fifties housewife, down to the monthly perm that was attended to as religiously as the weekly church service. Blessed with height, an overactive metabolism and a formidable nose, she was the yin to her husband's yang. Where Ian saw Jess's departure from the family home as an abandonment, Barbara saw it for what it was: an escape.

"Barb," he said. "I was just telling Ian that I thought Jess might show up at your place."

"The police said that might be possible," agreed Barbara. "You'd like us to call you if she turns up?"

"That would be great. I really need to talk to her."

"You two really should come over and spend a week in our guest house. It would do you both good to get away from your busy lives."

"We're fine," said Mark automatically. "We just had an argument."

"What you need is a child," said Barbara. "Haven't I always said so? I wasn't ever happy until my children arrived. It's how God intended."

Mark really didn't want to have this discussion again now. "It's not as if we weren't trying." The old mobile phone caught his eye, sitting on the table; the background image was of himself with Jess, both of them laughing, carefree, young.

"Obviously not hard enough," said Barbara.

The picture of Jess brought other memories to mind. Before it started to go bad. Before he'd started punishing her by seeing other women. He felt his body responding automatically.

"That," he said, "was never the problem."

He hung up.

II

The gods of fate had deserted Jeff Lang. He willed himself a quick trip to the hotel, to make up for his delayed departure, and was rewarded with nose-to-bumper traffic and every red light between here and Acapulco. Then in his distraction he left the binder of case notes in the cruiser and had to go back for it, and just when he'd finally made it inside a young family blocked the doorway as they exited the hotel.

It felt like an omen.

As he stood in the foyer he suppressed an urge to straighten the tie he wasn't wearing, brush his hair into place. He was not a teenager, and this was not a date. *This is* not *a date!*

Dr Ferguson was alone at a table near the front door, well aside from the mothers' groups. Her attention was fixed on her laptop as he stood in the

133

doorway and took a moment to stare. She was slim, dressed in a slightly old-fashioned outfit of loose slacks and a sleeveless blouse; in deference to the air conditioning in the bar she had wrapped a shawl around her shoulders. Her dark hair was unruly, too short to tie but long enough to fall into her eyes and require regular adjustment.

She was lovely, and quite clearly out of his league.

Will it into being. He squared his shoulders and approached.

She folded her laptop closed and tilted her head up at him. "Officer Lang, I assume. I'm Adele Ferguson."

"I know who you are, Dr Ferguson," he said. He didn't add, *we've met at least twice before.* "Thank you for looking at this for me."

"No, thank *you*," she replied. "It's the most interesting work I've had this year."

Her enthusiasm made his heart sink. He needed to reel it back — the more intriguing the case, the more disappointed she would be. He forced a smile. "It's a simple break-in. All part of the boring day-to-day work of a country copper."

Dr Ferguson shook her head. "It's no simple break-in. What you left me was a wedding dress for a teenager who lives in a palace. Somewhere on the other side of the world, probably. Marble dust, remember?"

She wasn't going to be mollified easily. "Can I get you a coffee?"

"Thanks. A soy latte would be nice."

While the young bar-girl made coffees, he glanced over his shoulder. Dr Ferguson was watching him from the table. She was well and truly hooked, and he was going to have to let her down.

"After we spoke, I did some more work," she said as he returned to the table. "I was fascinated by the cloth."

"It's a kind of silk, isn't it?"

"Not silk. It's a satin weave — at least the outer layer. Quality work — expensive. But that's not the interesting thing."

"You have resources about types of fabric?" Jeff folded himself into a seat, awkwardly arranging his knees under the low table. "I thought you were a botanist."

Adele seemed not to have heard the question. "Each thread is triple-stranded. I've never heard of triple-strand weave before. It's a kind of spiral - two threads wrapped around a third. It makes for really strong cloth. That's probably why they couldn't tear it." Her eyes were bright as she stared at him. "I don't even know how you could make it."

"You can't trace it to a particular manufacturer, or a place?"

"There's nothing like it in any of the databases I checked."

"Well, if it's not on Google, it probably doesn't exist."

She smiled with not much humour. "Compared to some of the databases I can access, Google's a child's encyclopaedia. No, Google didn't help.

"I did get a bit further with some of the particulates." Her coffee sat untouched on the table as she flipped her laptop open again and swivelled it to face him. A black-and-white photo of an alien face stared at him in high definition. "See this? That's pollen. See the sails? But it's not anything native." Her eyes were bright as she stared at him. "The closest I could find is a kind of flax native to eastern Europe. Even that's not a perfect match. That's not all." A new picture, a new alien. "This is a dust mite. I'm not an entomologist — I can't identify the species, but it's not the kind of bug you'd expect to find here."

"So," said Jeff. "East Europe. Palace marble. Unusual cloth you've never seen." He paused. "Have we found Anastasia?"

She looked at him blankly. "Anna who?"

"Anastasia," he said. "Empress of Russia in... never mind." He took a sip of coffee, needing the moment's delay. "This is... awkward. You've been really helpful. And I know it seems fasc— interesting."

She wasn't listening. She slid a sheet of printout across the table to him. "I've split my isolates into three groups. The traces I would expect to find: sand, dirt, plant matter from native grasses and shrubs. I told you about the blood. I've got hairs from at least four, probably more people. A couple of those have roots so you might be able to get DNA from them, but I'm not set up for that."

"That's great, but—"

"The second group I can identify, but not explain," she continued without pause. "The marble dust, of course. I found something that looks like metal shavings. That fourth item... I'm not sure, but it might be bone shards. Blood by itself could have come from anywhere, but bone says violence. Wherever this dress has been, it's not all roses."

"Marble, blood and bone, metal shavings," Jeff said. "Industrial accident of some kind?"

"It gets better," said Adele. "I showed you the pollen - I can't identify it. The cloth. There's another piece of plant matter, at least that's what it..."

"Hold on," said Jeff, finally interrupting, reaching out a hand to rest on her forearm. "This is all great. But I'm not on the case any more." He took a deep breath. "A federal agency's taken over. Looks like it might be a part of something bigger, something across State lines. Drug running." He paused. "Maybe. I don't know. But it's no longer in our jurisdiction."

"'Nothing out of the ordinary', you said." She didn't sound as angry as the words seemed. "So what does this mean?"

"I need to take the results you've found, add them to my own notes and investigations, hand them all over."

"You're kidding. What agency is this?"

"I don't know," Jeff admitted. "I just do what I'm told."

"Whoever they are, they'll need forensics," she said. "Tell me who's in charge and I'll speak to them."

"It doesn't work like that," Jeff said. "They won't be interested in anything we can offer. They don't care about people as... as provincial as us."

"*Provincial?*"

"Look, they'll have huge labs, hundreds of staff, equipment for every test under the sun. Why would they need either of us?" He stared unseeing at the bright chrome atop the bar. "So we hand over everything we've done — *you've* done — and they'll say thank you very much, and we'll never hear about it again. That's the way it works."

She seemed to consider for a moment before responding. "No."

"No... what?"

"You can't get me to look at something like this and then expect me just to give it up."

"I don't think we have a choice," Jeff said, despondent.

"Fine, then. They'd just get in our way, anyway. What if we kept looking at this in our own time?"

Jeff shook his head. "I have to give them everything. All your data. The evidence package. Don't worry, they'll pay you for the work you've done."

"I don't care about the payment. They can have all the data, of course I have copies. I'll just hang onto a fragment from the edge of the dress, they won't even notice it's gone. So long as nobody tells them."

"They won't hear it from me." That sounded too much like a concession, so he hastened on. "Look, I'm really sorry about this. I don't want to give it up either."

"Then don't," Dr Ferguson said. "They can have their federal investigation. We can have ours."

They weren't going to get anywhere. Without the resources of the police department behind them, a clandestine investigation would be a waste of time. He sighed and told her so. "We can't draw attention to what we're doing. We can't ask for outside assistance."

"You seem like a clever guy," Dr Ferguson said, "and *I* am little shy of brilliant. I'm sure we'll manage." She held out a hand across the table. "What do you say? Are you going to detect, Mr Detective, or are you going to hand it all over to the *federales*?"

For a moment he allowed himself the luxury of thinking about it. Without resources or authority they wouldn't get anywhere; without spending work hours on an unsanctioned investigation it would just be extended hours with no result. But maybe the result wasn't the point. It was the extended hours that mattered: time spent in company with Doctor Adele Ferguson was a very tempting idea.

He took her hand, and felt his fingers positively tingle at the contact. They shook, and he could tell he was grinning like a loon. "Partners in crime."

III

For a moment Jess was certain that the game was up. The policeman paused at the doorway, stared into her eyes: all over, bar the shouting and the arresting and the imprisoning. Surely he could see it on her face, the jolt of fear, the relief mixed with dismay. *Just when it was starting to be fun.*

But the policeman stood aside to let them pass, staring past her at the tables within. He was young and preoccupied, oblivious to the woman and two children he was passing. Jess hoped he wouldn't get into trouble later for having come so close.

Leaving the tall policeman behind, Jess led the children out into the glare of the late morning.

Vi nodded at a van parked opposite the doors, prominently in view. The spot directly across from the doors, under the ragged shade of a tall gum tree, had been empty when they first arrived. The van was unremarkable: Jess wouldn't have given it a first thought, but Vi seemed fascinated. Aran, too, was staring.

Jess frowned. "That van? Are you sure?"

It had once been plain white, painted windows preventing casual observation of the interior. At some point kids had got to it, and both sides of the van were covered in graffiti scrawl, unintelligible text mixed with surprisingly proficient art. "Much of that is meaningless," Vi said, "but not all of it. Do you see that loop there? The squiggle on its left? It is very clear."

"Your language again," said Jess. "So what does it say?"

"*Dahla.*" Vi paused, frowning at Jess's uncomprehending look. "It is difficult. There is not a word exactly like it in English. It means... someone who arranges things. A problem-solver. A... a *fixer.*"

"So do you think that man was a 'fixer' from... wherever you come from?"

"I do not know," said Vi. "But I want to find out."

It was only minutes later that Jess found herself walking alone across the car park towards the van. The last twelve hours had turned her paranoid; only yesterday she could have crossed a wide-open space without thinking twice, but now it terrified her. As she approached, she was assailed with visions of car-bombs, veiled men with machine guns, dark figures carrying fisherman's bags stocked with duct tape and scalpels.

As she drew closer, the front seat of the van became visible through the windscreen, but the cabin was empty. The wind gusting through the car park, sweeping dust into her eyes, was her only companion. The car park was still. No other guests arriving or departing.

All too soon she neared the van. She felt certain that it held more revelations, that it would further undermine the world she knew. "Hello?" Her voice was whipped away by a gust of wind, rocking the van slightly on its springs. Her fingers were sweaty on the grip of the *flinger*, under the hem of her t-shirt.

Maybe he heard her. Maybe he was watching from behind opaque windows. The rear doors of the van swung open, revealing a silhouette against the backlit windscreen. "For God's sake, get in here before somebody sees you coming."

The shadowed figure stepped back from the doors as she hoisted herself into the van, giving her plenty of space, a consideration for which she was grateful. As she stepped up she brought the flinger out and aimed at him while she waited for her eyes to adjust to the gloom. She hoped that the shadows would hide the shaking of her hand on the weapon. A lifetime of television indoctrination had conditioned her to expect sticks of dynamite and racks of AK-47s lining the walls, but the van contained neither terrorists nor serial killers. Instead, she saw she had stepped into the future.

It was a particularly low-rent kind of future, admittedly, more *Doctor Who* than *Star Trek*. Both sides of the van had been lined with cabinets that wouldn't have been out of place in a domestic kitchen. Atop the cabinets, most of the flat surfaces were taken up by electronic equipment. She was no expert, but she'd seen enough of the network engineers at her office to recognise computers and laptops, networking equipment, keyboards and mice secured with velcro, and a profusion of blinking lights and bundled cables. Monitor screens loomed overhead, secured to the ceiling of the van with extending arms. Chairs were bolted to the floor. It looked like a cross between an NSA surveillance van and HG Wells' time machine.

The tall man from the bar was standing towards the front of the vehicle, both hands on the back of a chair. He said something to her, but he spoke in whatever language Vi and Aran had brought into her life, and she shook her head. "Speak English," she demanded. "I know you speak English, you were using it before." She kept her left hand on the door handle behind her, ready to flee at the first sign of threat, but the man didn't approach.

"You don't need the weapon," he said. "If I'd wanted to do you harm, I'd have done it by now."

"You wanted to see me," Jess said. "You see me. Now tell me why. Why outside?"

His gaze flicked away from the weapon in her hand and up to an overhead monitor. "I needed to scan you. You're not at all what I expected."

"Terribly sorry to disappoint. You didn't answer my question."

He ignored her demand. "If it's not you, it must be those kids... don't waste my time denying," he added as she opened her mouth, "I've been watching you."

Jess tried anyway. "What kids? I don't know what you're talking about."

The man ignored her. "You're not from Zama," he mused. "You're local. So what the hell are you doing running around...?"

"I'm not local," said Jess. "I told you, I'm just passing through."

"Local enough. Comparatively speaking."

Comparatively. Jess didn't like to think about what that word implied. "Tell me who you are. What do you want with these kids you're talking about?"

"I think," the man said slowly, "that I should talk to them directly."

"You'll talk to me. Tell me what you want, right now, or I walk away."

"Yes, why don't you do that? I think that might be a good idea." The man suddenly smiled. "You don't know what you're into. This can be good for both of us. I'm exactly who you need. Walk away. I'll take care of the children. It would be best if you forgot you ever saw me, or them."

"They can make up their own minds. I doubt they're going to just walk into your clutches."

"Into my... who do you think I am? I told you, I'm not interested in hurting anyone. I'm on their—"

He froze, leaving the sentence unfinished, as a shadow moved behind him. A line of silver traced its way across the side of his neck. A sword.

Aran finished clambering through the front seat of the van. He'd moved so smoothly Jess hadn't seen him approach, even in direct view. "*Ve-tock chi claet sedti,*" he said.

"In English," the man snapped, carefully not attempting to turn his head. "From now on, everything in English."

"He doesn't know any English," Jess said. "It's inconvenient, but I don't think he's got much to say that's helpful."

The man raised an eyebrow. "Is he in charge or are you?"

"He thinks he is."

"Right then." He turned his hands over, palms up, resting his knuckles on the chair back. "I'm at your mercy. I'm unarmed. There's a misunderstanding here."

"You can start by telling me why you were following us," Jess said.

"That's my job. Your frightening friend here must have been told to expect me. He should have followed instructions and stayed put, I would have reached him sooner. Instead he had to go galloping off all over the country, and somehow picked you up on the way. Weren't you told to expect me? *Ach shedoc cleck?*"

Aran tilted his head in response, the muscles of his forearm relaxing. The tall man carefully turned his head to talk to the boy directly. *So much for 'everything in English'.*

Jess gave them thirty seconds for their jabber, but when the flow of meaningless syllables showed no sign of abating she coughed.

"Excuse me? I'm still holding the gun. You *do* know what this is?"

"Irresponsible, is what it is," the man snapped. "In the wrong hands, that thing could cause a war that would make the Second look like play time in the sandpit. Oh, wait... it *is* in the wrong hands. I should have said, *wronger*. Give it to me, I'll make sure it's dealt with appropriately. You know you can't keep it, right? It doesn't belong to you."

"Finders, keepers," Jess said.

"I'll pay you for it," the man said. "Good money. *Very* good money. You have no idea how valuable it is."

"I know it's the reason I'm in charge."

He frowned and changed tack. "Look. You seem to be a nice person. Polite. A *normal* girl. You've done a good job getting the lad this far. I really think it would be best for you... best for everybody... if you said goodbye now and went back to your real life."

"She cannot do that. She is with me." Vi stepped out of the shelter of the rear door and hoisted herself inside.

The man snatched another glance at his overhead monitor. "And here's the other one. And at least you speak English. We should be grateful for small mercies. Does that mean you're the leader of this little gang?"

"It does," said Vi. "Aran is my guard, and Jess has been kind enough to give us some help since we arrived."

"And what have you told her?" The man glanced sideways, as if to confirm Aran was still there holding the blade. "Have you told her what you did? Why they sent you?"

"I have told her the truth." Vi was sounding defensive.

Jess felt she could speak for herself. "She's given me a story. I'm not sure about 'truth'."

"All right, all right," the man muttered. "I've been chasing you since yesterday. Why'd you go moving without waiting for me?"

"We were not instructed to wait," said Vi. "We left in haste."

"They didn't tell you about me? What the hell is going on over there? You're just a kid. First it's family groups, now children. How am I supposed to do my job? I'm spending more time running around the country after you lot than I am running my business." He shook his head in frustration. "I'm sorry. It's not your fault. You should have been given a lot more preparation."

"We are not here by choice," said Vi.

He replied with a short bark of laughter. "Choice? Since when is choice ever the issue?" He sniffed, suddenly becoming serious. "Bugger it. If you

143

really weren't given the normal preparation... We got off on the wrong foot. Let's start over. My name's Jabe. It's my job to help people like you get settled over here. Whatever you were back home, whatever you did, it's over now. Time for a fresh start."

"Wait a moment." Jess was starting to feel sidelined. "Are you about to tell me that these kids really are from —" She swallowed, amazed she was actually going to say the words. "From another planet?"

The man sighed, his shoulders slumping. "She told you that. I wish she hadn't. A lie would have been safer."

"No," said Jess. "It's ridiculous. This is some kind of setup. I can understand the girl getting confused, delusional — might be the heat. Some kind of trauma. PTSD, maybe. But don't tell me you believe this rubbish. Encouraging them isn't going to help anybody. You ought to know better."

"I do believe it," the man said. "You see, she's not the first. We've been sending people here for decades. And I'm one of them. Been here for about twenty years, now."

IV

They gathered in the dining area adjoining the kitchen. One wall was marked with a deep rent in the plaster where a razor disc had missed its target, and a spray of blood to its left, remnant of the one that had not. There were no seats left around the table so Jarem stood with his back to the red splatter, but he could still feel it behind his shoulder blades, accusing him of complicity.

Captain Aesk and his soldiers didn't seem bothered. Three soldiers were on guard at vantage points in the house, but the dining space was crowded with ten, the soldiers lounging in the chairs or standing along the walls. Utara took the head of the table and the men left him a respectful buffer zone without being asked.

Utara's gaze roamed over the gathered men. "Congratulations on an efficient job." The soldiers around the table started to smile, and Utara smiled along with them, but there was something dangerous in his eyes. "Excellent work. A textbook assault on unarmed civilians, women and children, without warning. I'm sure you're proud.

"Once you're done congratulating yourselves, we can do what we came here for. The child is somewhere in the town. We can't afford to wait for nightfall, because with local help she might get away from us. We're not going home without that girl's head in a bag." Jarem flinched at the words, and Utara clarified the statement: "Preferably still attached to her shoulders."

On the wall beyond the General's shoulder a family photograph was mounted. In the photo the children were smiling, the adults close, arms around each other's shoulders. Loving and peaceful and happy, until Utara arrived and brought death with him. Until *Jarem* arrived.

The sharp crack as Utara slapped both hands on the table made Jarem flinch. The General was still speaking. "We're here for as long as it takes, even if it takes a year. I'm sure none of you want that any more than I do."

Please, no. They'd been here no more than half a day and already seven people were dead. How much carnage could Utara cause in a year?

When he closed his eyes he could still see the woman's beseeching stare.

"Master Jarem?"

He started when he realised something was being asked of him. What had they been saying? One of the soldiers had asked Utara a question. Jarem scratched through his memory for the man's name: Quain. Quiet, compact, and always watching — dangerous. What had Quain asked? Tracking the Empress in daylight — whether the drone would be too easy to spot. But Jarem had completely missed Utara's response.

The General repeated his query, his voice polite, neutral. Somehow that just made it more terrifying. "Can the drone still scan from inside its carrier?"

I believe so, he almost said, but Utara had already demonstrated his lack

145

of patience for prevarication. "Yes. At least while they're close. The range won't be good."

"What if they're not close? We lost the signal before we took the house," Captain Aesk reminded them. "Is it possible that whatever's shielding them is mobile?"

Jarem shook his head. "It's unlikely."

"They can't hide forever," Utara said. "We'll get as close as possible to their last known position and wait for them."

Dust rattled against the windows as the wind gusted, and the roof groaned like a giant.

"We can blend with the locals," said Aesk. He had already changed from his encrusted fatigues into clothing salvaged from one of the sleeping rooms in the house. The grey t-shirt's sleeves bulged around his biceps. His men were similarly attired in repurposed civilian clothes. At least they didn't look like clone soldiers any longer. "We should head into the town. Spread out around the area and keep a watch."

Utara nodded. "We have three people who can speak the local language. Our engineer is one. I took the language program. So did Rick."

"Rigge," Captain Aesk corrected.

"So, three groups. One translator in each. How many communicators do we have?"

The discussion turned to an audit of flingers and ammunition, breaching charges and Garron's seemingly inexhaustible supply of explosive weaponry, but Jarem tried not to listen. Why had the Empress had to run? If she'd just come willingly, this would all be over. Utara would never have come here and those children would still be alive.

Utara stood, conference over. "Get ready to fall out. And if that girl gets past any of your men," he added, directing the words to Aesk but making sure everyone heard him, "I'll be taking his eyes home in a pouch."

Captain Aesk marshalled his men, allocating tasks and filing with them from the room. Jarem gave them a moment to clear the doorway, then pushed away from the wall and turned to follow. Turning left, not right, to avoid bringing the stained wall into view.

Utara had not moved from the head of the table. "I have a question for you."

Jarem couldn't meet Utara's pitiless eyes. He fixed his gaze instead on the little scar on the General's chin. "What do you need?"

"Talk to me about these." Utara tossed a small pouch onto the table, and it bounced as it came to rest in front of Jarem.

In sudden dismay Jarem lunged for them, scooped up the bag and opened it. He peered inside but the little cubes looked intact. "We need my reader back. We don't have another. There's nothing on this planet that can read these."

"What if we can't get it back? If the boy has damaged or lost it?"

"I really hope not." If the data was lost — "I could manage. Get me some resources, some time on a computer. I'd need figures. From home. Then — I calculated it once. I can do it again. It would take... it would take a lot longer."

"Months or years?"

Jarem swallowed. "D-days. To calculate the vectors." Only, one mistake, a decimal point off by the merest fraction, and the Gate will miss. It took him years to calculate the first time. He couldn't redo it in days — weeks might not be enough. But he had to. They couldn't stay here for weeks. "Then, if Zama sends us what we need, depending how often they can open the Gate... a few days more. At least. Maybe another week."

Utara looked relieved. "A week we can handle. You'll have as long as you need."

Jarem took a deep breath. "Maybe longer. They don't... there's nothing here."

Utara raised an eyebrow. "Nothing?"

"Not even the basics. No magneto coils. No induction rails. Nothing at all I can use. We'll need to get everything from Zama."

"We'll get it," the General said. "Harke wants the girl. He'll spare no expense. When we get the girl, we'll retrieve your data pad. But if things go wrong, we'll be relying on your magic. Don't let us down."

"I have no intention on staying on this planet any longer than I have to," Jarem said.

"No need to worry about that," said Utara. "If you can't make good on your promises you're no good to me. I'll kill you myself."

V

There was a memory. Something relevant, Vi was sure, something she needed to know. It had a hazy feel to it: events she had never studied, events that never made it into the Lessons. She closed her eyes, trying to bring the memory forward.

We need a dahla. That was it: the connection. So close. It would...

They've put the man in a cell high in the citadel. Well-furnished and catered. They're treating him like an honoured guest rather than a condemned prisoner.

To the Empress Toni, the man doesn't seem monstrous. He's a small man, balding, still thin but with the genesis of a pot belly — too much comfortable living experienced too fast. She takes a moment to stare at him, gathering his measure. The prisoner's eyes gaze back at her with a distinct lack of deference.

It is he who breaks the silence. "Your highness. I didn't expect company, and surely not yours. Did my lawyer earn her pay and win me a pardon?"

"Your lawyer knows nothing of this meeting," Toni replies. "Nor

anybody outside of this room. There's no pardon on offer. Instead I bring... an amnesty."

"You have my attention," he says. "I don't much fancy spending the rest of my days in a penal colony in some wilderness."

"You understand you can't be allowed your freedom."

"Then why are you here? If not to offer me my freedom, and not to ship me off in chains to spend my life in the company of my trusty shovel?"

"Chains are still an option," the Empress says. "But let us not get ahead of ourselves. We have need of your special talents. I am about to offer you a choice. Whichever your decision, you won't be spending another night in this apartment. There can be no turning back, so choose well."

"My special talents are what brought me here," the man says, spreading his hands helplessly. "Now will they save me?"

"We need a dahla," says Empress Toni. "But not here. Somewhere else."

VI

Jess's eyes were adapting to the dim light inside the van. The more she stared at 'Jabe', the more certain she became that she'd seen him before. If only she could place it.

"I don't know what's going on over there," Jabe said, "but it can't go on like this. You weren't given even a basic briefing. You didn't come here in adult company? No parents?"

Vi didn't answer. She didn't seem to be paying attention, instead staring vaguely at the corner of the van.

"Just the two of them," Jess said into the uncomfortable pause. "In the middle of the desert."

Vi blinked and smiled, as if she'd just remembered something amusing. "You are the *dahla*. You provide resources, identity papers, an introduction to this world."

"They *did* tell you about me."

"They did not," said Vi. "How did you find us?"

Jabe shrugged. "There's a magnetic signature, anything that comes through the gate... I detect that signal. I'm supposed to drop everything and haul my arse across the country to meet whoever it is, before they get mugged or arrested. I was halfway across the Nullarbor when I realised you'd moved. Passed me in the other direction during the night."

Maybe he was a politician. Some anonymous back-bencher she'd seen around the edges of the chamber. A politician might have enough free time to go chasing around the country. But no — he'd said 'running my business'.

"There were others. More arrivals, shortly behind us," said Vi. When he nodded, she asked: "How many?"

"A fair number," Jabe said. "Definitely more than five. Less than fifteen. I'm not a miracle worker, you know. I can only deal with one arrival at a time. We need to finish up so I can get to them." He shook his head. "Fifteen. Madness."

"No," said Vi. "You do not want to contact these."

He raised an eyebrow. "It's my job."

It was the eyebrow that did it. Jess's eyes widened as the pieces fell into place. That was the *exact* look that the photographer had captured in the iconic image — a couple of years ago, and only seen the once. No wonder it had taken some time to bring it back to mind. She might have recognised him earlier, but the man in front of her was notoriously media-shy and rarely photographed. "You're Jacob Elliot," she said. "I saw you on the cover of *The Monthly*." She let the gun fall slightly, staring at one of the richest men in the country.

"The cover of *The Monthly*," sighed Elliot. "That damned article. They swore to me it was just going to be a two-paragraph profile. I should never have accepted."

"They called you 'Australia's answer to Bill Gates'," said Jess.

"In the article they did," Elliot said. "At least they had the decency to add a question mark on the front cover."

Jess laughed. "The founder of Elliot Industries is an alien from outer space. It's no wonder you're doing well, you've got the home team advantage!" Even in her own ears she was starting to sound a little hysterical. "What's your next invention, space travel?"

Elliot didn't deny the accusation. "I had help with some of my earlier inventions. Necessary seed money. That was a long time ago. Everything since has been genuine."

Jess shook her head. "I don't believe this. I'm in a van with Jacob Elliot, and he's an alien. I must have eaten something bad." Fever dream or not, the situation demanded answers. "So what does Australia's Bill Gates want with us?"

"I'm not interested in you at all," Elliot said bluntly. "It's the children I'm here for."

"We are not children," said Vi. "The boy with the sword to your neck is named Aran. He is an Imperial Guard in training. He may be young, but he is already blooded."

"*Bloodied*, maybe," said Elliot, indicating the boy's battered face.

"The man who did that was twice his size and would have killed us."

"If he's an Imperial Guard," said Elliot, "what does that make you? Are you on the High Council?"

Finally, something Jess knew that Elliot did not. She suppressed a giggle. "You don't recognise your Empress when you see her?"

Even as she said it she felt the last of her objections evaporate. She still didn't believe it, not a word of it. But... Elliot's unexpected support. The strange weapon in her hands. Their language, their sword-wielding pursuers. Maintaining scepticism felt like more effort than just letting the story sweep her along.

Elliot wasn't convinced. "You have trouble with the idea they come from a different world, but *this* you believe?"

"She is telling the truth," said Vi. "I am Vi Corala, nine hundred and eighteenth Empress. I bear the Crown."

Elliot started to lift his hands towards her, as if to ward away her words, but Aran shifted slightly and the touch of the blade reminded Elliot to keep his hands where they were. "If you have the Crown, you can tell me what I was doing before I was sent here. On Zama. Tell me my crime."

"That would be in my mother's memory," Vi said. "Those memories are lost. There was not enough time." The words were matter-of-fact but she spoke with the clipped tones of someone trying to disassociate.

"That's convenient," said Elliot.

"No," said Vi. "It is not."

"So how can I believe you, *my lady*? How do I know you're not just a liar? I've received my fair share of conmen, I assure you."

"I do not remember you," Vi admitted. "I *did* know your predecessor."

A calculating look came into his eye. "Tell me about him."

"*Her*," said Vi. "Empress Silka met Jera just the once. She was a senior diplomat in the Justice Guild, and she was corrupt. The Guildmaster took her actions personally. The *dahla* at the time was becoming old and forgetful, and it was time for him to be... retired. When I... when Silka heard of Jera, it seemed a logical solution. For her part, Jera feared being sent to the camps to which she had sent so many others. She would have seen exile as a safer fate."

"I never knew why she was exiled," Elliot said softly. "But if what you're saying is true... how can you be *here*? If you're the Empress, you should still... But you're... I don't understand."

"We are not here by choice," Vi said again. "The capital has fallen into the hands of rebels. I would have been captured also, if not for the Gateway."

Jess had to admit, the man recovered quickly. "Well. Coming here was not clever. There's no way to return."

"I *am* the Empress," said Vi, "and I bear the Crown. I will find a way."

"If you say so," said Elliot. "It changes nothing. Here, you're just another exile. You need to get by, just like the rest of us. My first priority is still to get you some identity papers and somewhere to stay in the short term."

"No," said Vi. "First must be to deal with the squad of soldiers sent to catch or kill us. They will kill you also if they find you."

Elliot glanced at the monitor again. "In that case we should talk about them," he said. "They're coming."

VII

The display was a meaningless swirl of dots and static that reminded Jess of nothing so much as a radar screen in a 1980s film. It was hard to discern the difference between a swirl of white fog in one segment of the circular display and the cluster of vague dots in another that represented the newest group of arrivals.

"I'd guess about ten or twelve," Elliot said.

Vi nodded. "Jarem said there was a squad. They are in one group?"

Elliot frowned as he tapped the screen. "Nope. A couple of them are heading off in a different direction. There's a third signal, a weak one. Maybe they're meeting up."

A third signal? More pursuers?

Vi was staring at the monitor. "We have been still for too long. They will catch us."

"They can't detect you in here," Elliot said. "The van's shielded. I needed to be able to scan outside. You're safe in here."

"Except," Jess said, "you've got a bloody big sign painted on the sides of the van that says *look at me*. That might be a clue."

"Ah," said Elliot. "I didn't think of that."

"This vehicle *is* obvious on sight," said Vi, who clearly hadn't thought of it either.

"I've never had to *hide* from new arrivals before," Elliot complained. "It's my job to find them and get them in here as quickly as possible."

"You don't want this lot in here," Jess said. "Can we hide the van?"

"The van gets garaged at the airport, but that won't help you. I don't know anywhere closer. But I have a different solution." Elliot turned his head gingerly and rolled his eyes in Aran's direction. "I need something from these cabinets. You're going to have to start trusting me eventually."

Vi gave Aran instructions. Aran nodded, reluctance on his face, and lowered the sword.

Elliot rolled his shoulders and stretched. "That's better. I'm not about to run off on you, and you've still got two weapons to my none."

"I believe him," Vi told Jess. "We must trust him." She nodded at the flinger, still held limply in Jess's hand. Staring at it as if she'd forgotten it was there, Jess slowly put the weapon back in its holster.

With slow and deliberate movements Elliot slid open a cabinet on the wall. He retrieved four large panels of what looked like fiberglass. "False sides for the van. In case I wanted to avoid police or the media. I've never needed them before. I need to step outside to attach them."

"Very well," said Vi. "Jess, go with him; I do not want him out of our sight."

"Apparently trust only goes so far. What am I going to do, run away on foot?"

"No," said Vi. "Because Jess will be with you to make sure you do not. Aran and I must confer."

"I'm not —" *I'm not going to shoot him*, Jess was about to say, but Vi was staring at her with raised eyebrows. Perhaps the threat of retaliation would make shooting him unnecessary. "Okay."

Jess ended up helping Elliot manhandle the panels out the back of the van; they were light but unwieldy. "Seeing as you're my chaperone, you can help me secure them," Elliot said.

He needed the help. The blustery wind kept catching the panels and it took both of them to hook the panels onto the attachment points along the roof. Wrestling the first panel into place, Jess nodded towards Elliot' hands. "Are you really married?"

"I am. Married, with two wonderful children." They struggled for a moment as a gust tried to free the panel from their grasp. "Are *you* really married?"

Jess glanced at her hands; she was still wearing her ring. It hadn't occurred to her to take it off. "Technically." Unwilling to let him change the subject, she continued: "But how can you have children, if you're not human? Is your wife an alien too?"

Elliot snapped the last fastener into place. "So far as I can tell, we're as human as you are."

"That's the most ridiculous thing I've heard all day," said Jess, "and today, that means a lot more than it did yesterday. I've never seen anything like this... this 'flinger' or whatever it's called. I've never been pursued across a desert by a bunch of guys with swords before. I can *just about* accept the idea that you all came here from Alpha Centauri or wherever."

"Zama," said Elliot. "This is Earth. Where I come from, it's Zama."

"Whatever." The second panel was proving easier to affix than the first. "But I can't believe that humans independently evolved on two different planets."

"That would be ridiculous," Elliot agreed. "There's a theory that our worlds were permanently connected, thousands of years ago. You do know that *homo sapiens* existed for a hundred thousand years before we got around to sharpening sticks? Maybe humans came to Zama the same way they got out of Africa. It's certainly true that Zama's magnetic fields shoot the gateway in this general direction."

"I guess that's no more insane than anything else in this whole mess."

Elliot appeared to take pity on her. "I understand this is all a lot to take in. My people considered making formal contact with Earth's authorities when we first opened the Gateway. For whatever reason, they decided against it. If Earth ever becomes aware of Zama, it could result in conflict. And frankly..." He paused, glancing sideways at her, trying to judge what her reaction might be. "Frankly, there's nothing here that Zama really wants, but Zama has resources Earth could use." He straightened from the panel and looked seriously at her. "I'm not sure I can say that fear isn't justified."

A succession of images marched through her head: deforestation, climate change, oil spills and overpopulation and air pollution. She thought of the world's armies and arsenals of nuclear weapons. She thought about China and India and their billions of space-starved citizens, just longing for somewhere nice and convenient for expansion.

"No," she said. "I don't think it's unjustified."

"That's where I come in," Elliot said as they hefted the third panel into place. On this side of the van they had some slight shelter from the wind and the work went quicker. "Zama sends someone here, they don't really care about them any longer; they're not coming back. But they also don't want to advertise to the world at large that we're dumping our convicts here."

"Wait... *Convicts*?" Jess stared at him, forgetting for a moment to lift her end of the panel. It banged back against the van, and Elliot lowered his end to the ground so he could suck his fingers.

"Yeah, convicts," he said. "What did you think, they were sending their lawyers? The people that get sent here, they're generally political prisoners. A few are worse. I don't ask questions. I'm not interested in whatever misdemeanour got them sent here... Did I say something amusing?"

Jess couldn't help it. It took her a moment to compose herself enough to say, "You're using Australia as a convict colony. Now *that's* ironic."

Elliot chuckled. "I guess it is. Well, you know what they say... such is life."

She was still grinning as they started attaching the fourth panel. "So, what was your crime? How'd you end up with the dirty job, earning truckloads of money, passing stolen technology off as your own, living like a king when you're not busy looking after the rest of your illegal aliens?"

"'Illegal aliens'. Clever. And my crime?" He grinned at her. "I was a forger. A pretty good one, as it happens. I got myself into the Noble classes and lived the high life for almost a year before I was found out." He stepped back from the van to get a better view. "What do you think? Pass muster?"

The panels, in brown and cream, transformed the van and completely hid the incriminating foreign symbols. "Very seventies," she said.

"Don't hold it against me. I had these panels made when I first outfitted the vans, almost twenty years ago."

"Maybe you could have repainted them in the last few years," said Jess. "I feel like I've stepped out of the *Brady Bunch*."

Elliot leaned back against the side of the van, obviously in no hurry to go back in. Jess joined him in the shade. Elliot pulled out a pack of cigarettes and offered her one, shrugging when she turned him down. "So," he said, whilst lighting up, "how did you get caught up with these kids?"

She told him about the roadhouse, about finding Vi and Aran in the desert. Aran's intent to harm the proprietors, and Vi's willingness to accept that. "Whatever else she is, she's gone through some kind of trauma," she said. "There's a wound on the back of her neck that I don't like the look of."

Elliot' reaction surprised her. "That fits. She said she had the Crown." He took note of Jess's blank stare and explained further. "The Empress wears a memory chip containing the gathered life experiences — the memories — of every Empress in history. At least, since the technology was invented."

"What technology?" Jess asked, somewhat disbelieving.

Elliot thought for a moment. "Back in the early days, when they first invented the computer, they used to give them instructions on punch cards." Jess nodded; she'd heard of this. "Well, on Zama, we do something similar. Only with brains."

"You're kidding."

"Okay, look. A memory is just a configurations of neurons. A collection of brain cells connected to each other in a specific pattern. Each time you learn something, new connections are made and another little collection of cells stores that memory."

"If you say so."

"So it's just a matter of recording these memory patterns — and then importing them into another brain. Learning is as simple as plugging in a chip and waiting for it to upload. You still need to use the implanted memories," he added, "access them, write them down or accomplish the task or whatever it is you're trying to learn. The brain needs to forge its own connections to the new data. But it saves the whole writing something down a few hundred times that you're stuck with over here."

"Sounds very convenient." She could think of more than a few things she would like to have learned by memory import rather than lived experience.

One example that came to mind: *Don't marry him.*

"Oh, it's convenient," Elliot said. "But it's also counterproductive."

Of course. There had to be a drawback. "How so?"

"Nothing ever changes," said Elliot. "Change requires innovation, but if you do anything different on Zama you're doing it wrong — and there'll be consequences.

"In many ways Zama science is ahead of Earth's. Unlimited free energy, quantum physics, antigravity — we have all that. We should be... they should be... spread out across the stars by now. But no, Zama sits and stews. There hasn't been a scientific discovery of note for decades. No ambition to travel to the stars. No drive to change the way we live."

"Why not? What's wrong?"

"The problem is perfection," Elliot said. "That's not how science works. It's not how a culture develops. Discovery comes from trial and error — mostly error. When you learn every technique, every skill, and can do everything perfectly the first time, you're never going to have those happy accidents that reveal new discoveries."

Jess thought back to her own training: four long years of constant cramming for exams and mining journals for essays. "Can't you build errors into the memories? Give your students a head start, but force them to take the last step?"

Elliot shook his head. "Not possible. *Editing* memories is a lot harder than copying them."

"Okay," said Jess. "You're saying the Empress doesn't have the memories just added to her brain. They're on a chip for her to wear?"

"It used to be worn," said Elliot. "The Crystal Crown, they called it. More recently, it's been an implant. The human brain is fantastically complex, it can handle many thousands of normal lifetimes of information. But it takes time to import memory patterns, and by now the Crown's data is enormous. So now the Crown is wetware. Every time they crown a new Empress, the memories of the last one are added."

"An implant? That cut on her neck." Another piece of the puzzle fell into place.

"If she really is the Empress, those memories are buried in her brain."

The Crystal Crown. That was what Utara wanted. Too easily Jess could picture the bald man in the desert, sinking a knife into Vi's neck to dig for the implant. She shook her head in an attempt to dispel the image, but the unwelcome reminder of their pursuers made her antsy for movement. "Well, unless we can work something out, that unbroken set of memories might end here. We're done?"

Elliot ground the butt of his cigarette under his heel. "We never invented smoking. If I ever go back, I might have to set up a franchise. I suppose we'd better get back in before your friends decide to try hacking my systems."

VIII

Jess led the way back into the van, realising as she stepped over the threshold that she was now comfortable enough with Elliot to have him at her back. Elliot might still choose to run, but she had other things on her mind. "You've been holding out on me. There are criminals from your world here. Political prisoners. And now here you are, come to keep them company. Safe to assume if you exile someone they're not going to be your biggest fan. You didn't think this might be a problem?"

Vi and Aran looked to have been interrupted in the throes of a mortal battle of wills, Vi glaring at Aran, the boy staring back defiantly. At Jess's words Vi broke the tableau, turning to face Jess. "Why? I do not expect to encounter any. There can be no more than a hundred. And were we to meet one, they have no reason to recognise me."

"More like four hundred," Elliot murmured.

Now it was Vi's turn to blink in confusion. "Surely not. Exile is a last resort, and the Empress signs every warrant. I would know."

"Evidently not," said Elliot. "I don't know where they all are now, but I'm clear on how many I've placed. How long was your mother the Empress?"

"The number was fifty-three on the day Jede was crowned. I do not believe my mother authorised hundreds of exiles in the last two decades."

"One decade," said Elliot. "I've had almost fifty in the past three months alone. Whole family groups, as many as four or five at a time. It's not easy to place a family of five without raising questions."

Vi nodded. "Many of the noble and professional classes went missing from the capital during the war. Perhaps they were sent here. But why?"

"You came here to escape," Jess pointed out.

"The war began two years ago, the siege only two months. If a hundred Zamans came to escape the siege, that does not explain the others."

"Maybe your mother's been getting impatient with people," Elliot said. "Or perhaps the work camps are getting full."

"There are always more work camps. There must be another explanation."

"I didn't ask," Elliot said. There was finality in his voice, a certainty that the conversation was over. "We're wasting time. The van is covered; you're safe for the moment."

Aran flicked at some switches on a nearby panel. The conversation in English had obviously left him behind some time ago and he must have been bored.

Elliot lifted a hand and started to reach towards Aran, then thought better of it. That was probably wise of him. Based on Jess's experience with the boy with the sword, he might have taken his hand off at the wrist if he felt threatened. "Don't touch that," Elliot said. *"Hecht orsh."*

"You say you want to help us. So help us," said Vi. "Drive us to... where were we going?"

"Adelaide," Jess answered.

"Not a chance," said Elliot. "I'll get you some basic papers. I can give you some support and somewhere to start. But I have a plane to catch. I'll be missed if I'm not on it; people pay attention to my whereabouts. I couldn't take you with me even if I wanted to."

Vi turned to Aran, started translating Elliot's words for him, her voice low and brittle.

"We really need your help," said Jess. "We have to get out of town without being caught by either the rebels *or* the police."

"The police are looking for you too? You didn't think *that* important enough to mention?"

"They may be," said Jess. "They probably are. But they might not be looking for us here. We *know* that the rebels are nearby. If they can track us —"

"I said I'll help you and I meant it, but there are limits. I can buy you an hour, but then you're on your own."

"Is it your normal practice to abandon the exiles once you have met them?" Vi demanded.

"We're a long way beyond *normal*," Elliot snapped. "I don't *normally* end up with the Empress and an Imperial guard to deal with. I don't usually have rebel assassins breathing down my neck. Try as I might, I can't seem to remember dealing with a fugitive from the police. *Normally*, people can afford to take a day or two to acclimatise and learn a bit about the world they're going to have to live in."

This wasn't helpful. If Elliot decided to dump them they'd be back at square one. Worse, with Utara and his men nearby. "We'll be grateful for any help you can offer. What *can* you do for us?"

Elliot took the proffered escape route with a graceful shift of tone. "Generally, I would put you up in a motel for a night or two. Provide enough paperwork for you to get by for a few days. Then I do an in-depth interview to find out what trade or skills the new arrival has, so I can build an appropriate new identity." He glanced at Vi. "I don't suppose you have any special skills or a trade?"

Vi didn't answer him; she just stared at him until he backed down.

"Kids. I have no idea what I'm supposed to do with you — Empress or no

Empress, you're still just a child. Nobody's going to take you seriously."

"We can't stay in a motel," said Jess. "The moment we step out of this van, Utara will be on us in minutes."

"They are closer." Vi pointed to the monitor. Then, for Aran: "*Lerri ec yrt.*"

Elliot barely glanced at the screen. "They're spreading out. Clearly they're looking for you. We have to get you out of town — you can't stay in the van forever. And I have places to be."

Jess stepped to Elliot's side, but she still couldn't make sense of the display. "I was planning to take the Stateliner to Adelaide. The next bus leaves at midday."

"That might work," said Elliot. "You'll need a head start."

"What we require first," said Vi, "is some information. You can tell me where I can find Hareth Rede."

"Hareth Rede? The name rings a bell," Elliot said slowly. "It's not recent, but if I've placed him, he'll be in my records. At least it will give you somewhere to start looking."

"Good," said Vi. "So look him up."

"I can't do that," said Elliot. "I don't have those records with me. I have a full system at the labs. There's databases to be hacked, catalogues to be edited, a hundred details I can't do from here. My records are there. I wouldn't risk them in a mobile environment."

"The labs? Where are they?"

"Brisbane. When I get back, I'll find your information."

Aran interrupted with what Jess assumed was a question, his voice rising on the interrogative.

Elliot shook his head. "Your *boy* is going to have to learn English, and quickly. Not being able to speak the language is going to get you both in trouble, sooner rather than later. Poor bastard, he's going to have to learn the hard way — I can't do memory patches. And English is a bitch."

Vi refused to be sidetracked. "The question stands. How is the van shielded?"

"It's shielded," Elliot said with exaggerated patience, "with three-inch thick copper coils with ten thousand volts running through them. Unless you want to wear a three-inch thick copper suit with a car battery strapped to your back, I don't really think it's going to help you." He paused, then scratched his head. Reluctantly, he added: "Maybe there's a way. I can't give you shielding. But maybe I can give you a brief advantage. A diversion."

"What kind of a diversion?"

"The kind that will flare out their trackers, at least for a short time. If I cycle full power through my scanners, then turn off the power to the shield coils, I can flare them out. Give them a signal that will swamp anything else for miles around." He frowned. "It won't last long. The moment I do this, they'll be forced to track me down. The van will be lit up like a Christmas tree."

The pieces were coming together in her mind. Disparate, random shapes combining to produce order, to resolve into an image that was whole. The thing she enjoyed most about her work as a draftsperson: the sense of fitting all the requirements into a smoothly interlocking whole. Tetris, with plumbing. She probed at the edges of the idea, afraid of losing the inspiration. "How long will this flare last?"

"Twenty minutes," said Elliot. "Maybe thirty. Certainly no longer. Enough time for you to get on the bus, if we time it right. When it clears, they'll pick you up again and you know they'll give chase, but if they're on foot they're not going to catch up in a hurry."

"Twenty minutes." Jess stared around the van, at the computer monitors suspended from the ceiling, the cabinets and the computers lining the walls. Cape Canaveral on wheels. "Okay. Can you get the internet on this thing?"

Pulse

I

Epiphanies, like misfortunes, come in threes. Jeff's first revelation of the day came to him behind the wheel of his land cruiser, surrounded by his trappings of office. The radio set on the dash, the GPS and traffic computers tucked away beside his knees, the .22 rifle behind the seat, even the navy blue of his trousers: reminders of how hard he'd worked to get here. Of how much he had to risk.

Whatever the gods of fate had in store for him, they were subservient to the all-powerful Captain Hartcher.

He couldn't risk throwing it away, not even for Dr Adele Ferguson. Maintaining an investigation after it had been taken away from him — withholding evidence — involving a civilian in a conspiracy — he could be drummed out of the force for far less. And pretending, play-acting at investigating a case he *knew* would go nowhere, seemed dishonest. The wrong way to go about wooing said civilian.

The tail-lights of Dr Ferguson's ute led the way into the car park of the college. Following her over the kerb he felt the engine drag as if reluctant to face the oncoming confrontation.

It's all a bit of fun until you enter into a conspiracy, but the structures of law don't tolerate such actions. There would be no surreptitious investigation, no long hours spent with Adele, poring over evidence.

The ice was broken now. She knew his name. That was progress. He could be satisfied with that.

Could she? The biggest risk now was that having the case snatched away from her would sour her towards policing, and towards him.

He brought the cruiser to a halt in the staff section of the car park, next to the doctor's ute. *There will be other cases.* This would not be his last opportunity to canvass her opinion on an investigation. Perhaps, in a year or two, another mystery would arise to likewise engage her fascination. *If* he was still in Port Augusta. *If* she was still teaching at the college and still interested in helping. *If* she wasn't hooked up with a local by then. Too many ifs.

Joining the doctor at the front of their vehicles, she was ethereal and beautiful and, once again, entirely unattainable.

Just before midday on a Monday, and the car park was largely empty. When he commented on this, Adele responded: "Not many classes during the day. It gets busier from mid-afternoon."

He trailed her into the buildings. The college was flat and square, several smaller buildings connected by corridors of glass. Dotting the buildings were small indoor gardens, lush and green under the cover of shade sails and constant attention.

The main entry was a wide space with lots of glass, lots of light and little to indicate this was a house of learning; a reception desk staffed by a lone woman and her three computers could have belonged to any office building. A board on the wall declaimed the names of "Chancellors" dating back as far as 1983. A layout map hung on another wall, but Jeff ignored this as he followed Dr Ferguson. "Been teaching here long?"

"A few years. I grew up around here, but there's not a lot of demand for microbiologists, so I turned to teaching."

"Do you get many students of microbiology here, if there's no demand?"

"Micro is a very useful set of skills," she replied, "for agricultural scientists and agronomists, and there's plenty of demand for those. I did my doctorate in Melbourne. There are research positions in Melbourne, if I'd wanted to stay there."

"Why didn't you?"

"Mum got sick while I was finishing off my thesis, so when it was done I came back to look after her. Then, when she passed away, it was just easier to stay."

"I'm sorry."

"It happens," she said. "So that's how I ended up teaching microbiology in a country town. You can see why I find the odd spot of detective work an interesting change."

Yes, about that... The timing wasn't right for that conversation. The timing would never be right. "Port Augusta's not country. I don't miss the big cities. We've got everything we need here."

"It's got a population of six and a bit," Adele said. "And four of *them* smell of sheep shit and want a wife who can carry eighty kilograms of hay on her back. This is me," she added, and it took Jeff a moment to realise she was pointing at the door to an office. She stalked past it without pausing, though, and Jeff frowned.

"Aren't we going in?"

"The lab's a bit further." She glanced at him sideways. "So how did you end up policing in a hick town like this? You didn't grow up here."

"I didn't. I'm from Adelaide. All recruits go on a rotation around the State as they go through the ranks. I don't mind Port Augusta. The town's big enough to have most every type of crime you can think of, but small enough that a jun—" He swallowed the word *junior* and found an alternative. "A new cop like me can get to the coalface. I've seen everything there is to see in policing."

"Glad at least one of us is enjoying the country," Adele said.

They approached a pair of double doors with etched glass inset. Hazmat, biohazard, and laser warnings were prominent. Adele stopped before the doors and held out a hand. "After you, Officer Lang."

"No, I insist, Doctor Ferguson," he said, sweeping a mock bow.

She grinned and pushed through the doors. "In here. I have it locked—"

She broke off in surprise, her steps faltering so that Jeff almost trod on her heels. The two men already in the room looked up, startled at the interruption. Adele blinked. "Excuse me, can I help—" she said, but she didn't finish that sentence either.

Jeff had a moment to take in the room. Fume cupboards lined one wall, cabinetry and glassware covering another; refrigerator units marched in rows down the centre of the lab, and a big wooden desk sat in one corner next to a technical-looking microscope on a stand, cables cascading out of the base of the lectern and drilling into the floor. A structured work environment: a place for everything and everything in its place.

But not any more. The lab was a mess.

One of the men stood amidst an ocean of broken glass. The cupboards he had been ransacking held plastic petri dishes and glass beakers and apparently the most efficient method of searching was to throw them to the floor and see what survived. The other man was systematically working his way down the line of refrigerators. Both were big men, defined muscle standing out on their forearms as they stared at him. Jeff was in good shape himself, but he was sure either of these men could tie him in knots if it came to a sheer contest of strength.

"Police," he announced. His uniform should have told the story. "Stay where you are."

The man at the fridges turned to face him. Jeff and Adele were in the doorway, blocking the men's exit. He placed a hand on Adele's shoulder and moved sideways, forcing the microbiologist to come with him. *Clear the door. Give them space.* The safest way to resolve this was to let them go. Chase them down later.

The man at the fridges raised a hand to point at them, and Jeff found himself staring down the barrel of a gun. *Shit. That escalated quickly.* He froze, his hands half-raised in front of himself. "You don't want to shoot a cop. I'm not armed."

The man by the cupboards snapped something at his companion. Jeff couldn't make out the words, but the tone was urgent. The man with the gun shook his head, but the other repeated his command. The fridge intruder scowled, but he lowered the weapon, and Jeff breathed a sigh of relief.

Back it down. He took a breath to say something else, but before he could assemble his next offering the man surged into motion. *Towards him.* Three quick steps closed the distance, and Jeff's back was already against the wall — nowhere to retreat. He lifted his hands. Too slow. A flurry of movement and a flash of light.

He was sprawled on the floor. How did that happen? His head ablaze with pain. *I've been pistol-whipped.* That was new.

Adele crouched at his side, pressing something against his temple, warm wetness leaking down his cheek. *Cold water, that's what you need, not hot.* Jeff brushed away wetness, then stared at the red on his fingers.

His attacker had stepped clear. The other intruder by the cupboards shouted at the man, his words angry but nonsensical. Perhaps the blow had stolen Jeff's ability to understand English.

"I tell him not shoot you." The intruder at the cabinets spoke in strongly accented English. Jeff blinked in relief. "You stay where *you* are, won't not be hurt more. You wait there," the big man continued, "wait until we finished."

"What do you want?" Adele asked, her voice low with fury. "You don't have to smash everything."

"Quiet," said the intruder. "We be quick." He followed this with more foreign language to his companion, who immediately turned back to continue along the line of fridges.

Jeff's head pounded with the beat of his heart. He ignored it and kept his voice low. "Where's the dress?"

"Desk drawer," she whispered. "You think they're here for that?"

Jeff nodded, then wished he hadn't. "What else? They're obviously not after the computers or equipment." He raised his voice. It took him two tries before his throat was clear. "In the desk."

The thief stared back. "You know what we looking?" Not waiting for an answer, he moved across to the desk.

"It's locked," Adele said, but the man didn't hesitate. One prodigious yank and the drawer leapt clear of the desk, spilling stationery. The second drawer was deeper, and rattled against the lock as the man pulled. Another heave and it too came open. The man lifted out a bundle of white, then shook it out and stared.

"That's the girl's dress," Jeff rasped. "That's what you're looking for."

The man nodded slowly. He shoved the dress into his backpack. "You stay. Not follow." With terse commands to his companion, he came in Jeff's direction, but he was headed for the door. Jeff winced as the man's shadow fell across him, then followed the two men out of the lab.

The moment they were gone, Jeff started trying to lever himself to his feet, ignoring the blaze of agony from his head.

"Don't get up," Adele protested. "Let me call an ambulance."

He ignored her, managing to get his feet under himself. He put out a hand and braced against the wall to steady himself for a second, but then lurched in pursuit. "Help me," he rasped, and reluctantly she did, putting a shoulder under his arm. Together they angled out through the door of the lab in time to see the two men disappearing around a nearby corner.

They followed, Jeff powered by the force of fury. Staring point-blank at a strange weapon, in danger of his life, he had come to a sudden realisation — a second revelation. Whoever these men were, whatever their relationship to the children in the desert or to the mysterious Ms Jessica McTiernan, they were part of the puzzle. Now he was personally involved. No way was he going to just hand it over to an agency whose name he didn't even know. Nobody could expect him to stand aside and not pursue every avenue open to him. Bugger the consequences. *They tried to kill me.*

The men were moving fast, though, running through the corridors, and

Jeff was finding it hard to keep his balance even with Adele's assistance. By the time they burst out of the front doors of the college into the heat of the day and the brilliant sunshine, the men had already disappeared from view. Jeff started to swear, until he saw the red Holden utility fishtailing in the car park, the tyres gaining traction and accelerating the vehicle towards the roadway. In the cab, Jeff could make out the men's shaved heads rocking as the driver gunned the engine. The ute turned onto the road and sped away, weaving between lanes.

"They're gone," Adele said.

Jeff pulled out his mobile phone and hit his first quick-dial. "Officer Jeff Lang," he said, giving his badge number. "I need to report a robbery. Two men, armed. Officer assaulted." Quickly he gave the relevant details. Signed off, then dialled a second number. "Pedro. Yeah, it's me. Yes, I know, I know, I'm on scene... Can you run a plate for me? ... Thanks mate. Yeah... lots going on. I'll bring you up to speed in a bit."

He turned to Adele. "Things are going to get very busy. There'll be police everywhere. Be honest; tell them anything they ask. Those guys just stole our evidence. You'll need to hand over your data. Just make sure you keep copies." He grimaced against the spike of pain from his temple. "We're not done with this yet. I don't care what the boss says. I'm going to have things to do, but I'll call you tonight, if that's OK." In the distance he could hear the first sirens approaching.

"They smashed up the lab," Adele said. "Who were they? Why would they want that dress? How did they even know it was here?" She seemed not to be expecting answers from him, which was just as well. He had none to give her.

"Maybe they're secret cross-dressers," he said, as the first ambulance arrived.

Soon the site was swarming with police. Medics shaved his temple and put a bandage on his head, but assured him the cut wasn't deep and he wouldn't need stitches.

His third epiphany for the day came about an hour later.

The registered owner of the red Holden ute lived at an address on the outskirts of Port Augusta. Jeff insisted on accompanying the rapid response squad, coming into the building on their heels, close enough behind them to witness their initial reactions to the scene. In a town the size of Port Augusta violent crime was not unknown and these men had witnessed assaults, murders, even explosions, but none of them were prepared for the cruelty they found inside.

The house held no enemies. No danger awaited the police; the violence here had moved on. As they progressed through the house, culminating in the bedroom at the rear where they encountered the final horror, Jeff realised that he had not, in the end, seen every crime there was to see in policing.

II

"You need to get moving," said Jacob Elliot. "The bus leaves at midday. Don't miss it."

"If that happens, we'll be caught for sure." Jess stood behind Vi's chair, the girl tilted back as far as the chair would go, a sacrificial t-shirt under her head. Jess's fingers were mobile, massaging the girl's scalp, and the fumes were making her eyes water. Finding a rapid-set hair dye during her shopping expedition had been the easy part; convincing Aran of her harmless intent as she approached the Empress's head with the clippers had been more of a challenge.

Elliot stood just behind the driver's seat, watching as Jess turned Vi's hair from auburn to black. "Not my problem. I'm not even sure why I'm helping you. Zama's not sending any more folks my way. My work here's done. I'm a rich man. I don't need you."

"Rich and famous," Jess agreed. "So why were you helping the people from... what did you say your planet was called?"

"Zama."

"Why keep helping the exiles, then? Does Zama have some kind of hold on you?" She stepped back, casting a considering eye over her handiwork. In the dim light of the van it seemed thorough enough. She reached for the bottles of water she'd retrieved from Aran's backpack and adjusted the position of the bucket under Vi's head.

"It would be worse if I stopped," Elliot said. "Imagine. Someone arrives with no idea how to survive. They'd be found out within hours. The first one or two might be locked up as delusional, but how long would that last? One person talking about other worlds might be dismissed as a nut. Two or three independent cases would change matters. Teams of scientists swarming over the countryside where the gateway opened. They'd start looking, watching for every gateway as it opened."

He seemed to hesitate. "Something else, too. Zama made me. They could unmake me. I have no interest in sleeping with one eye open, waiting for my replacement to come find me." He shrugged. "So if Zama's not sending any more people through, then it's over. I'm free."

"If that is your wish, I will grant it," said Vi. "I am Empress now. There will be no more arrivals — not until I know the truth. You say you have placed hundreds of Zamans. I do not see how that is possible. My mother would never have started sending people here without reason."

"Maybe you didn't know her that well."

"Keep your head still, honey," Jess said.

"I must know the truth. You have the answers I need."

"Maybe I do," said Elliot, "but now is not the time. You've got a bus to catch. You might very well be caught and killed by rebels. *If* you manage to get past them, I'll wait for your call."

"I will find a way to repay you for your help. If it is possible to return home to Zama, you will be welcome at my side."

"If I wanted to go back to Zama," Elliot said, "I could just join forces with your revolutionaries. I've no reason to be particularly fond of your Empire. Maybe they'd be willing to take me with them if I helped them catch you." Eyeing Aran cautiously, he added, "But I won't. My family, my

173

life, they're here. There's nothing for me back on Zama."

Jess stripped off the gloves and helped Vi tilt her chair back upright. The girl's newly short, glossy black hair changed her whole appearance, framing her face differently. It might not fool an attentive observer but it would have to do. "We're losing time. We need to get moving."

"You do," agreed Elliot. Swivelling in the chair, he slid open a drawer and retrieved a small cloth pouch. "Take this. When I find the information about your Hareth Rede, I'll send it to you. Stay on the move, but don't go too far from the capital cities; I have people in Adelaide, Melbourne and Sydney, and I'll need to get you better paperwork." He turned to Vi. "Your new identity. You're Vivian... I'll come up with a surname soon enough. Your brother is Aaron. You're immigrants from — I'll decide that, too. Those papers I gave you, they won't get you on a plane, but they should get you into the movies."

Jess tipped the contents of the pouch into her hand: a Nokia mobile phone and a small wad of plastic bills.

"Prepaid and in a false name," Elliot explained. "I'll contact you; don't try to call me, I won't answer. When I've sent through what you need to know, dispose of the phone. Take out the battery, not just the sim. Mobile phone hardware can be tracked."

"And the cash?"

Elliot shrugged. "I know it's not much. My standard 'welcome' package, and it's usually enough to put one person up for a couple of nights in a modest motel room. I've been thinking I might need to budget more if they're going to keep sending me families. Give me a couple of days, I'll have a bank account ready for your new identities. Until then, that's the best I can offer."

"It'll get us started," said Jess. She slipped the mobile phone into her pocket, then zipped closed her backpack. "The bus leaves in about twenty minutes; let's do this while we still can."

"Good luck," said Elliot.

The stillness was killing him.

During the interminable conversation with the *dahla*, the Empress
deigned to translate whenever she remembered to — far too infrequently.
He was always a few steps behind the conversation. They were making
plans without him. Aran was a Guard, with all his training, advanced
skills in subterfuge and concealment and combat, in tactics and strategy.
His was the responsibility for the Empress's safety. And he was utterly
useless.

He listened and watched as the conversation revolved around him, trying
to guess at the meaning of the body language and the tone of the voices,
and failing. Meanwhile the woman — Jess — rubbed an unknown, acrid
substance into the Empress's scalp that made Aran's eyes water. *Poison.*

Jess apparently had no intention to change Aran's hair. Instead, she
handed him a hat: a black scrap of cloth with a stiff visor, red cursive
writing he could not read. A plastic device with darkened lenses to prop
onto his nose. He found his own reflection in a polished panel and had to
grudgingly approve. Combined with his new clothing, he looked far
distant from the uniformed Guard who had first arrived.

A disguise wasn't going to get them very far, though. "Utara doesn't know
what we look like," he said when he had the Empress's attention. "He's
not trying to recognise us."

"This is for the local authorities," the Empress explained. "They will have
our description by now."

He had to admit the sense in that plan, but he did *not* approve of Jess
calling the shots. That should be *his* job. "She knows what she's doing,"
the Empress insisted. "Utara is near. We can't afford to wander. Can you
offer a better plan?"

Of course, he could not. They needed Jess and her situational knowledge.

"We have to trust her," said the Empress. "If she needs your help, she'll
ask for it."

But she didn't ask for it. Instead she spent precious minutes working on the Empress's face with unguents and lotions. Colourants. When she was done the Empress's face appeared changed: her cheekbones more prominent, her skin older. Jess stood back and nodded, then set about her own with the aid of a mirror.

The stillness. In the van he was constrained: useless, enclosed, trapped. In the open, on the move, he could be useful. He was a weapon, dangerous and skilled, but he could do no good while they kept him in a sheath.

Finally — after what felt like days — the conversations came to an end.

"We're going," the Empress said.

Aran nodded and took his place before her, pushing through the doors into the brilliant sunlight even as Elliot swung them open. Jumping down to the hard parking lot and turning in a circle, looking for threats. The open air tasted glorious.

That lasted mere moments. Then Jess was pushing past him to take the lead, setting a rapid pace across the car park. Elliot also was wasting no time. They were still only halfway across the car park when the van's engine coughed to life. They paused for a moment on the edge of the open space to watch the Fixer depart, for a moment silhouetted against the sun, staring at them as he turned the vehicle onto the road.

If he was flaring any kind of signal, if he was capturing the enemy's attention, there was no visible sign of it. They would have to take him on trust.

If Elliot was true to his word, this car park had just become ground zero. "They'll be coming," Aran said urgently.

The Empress nodded. "Jess knows where we're going. Keep up."

They ran. Movement was easier with the backpacks securely strapped to their shoulders, without the loose garbage bags on their backs; but the weight still slowed them and their movements were graceless as Jess led them into the street.

Aran kept his eyes in motion, taking a census of the surroundings. Civilians dotted the streetside, strolling casually from store to store, chatting to each other, blissfully unaware of the drama they were witnessing. Aran filed each face away in his memory, looking for the one that was out of place, the one set of eyes too intently focussed, the big man with no obvious purpose to be there.

Jess led them into the gap between two stores, a narrow laneway strewn with garbage skips and capped with a low fence. She immediately brought them to a halt. The Empress translated for her again. "We're far enough from the van. Now we move casually; we need to avoid drawing attention. Keep alert."

What did she think he was doing? He did not need that advice.

Jess led them back into the plaza. She kept them to a slow walk and maintained an inane, senseless chatter. Just a woman and two children, a family out for a morning walk. Nothing to mark them out.

They turned from the plaza onto a street, *cars* whisking by at their side, and Aran tried to ignore the passage of the vehicles just a couple of metres away. Far too close. An unguarded tree stood at the road's edge, making his fingers itch for the sword.

"There's only a short time until the next bus departs." The Empress kept her voice low — it wouldn't do for passers-by to hear her talking in Zaman. "We're aiming to board as close to departure as possible."

They approached a crossroad, and Jess increased their pace. She had her eyes fixed on something further down the street, possibly their destination in view. The extra speed would get them off the street sooner, but it made it harder for Aran to keep track, and so he almost missed seeing the man.

Almost.

"*Irri!*" Unheeding of her authority he put out a hand to snag the Empress's shoulder and draw her to a halt. Jess stumbled into stillness a few paces on.

The late morning was hot but not yet unbearable, and there were still people on the streets. Shops lined the streets leading away from the crossroads, and there was a light but steady traffic of window shoppers. On another corner a run-down cafe squatted in the sun, a gaggle of teenagers loitering. A third corner held a small park, low brushes wilting in the heat. A middle-aged couple strolled past the wooden pergola that anchored the park.

There was a man standing motionless on the corner where the streets joined, square-built and muscular, intent and motionless as he scanned the streets in all directions. Aran watched as the man carefully ran his eyes over the people strolling nearby the intersection; each person received a single once-over before being dismissed from his attention.

How do you identify a threat? Look for their interest. Drillmaster Warren had demonstrated the lesson by strolling to the side of the drill yard as his eyes remained fixed on the trainees. *Don't worry about what they look like, what they're doing, what they're saying; they'll be given away by the focus of their attention.*

The man in the intersection was dressed in local blue jeans and a plaid shirt that looked too small for his muscles and too hot for the weather; not a uniform, but Aran was willing to hazard a guess that they didn't belong to the man any more than they fit on him.

Aran ushered Jess and the Empress closer to the nearest storefront, taking cover behind other shoppers and a tree on the nature strip. "I think that's Utara's man."

The Empress didn't contradict him. "We need to get past him." She put a hand on Jess' shoulder and spoke softly. The woman's response was low and fervent, and the Empress nodded in agreement. "We don't have a lot of time."

"We're out in the open." Aran frowned. "He can't try anything out here."

"We can't let him see us or he'll know where we've gone."

By now Elliot' van was driving in the opposite direction, heading eastwards through the town, but evidently not all of Utara's men had taken the bait. Or else he'd been prudent enough to keep his men scattered rather than converging on the obvious target. In either case, Aran was as certain as he could be that the man ahead of them was watching for them.

Aran decided to give the man what he wanted.

"Wait for your chance. When the way is clear, go past. You'll know when. Don't wait for me. I'll catch up."

He ignored her objections as he moved away, edging along the storefronts as he neared the crossroads. His plan was a good one — but it was also dangerous. He might die. Worse, he might be caught. It didn't matter: this was his purpose as a Guard. To serve his Empress, with his life if need be. And in so doing, prove his worth.

So why was he sweating?

The park on the opposite corner of the intersection was dotted with benches, and one of them held his target. A girl, about the right age, sitting alone, deeply engrossed in her data pad. Both thumbs in rapid motion on the screen.

Aran broke cover and ducked across the street. No *cars* in sight, which he took as a good omen. He didn't dare look over his shoulder towards the soldier he knew was there.

He made it across the road and stepped into the park. Ten more steps brought him directly to the girl. He stood over her.

She looked up as his shadow fell across the bench. A frown of scorn flashed across her face as she looked him over, and Aran stopped feeling sorry for involving her in what was to come. She said something, her voice cold, but he didn't understand her words and he didn't want her for her conversation. He dared a glance at the guard across the street.

The man was coming.

Aran raised his voice, speaking loudly in Zaman. "We need to keep moving." He reached out a hand to the girl's shoulder and plucked at her sleeve. She tried to brush him off, but he persisted, and then she stood. She was at least six inches taller than him and he lost his grip on her shoulder, but the desired effect had been accomplished. If the soldier hadn't been convinced before that these were his quarry, he certainly was now.

Aran ignored the girl's angry protests. Even if he'd been able to understand her words, he wouldn't have responded. "Sit down and rest later. We need to get under cover." The words in Zaman were meaningless to her, but they weren't intended for her ears.

And then the guard was there. Aran hadn't fully recognised how large the man was until he pushed Aran aside and reached for the girl; he was a solid wall of muscle. He pushed Aran out of the way effortlessly as he grabbed the girl's wrist.

The girl, truly alarmed now, shouted in panic. "Shut up," the soldier said sharply, "be quiet or I'll have to hurt you."

Determined to keep the ruse going, Aran shouted at him. "Let her go! Leave her alone!"

The girl's hysterics were increasing. Aran could barely keep from grinning as her shrieks for help pierced the air.

The commotion drew attention, passers-by gawking; a few bystanders cautiously approached. Some of them got out their *phones* and pointed them at the soldier. Aran made a half-hearted attempt to push the man away from the girl, but it was like pushing at the side of a building. "Give it up, boy," the man growled at him. "Be thankful there's witnesses. Run away while you still can." To the girl, he snapped, "Be *quiet*! I don't want to hurt you."

The crowd were becoming more indignant as they made sense of the scene before them. A young man stepped forward from the surrounding public and shouted something. Meaningless words of demand: *Let go of the girl!* The soldier was trying to pull the girl with him away from the witnesses, but she was resisting and thrashing and screaming. Traffic on the road was slowing, and somebody sounded their horn in protest.

The young man who had shouted stepped forward and reached for the girl. The soldier saw his approach and reacted instinctively, his spare hand lifting his flinger out of its holster. That was a bad move. A nearby woman saw the gun and screamed, and then all hell broke loose.

The soldier never got off a shot, as another man from the crowd lunged forward and trapped his hand, wrestling it towards the ground. The soldier lost his grip on the girl as several more bystanders braved the danger and entered the fray, and suddenly the soldier was fighting for his freedom, three men trying to bring him to the ground. The flinger was dislodged from the man's fingers and skittered away onto the grass. The girl fled, sobbing and clutching her wrist, and it was time for Aran to go. Past time.

He glanced for a second at the flinger, untended on the grass, but it was too close to civilians, underfoot, and he wouldn't be able to get it without endangering his own escape. Instead, he looked for a gap in the encircling crowd, and ducked in that direction. Fingers plucked at his sleeves, hands reaching for him, but for once being small was an advantage, and he avoided the questing grasp and stayed low as he cleared the crowd. And then he was free, a glance over his shoulder confirming that nobody was following.

His heart rang with exultation. Evaluated, planned and executed perfectly. *Keres, eat your heart out. This one's* mine.

IV

They approached the bus depot separately: Jess and Aran together, Vi waiting several minutes before following. Any observers looking for a girl and a younger boy travelling together, with or without an adult woman, would go unrewarded.

It had seemed clever when Jess first thought of it; maybe the first thing she'd done since leaving the roadhouse that wasn't abject stupidity.

Mobile phones have unique identifiers that can be tracked. Jess had known this even before Elliot told her, that every mobile phone has an IMEI number — a digital fingerprint to track the device wherever it went.

Since arriving in Port Augusta, Jess had used her phone blithely and frequently, making and receiving calls and attempting internet searches. She'd used her own credit card when buying clothes and cosmetics. If the police were looking for her, she might as well be wearing neon.

Well, she knew better now. Which led to the next problem: how to pay for three bus tickets to Adelaide? Her credit card wouldn't do, unless she wanted the federal police waiting for the bus at the other end of the road. That might happen anyway, but there was no point in advertising their destination.

That left only the meagre cash Elliot had given them. He'd flat-out refused to withdraw more before leaving them. "Bank accounts are the primary way of tracing a person's movements," he'd said. "I'm not here. I'm a thousand kilometres away, and I have a good alibi prepared to prove it if anyone asks. But the moment I break out the plastic, I might as well kiss all that preparation goodbye."

Now Elliot was gone, and as far as official records were concerned he'd never been here. Even if she'd been blazing a digital trail of her movements, Jess was determined that it should go cold here. Horses and stable doors.

Jess held the door to the ticket office until Aran pushed past her. She paused on the doorstep for a second longer, sweeping her gaze across the street. A dozen people were in sight, teenagers and strolling mothers pushing prams, and any one of them could be a plainclothes cop.

Or none of them. *Pull yourself together.*

The ticket agent was an elderly man with thin silver hair and bad teeth. He barely looked at her as she paid in cash for the tickets, his attention glued to a tiny television screen beside his knees. With a face wreathed in creases he might have been an interesting subject for a portrait, but Jess wasn't in the mood for verité.

The bus was already at the roadside with its engine idling. Jess stood on the step halfway into the vehicle and gave the street another once-over. Still nothing suspicious.

They should have been caught by now. The streets should be swarming with divvy-vans, their faces on every television screen. Bruce and Dot surely had reported the robbery by now. But the encounter on the road, Ivan's truck, Aran driving a knife into the big soldier — that all happened in the middle of nowhere with no witnesses. Was it possible the police didn't know?

After giving cash to Vi to cover her ticket, paying for Aran and herself, there was little enough left of Elliot's thin envelope of cash. Jess folded the remaining fifteen dollars into her purse and wondered how they'd scratch through the next days. The bus was due to arrive in Adelaide by four in the afternoon. After that they might have to sleep rough for a night, unless Elliot came through with his promised counterfeit bank account. *We can do that.* Or maybe they could break into another motel.

She took up a seat as close to the rear of the bus as she could manage; the rear bench was taken up by a pair of dishevelled kids, all ripped denim and heavy metal t-shirts and too much attitude. They ended up under the air conditioning vents, a stream of cool air combating the heat from the windows.

A few tense minutes later, with the bus almost due to depart, Vi boarded. Jess almost didn't recognise the girl as she climbed the steps. With her shortened hair and some subtle make-up effects, she looked a good ten years older. But it wasn't the cosmetics or the hair that sold it. Vi walked with a different gait, her mannerisms subtly different. She seemed to have tapped into the behaviours of an older woman. Unbidden, the thought occurred to Jess: could she *really* have the experiences of generations of women in her head?

If she was truly from another planet, then maybe anything was possible.

With a rumble of engine and a hiss of brakes, the bus lurched into motion and they left Port Augusta, with its complement of interplanetary rebel soldiers, behind them.

Actions in Transit

I

An autumnal breeze was sighing through the rose bushes and murmuring through the low foliage, setting the wild bursts of colour into waves of gentle motion. Spotted around the palace gardens the smaller trees and shrubs had not yet lost all their flowers, profusions of white and yellow. Dotted in their midst charred stumps remained of the larger trees. The gardens had been left untended for months, the groundskeepers fled with Harke's amnesty. Accordingly, in preparation for Harke's entry, Joteun had tasked a squad of soldiers to venture inside and torch any trees large enough to harbour a barker.

The morning was sunny and clear, but the breeze had teeth. He had Jede brought to him in a small glade, surrounded by explosions of flowers and just out of sight of the blackened skeleton of a tor tree that had grown too large for safety. As his soldiers escorted the past Empress into view he greeted her with a smile and gestured her to the bench seat next to him.

Jede's return smile was insincere. "*Mister* Harke. I am advised that we met previously. I have little memory of it. My mind is not what it was." Her guards were receding, leaving them some privacy, but Jede appeared reluctant to take the seat at his side.

"Please, sit," he insisted firmly. "I just want to talk. You appear better than you did at our last meeting."

"I have good days," Jede said. "More often now, my days are bad."

"My physicians think your condition may have something to do with the removal of the Crown. Are they correct? Is there anything I can do for you?"

In precise movements, the past Empress perched herself on the very edge of the seat, as far from him as the bench would allow. "There is a reason that the Empress has the title for life. While you bear the Crown, you are... connected. The presence of all the Empresses of the past. It is unlike any other feeling... your mind expands, adapts. There is a price. No Empress has ever lived far past Transition, and few went gracefully."

"Is it worth it, then?" It was a serious question. "A lifetime of service with no possibility of ever laying it down. It's a wonder anyone wants to be Empress."

"It is an honour and a privilege. The Crown is at the source of our Empire's stability. And you're trying to tear it down."

"Oh, I'm all for stability," Harke disagreed. "Nobody likes war and disorder. I brought the war to the Capitol so we could get it over with as rapidly as possible. My vision for Zama is not all that far from yours, you might be surprised to learn."

"You would see the Crown destroyed simply because you will never be able to wear it," Jede snapped.

"I certainly want it destroyed. If I ever lay my hands on your daughter, I'll pull it out of her skull and crush it on live television. But not out of jealousy."

"Really? Because I thought you were hell-bent on killing the nobles. You're desperate to crush the Guilds."

He shrugged. "Not crush: fix. With a few changes, under my rule Zama will continue as it always has. There'll be more freedom for all; in my book that's a good thing. But things aren't working out quite as I hoped."

One of the Lady's eyes was watering and she wiped at it absently as she spoke. "Of course they're not. It's never that simple."

"The war won't be over until the Regions accede to the change in leadership." Harke shrugged to indicate his helplessness. "They're not cooperating. I *was* hoping that by capturing the Crown and proving that it was destroyed that I'd forge an undeniable sign that things were changing. You've denied me that sign."

"So you haven't found her," Jede said softly.

"Oh, I know exactly where she is."

When he said this her face collapsed, a momentary sign of distress. She rallied, a brittle smile on her lips, but Harke knew better.

"I've sent my best people after her. But I haven't heard back from them yet and there's no telling how long that will take, and while we wait more people are dying. Your general Beryn has rather a large army encamped on the mainland. I'm getting tired of shooting down his planes and he's getting tired of sending them, so it can't be long until he decides to try boats. That won't end well for him, I'm afraid. I'd prefer to avoid that outcome, which is where you come in."

She turned on the bench to face him directly, her eyebrows raised in astonishment. "You expect me to help you?"

"It would certainly be helpful if you'd order General Beryn to stand down. For his own good and the good of his men, if nothing else."

Jede shook her head. "No. I trust my generals. I think I'll wait for him to surprise you and kick you back into the sea where you belong."

Harke sighed. "I suspected you would feel that way. But you will be helping me. There are... other avenues open to me."

Jede smiled. "It's strange. I'm actually glad that I'm going to go insane. I won't help you. I'll die before I sign your writs or make a statement or whatever you have in mind."

"The ceremony I have in mind doesn't require more than a few words," Harke said. "I'll just have to hurry up and marry you while you're still able to stand upright."

Her shocked stare was almost worth invading a city for.

II

Jess had been running for too long on too little sleep and too much adrenaline. As the bus left the port town behind and passed back into open country, the scenery outside the windows reverting to empty scrubland dotted with sheds and barns, she sat in a stew of heartburn and wished for antacid. Her headache had returned worse than ever. The rumble of the bus, the heat radiating through the windows and the blast of chill air from the vent all merged into a jangle of sensations that set her teeth on edge.

She had to wait until they were outside the town centre before Vi moved back in the bus to join her and Aran. The girl had barely seated herself before Jess confronted her. "You could have gotten yourself killed," she hissed. "Tell him that. He could have got that poor girl killed."

Vi's translation sounded less angry than Jess had intended it. She listened while Aran answered, then turned back to Jess. "They were in the open. Aran judged that the man wouldn't take the risk of hurting them in public. And if he had," Vi added, "I believe Aran could have responded with force."

Jess could believe that. She hadn't forgotten the boy's comfort with a knife. "I don't care. I don't ever want to see him trying something like that again."

Vi and Aran took up a low conversation; Jess heard snatches of English and assumed that Aran was receiving further lessons. Temporarily ignored, Jess gazed out the window, but her thoughts were not for the endless succession of paddocks.

What's happening to me? Why was she so concerned about the risks Aran had taken? He wasn't her responsibility. He had threatened her, he had threatened innocents around her, he had attacked a man without hesitation. He obviously didn't trust or like her, so why should she care? They'd be better off without him.

But she did care. Somehow, she had started to feel protective of him. Of both of them.

Damn it. They're not my kids. But tell that to her brain, which had come to consider them under her care. True, she had always wanted children. She had always... mostly wanted children. She and Mark had tried: made their plans, prepared themselves for the next phase. But life got in the way, work and stress and fatigue eating into their time and into their relationship. And children had not come.

Now she was thirty. More than thirty if nobody was listening and she could be honest. Thirty, and alone. Her chance for children was slipping away from her. Little wonder she might be in danger of adopting strays.

Not my kids. She hadn't given them birth, hadn't watched them grow from infants to *enfants terrible*. Hadn't experienced any of the joys of parenthood to make the responsibilities worthwhile. It wasn't fair for her to feel so attached, after less than a day in their company. So protective. So *responsible*. It was like bad breath without a good smoke as an excuse, and it was not fair at all.

For the first time in ten years, she thought she would like a cigarette.

III

They were on the Augusta highway by now, traveling through open country, the town no more than a smudge out the rear window.

The bus might not have been a good idea. *He'll find transport*, Vi had said, and after Ivan's truck, there was no reason to doubt it. And here they were on another long, straight highway. At least in her car she'd had some control over the chase. In the bus they were at the mercy of the driver.

It wasn't like they'd had a lot of alternatives. She didn't know how to hotwire a car. And a train would have been, if anything, worse. In the bus, if Utara caught up they could threaten the driver, convince him to change the route—

That's not me. Jess realised with a shock that she had been seriously considering threatening violence against the driver; that the only thing that stood between her and theft of a motor vehicle was capability.

There was a claustrophobic toilet at the rear of the bus. On legs shaky with adrenaline and caffeine, Jess took a few minutes to splash water on her face in a vain attempt to cool her throbbing skull.

She wasn't the only one suffering. Slipping back into her seat, she nodded at Aran's bloodless face and fixated stare out the window. "He looks like I feel. Is he okay? He'd better not get sick on us."

"The noise," Vi said, her voice faint enough that Jess needed to lean closer. "This is very loud. Rough. And it smells."

"It's not that bad."

Aran groaned slightly as the bus passed a herd of cows, clustered up against the wire fencing that lined the road here; the animals regarded the passing bus with dull-eyed disinterest.

"We are on the ground," said Vi. "Back home, we use magnetic rail. For urgent travel, we use anti-gravity flyers."

"Of course you do," said Jess. "Flying cars. I should have guessed."

Vi glanced at the window, then recoiled, fixing her eyes on the back of the seat in front of her. "Everything is too close. How do your vehicles not collide with each other? With people?"

"They do," Jess admitted. "There's a lot of rules about road travel, but we still have accidents."

"It is hard to breathe," Vi said, and her voice sounded like mourning.

"Maybe we should have taken the train," Jess said.

Vi changed the subject. "Noble girls train from youth to become Empress. We study the Empire's past, what life was like a hundred, five hundred, a thousand years ago. We do this to understand the choices past Empresses made. To understand their experiences. I have studied the lives and cultures of thirty eight Empresses and I know them all by name.

"Now I am Empress. And I have their memories in my head. If I concentrate on something I know, something I learned in those history classes, I can bring to mind the experience of the Empress who lived it. That is... difficult." Vi shook her head and Jess was reminded again how young she was. "So many memories. I need to concentrate to bring out a specific recollection." She gave a tentative smile. "I am hardly the first Empress to learn this. I can remember learning that it will become easier."

"Why are you telling me this?"

"There is another way that memories may arrive," said Vi. "Sometimes a sound, or a smell, or something I see, will trigger a memory. *Those* memories are vivid, real. Absorbing. Caught up in another person's experiences, I may forget where and who I am. I have experienced this twice since we rested last night. And the memories are growing stronger.

"I am holding them at bay, but... I do not know how long I can continue. This world reminds me of Zama of long ago. These smells, these sights and sounds, they are unfamiliar to me — but my forebears knew them.

"If I seem vague," she finished, "that may be the reason. If I get lost at the wrong moment, it could be dangerous. If that happens, you must return me to the present. I give you permission to strike me."

Permission. This was not the first time Vi had seemed to assume superiority. Whatever else she was, she was used to authority. Perhaps she really was an Empress. Jess was willing — even pleased — to help a young girl in need. She was less comfortable with assuming the role of a servant. *She's not your daughter. She's just acting like it. Like she owns you.*

"Don't worry, honey," she said. "I will."

IV

Jess jerked awake, her cheekbone aching. The bruise where Mark had hit her had been jostling against the window of the bus, and she was startled that she'd been able to sleep at all.

She struggled to her feet and stretched. Bracing herself on the seats, she worked her way to the back window of the bus, intent on searching for signs of pursuit. The teens in the rear seats were being as deliberately forbidding as only teenagers know how — sprawled across the width of the bus, feet carelessly thrown up onto the seats and bags deliberately placed to take up the extra space. They glowered at her as she craned to see out the back window, but after being threatened by guns and swords, a couple of teenagers held no fear for her.

The road behind the bus remained empty.

Returning to her seat, Jess sought another form of distraction. Vi had moved across into the window seat and was staring out at the passing countryside. "Tell me about this Utara," Jess asked her. "Who is he? You speak about him like he's Genghis Khan."

Vi ran a hand through her hair. Alcohol wipes had removed the worst of the caked makeup; the remaining traces made her look tired. "Utara is amongst Harke's most trusted generals. Harke has few real soldiers amongst his men. His is a movement of discontent, and most of the military is perfectly happy with their lot so they have been hard to suborn. That means the generals have many fighters who used to be civilians. They joined because they are angry.

"They are not used to taking orders. Not disciplined. When they win a victory..." The girl swallowed, and for a moment she seemed younger, as she continued: "When they win, rape and murder are common.

"So the generals have to be cruel to maintain their authority. They must be harder than their men, angrier, more dangerous. They win the respect of their men through fear. And Utara is amongst the worst.

"There is a story they tell, about the man who gave him his scar. Some have it that the attacker was a mutineer, a man with too much ambition and too little sense. Others say it was the leader of a city garrison that was slow to lay down its arms. Whatever the case, Utara chose to make an example of him. He took the man's fingers, tongue and nose. He had his eyes put out, and he had his men pierce his eardrums with a hot needle, but not before leaving him a last message. He said that one day... when

191

the man had somehow put his life back together, had found whatever measure of peace his life might still attain... that was when he would return. To finish the job."

Jess stared at her, horrified. "That must be an exaggeration. Nobody's that cruel."

"Even if he is only half as terrible as his reputation, he is not someone I want to meet. He wins most of the fights he picks. And truly he is ruthless when he captures a settlement. I have heard of towns laying down their arms to avoid having to fight him, to avoid the certainty that they will lose. To avoid the reprisals."

"Okay," said Jess. "I understand why you're frightened of him. But this isn't a military campaign. He can't just walk in, grab you and fight his way out again, or he'd have already done so. They had plenty of time." She frowned. "Last night, the soldier Aran attacked, he was in tactical gear. But his man on the street today was in civilian clothes. They must want to avoid too much attention."

Vi glanced across the aisle at Aran. "That seems unfortunate."

"So it's a different kind of fight," Jess said. "Maybe Utara's not cut out for being subtle."

"Subtlety is not his style," Vi agreed.

Jess tried to keep her next question gentle. "So why do they want you? If they've taken the capital, overthrown the government, and you've gone away to a whole other planet, what can they possibly want with you?"

"Will they try to take me alive, you mean?" Vi nodded. "They might. If there really is a way to return to Zama, perhaps Harke fears that I will return to lead a counter-rebellion."

Jess thought about everything she had heard about Vi's world. "Is that likely? I get the impression your rule is not exactly popular."

Vi shook her head. "The Empress is well loved. People are ruled in their own communities; the Guild councils and the Low Council see to regional needs. The High Council and the Empress are involved in global matters. If people are dissatisfied, they bring it to their Guild. The High Council takes credit for everything good. My mother once told me, the Empress is a figurehead. She proves that there is someone in power who cares for them and will attend to their needs — even where the local Guild Heads are not on the Low Council, the Empress is concerned for every Region. My mother also said they could enthrone a horse and the people would still come to throw flowers at the balcony. So yes... I think it would be possible. When I return, I will find support."

Guild councils, Low Council, High Council... too many councils, too many things Jess didn't understand. "My head hurts. Your government makes ours seem like a fete committee. So what's this war about? If the people all love you, who are you fighting?"

"There are some who seek a different way of society. They are unwilling or unable to accept their rightful place in society. They think they deserve more power, more responsibility, than they have earned."

"I'm almost afraid to ask," Jess said. "Their rightful place?"

"My mother said that they all want to be nobles." Vi paused before continuing. "I am not so sure. Many are trapped by circumstance. Those who are expelled from their Guild, or cannot advance in it. Those who will not choose a path, or are incapable of doing so. The higher classes will not willingly take on somebody from a lower one. Those without a Guild do not have an easy life. Harke found some of these easy to seduce."

"I'm sorry, you've lost me," said Jess. "Higher classes? You mean, middle-class, working class, yuppie?"

Vi looked blank. "Class is not a formal distinction. Each Guild jealously guards its own ways, yet all recognise that some Guilds have higher status than others. A person with no affiliation may join a Guild of higher standing but it is rare. Some people find themselves outside of the Guilds through their own poor choices."

Jess absently rubbed at the aching bruise on her cheek. "Does it really matter? Not being in a Guild?"

Vi shrugged. "They can rely on the generosity of family, or they can beg on corners. But it is entirely their own choice. The menial classes will always accept neophytes."

"Wait," said Jess. "Do you only get paid if you're in a Guild? And if you can't make it as a… as an architect, say, your only option is to become a labourer?"

"Of course not," Vi said. "There are a hundred guilds between architecture and menial labour. You will, of course, have to start as a neophyte, when you join a new Guild."

"Oh my God," Jess said. "My dad was a bricklayer. My mum was a typist. You're saying, on Zama I wouldn't ever have become an architect — it wouldn't have been allowed? I don't think I like the sound of your world."

"My world," said Vi, "has been stable and peaceful for five hundred years. Can you say the same for yours?"

V

Port Augusta to Adelaide is four hours on a clear road. Jess felt every minute of it.

Occasionally the bus passed through small country towns along the highway, sparse buildings barely warranting a name on a map. One town consisted entirely of a pub. At another point, they passed a beaten weatherboard church standing amidst open fields, giving its congregants an excellent view of the breadth of creation.

Apart from these occasional interruptions, the Australian outback was as barren and shapeless as porridge. This was grazing country, both sides of the highway lined with acres of paddock. Occasional clusters of trees to bind the soil and offer scant shade to livestock broke up the otherwise featureless desiccated earth.

Vi and Aran passed much of the journey in low conversation, either continuing Aran's education in English or laying plans for world domination. There was no point her trying to listen to either.

Higher standing. Jess kept a sidelong eye on Vi, the child Empress's casual authority gaining new significance. She talked to Aran in the sure knowledge that he would respect and obey her. For his part, he attended with a discipline and seriousness Jess would not have credited to a boy of his age. No fidgeting, no distractions, no interjections; whatever a *guard* was on Zama, the boy had left his childhood well behind him. Jess pitied him, but she also feared him. What he meant for her understanding of Zama.

Unwilling to accept their rightful place in society. Which was all well and good, but *rightful place* was typically decided by others. *Rightful place* was invariably below the place of the one assigning the right. And Vi was on top of it all.

The Guilds. The Councils. The Nobles. And at the top, the Empress, ruling with a velvet glove — supported by the Guards, whose children were ready to kill before they should have been out of school.

No wonder this Harke wanted change. Jess wasn't sure she wouldn't choose his side, if it came to a choice.

She doesn't know any better. The girl had grown up in a world segregated by class and no doubt had been taught for her entire life that this was the best way. Yet that wasn't much excuse. If she really had the memories of generations of Empresses, she must remember a time before, a time when people might have been free. More — she had the memories of the Empresses who presided over building the system. Who were responsible for it.

Little wonder she didn't question it.

Perhaps it was up to an outsider to raise questions.

"You told me a while ago that you don't become Empress by birth, but by merit," Jess said, during a lull in Vi's conversation with Aran. "So what was that about? How did you get to be Empress?"

Vi seemed happy enough to reminisce. "It is like any other Guild, any profession. There are annual Trials."

Jess raised her eyebrows at the girl. To her credit, Vi seemed to understand Jess's confusion.

"Every noble girl dreams of becoming Empress. We all train for it, learning the histories, seeking to understand the Empresses. And once a year, there are the Trials. Every Guild runs them, allowing those seeking advancement to prove their abilities. In the Capital, the Trials test our recall, our strength of character, our drive to exceed. The highest qualifier in the Trials is named Empress-elect for the year. Should tragedy strike and the Crown need to be passed on, it is the elect who will become the next Empress."

"I guess, with your mother being Empress, it must have helped you prepare," Jess said.

Vi looked at her feet. "I was never the Empress-elect. This year, I was eighth in line. I should not have been the one to inherit the Crown. But there was nobody left."

Jess blinked. "But your mother —"

"My mother was generous with her advice, her wisdom," said Vi. "But the Trials are about more than common-sense, more than the cunning of politics. My mother gave me what I would need to *be* a good Empress." She shrugged. "Not to *become* Empress."

Beyond the window a herd of cows watched as they passed.

"So now you're the Empress." Jess frowned. "And you're here. What's happening without you, back on Zama?"

Vi shook her head, not looking up from the floor. "I do not know. Harke will not have attempted to capture the Capital without a plan of what he intends next. I can only hope that my escape has thrown those plans into disarray."

This was an opening, and Jess jumped on it. "So how does Harke want to change things? What's his revolution about?"

"He has told his followers that he intends to dissolve the Guilds," Vi said. "I do not believe this is true. If it is true, I fear for my people."

"Your Guilds sound like a kind of prison," Jess said, as gently as she could. "Perhaps it's not a bad thing for them to be dissolved."

She expected Vi to argue, but the girl smiled sadly. "Perhaps. There are some who argue for alternatives. But there are less disruptive ways of bringing about change than to burn it all down."

Here was an area where Earth history could contribute plentiful examples. Jess nodded. "Revolutions have a way of breaking more than they fix."

VI

"I have told you of my childhood," Vi said, a little later. "I would like to hear of yours."

Jess's life was not the girl's concern and under other circumstances Jess might have begged off, but there was nothing in sight behind or in front of the bus as far as she could see, and any conversation was better than sitting ignored for four hours. "There's not much to tell." Her foot had gone to sleep and she shifted in the seat, gingerly settling her weight to the other side and turning to face the girl. "I grew up in Perth. We don't go in for princesses and Empresses there, so I don't have a story like yours."

"Nevertheless there is a story," Vi said. "When we met, you were returning to your hometown, to your parents, were you not? You have been away for some time. Or have I misunderstood?"

"No, that's all true enough. My parents and I... we don't get along." Which was partly true. It was ambition that had driven them apart — her desire to become more than her parents had ever achieved. She'd never understood where her ambition originated from because she hadn't inherited it from either of them.

"They never thought I would amount to much. My father thought I was going to marry some mine engineer and have lots of babies," she said sourly. "That was about as far as his imagination could stretch. Mum was slightly more ambitious; she thought I might make a good secretary.

"I don't think either of them ever quite accepted that I could do something more worthwhile with my life. I put myself through college, got my degree. Did some odd jobs for experience. There wasn't much available in Perth for graduates. There were good jobs in Melbourne, paying big money for senior builders."

Vi nodded. "You moved for your work."

That wasn't entirely true. She'd moved for love — or what she'd thought was love. When Mark asked her to come east with him, getting a better job had been the furthest thing from her mind. But she didn't want to revisit that ground with Vi now, and defensiveness made her reply sharper than it might have been.

"Is there something wrong with that? I assume people on Zama move when they're offered a better salary."

"The question is meaningless." Vi smiled, as if to rob the words of any implied criticism. "People on Zama will never be offered a higher reward for moving, nor for taking on a new job."

"Oh god. This is a *Star Trek* moment, isn't it? Don't tell me, you no longer use money."

"We have money. We simply do not allow it to become a reason for anybody to become dissatisfied with their lot. You are paid more for being better at your job, not for moving to another one."

"That doesn't make any sense." Jess grabbed for the most obvious example for her protest. "We pay — for instance, we pay surgeons more than nurses, because the job is harder. Because the job is more important. We want the best people to be surgeons, so we pay more to attract the best candidates."

"In that way, we are different. We do not compete for talent. In this way we ensure that nobody leaves a job that satisfies them for the lure of money."

"But how do you get the best people for the best jobs?"

Vi didn't answer immediately, frowning as if she sought the best way to explain. "Some argued as you do. Successful men and women, for whom the system had been a gift. They protested that we could not limit what people would earn, and pretended they were not concerned for their own earnings. They argued that establishing limits would lead to stagnation, as people would stop trying. They argued that the market had to be free.

"I had them all executed."

Jess's breath hitched and she stared aghast at the girl in the seat next to her. Vi stared back dispassionately...

The glint in her eye gave it away.

"Was that... was that a *joke?*"

Vi smiled and nodded.

"It wasn't funny," Jess snarled.

For a moment Vi's smile held, then it collapsed, her brows furrowing. "Oh. Oh. I am sorry... I did not mean to offend. Empress Talia has — had a dark sense of humour."

"So you didn't... didn't execute them."

"No. The Empire is not a dictatorship, and the strength of the Crown is in patient strategy, not brute force. It took the reigns of four Empresses to fully implement the vision."

"What vision?"

"When you reward people more for different kinds of work, it becomes impossible to fill the jobs that society requires. If a financier earns more in a year than an educator in a lifetime, why would anybody choose to be an educator? You create a dichotomy: work that everyone wants to do, and work that nobody will choose.

"Understand, also, that many of our citizens work in the same profession as their parents before them. The son of a builder will go through learning programs that provide him the knowledge he needs. After this he must apprentice to a builder. How better, than to join his father? But if the son believes he will be better rewarded as a junior surgeon than as an elite builder, and if the surgeons' Guild will not accept him, you seed resentment.

"So it was decided to standardise rewards for each level of Guild seniority. It took many years to achieve the goal. The system was entrenched and nobody had the power to effect change. Nobody but the Empress. I had to act.

"What I started, I... Empress Xantha..." Vi's voice had changed, deepening and taking on a stronger accent, but now she paused, apparently confused. She blinked several times, and as her eyes focused on Jess, there was a flash of dismay in them. "Empress Xantha, four Empresses later, finished the process. It would not have been possible if not for the continuity of the Crown.

"This is at the heart of the Empire's stability. One may choose to be an educator or a banker, a builder or an electrician, according to your heritage. You will be paid the same. If you excel you will rise through the ranks to greater seniority and reward. But you will never earn more than you would have been able to earn in another job. A plumber, at the first Guild rank, earns the same privileges as a first rank lawyer."

"But what if you'd be a perfect surgeon, but you're born into the family of a carpenter?"

"Then you will make a perfectly adequate carpenter. And you will be satisfied."

"Not everybody," Jess said. "General Harke, for instance." *And me.*

Two and a half hours out of Port Augusta, they passed through Lochiel — another tiny outback town whose chief export industry seemed to be roads leading elsewhere. The last of the buildings was falling behind them when the phone in Jess's pocket chirped at her. It took her a moment to recognise the cheerful tones; the phone given to her by Jacob Elliot was unfamiliar. She fumbled it out of her pocket, sure she would already be too late, but it continued to buzz at her as she flipped it open.

The message was short and to the point.

PROFESSOR GARETH REED UNIVERSITY OF BALLARAT LECTURER SOCIOLOGY GOOD LUCK

Ballarat. Further east. At this rate she was never going to make it to Perth.

"Elliot has found your Hareth Rede." She tried to show the phone to Vi, but the girl shook her head.

"I can speak English," she said. "I cannot read it."

Jess had to explain *lecturer* to Vi. "We teach by telling people what they need to know, and then they have to go away and learn it. Professor Reed will be an expert in his field and his job is to structure the information into lessons, and then to evaluate the students' success in remembering what he told them."

"An inefficient method of teaching," Vi said. "But Hareth Rede must have done well to become an expert."

"Probably depends on how long he's been here. We can ask him how he managed it when we see him."

"So how do we contact him?"

"When we reach Adelaide," Jess said, "we'll call the university. We should just about have enough time. Either we'll get onto him directly, or the University might be able to tell us where to find him. What do you want to ask him when we contact him?"

"Can we not call him now?"

"If I turn my phone on, the police will be able to tell where we are. If they're looking for us."

Vi nodded at the phone still in Jess's hand. "What about that one?"

"Elliot told us not to make calls on it."

Vi turned to Aran for a quick conference. Eventually the girl turned back. "Hareth Rede is the one person I was told could help us. My mother did not mention Jacob Elliot at all. I am inclined to trust my mother's advice over his — for all we know, he is collaborating with the enemy. I want to make the call."

"This is a bad idea," said Jess. "You don't want to piss off Jacob Elliot," but even as she was saying this her fingers were tapping in the number for directory services.

It took three calls to be put through to the appropriate department at the University, and thirty seconds to receive an unwelcome answer to her query. "Professor Reed is away from the University," Jess told Vi. "He's attending a conference in Melbourne and he won't be back until Friday. Five days from now."

"We cannot wait five days," said Vi. "Where is Melbourne? Can we get there easily?"

"Further east," Jess replied. "I live there... I *used* to live there, until three days ago." She paused. "This bus goes to Melbourne."

"That is fortunate," said Vi.

"We don't have tickets for Melbourne. And I don't have the money to buy them."

"I am sure you will think of a way," said Vi.

Hareth Rede

I

Melbourne is a night city, after dark thrumming with life and activity. Every day of the week there are *al fresco* cafes open until late, late-night shopping arcades, hotel pubs and nightclubs and strip clubs.

It was well after eleven by the time Jess and her companions emerged from the bus terminus and made their way into streets. People were still walking under the streetlights, couples hand-in-hand and businessmen avoiding their homes. Melbourne on a Monday night; more active than Perth on a Friday. Today's dawn had ushered in the back half of January, but the Christmas season wasn't done with the city yet. Neon Santas and Christmas tree ornaments and nativity stars cast their glittering hues across the faces of the pedestrians and reflected off the wet sheen of the road. The trees lining the streets were festooned with tinsel ribbons and light strings, tied together like neurons; Tarzan would have been right at home, had he discovered a predilection for tinsel.

It had rained prior to their arrival and the air hung heavy with wet. The day's heat was still radiating from the brick buildings. The city smelled of wet dust and pine needles.

The bus had terminated outside the rail station popularly and unofficially known as Spencer Street, an expanse of curving roofline with all the aspirations of a European rail station and none of the colour.

Hotel Ulupna was on the other side of the CBD. With her scant remaining funds Jess bought them a tub of potato wedges, fortification for the walk. Vi and Aran ate with enthusiasm as if they'd never tasted sweet chili before. Jess wanted a Coke, but the extent of her remaining cash was four dollars and sixty-five cents in coin, and she decided to hold onto it in case of a sudden need for a payphone.

They were all in the same rumpled clothes they had worn back in Port Augusta, fifteen hours and a thousand kilometres away. At her side and taking two steps for each one of hers, Aran was nervous, fidgeting with the straps of his backpack. He flinched every time a pedestrian jostled him, as if he were unused to crowds. More times than she could count, a night walker would deviate directly into their path, swerving around them at the last moment, and each time Aran reacted visibly, all but reaching over his shoulder for a weapon. *He'd better leave the sword in his bag or he really will have something to worry about.*

They made it across six wide blocks without incident and stood outside the Hotel Ulupna. Inside was the promise of rescue — a name, one unlikely saviour. Professor Gareth Reed, also known as Hareth Rede. How he might help them Jess couldn't imagine. Perhaps he could take on the responsibility for the children, let her return to her car, her belongings, her life.

Perhaps she didn't want him to.

The hotel that was hosting The Australian Sociological Association national conference was set back from the road by a curved driveway, the entrance understated glass-and-wood leading to a small lobby in marble and oak. The space was dominated by an enormous Christmas tree, fifteen feet high and festooned with gaudy decorations, too perfectly conical to be natural. It drew the eyes upward to the first floor of the hotel, an open balcony overlooking the lobby like stalls in a theatre.

To their right a low bar area was still open, a few patrons visible at the counter; on the left, the reception desk. Directly across from the entrance a bank of lifts stood invitingly open. Closer, a small easel announced the itinerary for the day just gone. The TASA welcome and opening drinks had been held in the bar. A glance over her shoulder confirmed that there was a lot of drinking and not a lot of socialising going on.

Maybe that was how sociology lecturers partied.

A single attendant in a formal uniform that looked better suited to a cruise liner sat behind the reception desk. A badge on his chest, gold on brown, announced his name as B. Clarence. He looked up from a novel as Jess approached. "How can I help you?" His voice was courteous and betrayed none of the boredom in his eyes.

"We need to speak to Professor Reed," Jess said. "He's here for the conference. Sorry we're a bit late."

B. Clarence blinked owlishly at her. "I'm afraid I can't..."

"Professor Gareth Reed," Jess interrupted. "I'm his student. We were supposed to meet here today but we got held up." She smiled at him, attempting her best studious look.

"It's very late," the young man replied, his voice doubtful. "Can't you call his mobile? I'm not supposed to disturb a guest after nine."

"Well, Ben," said Jess, guessing, "I would, but the Professor doesn't keep a mobile. Could you just call up for me? He'll want to talk to me. I promise."

"I'm very sorry. I really can't."

"Then can you just tell me which room he's in? I really... I just need to talk to him." The hitch in her voice was unintentional but it seemed to convince him.

"What did you say your name was?"

"Jade," she said. "Tell him it's Jade. If I can just have five seconds, I know he'll tell you it's okay."

"Jade," said the attendant. He lifted a phone handset and punched in a number. They waited while he spoke briefly into the phone. "She says her name is Jade. She wants a quick word." Vi watched as the young man's eyes clouded over. When he handed Jess the phone, deep suspicion resided there.

Jess lifted the handset to her ear. "Hello?"

"Who is this?"

Carefully, Jess repeated the syllables Vi had taught her. "*Ui-latti es jirult,*" she said. "*Flen dirack, scald.*"

The approach of using Zama's native language had worked for Jacob Elliot, but now the silence stretched on for so long that she started to wonder if the Professor was still there. When he did respond, his voice was slow and deliberate; the voice of a man scared and trying not to show it. "You'd better come up."

"Thank you," she said. "We'll see you in a minute."

Whatever the Professor said to the attendant was sufficient to lower the drawbridge. Clarence resettled the phone into its cradle and nodded to the lifts. "The Professor is in room twelve-fourteen," he said. "Twelfth floor."

Jess smiled sweetly at him. "Thank you very much for your help." She didn't wait for a reply as she started across the wide expanse of floor towards the lifts.

II

Vi thought she knew hotels. She seemed to have spent half her childhood in them, dragged with her mother on one interminable state visit after another. Whatever the city, in every Region, hotels on Zama were cut from a single cloth. The Guild had settled on the ideal design for hotels a century ago and any variations since were attempts to improve on perfection.

Ulupna was nothing like them. For once, the voices in her head were silent.

The core of the hotel was its central tower, anchored on the lifts — a bank of four, two of them locked down and dark at this time of night. From this central tower two wings arced away, gently curving to east and west. On the twelfth floor the lifts opened onto a wide space carpeted in muted green, decorated with sickly pot plants and indecipherable abstract paintings. The numbers on the wall by the lifts indicated room ranges, but

Vi couldn't read them, and was happy to let Jess lead the way.

Room 1214 turned out to be the penultimate room on the wing. The curve of the hotel was just enough to take them out of sight of the lifts as Jess knocked on the door. Vi stood behind her left shoulder, far enough aside to have a clear view of the doorway past the taller woman.

Find Hareth Rede. He'll help you. She wanted to see this man that her mother knew by name.

The door swung open before Jess could complete her third knock. The man inside glared at her. "Quiet," he said in English, his voice a low but emphatic whisper. "I'm sharing. No need to disturb Doctor Hawthorn." He blinked as he registered the presence of Vi and Aran standing behind Jess. "I didn't expect—" He took a deep breath. "There's somewhere we can talk, downstairs."

Professor Reed led them back towards the lifts, his shoulders stiff as if it were taking all his effort not to peer back at them. His age was indeterminate; on the wrong side of fifty, older than her mother, at least. He still had energy, setting a spry pace along the corridor.

He had dressed in haste. His shirt hung out at the back and one point of his collar was caught under the edge of his brown vest. "You'll have to forgive me," he said as they walked. "I've been speaking nothing but English for twenty years now. My Zaman is rusty."

"I prefer English," said Jess. "Thank you for meeting us."

Rede pushed the call button for the lift before turning to face Jess. "I was hoping... no, never mind. You said you had a message from the Empress. I could hardly ignore that. Even after all this time." He shook his head, and murmured again, "All this time."

His face, his voice. Vi frowned. Something nagged at her, teasing at the edges of her memory.

A head full of other peoples' memories, there were bound to be a million faces she had known. It would be astonishing if she met someone she *didn't* think she recognised. Rede didn't look like any kind of a hero;

certainly not the saviour they had been promised. He was tall, and perhaps once he had been fit, but now he carried extra weight. His hair was black tending to silver, and he squinted from behind wire-rimmed glasses. He bore the appearance of an archivist or a technician — academic, studious, probably very good at a dry, dusty job.

They needed a General, not an academic.

They exited the lift on the darkened third floor of the hotel. "I didn't think we should have this conversation in front of my colleague," Rede said. "His mind is narrow, and I don't feel like trying to expand it at this time of night." The old man led them along a corridor much more deeply carpeted than the residential floors, until they came to a pair of double doors. There he swiped a card against a reader and led them into the room beyond.

The theatre had been set up for the next day's conference. Rede operated a switch panel by the door and dim ceiling lights across the room came to life; a brighter spot threw the lectern at the front of the chamber into brilliant clarity. Chairs were arranged in angled rows facing the lectern: sixty chairs in rows of ten. This chamber could have comfortably seated five times that number, so the small crowd of chairs at the front swam in an empty hall. At the back of the room a trestle table hosted an urn, cold and lonely.

"I guess your conference isn't huge," said Jess, waving a hand at the audience of furniture.

"This is for breakaway sessions," Rede said, somewhat defensively. "But no, it's not a huge crowd. Sociology isn't as sexy as climate change or terrorism. But you didn't come here to talk about my lectures. Do you have a message for me?"

Had she known him? In a previous life? The memories felt clearer than mere resemblance, painfully just out of reach. Vi felt certain she'd met him before. Why couldn't she remember?

She jumped at a touch on her shoulder. Aran was there, hovering and tentative. "What?"

"I must do my checks," the young Guard said. "Approaches and exits."

"Very well, do that." Aran was a distraction, when she was so close to discovering how Hareth Rede could help her. How did her mother know him? She barely noticed as Aran withdrew.

Rede was staring at Jess. Jess was staring at her. Of course... the promised message.

She shook her head to clear it, took a breath to reply, then reconsidered. *English*. Partly for Rede's benefit, partly for Jess. "Jess is here on my behalf. *I* am the one who needs to talk to you." She faced the old man squarely. "Before we begin, please tell me about yourself. I am seeking one specific person and I need to be sure that you are he."

The old man arched an eyebrow. "*You* came to *me*. I assumed you already know who I am. My name is Gareth Reed. I'm Professor of Sociology at Ballarat University, and I'm in Melbourne for a conference. What else do you want to know?"

They didn't have time for him to be obstructive. Vi focused on channelling Calla's imperious voice as she faced the professor. This was not a time for youth and deference; firmness was needed, and Calla had been nothing if not firm. "Let us start with truth. Your name is not Gareth. It is Hareth Rede, and you were born on Zama. This much we know." His reaction to their message had dispelled any lingering doubt. "I wish to know why you are *here*. What brought you to this world? For what crime were you exiled?"

Rede was silent for a long moment. When he answered, his voice was steady. "No. That's not fair. That question is personal and I don't care to answer it. Will it satisfy you if I say that I am here by choice?" His face was set and resolute, a face that was so familiar, and the memory was *so close* to the surface —

The guest wing of the palace faces west and the sunset is low to the horizon as she stalks along the corridor. Boiling out of the north and directly overhead, storm clouds are gathering; a deluge threatens. The ominous weather reflects the Empress Calla's own mood as she pauses at the door.

"Wait here," she tells the guard before she enters.

The young man looks up, startlement on his beautiful face, before he surges to his feet at the recognition of his visitor. Data pads scatter across the tabletop as he lets them go. "My lady," he says, "I am honoured by..."

- NOT NOW. Unaware that she had mouthed the words, had almost voiced them, Vi forced the vision down, back into her memories, blinking rapidly to clear her eyes. *Focus.* What had he been saying? *Will it satisfy you...* "It will not," she said. "I must know who you were. What skills you possess. And I *must* know the crime for which you were sentenced."

Rede appeared to consider resisting further, but Vi kept her face unyielding. After a moment he seemed to deflate. "I'll say this much. Yes, I'm originally from Zama. A long time ago. I was an archivist, a historian. Now, I'm a sociologist. Not a great deal of difference in practical terms. In terms of skills, that's an easy question: I have none. At least, none that I can offer to you. I am fluent in English; I have some small amount of practice with libraries and journals. If you need somebody who knows the history of both Earth and Zama, then perhaps I may have some use to you. Otherwise, I don't know how I can help. But you haven't told me yet what you want of me." He raised an eyebrow. "Maybe you really do need a librarian."

Vi was almost satisfied but didn't let it show. "And your crime?"

Reed's eyes flickered away. "My crime." He paused for a second. "I don't think of it as a crime. Perhaps it will suffice to say... I fell in love with somebody I should not. Somebody with power — enough power to protect me, but not to save me. In the end I was given a choice between the work camps and permanent exile here. Given those options, my choice was a simple one."

"If people can be sent to Earth simply for falling in love with someone from another caste, there would be a hell of a lot more of you here," Jess protested.

Even if she could hardly credit it herself, Vi felt she had to defend her forebears. "There must be more to this story."

"My case was special," said Reed. "Is that enough? I've told you what you want to know. Now give me this message, or leave me alone. Maybe I'm not that curious after all."

"*Ui-latti es jirult*," Vi said, the words flowing much more fluently off her tongue than Jess had managed. "We did not say we had a message from the Empress. We said that the Empress has need of you." She paused. "*I have need of you. Your Empress is asking for your help.*"

Reed's face froze. He ran his eyes over her, evaluating. "Are you saying... the Empress? *You?*" When she nodded, he sucked breath through his teeth. "But you're *young*. Calla was Empress. She was old when I knew her. She must have been ancient at her succession. How long? How long have you been Empress?"

"Jede was Empress after Calla," said Vi. "I have held the title for less than two days."

Reed's eyes flickered, as he added up years in his head. "Jede was Empress?" His face fell. "But now... now you are Empress. How does this come to be? Jede would still be young. Is... is she..."

"Dead?" Vi asked. Her voice came out unintentionally harsh but she couldn't rein it back. "I don't know. She was well when I last saw her. She may well be dead now."

Reed's hands shook slightly as he felt behind himself for a chair to sink into. "But how did you come to be Empress? Jede is... too young. Too young to be passing the Crown. I don't understand!"

"Tell him about the war," said Jess.

"Let *me* talk to him," said Vi. Jess raised her eyebrows and closed her mouth, but the words could not be unsaid.

Reed stared at Jess. "War? On Zama?"

Vi sighed. "Yes, war on Zama. The capital has fallen to rebels. Passing the Crown was the only way to preserve it. Coming here was the only way to preserve *me*. But we have brought the war with us. We have been followed."

"And you come to me looking for help? I'm just an old man. What do you need from me? I'm no soldier."

His words confirming her own doubts did her confidence no good at all. Still, there must have been a reason Jede had given her his name. "I am not looking for a soldier." *Although a warrior might have been nice.* "We are here because the Empress told us to find you. She said you would help us."

"Did she?" Reed shook his head. "She never forgot me. She still expects more of me."

"She may have held expectations," said Vi. "I do not. I come to you only with hopes. I do not know you, and there is little reason you would help me. I am the Empress... but I would be foolish to think you still owed the Empire allegiance after so long here."

"Oh, of course I'll help you," said Reed. "If there's anything I can do, I will. For the sake of the Crown, if nothing else." The old man took off his glasses and rubbed them absently on his vest. "Is she in there? You have her memories — is there any part of her personality in your mind?"

If only it were so. "The Crown contains only memories. Memories are not personality. In any case..." She swallowed. "There was no time for Jede to merge. Her memories are lost."

"Lost," breathed Reed. The corners of his mouth twitched. "Lost... and maybe dead. I'm an old man. You're not bringing me good news."

"My mother said to find you. Your name is the only hope we have."

Reed stared at her. "Your mother... You are Jede's daughter?"

"I am Vi Corala," said Vi. "Jede is my mother."

Rede stood from his chair, then bowed stiffly. "I... knew your mother. I was privileged to spend time with her in the Capital. And now I am likewise privileged to meet you. I'm sorry my hospitality cannot be greater."

That bow convinced her: she had known him. With that recognition came a sudden deluge of memories. *Not now!* She struggled to stay present, to stay focussed. She forced a smile. "Any hospitality you can offer is welcome. But we need more than a place to stay. How can you help us?"

The pressure was building — the memories were coming, demanding to be witnessed, crowding out the present in favour of another time and place. *She had known this man.* Her mind needed to remember.

Reed's voice was coming to her from a distance through water. "I'm sorry. I have no special skills to offer. I have no idea how I can help you."

She hadn't had the time or training needed to build her defences. She didn't know how to hold off the deluge of experience that was approaching. *You're going to lose yourself.* Garth's prophecy. With time and practice, she might be able to build walls, to integrate the memories into her own mind without being overwhelmed by them — but in front of her was someone she had known. Her inherited memories of him demanded reconciliation. It was too strong, too overwhelming, and she resolved to let go and get it done. Get through it, learn what you need to know, move on. Just remember to come back. *Remember who you are.*

The memories swept her away.

III

Guard training included an entire unit on the protection of dignitaries in hotels.

Of course, it had never been considered that a single Guard might need to cover an entire hotel alone. And that wasn't the worst of it.

Where's the security net? Where are the secondary accesses? Aran could see no sign of corridors dedicated to menials. Hotel guests and servants must use the same corridors, the same lifts. That cut down the number of possible approaches, but also the avenues for quick exit. In a proper hotel, with the proper layout, he would have been hard pressed to defend his charge against an assault by multiple assailants. Here, it would be impossible.

This was barely a hotel. But this was still a building, and there were protocols for buildings. Aran walked through the corridors, eyes flicking left and right, and remembered Drillmaster Warren's voice. The grizzled old soldier had ticked the list off his fingers. *Identify the directions from which your enemy might approach. Prepare plans to extract or protect your ward. Approaches and exits! If you can't extract, find a strong point for defence and claim anything you can use as a weapon.* Aran shook his head. Nothing here but lightweight pot plants less lethal than his bare hands.

The western arm of the hotel held five large rooms identical to Rede's conference hall. Some populated with rows of chairs, others only bare carpet. The partitions between them were hinged panels, able to be folded aside: potential for new avenues of escape. He folded and unfolded them with curiosity. Each room possessed large plate-glass windows overlooking the curved drive below and the street beyond. Despite the late hour the street still seemed colourfully lit. He stood at a window for a moment, imagining that it was Capital Island below him, pretending he was home. But any of the tiny figures moving about down there could be an enemy and he didn't dare linger in view.

A large door capped the far end of the corridor, bearing a boldly lettered sign that he couldn't read. Behind the door a narrow concrete stairwell stretched up and down. Another exit. He eased the door closed gently and retraced his steps.

The Empress was still deep in conversation with Hareth Rede, the old man waving his hands in animation.

Jess stood at the side, the flinger tucked into her belt. He had to admit that Jess had shown them nothing but good faith. Not that he was willing to trust her to protect the Empress, but the old man didn't seem threatening. The Empress had sent them here with a name, sent them to find this old man. She would hardly have done that if the old man were a danger.

They didn't need him right now, and he still had work to do. Half of the hotel remained unexplored. He let the door swing closed and turned towards the central tower.

An old man. Aran had been certain the Empress had sent them to find a soldier — had dreaded the encounter, even if it was his duty to make it happen. Hareth Rede was going to turn out to be a veteran, someone to supplant Aran, who by his strength and training and local knowledge would be everything that Aran was not. Aran knew his limitations. His youth, his inexperience, just a boy lost in this alien world where nothing was correct and everything was unexpected.

Aran was the best the Empress had, and he was not enough.

But Hareth Rede was no soldier. Aran could have cheered when he first laid eyes on the old man. Rede might prove to be a guide, an interpreter. But he would not fight for them. Aran was still needed.

He paused at the bank of lifts and took stock of entry points. Four lift shafts — two lit and active, two dark and disabled; another stairwell. The lifts and stairs formed a single entry, a chokepoint. If only he had a team to protect it.

Lifts. He ran the unfamiliar English word across his tongue. Not a good option for escape: once locked into that claustrophobic metal room, he'd burst into instant nervous sweat. Anybody could be waiting beyond those doors and you would have absolutely no warning. Stairs were better.

Beyond the lifts, on the other side of the hotel, the layout changed. He found a succession of small meeting rooms — nothing but empty cabinets, closets stacked high with chairs. Plate-glass windows that overlooked the street below and did not open.

There was another large door at the end of the corridor, another identical stairwell. Stairs at the end of each wing, and a third set in the centre with the lifts. Aran took the stairs upwards two at a time until he reached a landing, the stairs switching back on themselves. From here he had a sight-line on another landing and another door. The fourth floor. He plunged down a flight to another landing, another door. He nodded and retraced his steps.

The door to the third floor had swung silently closed behind him, and now would not open.

Stupid. Stupid. A child's error. He allowed himself the luxury of self-recrimination for the merest of moments — no longer. He flung himself down the stairs to the second floor and tugged ineffectively at the stairwell door. The stairwell doors could not be opened from the inside.

He had his communicator. The sliver of metal curved over his ear and nestled against his data contact. The Empress was wearing its pair, he'd made sure of it. He could ping her. Ask her to come let him back in. He could ask the Empress to rescue him. Her Guard.

He'd rather die.

The stairwell had to open at the ground. It must, in case of fire or emergency. From the lobby he could check the central shaft, find out if the stairs there were also a trap. If he must, he could use the lift to return. If there were no other choice.

He started downwards towards the lobby.

IV

The young man glances up as she enters. Recognition comes; he rises and attempts a bow. He's not been trained to bow properly and he makes a hash of it, but there's no uncertainty in his voice. "My lady, I am honoured by your presence. How may I serve?"

She doesn't immediately answer him, simply fixing him with her sternest gaze. That stare has destroyed her opponents in the Council chamber, and this boy visibly wilts under it; yet he manages to keep his eyes level. Despite herself, she's impressed.

It's not hard to tell what women see in him. He's handsome — a classic male beauty that would not be out of place in an oil painting. Matched with a will strong enough to even attempt to stare her down, he is likely a menace to any woman who catches his attention.

But she is the Empress Calla, and she is above such distractions.

He swallows. "Have I given cause for offence?" he asks now, as if he doesn't know why she's here.

She glances over her shoulder. The door behind her is firmly closed, the guard outside as commanded. Only when she is certain of this does she turn back to the young Hareth Rede. "You are not only foolish," she says softly, "but you're hopelessly naive. Did you think that nobody would know? Or is it worse — do you simply not care?"

He knows what she's talking about, and she knows that he knows, but the game must be played. "Care? Know? About... about what?"

"Jede", says the Empress Calla, and there are volumes of meaning in that one name.

"You know," he says, visibly deflating. "We thought we were keeping it secret."

"There are no secrets in the palace," she says. "Of course I know. And I am not the first. Others know as well... or they suspect, and where they suspect, they will soon find out the truth."

"I don't understand!" Now he drops his gaze, as he glances down at the table and uses a fingertip to push a data pad back from the edge, buying himself time before looking back into her eyes. "We never meet in public. Nobody could have seen."

"They don't need to see. Your absences coincide with hers. Her distraction and her moods. Your own changes of habit. These are obvious signs. Do you think this is a new story? For some of us who are grown adults, the truth is obvious."

"We love each other." As if that makes it all right. As if that's an excuse.

"I'm certain Ophi will be delighted to hear that when she brings her suspicions to the Magistrate," the Empress Calla says. "How does this end? Were you expecting to keep this secret forever? Are you planning to destroy her life — or simply to break her heart?" If it were possible for a person's stare to break stone, Hareth Rede would have been dust.

"I don't know," says Rede, and she can tell by his voice that it is true; he has been trapped by reality but at least he's recognised it. "I keep trying to stop — to leave — but I can't. She wants to marry me."

"Never. I will not allow you to destroy my dynasty."

The setting sun through the tall windows is directly in his face, turning his skin to red. "That has never been my intention."

"Then you're truly foolish," she snaps. "Allowing this to begin. And you're a worse fool for not thinking about the outcomes."

"Forgive me my impertinence," Rede says, his own frustration driving him to defiance. "You're not infirm. Jede is already nearly thirty. I'm not going to prevent her becoming Empress; you're doing that all by yourself."

"You blind idiot," Calla says. "Jede will have children some day. Jede is my only heir. I won't allow her to throw away her title, nor to squander her legacy. This — between you — must end."

"So what do you suggest?" There is a clear lack of repentance in his gaze.

She doesn't let herself soften. She came here with a singular intent and she is not leaving until it is accomplished. "That, boy, is up to you."

V

Vi was lost in some kind of trance, her eyes half-closed, unaware of her surroundings. Her pupils danced left and right as her unfocused gaze roamed the room like an unmanned searchlight.

Professor Gareth Reed stared in consternation. "Is she unwell?"

"I think it's the memory implant," Jess said. *Fighting off memories of the past.* "I think she'll snap out of it in a minute." Saying the words did not make her more confident they were true.

"I've heard of the Crown, of course," said Reed. "Never thought I'd see it in action, though."

"It's been getting worse. She's completely gone this time." She waved a hand in front of Vi's eyes with no visible response. "I don't know exactly how... your memory stuff... works. I don't know if this is normal."

"Memory patches have variable effects," Reed admitted. "It depends on the complexity of the program. I've seen catatonia of up to half an hour. I probably wouldn't get worried yet." He bent down to peer into Vi's eyes. "I can see her mother's features in her. The hair's darker."

"We dyed her hair."

"Really? Did that help?"

"We thought it would be better not to take chances."

Reed straightened and turned on a heel to face her. "How did you get mixed up in this little mystery? You're obviously not one of us."

"Typical story," she said. "Wrong place, wrong time. Vi needed my help and she... found a way to convince me to give it."

"She seems a very determined young woman," Reed said. "That lad she has with her... a friend? A brother?"

Jess shook her head. "Believe it or not, he's the bodyguard. He's dangerous. Old enough to cause violence and too young to understand why he shouldn't. Try not to anger him. He's already hurt one of the men chasing us."

Before she knew it she was telling the whole story, words spilling out of her. Professor Reed listened with fascination as she told him about her initial encounter with the children at the roadhouse; the possibility that the police might be seeking them. She described the surreal chase across the desert, the confrontation with Jarem and the unexpected cooperation of the driver carrying them back east to Port Augusta. Their encounter with Jacob Elliot.

Reed nodded. "Jacob Elliot. He was young when I met him. Just starting to make a bit of money." The professor glanced at his own threadbare vest. "It appears I chose the wrong career two worlds in a row."

Jess went on to describe their flight from Port Augusta. "We've been on a bus for almost twelve hours. We got to Melbourne just a little while ago."

Reed tilted his head. "I'm glad she found you. You've been a great help to her. I doubt I will be nearly as useful. Please, stay with me for the next few days. I'll take a room in my own name. If your name isn't on the register there's no reason the police should trace you here. That should give you a few days to take stock."

The offer was appealing, but impossible. "Thank you. But... it wouldn't be safe. We'd put you in danger. Utara's tracking them, somehow. As long as we're here, you're in danger." She paused. "You came across the Gateway yourself. I assume the trace fades over time." *Or else Utara might track you down.*

"You'd need to ask a physicist. I'm useless at anything that sounds like real science." Reed frowned. "As it happens, I do have a few friends in the Physics department. You said that Elliot's van was able to shield you from detection. Maybe we can get some advice on that — they might be able to work out a way to block any signal."

"That would really help," said Jess. "Elliot said the van was shielded by coils of copper wire. Might be somewhere to start."

Reed seemed pleased to have something to offer. "Great. I'll make some calls in the morning."

Jess glanced at Vi, who still appeared lost in memories, her mouth hanging slack and her eyes flickering. Jess nodded and turned her attention elsewhere. "I've been awake for about thirty-six hours now. I am *desperate* for coffee. Want one?"

"Tea, for me," said Reed. "I'll get it myself, thank you." They moved to the urn together and Jess took a moment to work out how to turn it on. While it heated, she rested her backside on the table and regarded the professor.

"So how does a historian from another world end up lecturing in politics at an Australian university? It must have taken you some time to get your head around our system."

"Political history, and it wasn't as difficult as you might think," Reed answered. "I had plenty of time to study. When I arrived… let's just say I had special consideration and the *dahla* ensured that I had plenty of money. More than plenty. That man's a very accomplished hacker and he must have had a lot of spare zeroes." He shrugged. "I've never *needed* to work. But he helped me generate a back-story and some qualifications and after I spent a couple of years studying, I joined the university as a tutor. Turns out, I liked the academic life."

Reed's movements were curiously delicate as he bobbed his teabag. "Now you can tell me something. As her protector — what's your plan? I don't mean just getting away from your pursuers. Assuming you manage that, what's next?"

"You'll have to ask Vi. I'm just looking forward to getting back to my life," said Jess. "I didn't exactly choose to be here, let alone chased by soldiers from across the galaxy. Once your Empress finds someone who can be a better protector to her than I can, I'm gone." *That protector was supposed to be you.* The words hung in the air, unsaid but mutually understood. He knew both worlds; he was already dedicated to the Empress, had promised his support of his own free will. But while his contacts might be helpful, he didn't seem to be the kind of man to be protecting a young girl from a posse of assassins. His next words reinforced that view.

"I'm just an old academic," said Reed. "I'm no hero."

"Do *I* look like a hero to you?"

Reed lowered his head to stare at her over his glasses. "Heroism isn't about appearances. Heroism is ordinary people caught in extraordinary affairs. A *hero* isn't something you are. It's something you *do*."

Jess shook her head. "Not me. Sometimes ordinary people stay that way."

The coffee was a granulated instant, two steps up from coffee-flavoured mud. Jess didn't care. She could have eaten it dry for the sake of the caffeine. She took a deep mouthful and felt sudden invigoration flooding through her from her stomach out into her limbs. Buoyed by new energy, she threw caution to the wind. "You had an affair with the Empress, didn't you? The last Empress. This 'Jade'."

He stared at her and she took his silence as assent.

"She was the 'wrong person... someone with power' you were talking about. So why didn't she just pardon you? If she cared for you, and if she's the ultimate authority in your empire, why couldn't she just say it was all forgiven?"

The professor sighed heavily. "She wasn't Empress at the time. And it doesn't work like that. Marrying outside of the nobility — it's like abdication. When I saw what the results would entail for Jede I chose to come here." He glanced away from her. "It's hardly an imposition. I've been comfortable. And this world's history is fascinating."

"Fascinating," Jess repeated.

Reed nodded. "Sociologically. It's like a snapshot of Zama's past. Democracy, free capitalism, the internal combustion engine. We tried them all. It's a great way to witness the past in action."

"I'm glad our primitive culture amuses you."

"Don't get me wrong," said Reed. "I've been here nearly sixteen years. Zama isn't home any more. I barely think of it."

Jess nodded. "Who knows how it's changed in a decade and a half?"

"Oh, I'm certain it hasn't changed at all," said Reed. "You're used to a changeable society. Every day brings new devices, new wars and revolutions. The 24/7 news cycle. But not on Zama. Everything in Zama's culture, *everything*, works against change. It's the most stable culture you can imagine — and the most boring. You know, you ought to read my book."

"Does *stability* include civil wars? We have rebel soldiers hunting the Empress across another planet right now. Doesn't seem that *stable* to me."

Reed seemed ready for the question. "It's hardly surprising. On Earth, if you're in need of change you can move somewhere else, take a new job, make new friends. You take up graffiti as a hobby or run away to join a circus. Not on Zama. Before you're born it's already known what job you'll do, where you'll live, how your life will be lived. A lot of people find that comforting. But there are always some who find themselves trapped by expectations.

"There have always been uprisings. People are always wanting a way out of the structure that our society imposes. There will always be some who don't fit the mould, who fall outside of society's norms. They flail about a bit, make some noise, do a bit of violence. None last."

"This one might," Jess said. "The capital has been captured. The government's fallen. The Empress is exiled to another planet."

"Zama will find a new equilibrium. It might not be all bad. If there's one thing I've learned from studying history it's this: if you want growth, you need to experience loss."

VI

The stairwell opened onto the rear of the bar, next to the toilets.

The bar was emptier now than earlier. A few die-hards remained slumped over the bar, but most of the lights were off now. The suspicious eyes of the barman tracked him as he approached the lobby. Even as he stepped out onto the marble floor, the barman continued staring, either at him or his bulging backpack.

The fake tree in the lobby distracted him. *A tree — inside a building*. He didn't try to make sense of it. It would serve as cover in a firefight: the plinth it stood on at its base was wide enough to provide shelter. A fit man might be able to climb the tree from the lobby floor to vault over the first floor railing to the balcony.

The concierge, behind the desk, was trying to give the impression of being absorbed in his novel. He held the book low enough to peer over, and he watched as Aran moved back to the lifts. Aran half expected a challenge as he passed. They didn't share a language: any conversation would be a waste of time.

He considered the call button — helpfully marked with an upward-pointing chevron. It seemed that some icons at least were universal. But he'd had enough lifts for one day. *Try the stairs first.*

At the first landing he tried the door and was pleased when it opened smoothly, revealing the broad expanse of the first floor balcony. The stairwells on the ends of the wings only opened at the ground; these ones were usable. He stepped across to the balcony railing and surveyed the layout below.

He had a good view of the expanse of the lobby. Most of it, anyway: the front doors were obscured by the tree. He sidled along the rail until the doors and the reception desk came into view. *A good spot for a reception team.* Half a squad would be more than enough. He didn't have half a squad. By himself, with a flinger, he could cover the front doors, and the balcony railing would give cover and allow a crouched defender to cross from side to side. The front doors would be a long shot, but he could do it.

He didn't have a flinger either. The woman had that, not that she'd know how to use it.

He turned on his heel to head back to the lifts. He'd seen enough; there was still another floor to review. He had taken three steps back towards the central lifts when he heard it, and his body responded automatically, sending him instantly into a crouch below the level of the railing, almost before he registered the sound.

Zzip... tchack.

The distinctive *zip* of a razor disc leaving a flinger, and the metallic *snap* of a new disc ratcheting into place. Couldn't be anything else.

Late-night visitors: two dark shapes in the doorway. He had been turning away as they entered, he'd barely seen them. Had they seen him? Probably not, unless he was unlucky.

Utara's found us.

How many of them? Two, at least; there might have been more coming in behind. He had to know. Risking being spotted, he lifted his eyes above the railing to peer down into the lobby below. A quick sweep of his eyes across the floor and he had fixed the position of the men in his mind. Two men, neither looking upwards. The man with a shaved head and a bandolier was at the reception desk; no sign of the concierge. Shave-head moved from left to right, peering through the open doorway behind the desk, checking the angles. *Looking for targets.*

The second invader had plenty of hair, dense sideburns and a shaggy beard. He faced the bar until Shave-head joined him, then together they moved in that direction, behind the tree and out of sight.

Ten seconds had passed since the men entered the lobby.

The men were heading for the bar, where the suspicious barman and his customers could have no idea what was coming for them. There was nothing Aran could do for them. Not his responsibility: his charge was the Empress, two floors above.

Attacking civilians was a desperate move. Utara must be certain of his quarry's presence to be willing to risk it. Would he just use two men? No, these were the scouts. Once the entrance was cleared Utara would enter in force. Outside, men would be moving to cover the exits.

Where to go? *Think. You've done your scout.* Head upstairs to rejoin the Empress? Guide her to a stairwell?

Utara had a full squad: more than enough to cover front and rear doors, two sets of stairs, with plenty to spare. Trapped like rats on a sinking ship; they could head up, but it wouldn't take long for them to run out of *up*. It would buy them time, nothing more.

He reached up and tapped his earpiece communicator. It chirped at him, confirming that contact was open. "Utara is here," he whispered. "They're in the lobby; they'll be coming in a moment. Head *up*. I'll come meet you."

That was all he had time for: the two men were returning from the bar. Instinct made him want to crouch lower behind the barrier, but he suppressed that reaction. The tree would obscure him from a casual glance, but movement would draw the eye and give him away for sure. *Break the silhouette. Remain still.*

Hairy was tapping his own temple; a momentary glint of blue confirmed that he was wearing an earpiece of his own. He didn't bother to keep his voice low as he spoke. "Lobby secure. Come in."

Moments later more men flowed through the doors to join the first two. Aran counted six newcomers — a total of eight. The man at the rear was bald and limping; Captain Aesk with his wounded buttocks. The men were led by a shorter figure, long auburn hair flowing over the shoulders of his suit. It was too far from Aran's vantage point to make out the famous scar, but whether because of the man's confidence or the way he carried himself, that had to be Utara himself.

Shave-head nodded in the direction of the reception desk. "There may be more staff in the back."

Utara nodded. Wasting no time, he used economical hand gestures to signal his men to secure the service area behind the reception desk. Aran's lips twitched as Utara's men stared blankly. *Not trained in hand-sign.* Utara's signals, on the other hand, had been precise and clear. The commander was trained and experienced and not to be underestimated.

Sighing loud enough for Aran to hear, Utara turned to the men who had entered with him. "No civilians this time. Quain, Rodd, clear the area. Go quietly and be quick."

Aran watched as Utara sent one man to cover each stairwell — east and west — in case his quarry should attempt to use them to escape. No more or less than Aran had expected, and the verification gave him no comfort as each avenue of escape was progressively sealed. Utara took the rest of his squad in the direction of the lifts.

Eight men — the rest outside. One each at the indoor stairwells. That left six.

He couldn't fight six men at once. But he might be able to disrupt their plans. *Take out the leader, watch the undisciplined forces collapse.* Utara's command was the glue that held this squad together. Eliminate him, and the squad might well disintegrate. He might have to finish the job with Captain Aesk as well if he wanted the squad to fall apart. His bruised cheek tingled at the thought.

One of the men was carrying a crate, two-handed. *The drone.* That didn't leave a hand free for a flinger. Why would they bring that inside? They already knew the Empress was in the building. A moment later he realised: they would use the drone on each floor to locate their target. No need to knock on doors. Less chance for alarms or disturbances.

None of the hotel training scenarios had given the enemy sensor drones. Aran tried to remember if he'd ever heard of a way to hide from a sensor drone, but he feared that those Lessons were in next year's learning program.

There had been no response through his earpiece from the Empress, no indication that she'd heard his warning. He tapped it again: the confirming chirp told him that its pair was awake and transmitting audio. She must have heard. No reason at all she wouldn't respond, if only to acknowledge his warning. Unless she'd taken off her earpiece. Or unless Hareth Rede had turned out to be less of a help than expected — if he'd proven to be a threat. If he'd harmed her. And Aran had left her alone and undefended with him.

Aran's English vocabulary was still limited, but there was a word he'd learned directly from Jess. Even though his pronunciation was imperfect, the sentiment was heartfelt.

"*Thit,*" he said.

How sociologists party

I

Professor Reed was attempting to explain the intricacies of Zama's ruling class. "Jede wasn't the Empress at the time. Being the Empress's daughter doesn't count for much; it's not hereditary."

Jess nodded. This much she knew already.

"There *are* no hereditary positions on Zama. So there was no reason to expect Jede would ever become Empress. Calla was in her mid-fifties and seemed healthy. Empress for thirty years, there was no reason to think she wouldn't still be Empress for another thirty." He shrugged ruefully. "How little we know. Anyway, Jede was already in her mid-twenties. It's very rare indeed that the Crown does *not* pass to a lady trained within the previous three years. Noble girls don't retain their level of knowledge for long after they leave the Lessons.

"When I... left... Jede was already two years past the Lessons. We thought we weren't losing anything but we didn't consider what our relationship would mean for any children we might have. But Calla considered it. She wasn't willing to allow her grandchildren to forfeit a place in the nobility. She saw herself as part of a dynasty and she wouldn't countenance her descendants being ineligible to be Empress."

Jess rested her paper cup on the table and frowned. "You can't marry into the nobility?"

"Absolutely not," said Reed. "It's not a guild. Jede would have forfeited her rank. We could have coped with that, but like I say, Calla had higher ambitions for her grandchildren."

Expectations. Jess, who had grown up without any, found it hard to imagine what it must have been like for Vi, growing up with the weight of others' aspirations on her shoulders. Even before she became Empress, the girl must have been denied a normal childhood, with her grandmother, her mother, looking at her not as a girl but as Empress-in-waiting.

"So have I got this right? Most children follow in their parents' footsteps. They take a memory pill or whatever and suddenly they know everything there is to know about woodworking or brain surgery."

Reed nodded. "Not everything, a subset. There are levels. But yes, in essence. It feels like remembering something you used to know but had forgotten. Memory by itself isn't enough. All students combine their new knowledge with a practical program. Almost all education is via what we would recognise as apprenticeships. For most people, that apprenticeship is with your close family."

"Okay. But if you don't want to be a brain surgeon, you can join another guild."

"Sure. If you find a sponsor, someone willing to take you on as an apprentice. There are people willing to take on a neophyte — those without their own children to follow them, perhaps."

"But you can't join the nobles. They don't have — what did you call them? Sponsors."

"You become a noble by birth, or not at all." Reed paused and took a sip of his tea while he collected his thoughts. "Anyway, few people would want to join the nobles. It's not as glamorous as it sounds. Nobles make up the High Council, but the High Council has little legislative authority. So mostly, what the Nobles do is lounge around having parties, while the girls learn history, economics, politics."

"What a terrible life that must be."

"Is that sarcasm I hear? Try living that life for a few years and you might change your mind. Jede wanted nothing more than to escape that world. I thought I could offer that escape."

"You have no idea."

The voice was low with fury and it took Jess a moment to place it. Vi was advancing on them across the theatre, thunderheads on her brow. "You've had sixteen years to consider. Sixteen years, and you still don't understand. There is *no higher calling* than to be Empress." Vi's voice was strange: a deeper timbre, a rounder accent. It made her sound older. "History rests on her shoulders. The traditions and rituals to which she is born have existed long before she was a speck and will continue long after she is dust. There is honour in that title — and it must go to those who are strong enough, *true* enough, to be worthy of it."

Reed stood to face her, his eyes darkening. "Rich enough. Pampered enough. Born to rule. You should at least admit it — most of the nobles are corrupt fools. I've met a lot of people since I came here and some of them would be a lot more *worthy* of the title of Empress than most of the nobles I used to know!"

"Do you think it's easy?" The mouth was Vi's but the words and the anger belonged to someone else.

Jess raised her hands, placating. "Vi, honey? Are you okay?"

The girl ignored her, continuing her advance on Reed. The professor retreated. "You spoiled my daughter," Vi said, her voice shaking. "You almost destroyed her, poisoning her mind with impossibilities. Now my granddaughter comes to you. As if you could help her! I won't let you destroy her with false hopes. You have no place in her life!"

You need to bring me back to the present. I give you permission. Vi's words to her on the bus. At the time Jess had enjoyed the idea, but now the challenge was real. Her parents had not spared the rod, but Jess had sworn not to be like them. Striking a child was not in her nature. *This whole business started with a punch.*

Reed had run out of space for retreat, backed into the corner of the lecture hall. He raised his hands, ready to fend her off. "You *are* her granddaughter. You are not the Empress Calla. You are Vi Corala. You are the Empress Vi. You are *not* Calla."

Vi had closed to direct contact with him. The girl was half a metre shorter than the old man and she had to crane her neck to glare up at his face. She balled up her fists. She might hurt the old man — or he might shrug off her feeble blows. It wasn't clear which would be the worse outcome.

"Leave her alone, you *crek*," Vi said. "Send her away. I don't want you anywhere near my grand-daughter."

"She is *Jede's* daughter," the professor said, his voice low, "and I will help her if I choose. You stood between me and your daughter once. I gave up my life for it. For *her*. I sacrificed everything for her sake. No — for *your* sake. But not this time. Not here."

For a moment the tableau was still: the girl glaring up at Professor Reed, his back to the wall but unrepentant. Vi's shoulders shook with rage or with tears. Jess started to reach for her —

The girl span on a heel, fast enough for her hair to billow. Turned toward Jess and took three rapid steps, closing the distance between them before Jess could think to react. The girl lashed out and Jess flinched, not understanding why the girl should suddenly change her target, but Vi wasn't striking for her face. She went lower, and Jess felt the weight vanish from her belt before she saw the flinger in the girl's hand.

Vi pivoted and lifted the weapon, pointing it directly at Reed's chest. "I won't allow it. I *will not*."

Jess slapped her.

The blow was light, but the recoil seemed to ricochet up her arm and straight into her heart. The sound of the slap was a sharp retort in the empty room, and the girl stumbled. With a muffled *zip-clack*, the flinger discharged, bucking in the girl's hand. A jagged rent appeared in the plaster of the wall beside Reed's head and a line of bright red started to well on his cheek.

Jess found herself staring at her open hand, feeling the palm tingle; her other hand had risen to her own cheek, feeling gently at the skin which was still tender where Mark's bruise had not completely healed.

Bring me back to the present. She hoped that she had been successful. She would not be capable of striking a second time.

Vi stumbled at the blow but didn't fall. She glanced at the weapon in her hand as if she had no idea how it had arrived there. Her other hand went to her cheek.

"I'm so sorry, honey," said Jess. "I had to."

Vi didn't look up. "No. That was... exactly what I needed. I was forgetting myself." She turned to Reed. "I am sorry. I might have hurt you."

Reed took off his glasses and polished them on his lapel, his hands shaking. Returned them to his nose, then brushed at his cheek, blood on his fingers. "Not your fault... That was memory leakage. Worst I've seen."

"You cared for my mother. I now know something of why you chose as you did. Calla is... *was*... a very determined woman."

"She certainly was that."

Vi looked at him intently for a long moment, and Jess wondered if she was about to start threatening him again.

Reed seemed to find the attention discomfiting. "What is it?"

Suddenly the girl's stare broke, her eyes darting sideways. The colour drained from her face. "Oh no..."

The sudden fear in Vi's eyes made Jess's own heart race. "What's up? What's the matter?"

"Utara is here."

"Shit," said Jess. "How do you know?"

"Aran's watching them now," Vi answered. "Eight of them in the lobby. They're heading for the lifts."

All their efforts, their headlong flight, and still they'd barely stayed one step ahead of their pursuers. On the road, with Ivan and his truck, there had been just two of the enemy; a single soldier in the town of Port Augusta had nearly caught them. How could they fight against eight in the enclosed space of the hotel?

Obviously they couldn't. "We have to move," Jess said. "There'll be a rear exit behind the kitchens. We can't stay here."

Vi offered her the flinger. Jess stared at the outstretched hand and made no move to take the weapon. "I don't know how to use that. I'm not a soldier. I have a rule about not shooting people."

"Please," Vi implored. "They might want me alive, but they will certainly kill you. And Rede, and Aran." The girl's voice was bleak but resolved as she spoke, each word a stone of cold logic. "I have brought my war to you, and I don't want you to die on my account. These are bad men. If you get the chance, shoot them. Not for my sake, for yours."

Jess reluctantly took the outstretched weapon. "Maybe I can give us some cover. I'm not killing anyone."

Vi ignored her protest. "Utara has people at each exit," she said, one hand cupping her ear. "We cannot go down. They are at the lifts."

"There's no way out," said Reed. "We have to hide."

"Aran says to go up," Vi said. "We need to buy him some time."

"Okay," said Jess. "We go up. Professor Reed, we need your key."

"I'll bring it," said the Professor.

"They're not looking for you. You'd be safer staying here."

Reed shook his head, silver hair swaying. "I'm not leaving you. I've been waiting twenty years for proof that I made the right decision to come here. I don't want to go another twenty wondering if they caught you or if you're going to turn up on my doorstep again some day."

"Okay," said Jess. "Keep up. If you slow us down, we can't wait for you."

"I'll keep up."

II

The whisper of steel as Aran unsheathed the sword, slow inch by precious inch, was so quiet as to be almost inaudible. Still, Aran chafed at the delay. Releasing the weapon from its scabbard was bad enough; opening the backpack had been worse, an exercise in jaw-grinding frustration as he moved the zipper tooth by tooth.

The extra time was worth the effort. The men below remained unaware of his presence as he rested the scabbard with his backpack against the balcony barrier. It comforted him to feel the weight of the sword in his hands: a false confidence. All the men below had flingers *and* swords.

His fingers itched for a flinger. From this height, with the advantage of surprise, he could thin their numbers by two or three at least before they found him. But the Empress had ignored his advice and left the weapon with Jess. Much good it would do her; she was more likely to shoot herself than the enemy.

He again raised one eye above the level of the barrier to peer at the lobby below. It was a risk: if they were attentive they might spot the movement. But he had to know what they were doing. Ignorance would kill him faster than overconfidence.

He need not have worried. The men were clustered around the lifts as Utara gave instructions. In the silence of the hotel lobby the words carried to Aran's ears.

"If you see any locals, put them down. I want no alarms," Utara said.

"We'll attract attention." Captain Aesk showed no sign of his injury, his face impassive. "They'll come looking for us. And we can't burn this building down."

Utara's voice was strained. "When we get the data reader back from the boy, we're halfway home. No more delays. We grab the girl and head out. We'll be gone before they catch up."

Aesk turned to his men and with quick commands deployed them. The lobby, the lifts, one man behind the reception desk.

There was a hitch as Obi objected to his assignment. "The stairs? Why do I always get the stupid jobs?" The big man was the one who had almost stopped them in Port Augusta. Aran recognised the plaid shirt straining across the biceps.

Utara grinned without humour. "Because they're what you're best at. Brec patches wounds. Garron collects weapons. The captain *loses* weapons. Quain gives us strategy and Heth gives us pointless jokes. And *you* do the heavy lifting and the climbing up stairs. You have a problem with that?"

"No problem," said Obi in a voice that belied the sentiment.

"I'll take the stairs," said another soldier. "I don't like enclosed spaces."

Utara's gaze swung to glare at the soldier who'd spoken but it was Aesk who replied. "Next man who questions my orders gets left here to rot. Rell, you have the drone, so you're in the right tube with Heth. Does anybody else require me to repeat their orders?" This demand was met with silence and Aesk nodded. "We all want to go home. So let's get this finished. They're still above us?"

It took Aran a second to realise what the question meant. Then the soldier with the discomfort for grav-tubes raised the case in front of him, turned a full circle on his heel. *Scanning.* Aran had to assume the device would point to his location like a compass. *Time to move.* He ducked below the level of the barrier and started a low scuttle towards the stairs.

Behind him the soldier's voice floated over the railing. "Two distinct signals. One's a long way up — but the other one's close. *Right there.*"

Then Aran was on the stairs, the door swinging closed behind him. He bolted upwards, the enemy's eyes already on his wake.

III

Jess took the lead up the central stairwell. With Utara at the controls in the lobby they couldn't use the lifts, so they were forced to climb nine flights of stairs.

"Where are we going?" The exertion was slowing Reed, but the old man was doing better than Vi, who was struggling at every step upwards. They couldn't afford to slow. *Buy him some time*, Vi had said, but what the boy could do against a squad of soldiers Jess didn't want to guess. If he was sensible he'd barricade himself somewhere. Even if not, he wasn't coming to the rescue.

"Your room," she replied. Breathlessness made her voice terse. "We need a phone."

"How can we fight them?" Vi asked, her voice coming in little puffs between stairs. "Aran won't hold them all."

"We don't have to beat them. We just need to hold them back." Jess waggled the flinger and made sure there was more confidence in her voice than she felt. "I'll make it hard for them to get close."

"We have no spare cartridges," said Vi. "Only twelve discs. That will not hold them back for long."

"Eleven discs," said Reed, fingering the line scored across his cheek.

"Trust me," said Jess. "I know what I'm doing."

"On Zama, women aren't considered capable of fighting," Professor Reed said breathlessly, seemingly at random. "There are no women in the army. It's common wisdom that women don't make good soldiers. They're not aggressive enough."

Jess grinned a ferocious grin. "They never met my mother."

IV

Aran waited on the second floor for the enemy to come to him.

Combat is chaotic, Drillmaster Warren had lectured. *Do not allow the chaos to control you. Retain a sense of stillness. You must rise above, remain outside the fray even while you are at its centre. If you cannot do this, you have no place on the battlefield.*

Aran had never found that place of calm. In the exercises, and later in conflict with his peers as they tried to bully him out of the service, he had always been in the moment, responding on instinct to the threats. It had always been enough. Perhaps it would be enough today.

The first-floor balcony was too open; against an enemy armed with flingers, he stood no chance. Here on the second floor there were rooms, doors, curving corridors; potential cover. Enough, perhaps, to earn another few minutes. He could do a lot in a few minutes.

He stood close to the lifts, close to the adjoining stairwell. The reluctant soldier hadn't been wrong about the dangers of an enclosed space. When the doors opened, Aran would be inside with his sword before Heth and his companion could react. In that enclosed space, they couldn't fire their flingers for fear of shooting each other. And Aran would give them no time to respond. He felt confident he could clear one lift.

Then he would be trapped in an enclosed space with the enemy at his back, but he had no better ideas. That would require remaining outside the fray, and he had never achieved this.

The stairwell door opened before the lift arrived.

Obi came out of the stairwell at a rush. All Aran's plans, his preparation, fled at the sight of the oncoming mountain. The man filled his vision and for a second he was just a boy, frozen in panic.

The big man's eyes widened as he registered Aran's presence, but faster than Aran would have credited, he had his flinger out and was bringing it to bear. *Move!* Aran lunged, leading with the sword, but the freeze had lasted too long. He was already too late as Obi pressed his trigger.

Instead of the characteristic *zip* of a disc being launched, Obi's flinger gave a dull metallic *thunk* — the sound of a flinger with misaligned rails. Damaged — probably when Obi lost it in the crowd. *The flinger trampled underfoot, Obi fighting his way clear of the men clinging to his arms.*

Aran put the vision aside as he closed the distance to the big man and brought the sword down towards his head, letting free a shrill shout to give extra force to the blow.

For such a big man Obi moved swiftly, his own sword coming up in a blur of steel, barely in time to deflect the strike. Growling, the big man threw aside his useless flinger and shifted his grip on his sword, taking an offensive stance and coming at Aran with all his considerable weight.

Trying to block the man's blows would be foolish. Two blows from that giant would be enough to numb his arms; within three he'd be struggling to hold his sword, in four at most he'd be defenceless. *Don't block, deflect.* Aran used his weapon to turn the blows aside, using each impact to aid his own flowing movements. Using Obi's own force against him.

One strike turned. Two. And Aran realised the startling, wonderful truth: Obi was no soldier. Somebody had put weapons in his hands, but not taken the time to train him to use them properly. The most basic of maintenance would have detected the flinger's misalignment and repairing that kind of damage was simple. His technique with the sword was blunt and untrained. Obi relied on muscle. Any strike could sever an arm, were it to cut home, but he telegraphed his every move and Aran avoided the blows with ease.

Aran deflected another strike to the side, and when Obi tried to bring the sword back with a wild and barely controlled return swing, Aran swayed back, out of reach, then flicked forward with a strike of his own. A line of red opened on the big man's bicep. Obi roared in outrage, but now he was on the defence. Aran's sword danced as he advanced, driving his opponent back towards the open stairwell. Mere seconds had passed but now Obi was forced to retreat, barely able to block Aran's cuts.

Aran nearly laughed. The man was twice his size, but his attacks were consistently too high, and he wasn't even holding his sword properly. A sideways parry caused the sword to twist in Obi's hand and the big man almost lost his grip entirely.

Behind Obi, the lifts chimed. Obi flinched, his eyes flickering at the unfamiliar noise, and the fractional loss of attention was enough. Aran lunged, twisted, and his blade caught Obi's weapon and turned it aside. In the same movement Aran pounced forward and struck home.

The resistance of cloth and flesh as the sword punctured the big man's sternum and ran him through felt like surrender.

Obi stared down at the hilt of the sword in his chest, Aran's hand still wrapped around the pommel, then started to lift his eyes to meet Aran's stare. Before his eyes were level, he was stumbling backwards into the stairwell, twisting as his legs failed, tumbling.

The blade had slid through the man's torso like silk, but now it bound on bone and against the dead weight of the big man's body Aran had to let go or be pulled after him. The sword was torn out of Aran's grasp as Obi's body fell backwards into the stairwell.

Aran took one step after him — one step towards the stairs — and froze. If he entered the stairwell with enemies behind him and soldiers below, he would be lost. No cover, no exit, no escape once enclosed in that small space. The lift doors were starting to slide apart, and he was out of time; his momentary indecision had lost him whatever fraction of a second he might have used.

It didn't matter. The entire fight with Obi had taken mere seconds. His heart was pounding from exertion — or from exultation. He stood empty-handed before the lifts, and he didn't care. He could barely keep a grin off his face as they opened, doors sliding apart with glacial slowness. Aran waited, his empty hands in the clear. With the slump of his shoulders, the curve in his spine, he sought the appearance of someone beaten; someone who knows they are outmatched. He was not outmatched.

These men were not soldiers. They were thugs with guns. They had the weaponry, but they were no match for him.

As they would soon learn.

V

Professor Reed's swipe card unlocked the door to room 1214. As Jess waved her two companions into the room, she stared down the length of the corridor. The gentle curve of the wing had taken them just out of sight of the lifts. The element of surprise — from here, she would see them coming before they saw her. The unfamiliar weight of the flinger in her hand gave her no confidence, but all she had to do was make them hesitate. Demonstrate that they couldn't get close without her shooting them. Then she wouldn't have to shoot them.

She paused just inside the room as Reed turned on the overhead light. The twelfth-floor suites were comfortably furnished and spacious. Two interior doors led into bedrooms, and a floor-to-ceiling window made up one of the lounge area's walls, overlooking a twelve storey drop to the concrete drive below.

She needed cover, some kind of barricade. She considered and as quickly dismissed the dark leather couch as well as the television it faced. Twice she had seen razor discs carve through plaster and wood, and the couch would hardly do better. A low coffee table in chrome had a glass top, which would be worse than useless.

Her eyes came to rest on the credenza. Low and solid and ubiquitous. Identical to those found in every hotel room she'd ever inhabited: she would have laid odds on something similar populating Zaman hotel rooms. The doors on this particular piece of furniture slid open freely, revealing the expected bound folders full of pamphlets advertising *What to See While You're In Town*, *How to Get Around* and *Places to Eat*, as well as two-volume copies of Yellow Pages and White Pages. An encouraging start, but not nearly enough.

She hooked her fingers under one end of the credenza and discovered it was as heavy as it looked. Excellent. "Find me a phone," she told the Professor. "Then come help me with this."

Reed looked at her with an expression of helpless confusion, but then did as she asked.

Vi took a corner and tried to help Jess, but her contribution was negligible. "Why do you need a phone?" Considering the peril, the girl seemed calm, betrayed only by the rapid pulse at her throat.

Reed returned from the small bedroom, clutching a phone handset. The wire from the phone trailed behind him.

Jess had managed to swivel the heavy credenza on its end so it stood out from the wall. She paused in her efforts and looked up at the professor. "Call triple zero," she said. "Get the police out here."

"The police? I thought you..."

"Lesser of two evils," said Jess. "They're not likely to kill us, and if they run into Utara's people we might be able to escape in the confusion. It's worth a try. Unless you have a better idea?" Aran's trick in Port Augusta had inspired the idea, but they needed something other than passers-by; she didn't want to put innocents into harm's way.

Reed's eyes flicked from Jess to the phone, back to Jess. "What do I say?"

"Bloody hell," said Jess. "Pass it here." Accepting the phone from the professor, she punched in the emergency number. She injected urgency into her voice as she spoke into the phone. "Police! I need the police. There's men with guns. They're shooting people. In the Ulupna Hotel. Oh God, help us! I saw... there's about a dozen men, I don't know! Please come quickly!"

Without hanging up, she flung the handset aside and didn't wait for it to stop bouncing before she turned back to the cabinet. "Give me a hand here," she ordered.

The commotion and the light had drawn the attention of the room's other occupant. Reed's roommate, Doctor Hawthorn, was tall and skeletal and in his dressing gown as he stood in the doorway to the bedchamber. "Are these your students, Gary?" His eyes widened as he took in the scene — Jess levering the credenza out from the wall, Reed staring on helplessly, the teenage girl in the corner. "Do you know this woman? Who is she?" A pause, then: "Why is she stealing our furniture?"

"Don't call me Gary," snapped Reed, with an irritation in his voice that said this wasn't the first time. "And she's not stealing it. Make yourself useful... help me with the other end."

Hawthorn blinked at the peremptory tone, but followed instructions. As he and Reed strained to lift the cabinet off the carpet, he went on. "What is all this? Care to explain yourself?"

It was Vi who answered. "You are in grave danger. There are men coming towards us as we speak, and if we cannot stop them they will kill all of us."

"You're kidding me," said Hawthorn, but he didn't let go his end of the credenza. Together, the three adults got it out the door of the room and lowered it to the floor in the corridor.

"It's no joke," said Jess, shaking her hands to get feeling back in her fingers. "Believe me, I wish it were; I'm about to try to shoot some people. It's a bit of a step up from rabbits." She paused. "I need books. Any books you've brought with you. I assume you brought books?"

Reed grimaced. "We're academics. Does a vegetarian piss green?"

"I figured," said Jess. "Bring them here. Then, all of you, get into the bedroom and stay there. Barricade the door if you can." She shot a sour look at Vi. "I'll hold them off as long as I can. Hopefully until the cavalry arrives."

Vi nodded. "A good plan," she said, as if Jess were a general proposing a tactic for a far-distant war. She hesitated, about to say something more, then turned back into the suite. Professor Reed had to grab Hawthorn's arm and drag him back into the room.

Jess took up a position behind the credenza. She needed to buy some time. She lifted the flinger and pointed it shakily down the corridor: if she could present a formidable enough threat, it might give the enemy pause, give the police enough time to arrive. Please, let them pause. One shot from the weapon ought to be enough to show Utara that she didn't know how to use it.

VI

Aran stood invincible and felt no fear.

Not that the enemy could see that. The image he presented them was a pitiful sight: a boy, a mere child, hands empty and open in the air.

Cowering before them. No threat at all. Just as well they couldn't see the state of his singing heart, feel his tingling fingers. It should have been *them* feeling intimidated.

There were five of them in all. Too many for him to take on at once. Aran bided his time.

Utara was coiled and calm, a snake ready to strike. Up close, the scar that stitched from the general's chin to his eyebrow stood out as a pale line against the sun-darkened skin. The man carrying the drone — "Rell", Aesk had called him — held it in its case, awkwardly extended in his left hand, a flinger in his right hand aimed too low. Standing beside Rell, Heth was either left-handed or had injured his right as he held his flinger to that side. Garron, with shaved head and a bandolier, stood with the clean-shaven soldier called Rodd, two steps behind the general.

"That's him," Rell said needlessly. "The boy. What do we do with him?"

"He has our cube reader, or else he's hidden it somewhere," said Utara. "Ask him about it. I'm going after the girl. Where is she?"

Aran's cheeks burned. Not worth Utara's attention. To be fair, that was exactly the impression he was trying to give, but it still hurt.

Rell turned his eyes to the ceiling. "Further up," he said.

"When you've secured the pad, follow us up." Utara paused, glancing at Aran. "I think he's going to be smart and cooperate. If so, let him live. Just make sure he doesn't cause us trouble from behind. Rell, with me. The rest of you, don't take long. Remember, quick and quiet."

Aran watched Utara and Rell as they returned to the lift. He didn't blink until the doors were closed. Three left. No chance to take on Utara — not yet. The general wasn't even looking at him as the lift doors slid closed, Aran losing sight of him — and perhaps even more important: the drone. That drone had to be how Utara tracked them here. If he could destroy that, it wouldn't matter how many men Utara brought. They wouldn't find them again.

Rodd, nudged Heth's shoulder. "I say we shoot him. He cut the Captain."

"Let him live, he said," Garron snapped.

"A shot to the knee won't kill him," said Rodd. "Might make him more cooperative."

"Don't shoot me," Aran said, trying to sound frightened. "I'll be good!"

"Aw, he's just a kid," protested Heth.

- *He's just a baby*. Aran felt his face freeze as he recalled Niosk's frequent refrain. *Go on, baby, run back to your daddy*. Don't let your fury show. Let him get a few steps closer. Just a few steps.

Heth lowered his flinger as he advanced towards Aran. "Look at him. He's not going to give us any trouble. Are you?"

"I won't give you any trouble," Aran agreed. For once he didn't care how young his voice sounded. He focussed on the image he was trying to convey: *just a harmless boy. I'll be good*. "I'll show you where I put it."

"Go on then, take him. But hurry up about it," said Garron, glancing over his shoulder; the left lift stood invitingly open.

Quiet, now. Aran took in a slow, deep breath, filling his lungs, as Heth approached, a hand reaching for Aran's shoulder. Compared to training, the man was laughably slow. Against his peers in the Trials, he could beat three opponents in a melee. Just. Against these men, there was no contest. Heth had holstered his weapon. Rodd's flinger was pointed harmlessly at the floor and half of Garron's attention was still on the lift-tubes. There would never be a better time, and Aran flowed into motion.

Within a second he had swayed around Heth's reaching fingers, moving instead for Rodd. *Control the weapon*. By two seconds, he had broken Rodd's nose. In the same motion, striking with his palm he knocked the flinger out of the man's hand and sent it flying along the corridor. Rodd was reeling, falling, but he had not yet hit the floor and Aran was ready for his next target. *Three seconds*.

Garron was four steps away, eyes just starting to widen at the sudden violence. Heth was closer. Aran tucked a heel and went low, taking Heth's legs out from under him. Then it was the simplest thing, as the man fell, to be in *just* the right place. *So simple.* Under the man's descending chin was Aran's left hand, and in Aran's left hand was the big bowie knife that he'd kept at the small of his back.

The sheet of blood that swept over Aran's hand and forearm was hot and shocking and slippery in its sudden vivid red. His training had never included that. Aran lost his grip on yet another weapon, Heth spinning to the floor with his hands grappling for the knife still buried in his throat. The knife had gone deep and the man didn't realise yet that he was dead.

Five seconds.

Too long — long enough for Garron to react. Both Heth and Rodd were on the floor and Aran was too promising a target to refuse, and the bald rebel was firing.

Too fast. The disc spun past Aran's shoulder and punched a hole in the wall behind him. The *zip-tchack* of the flinger seating a new disc seemed to take forever. It takes seconds for the magnetos in a flinger to recharge the capacitors. Seconds were all Aran would need to take the weapon out of Garron's hand, but without his knife the odds had suddenly turned. Rodd was scrambling to his feet, blood streaming down his face from both nostrils as his hands quested for his sword. Garron was using his left hand to steady his flinger. From this short range, it was unlikely that he would miss a second time.

No time to waste. *Have to get upstairs.* But he couldn't achieve anything if he was dead, and he would be dead if Garron got to shoot again; he would be dead if Rodd could bring his sword to bear. He needed that place of stillness, he couldn't find it. *No, respond by instinct.* When he moved, he moved away from the two men.

His fingers quested for Rodd's lost flinger, sitting on the carpet of the corridor. Behind the weapon, the door to the ballroom stood unlocked. One chance, one only; if he missed either target, he was dead. But he didn't miss, scooping up the weapon as he ran past, and the doors, tested earlier to ensure they would open freely, exploded aside under the force of his shoulder.

The ballroom was a vast empty space before him. He'd bought himself seconds, no more.

He could do a lot in a few seconds.

VII

Not aggressive enough.

She hadn't *asked* for this. She didn't want the weapon and she didn't want to be in this corridor, taking cover behind a piece of chintzy furniture, waiting for rebels from another world to try to kill her. But now she was here, she was damned if she was going to let being a mere woman stop her.

Still, it had been a long time since she had shot anything.

Her father had used to take her out rabbiting. Some of her earliest memories were of early mornings in the scrub — creeping through the pre-dawn chill, clutching a .22 almost as tall as she was. Waiting for her father's big hands to fold over hers and help her shoot safely. She had never been very successful, and those rare occasions when she'd managed to hit her quarry had been times of celebration, but killing rabbits had never really been the point.

She had always been better than her little brother; he'd started coming along as soon as he turned eight, under their dad's careful supervision. For a time, Jess had been jealous of the loss of her father's sole attention, but there was always another rabbit and over time she learned an appreciation for the sport. When they came home with a brace of rabbits her mother's wordless disapproval would earn her an encouraging smile from her father, and before long the weight of a weapon in hand came to be a comforting sensation.

It wasn't comforting now.

A rifle had a precision to it that the flinger lacked. With its stubby shape and its square barrel, this felt dangerously imprecise. Like trying to photograph a game of football with a point and shoot camera with no auto-focus and only twelve frames of film.

Eleven.

After Jamie died, her father had never taken her hunting again. Fifteen years. A long time to fall out of practice.

Reed had been true to his word. He had retrieved one large suitcase on wheels, containing what appeared to be half a bookcase worth of texts. Hawthorn also had volunteered his reading material, although he'd taken more convincing before he was willing to sacrifice his half dozen textbooks. Now the credenza was satisfyingly full of paper. The thick reference books and journals didn't entirely fill the credenza but the top shelf was stuffed, and Jess used cushions and pillows to fill out the bottom. Not enough to stop a bullet — or a disc, probably — but it might help slow it and reduce the damage.

Who was she kidding? In a firefight between herself and trained soldiers, she knew where her money would be. All she could hope for was to keep them off balance, delay them long enough. Shoot them in the legs; that would slow them enough. Her rule about not shooting people might be flexible enough to concede that.

Sudden shade in the corridor, near the lifts. She hadn't heard the bell. But now there was definite movement... more than one person down there. She waited for the approach; five seconds; ten. Nobody came into view. Perhaps they were regrouping. The corridor was wide enough for two abreast — if they came at her in a rush she wouldn't be able to hit more than one or two of them.

Even with cover this was starting to seem like a stupid idea.

A flicker of movement, and she almost fired. *Almost*. But the head and shoulders ducked back out of sight before she remembered the simple action of squeezing a trigger and then the moment was past. Just as well, she would have wasted a disc and she didn't have any to spare.

She'd been spotted: the only possible reason for his retreat. Good: at least she wasn't going to shoot a civilian by mistake. The man had been advancing carefully, ready to back off instantly, and that meant he was expecting resistance.

Okay then. She would give him resistance.

They came at her in a rush, two of them rounding the corner together, and for a long second she hesitated, her finger taut on the trigger. *Can't do this. I'm not shooting anyone!* She had a rule... One rebel was on the floor, rolling past the bend in the corridor, on his stomach with a flinger at full stretch. The other man was high and fast and running at her. Shooting at her. Scalpel-sharp metal punched into the credenza, puffs of shredded paper erupting into the air like blood.

Shooting at her. They didn't know her, she could have been an innocent. Bugger that — she *was* an innocent, and they were trying to kill her. Moral questions evaporated. Scraps of paper were fluttering down onto her, and they were trying to kill her, and suddenly it was all very simple.

The trick about shooting rabbits is quick reflexes. You never know quite which direction they're going to bolt when they're flushed; you might only get one chance. Jess found herself thinking about the family dog — Barney — he'd been terrific at flushing the animals from their bolt holes, and she *squeezed* and the flinger bucked in her hand, making a noise like a hose reel coming to full stretch, and a line of distorted air drew a laser-straight path from her hand to the running man's chest.

The force of the disc slamming into his torso flipped the man around and over and he was crashing face-first into the carpet even as Jess ducked back behind the dubious shelter of the credenza. She'd never killed a man before. She could meditate on how she felt about this later. She paused long enough to take a breath, but this was long enough for her to imagine the other man rising from his prone position and closing the distance. Running, it wouldn't take more than a few seconds to reach her cover. She straightened, ready with the flinger.

The other man was on one knee, aiming down the corridor. *Ready for her.* Jess was still bringing her own weapon to aim, and he had the drop on her, and he did not shoot. She had her flinger up and aimed and still he did not shoot. She depressed the trigger and still he did not shoot.

The weapon in her hands remained silent.

What the hell —

She flung herself sideways and down, even as the other rebel finally fired, a disc stitching through the air where she had been a millisecond earlier. She hit the floor with her left shoulder, pins and needles shooting instantly down her left arm before it went numb.

Feet, pounding. She rolled, trying to get her feet under her, as the soldier loomed over her, leaping atop the credenza. His hands were empty, his fingers reaching for her, grappling for her flinger, for her throat.

She tried to get the flinger between them, but the pressure of the man's big hand over hers was too much and the trigger depressed; *now* the weapon fired, a disc punching a hole harmlessly in the ceiling. Plaster rained down on them as the man's other hand grasped at her throat, trying to get leverage to squeeze. Her left arm was nerveless and her attempts to batter his hand away were feeble and useless. Behind him the corridor darkened as another man came around the bend at a run. Or perhaps it was her vision going dark as the air left her lungs.

"Bastard," came a shout behind her, and then Professor Gareth Reed hit Jess's assailant in the face with a saucepan.

The pressure at her throat was gone. The man reeled backwards, clutching his head, and Jess fell back to the carpet, Reed standing over her. Jess was coughing, spots dancing before her eyes, and she barely saw the professor reaching for the flinger on the floor where it had fallen from her nerveless fingers.

Don't, she tried to tell him. *Not working*. But she had no air in her throat and the words wouldn't come out. Reed stood, holding the weapon two-handed. Ignoring the closer soldier, still on his knees with his head in his hands, Reed took aim instead at the red-haired man who had come around the corner, who was now mere steps away.

Reed and Utara fired together.

The Professor's aim was poor and the disc spun harmlessly down the length of the corridor. Utara's aim was truer. The professor let out an explosive *whoof* as the disc propelled him backwards, driving into his sternum square and centre. Jess was spared the look on his face as the force drove him almost double. The flinger dropped from his hands and tumbled into Jess's lap like a benison.

Jess used both heels to piston back into the room as Utara closed the gap between them. The man's face was distorted in rage, the scar on his cheek standing out flushed red, for the one moment she had to see it before she got her hands on the door and swung it closed with as much force as she could muster.

Through the door she heard a muffled shout and she hoped that she had broken the man's fingers.

The hotel door had the kind of latch that allows a guest to secure the room against uninvited service. The door shook as a heavy weight pounded into it. It wouldn't hold long.

Jess burst into the bedroom to find Vi had armed herself with a steak knife from the rudimentary kitchen. In the corner of the room, Doctor Hawthorn stared at her in horror. Jess followed his eyes to the blood running down her right arm, dripping from her fingers. She flexed her fingers and was relieved when they all responded. A flesh wound, then. Her left hand was coming back to life and she welcomed the pain there. Her left hand was her watercolour blocking hand and she would have been badly upset if it were permanently hurt.

"Change of plans," she said. "We're getting out of here."

VIII

He had made a mistake.

What part of 'Never rely upon the enemy to act as you expect' didn't you understand? Drillmaster Warren had drummed the adage into them early on in their tactics classes, but Aran appeared to have forgotten that piece of advice.

The ballroom was a darkened, cavernous space, the fake-wood floor bare from wall to wall. Stacked chairs lurked at the perimeter. Across the chamber, on the left side of the front of the room, a low stage resided, and on the right side of the hall a low-slung grand piano was a dark silhouette.

Aran faced the double doors that served as the room's main entrance. If Rodd and Garron wanted him they would have to come through those doors and find Aran waiting for them. And that was his mistake.

He was relying on the enemy to follow him into the ballroom. But why should they? This room was not an ambush; it was a trap. The enemy had no need to come after him, and the longer he was waiting here for them, the closer they drew to the Empress. Moments stretched into minutes and the certainty that he had trapped himself became too terrible to ignore.

He padded across the floor in silence and laid his ear against the gap between the doors. There was no sound out there, nothing louder than the beating of his own heart. He reached his left hand for the door handle, took a deep breath, raised the flinger —

He paused.

Never rely on the enemy to act as you expect.

Coming into the ballroom, he had turned the tables; he had allowed the enemy to take the lead. *Don't let him come up and cause us trouble,* Utara had said, and surely they wouldn't just leave him free to follow. They were waiting for him.

Time to do something they *weren't* expecting.

The grand piano at the side of the room was on wheels, but it was heavy and tended to swing left; the big instrument didn't want to travel in a straight line. Once Aran got it moving, straining with all his young muscles, it rolled freely enough and he put his attention towards directing it. On the hard dance floor it picked up momentum and Aran was barely able to keep it from striking the doorframe rather than the doors themselves. A last heave with his shoulder and the piano veered right, striking the double doors centre-on. Even as it struck Aran had his flinger in hand, shifting his weight to vault over the instrument as the doors burst apart in shattered wooden panels.

He made it no further before a wall of superheated air blasted him off his feet.

The explosion could have shredded him, but the piano took most of the force and sheltered him from the worst of the concussion. The world turned into a swirling haze of red and black. Aran was flung back into the room, a chaos of wood and steel and ivory swirling around him from the disintegrating piano, high-strung metal wires lashing the room like an enraged octopus. One strand struck Aran across the side of his head and the unearthly jangle of the piano disappeared under the sudden high ringing of bells.

He was seeing double; the bright doorway was two overlapping rectangles. Aran was on his back, partially covered by a wood panel that had been part of the piano's frame. His hand was empty, the flinger lost. His foot was a blaze of wrenching agony, trapped somewhere under the detritus. Desperately, Aran felt around himself, trying to recover his weapon.

Before he could move to free himself, the doorway darkened. A man leapt inside, clambering over the remains of the piano. Rodd — the rebel's nose still streaming blood, red dripping from his chin. The doorway was filled with streamers of smoke, uneven wood and mangled iron underfoot, and Rodd's shape became clearer as he took two more steps forward, testing his footing with each advance. Now he was within a metre, his front foot putting weight on the panel that pinned Aran. Rodd grinned a bloody smile as he brought the flinger up.

Aran ignored the scream of pain from his foot, ignored the ringing in his ears, as he lurched off the floor, the wooden panel shifting, his enemy stumbling as his footing dipped. Aran went at him, tasting blood in his mouth from his bitten tongue, seeing red in the swirling smoke, and he let forth a keening scream of rage.

Rodd froze, sudden panic on his face. An accountant before enlisting in Harke's army, or maybe a vacuum cleaner salesman or a teacher. Not a soldier. Faced with pure violence he tried to retreat but Aran didn't let him, closing the distance, a loop of piano wire in his fist as his only weapon.

The flinger was still thrust forward, and Aran wrapped the piano wire around Rodd's hand, pulling down and to the side. Rodd went to his knees as his footing failed him, the wood shifting under them again. Aran skirted the man, coming up behind him; brought the wire up to the man's throat and pulled it taut. Rodd fought him, using his trapped hand to try to pull the wire away, but Aran planted a foot on his back and used it for leverage, and held the pressure until Rodd stopped struggling. Even then he held, reluctant to let go too soon.

Finally Aran let wire drop, allowing Rodd to slump. He reached down to wrench the flinger free of the dead soldier's slack fingers.

He was out of breath, his foot was a blaze of agony — but it could bear his weight. He would make it bear his weight. The Empress was upstairs and Utara was on his way.

Aran flung himself out through the broken doors, staying low, rolling across the carpet, Rodd's flinger in one hand and Heth's at his belt. The corridor was empty but for Heth's body; Garron had gone. Following Utara upstairs, probably.

His left hand was on fire, his right foot blazing with every step, his ribs ached and his hearing hadn't returned. The side of his face was warm and wet. He ignored it all as he came to his feet. He unconsciously used a hand to wipe at his ear, blood spattering the carpet, as he ran, limping, for the stairwell.

IX

"A lot of hotels are framed with partition doorways," Jess said. "Put in a sheet of plaster, you've got separate rooms. Put in a door and they're connected. Design flexibility." She tapped her knuckles on the bedroom wall as she moved along it, noting the dull reverberation when she met the frame behind the plaster. "Here," she said, stopping. Near the bedroom's doorway. "Just plaster. We can knock out a hole to the next room."

Doctor Hawthorn was deathly pale. "What are you? A hotel manager? I thought you were a student."

Jess shook her head. "I design buildings," she said. "Now shut up and do as I say. Bash a hole in this wall."

Hawthorn glanced at the iron in his hand. Old, heavy and solid, it would make a formidable weapon. "This can't be happening," he said miserably as he swung the implement at the wall. The only effect he had on the wall was to scar the paint.

"You're trying to break it, not flatten it," Jess snapped. She pulled the flinger from her belt and turned for the doorway. "Vi, you're in charge. That's our way out."

Another heavy thud shook the room's front door as she returned to the lounge area. The door's privacy clasp bent further and the door was already splintering around the handle. It wasn't going to last. *Where the hell are those police?* She'd spent most of the past few days trying to avoid the police; now, when she wanted them, they were staying at a distance, until they were too late.

Jess took up a position behind the couch. It wouldn't provide much shelter but the cover might give her a shot or two before they found her. She waited, listening to the pounding behind her as Hawthorn worked on the wall, and in front of her as Utara worked on the door. She glanced at the big windows, for a second wondering if they could climb for escape, but dismissed that thought as quickly as it had arrived.

Another pounding impact, and the door clasp broke free of the wall, the door sagging inwards, held only by its latch. Light from the corridor leaked through where the door didn't meet the frame near the carpet. One more strike and they would be inside. She would get one shot, one chance. Convince them to keep their distance, delay them, just long enough.

But the final assault didn't come. *That's right. Take your time. Take as long as you need.*

The light around the malformed door shifted: someone standing right outside. Jess sighted along the stubby rectangle of the flinger, breathing deeply and slowly, her hands steady. The doorway was perhaps three metres away — an easy shot even with this weapon. Could she hit him in the leg? From this distance, she thought so. She hoped so; she had already broken her record for most people murdered in a single day.

Through the gap at the base of the door popped a thin chrome tube.

It looked like no grenade she'd ever seen but there was nothing else it could be. "Fuck," she said, and dropped below the couch as the room exploded into a maelstrom.

No flame or heat, just a pounding concussion that sprayed fragments of metal across the room. The couch bashed back into her knees as the glass coffee table, the flat screen television and the writing desk all disintegrated, the walls around the living area suddenly peppered with holes. The floor-to-ceiling window frosted white for an instant before it exploded outwards; at this height the air outside was cold and it gusted around the room. Something sparked in the ruins of the television and smoke began leaking.

Jess had barely a moment to draw a breath of suddenly cold air before the door to the room was erupting inwards and the enemy were making a final assault. Bald, narrow-faced and furious, the man's eyes fixed on her as he stepped through the doorway. Instantly he leapt at her, his sword rising over his shoulder as he came.

Jess raised the flinger and shot at him, but everything was moving too fast; she didn't even see where the disc went. She dropped the weapon as her assailant's sword split the air in front of her. In panicked instinct she thrust a heavy cushion from the couch at him, an improvised shield, but a downwards slash of the sword split it in two, wisps of cotton puffing into the air and blowing in the cold wind from the shattered window.

Jess stumbled back from him, barely avoiding another strike, and then the ruins of the coffee table met the back of her thighs and she toppled backwards. The sword flashed over her head as she fell onto carpet littered with shards of glass, a myriad of sudden stabbing pains flaring at her back. She ignored the lacerations as she rolled, barely avoiding being skewered as her attacker stabbed downward at her. Another man was entering the room but she couldn't spare any attention, she was focussed on staying alive for the next five seconds. Kicking at the twisted metal of the coffee table's frame, she forced her attacker to step backwards or take its impact on his shins. Jess rolled again, cutting her hands open on the carpet as she came back to her feet.

The flinger was back in her hand. She tried to steady the weapon as the man with the sword rushed back at her. Sharp metal slashed at her, and pure reflex pushed her backwards out of range. Again her flinger discharged; the disc spun a tunnel through the air across the room and punched through the opposite wall. The red-haired man who had entered behind her attacker was now mere feet from the bedroom, and he faltered in his stride, shooting his gaze in her direction; the disc had missed him by a handsbreadth. Jess couldn't spare him her attention.

Back she retreated, and back again, each time the tip of the sword missing her by smaller increments. And then there was nowhere else to go. At her heels yawned the open window, cold breeze plucking at her cotton sleeves and cooling the fire of her glass-studded shoulder-blades, and the thin soldier grinned viciously, raising the sword high overhead for the final blow which she could not evade.

Jess flung her right hand forward in desperation, and her opponent forgot his killing strike as four dollars and sixty-five cents in coin pelted him in the face; reflex brought his hands together at his face, too slow to block the flying metal. And Jess lunged forward, grabbed the bandolier slung over his shoulder, and *heaved*. She let herself fall backwards to the floor as she pulled, and the man came forward with her, unbalanced and blinded. With an inevitable gracelessness he stumbled two more steps forward, and then he was over the edge. At the last moment understanding his situation he grabbed at Jess, questing fingers brushing the front of her t-shirt, and then he was falling.

Jess watched him all the way down.

It took her a moment to recover her breath, but a moment was all she could spare. With the glass of the window gone, the sounds of the city at night were audible; she could hear the approach of sirens. They were close and getting closer, but they would be too late. Reclaiming the flinger from the floor, she stepped into the bedroom.

Redemption

I

Doctor Hawthorn, kneeling by the bed, hands and forehead flat on the bedspread in surrender. Jess could hardly blame him; he was a civilian, a non-combatant. *So what am I?*

In the far corner of the room, in the cramped space between the bed and a small occasional table, stood Vi. She held the kitchen knife in front of her, but it was a small and futile gesture.

Jess glanced at the wall. They'd been unsuccessful in carving a passage into the next room; the plaster sagged in a ragged patch but the wall on the other side of the partition was intact.

Between Jess and Vi stood Utara. He held his flinger steady and level, directed at Vi's chest, but he turned his head to face Jess as she entered. Close up, he was classically attractive; a square jaw that might in kinder light have been called "chiseled", piercing blue eyes, red hair tending to brown. The scar across his cheek added character.

"I assume Garron will not be joining us," Utara said. His voice was a rich baritone, strongly accented.

Jess hesitated, but the words had already come to mind. "He left the building."

"A pity. He was not a clever man, and he had an excessive fondness for his toys, but he was loyal. I value that. You are causing me a great deal of trouble."

"Sorry not sorry," said Jess. "I didn't ask to be a part of this. I'm not involved in your little war. But Vi's just a child. I can't just let you shoot her. I — if you do, I'll shoot you next." She hoped he didn't hear the hesitation that declared it a lie. She had already killed — No more. She didn't think she could pull the trigger again.

"If I wanted to shoot her," Utara pointed out, "I would have done so already. I'm supposed to bring the Empress back to Zama — alive, if possible. Whilst I would take a great deal of pleasure from killing her, I have a reputation for success." He raised an eyebrow. "Besides, there is something I want more than her head and I'm willing to be reasonable. But if she continues being obstructive, I *will* shoot her."

"Then I'll shoot you," said Jess. "Perhaps you'd better come up with a plan B."

"I have another eight men," Utara said. "They're coming now. When they join us, I won't stand in their way. You've killed two of their friends. Maybe *you* require a 'plan B'. You should leave. I won't stop you."

Vi interrupted him. "You have fewer than you think. Aran may be young, but he is a trained Guard. Your men may have underestimated him."

"I arrived here with ten men. I can spare a few," Utara said. "Now I have the best bargaining chip available; I have you. All I want is the data pad your boy stole from my engineer."

"I'm perfectly willing to *trade* it back to you," said Vi. "In return for your tracker. You say you want your data pad more than you want me? Prove it."

Utara shook his head. "You bore me. Do you think that toy will scare me? Lord Harke asked for you alive. He didn't specify intact. Maybe I'll cut off your hands. Then you won't cause any trouble."

Jess felt the need to remind him of her presence. "I *will* shoot you."

His head snapped around to glare at her. "Then stop talking about it and just *do* it. You've had plenty of opportunities. You can kill me if you want, but my last reaction will be to shoot your little Empress in the heart. Or we can stand here and banter until my men arrive behind you." His eyes focused over her shoulder and he gave a tiny nod.

It was the oldest trick in the book, but old tricks still work because a human can't fight against a million years of evolution. Before she could think to stop herself, Jess turned her head.

The doorway stood empty. Of course. The distraction fooled her for no more than a second, but that was all Utara needed. By the time her head was turning back towards him, he was upon her.

She tried to react. Brought the flinger up where she'd let it droop, shifted her weight, ready to dodge. But her reactions were slowed by her injuries, the pain that accompanied every movement, and before she could squeeze the trigger Utara knocked her hand aside. For a fraction of a second she watched his fist coming, noting the details — the callouses on the knuckles from bar fights, the veins making furrows on the skin — and then it drove into her jaw and the world flashed white. Another second and Utara kicked her in the stomach hard enough to lift her off the floor. The breath was driven from her lungs and her legs went out from under her as she collapsed in the doorway.

The flinger was still in her hand. Useless. Retching for breath, it was all she could do to keep her eyes open as Vi threw herself at Utara's unguarded back. As she came she lifted the knife. But Utara was already turning, warned by some instinct, his reactions faster than Jess's had been. Casually Utara swept the girl's knife aside, his big hand closing over her fingers. He spread his left hand over Vi's face and pushed her backwards and onto the bed. Vi screamed as her fingers bent, and then she was on her back, clutching her right hand to herself as Utara tossed the knife aside.

The knife skittered across the carpet and came to rest next to Doctor Hawthorn's knees. Utara didn't even glance at the sociologist, instead turning back towards Jess in the doorway. Hope sprang to life... flared, and died. Doctor Hawthorn didn't move except to close his eyes.

Jess could hardly blame him, but in that moment she hated him anyway.

With the last of her strength, she managed to get her left hand under herself, started trying to stand. Utara took three strides towards her; with his toe he ground the flinger to the floor, her fingers pinned underneath the weapon. With a flick of his boot he sent the firearm skittering through the doorway.

The pain from her fingers felt distant, less important than a sense of horror as Utara smiled gently and again drove a boot into her side. It hardly mattered any more; she couldn't have resisted him to save her life. She could only endure as he kicked her again, and once more.

After what seemed like an eternity but was surely only moments, the beating stopped. Jess tried to curl into a ball, wrapping herself around the hot pain in her side, but then there was a strong hand at her throat, lifting her. *God, he's strong!* Utara lifted her and drove her backwards into the doorjamb, using his weight to hold her there.

In his other hand he held the knife, and he waggled it in her face as he stared at her. From this distance there was no mistaking the disinterest in his cold blue eyes; the uncaring of ice. If he had ever seemed attractive, a close look at those eyes would have dispelled the illusion.

"Athara was annexed by the Empire three hundred years ago," Utara said. "My homeland. My people. We were the last to bow."

Jess would have responded but her throat was a lake of fire and she could barely breathe past Utara's hand. All she could do was stare at the knife as it weaved back and forth.

"When my homeland was absorbed by the Empire, the sacred traditions of my people were outlawed. The Empire disbanded our slave workforce, abolished our currency, outlawed our language. They did everything in their power to destroy our culture, our heritage. Three hundred years, but some of us remember the old ways."

Utara brought the knife forward until she could no longer see it, but she could feel its sharp point on her forehead. For a second Jess took one hand away from her throat, from clawing at Utara's hand, but without its support her breath was completely cut off and she had to bring it back.

Utara grinned. The knife moved, tracing a path across her brow.

"It's a tradition stretching back a thousand years. Each clan's slaves are branded with a mark of ownership. My family's mark starts *here*, and runs across the forehead and down the cheek. Just like this."

Against the fire in her side, at her throat, Jess barely felt it, barely registered it until blood started leaking into her right eye, filtering through her eyelashes. She could do nothing but wait for it to end.

"I gave you a chance to leave," Utara said. "I'm glad you stayed. Perhaps you've realised by now that I don't care about the boy. I don't care about my squad. The girl can live or die, it's no matter to me. I promised to deliver her alive, but I'll bring her head home in a box if I need to. But you've wasted my time. And that makes me angry." He glanced out the door towards the shattered living room. "I only wish I could take the time to do this properly, but I believe those sirens indicate that whatever passes for law is on its way."

Her vision was blurred around the edges. She was moments away from losing consciousness, but Utara had other intentions for her. Abruptly he let her go, and she slid down the doorway to sit on the floor. Her breath wheezed as she found herself once again able to find air.

Utara turned the knife over in his hands. "I marked you with this. Now I can't use it to end you. Tradition. No matter." He stepped over her outstretched legs, into the living room. He scooped up Jess's discarded flinger and examined it. "Yes, this will do."

"Don't," said Vi. "Please don't."

"I'm done listening to you, Empress." He lifted the stubby weapon until it filled Jess's vision.

Jess tried to get her hands under her, but it was too much energy and she couldn't raise herself.

"You're mine now," said Utara.

There was the *thunk* of metal meeting bone.

Utara lurched, his eyes rolling upwards, and he fell. The flinger tumbled from his hands.

Behind him, standing in the living room surrounded by broken glass and metal, stood the very last person Jess would have expected to see. In his hand glinted a metal pole; a fragment of the frame of the destroyed coffee table. His eyes were wild with fear and disbelief. It was impossible — ludicrous. She must be dreaming. Or her injuries had given her concussion, delusions.

"What the *hell* have you gotten yourself into?" demanded Mark McTiernan.

II

"Yes, this will do."

Vi nursed her fingers against her chest. Apart from the bruises there she was unharmed, and yet everything was lost. In a thousand years of lifetimes, none of the Empresses had come so close to ruin, or if they had, their experience eluded her now.

Jess was slumped in the doorway, legs splayed, her head lolling, blood running from the ugly weal across her forehead, down her cheek and dripping from her chin. Her breaths came in ragged gasps. Utara turned the flinger over in his hands and nodded.

Aran was lost somewhere in the building, facing impossible odds, probably dead. Hareth Rede was dead in the corridor, his tenuous connection to her mother unexplored, his salvific potential vanished almost as soon as they'd found him. In moments, Jess would be dead too. And it was Vi who had brought them all here, gathered them together to this end.

"Don't —" Vi said. There was nothing else she could do, no act of heroism remaining to her. Utara wasn't lying when he promised to maul her. The light in his eyes as he marked Jess showed him for what he was: he would do it, cripple her, and smile as he did it. Vi had no weapon, no power, no help beyond her voice. There was no hope.

And then there was.

Movement — a shadow, a person in the room behind Utara's back. Vi blinked, desperate not to stare. Utara wasn't looking at her, focussed instead on pointing the flinger at Jess's face, but he'd shown his preternatural senses before. She needed to keep his attention. But she had no words. Generations of Empresses in her head and none of them could give her the words to change this monster's mind. Vi did the best she could. "Please, don't."

Utara lifted his eyes to meet her. "I'm done listening to you, Empress." He grinned, a promise that said *you're next on my list.*

Jess shifted her weight and Utara looked back down at her. "You're mine now," he said, and lifted the flinger, and behind him the stranger swung the metal pole he was clutching. It was a decent blow, enough to stun at least, and Utara collapsed like a felled tree.

The bent pole tumbled from the stranger's hands and bounced on the carpet. The man stood in the doorway and he looked, not at Vi, but at Jess crumpled on the floor. "What the *hell* have you gotten yourself into?"

Jess seemed to want to answer, but her strangled croak was unintelligible. Then, for a moment that stretched out into what felt like years, there was quiet: the man in the doorway, Jess forcing the air in and out of her lungs, Hawthorn with his face buried in the duvet as if in hopes he could go unnoticed.

Vi levered herself off the bed, straightened her shoulders and put on her best command voice. She ignored her stinging fingers and nodded at the door. "The corridor is clear?"

"I don't know," said the newcomer, sounding manic. "Do dead people count?"

"Corpses are a problem for tomorrow." She hooked her hands under Jess's armpits and tried to lift, but the woman was too heavy. The newcomer hastened forward to take an arm and together they got her to her feet.

Blood dripping from her hands, purpling bruises on her throat and jaw, Jess could barely stand on her own. Vi glanced at the stranger, their saviour. "Forgive my bluntness, but who are you?"

"Mark." His eyes danced about the room, wide enough to show white around the irises. "Mark McTiernan."

He was a tall man, lean and very fit, but he was one sharp shock away from dissolving into panic. He needed a task to keep him occupied, keep him moving, and she had just the thing. "Mark, you need to help her. Her name is Jess. We need your help to get out."

"Who *are* you people?" The question came, not from Mark, but from the thin scholar at the bed. Doctor Hawthorn climbed to his feet, carefully keeping his eyes averted from the crumpled man in the corner.

"There are some questions," Vi said, "where it is safer not to know the answers."

Jess was starting to regain, if not her strength, at least her stubbornness; she pulled away from Vi's grasp, pushed away Mark McTiernan's hands under her elbow, stood on her own. She swayed as she turned to face Hawthorn. Her voice came out as a rough rasp. "The police will... questions. Tell them... don't know anything."

"I *don't* know anything," complained Hawthorn. "If anyone asks I slept through the whole thing." He paused, took a deep breath. "Wait. I can make some guesses. Before you go, take this."

Vi waited with growing impatience as the lecturer rooted through a suitcase beside the bed. The seconds stretched out, and she was on the verge of turning on her heel when Hawthorn turned back. In his hand he proffered a slim paperback.

"What's this?" Jess asked as she received the gift.

"He didn't ask you to read it? That would be a first. It's Professor Reed's only foray into fiction... if it *is* fiction. I'm not sure what I think any more." To Jess's uncomprehending glare, he added, "Read it, you'll understand."

"We must leave," said Vi. "Now."

She didn't wait for them, trusting Jess to follow. She led the way back out into the corridor, ready with Jess's flinger in case any more of Utara's men had followed him up the stairs. In a long succession of lifetimes she had rarely laid hands on such a weapon and never fired one in anger, but Jess was currently incapable.

The corridor was as clear as Mark had promised. Vi paused in the doorway and looked down at the body of Hareth Rede. The old man's eyes were open and glazed, his body sitting at the base of the wall upright and his legs akimbo. If you ignored the blood that had poured down his front he could almost have been resting.

The revelations of his past... and what it meant for her... she would think about later. They could do nothing for him now. He could do nothing for them now.

Further down the corridor, one of Utara's men lay dead on the floor; he had crawled a few feet from where he first went down, but he was dead now.

Beside his outstretched hand a carry-case lay on the floor. Vi took a sharp breath. "Wait." She flipped the catches and lifted the lid. Inside, the sensor drone was matt black and ugly and inert.

Outside the sirens were nearing, but she needed to take the time for this. The dead man still clutched a flinger, another seven or eight discs remaining in the cartridge. She peeled away his fingers, then stood over the drone in its case. The first disc carved through the device like a knife through cake, thin aluminium sheeting and cabling and magnetos alike crumbling. She followed with another shot. And another. Until the flinger vibrated in her hand, all its ammunition spent, and the drone was a smoking tangle of metal.

Utara's forces were decimated, the general himself was unconscious or dead upstairs, the hotel would shortly be crawling with local authorities, and now the enemy's sensor drone was destroyed. Vi allowed herself a thin smile, but only for a second. "We must find Aran."

They found him in the stairwell; she almost shot him by accident as he rounded a bend on the stairs below them. Even Jess was taken aback and Mark came close to flight when they saw Aran's condition. Aran was a red revenant — splashed and coated in grue from his hairline to his boots. His face was mottled with lines of brown, like warpaint, but his teeth were brilliant white as he grinned. Over his shoulders stood the crossed pommels of two swords strapped to his back and multiple flingers dotted his belt.

"For God's sake," Jess rasped, "we can't go anywhere with you looking like that. People will *notice*."

"That is not our concern today," said Vi. "We are not out of danger yet." Below them, the lobby awaited. Aran had warned them of Utara's troops covering the exits. *There'll be more work yet to do.*

They paused at the first floor landing and waited for Aran to retrieve his discarded bag. When he returned, shrugging his reclaimed backpack onto his shoulder, he looked disappointed. Below them the lobby was empty of foes. Perhaps they'd been driven away by the approaching sirens. There was little enough time for Vi's group to escape; after surviving Utara's assault, it would be bitterly ironic to be captured by the police now. As Vi led them out of the stairwell on the ground, red and blue lights were starting to wash across the marble floor, police cars gathering in the driveway like sharks. It could only be moments before the lobby flooded with uniforms.

As they stepped out of the stairwell, Vi brought them to a sudden halt. If she was startled to see him, the man before them was even more so; the tall bald soldier was jogging towards the lifts, his boots ringing on the floor as he stumbled to a halt. *Captain Aesk.* For a long moment, their eyes met, frozen in awkward stillness. Beside her, she sensed Aran belatedly lifting his own weapon.

"Lower your weapon, Captain," she told him, her voice low with urgency. "There's been enough killing."

Slowly, the Captain lowered his half-raised flinger. His eyes ranged over their group as he slowly relaxed his stance. "You think so?"

"Let me kill him," Aran said. "You promised."

Yes, she had promised. But glancing across at their new helper, this 'Mark', she hesitated. She'd seen that expression before: the look of a man on the edge of breaking. An act of violence in front of him might be enough to push him over the edge, and if he left them she didn't think she and Aran would be strong enough to keep Jess upright.

"If he takes one step in our direction you may kill him," she said, hoping that would be enough to hold Aran back. "Captain, your general is upstairs. Do you hear those sirens? Leave him. Go home."

"I can't leave my men," Aesk said. "Even him."

"You won't like what you find. This is over. We're going now. I recommend you do the same."

Captain Aesk stayed carefully still, just his eyes following them as she led her little group around the reception desk and through the doorway into the administrative area. Only once he was well out of sight did Aran relax his taut grip on his flinger, and he fell to the rear in case the Captain should change his mind and come after them. Vi was confident that he would not.

There was a maze of corridors and rooms behind the reception desk, chambers full of arcane machinery whose purpose she couldn't guess, but entirely bereft of staff. Utara's men had been thorough; they encountered two more hotel employees as they explored: dead. Murdered in a war they didn't even know was being waged.

They found a door at the rear of the kitchens unlocked and unguarded, flanked only by garbage skips and a stench. No police here, and none of Utara's men lying in wait. As they stepped out into the night air, Mark stepped forward as if to take the lead. "I have a car," he said.

Jess used a strip of cloth she tore off the bottom of her shirt to wipe ineffectively at Aran's face, and from the backpack he carried they rescued a lightweight jacket to hide the worst of his appearance. They needn't have bothered; in the early hours of the morning, Melbourne had finally gone to sleep and they made it to Mark's car without incident.

Red and blue lights were spreading like a cancer, squad cars finally pulling up to the rear of the hotel. They left the commotion behind and drove into the night.

III

She was tired. God, she was *so* tired. Slumping in the bucket seats of Mark's sports car, Jess could just about put her head back and close her eyes and drift. But when she reclined into its embrace her back and shoulders screamed murder at her from a thousand cuts and glass splinters, drowning out the cacophony of hurt from her hands and her side and her face until she leaned forward again to relieve that specific pain.

Mark drove them east on St Kilda Road. There were faster roads and highways out of Melbourne, but they were tolled, with cameras standing sentinel. Staying resolutely below the speed limit on public roads reduced the chance of being quickly traced by the authorities. Earlier in the day she had been surprised to remain at liberty; she'd almost begun to wonder if the police were actively seeking them at all. Once they saw the footage from the hotel cameras, they would most definitely start.

In the quiet of the car, Queens of the Stone Age sang about keeping secrets. Trying to keep up with the 20-something cool kids in his agency Mark made a point of listening to the latest popular music, but he couldn't stand the music so he kept the volume down to relegate them to background atmospherics.

They had left the CBD and its sirens far behind them when Jess turned her head to look at her husband, his knuckles white with tension on the steering wheel. "How did you know where to find me?"

The depth of his concern and confusion was evidenced by his frequent sidelong glances, but showing unexpected restraint he had not pressed her for answers to his many questions. "Your mother called me. You know, if you want to keep your destination a secret, don't ask your mother to buy the tickets."

Jess had to swallow twice before she could get her next question out. "Why?"

"Why shouldn't you ask your mother? Or why did she call me? Well, that woman has never kept a secret in her life. You know that. And she called me because she thought you might need help and I might be able to give it." He paused, and his voice was softer when he added, "And for some reason she likes me."

"I asked her not to tell the police."

"She didn't tell the police. She told me. And it's a good thing she did. It wasn't hard to find out when and where the bus was coming in and I was able to follow you... and your *posse*... easy as."

"But how did you get into the hotel? They were watching the exits."

"Nuh-uh, my turn now. I've answered a question, now I get to ask one. Just one question, but it's a beauty. What in the name of God have you gotten yourself mixed up in here?"

"You wouldn't believe me if I told you," Jess said, turning her face back to the windscreen.

He appeared to consider this for a moment. "I just hit a man with a gun over the head with a piece of furniture. I had to walk over corpses to get to you. I have two kids in the back seat of my Aston Martin bleeding on the leather. One of them looks like the son of Jack the Ripper. I'm trying to avoid being caught by the police, who seem to think that you're caught up in some kind of interstate racket. I *already* don't believe you, so go ahead and try me."

Jess closed her eyes for a moment. Where to start? How much to tell him? He didn't deserve her time or her respect; she was done with him. But then again, he had just saved her life.

"It started after you hit me," she said after a moment, deliberately vindictive. "You might have noticed I packed my things and left you."

In the dark of the car's interior she couldn't clearly make out his face; it could have been contrition or anger. His words supported the former. "You had every right."

She ignored the olive branch. "I was headed back to Perth and I stopped in at the Yallara Roadhouse. You remember it — it's still Bruce and Dorothy there, carrying on, *happily married*. I was just trying to refuel. But while I was there, we saw these two kids in the desert."

She found herself telling him the story from beginning to end. Talking in the darkened car, Mark occasionally providing an encouraging prompt, seemed to help her gain some distance from it. Describing the story made it feel like a narrative that had happened to someone else. Occasionally she would forget a point and she found herself jumping back to make sure it was clear.

She told him about the roadhouse, rescuing the children, the threat to Bruce and Dot, their eventual departure from the roadhouse leaving the owners behind bound but unharmed. The surreal chase across the desert. Ivan's assistance. She didn't neglect to give credit where it was due. "Aran — the boy back there — he attacked the biggest guy I've ever seen and gave us the distraction we needed."

"Now do you understand why I wanted girls?" Mark said. He meant it as a joke, to lighten the tone, but it hit too close to home, tweaked nerves that Jess hardly realised she still had. *They're not your kids.* Jess had never felt less like laughing.

Still, she didn't cease with the story, telling him about the Fixer and their escape from Port Augusta.

"Wait, *the* Jacob Elliot? Elliot Superconductors Jacob Elliot? The richest bloody man in Australia Jacob Elliot? The union-bosses-are-my-friends-since-their-knees-healed Jacob Elliot? You're kidding."

"*That* Jacob Elliot," agreed Jess. "Not kidding. We really met him. And he's really from another planet."

At this time of night, traffic on the wide highway was sparse, and as she talked, as the car rolled smoothly towards the suburbs, Jess glanced occasionally at the rearview mirror. Vi sat quiet and still in the rear seat;

she had seemed just shy of catatonic since stepping over the body of Hareth Rede in the hallway. Jess could sympathise; they now had no clear destination, no mission, no idea what to do next. The girl had pinned her hopes on Hareth Rede being able to help her as her mother had promised, and now he was dead and falling ever further behind them. Jess didn't have any ideas of how to help the girl, so she gave her the space and concentrated on getting the details right for Mark.

As she came to the end of her tale, describing the battle in the hotel until the point of Mark's arrival, she wondered if Mark would object, would suggest that she was crazy or lying. She almost hoped he would. It would make things simpler. But he drove in silence for a minute, before taking a deep breath. "That's a lot to take in," he said. "This is... this is huge. I'm sorry, I'm finding it difficult to wrap my head around it all. I mean, look at you... you're handling this way better than I ever would." He shook his head again. "You were always the adventurous one."

"Adventurous?" It was not a word Jess would have used to describe herself, but Mark was shaking his head.

"You're the one who threw her old life aside to come with me back to Melbourne," he said. "All your friends and family, your job, your hobbies..."

"I was working at Safeway," she said sourly, but she couldn't help smiling.

"So what do you want to do now?" Mark asked. "We need to talk to the police. Make them understand. Come home with me, they'll be watching the house."

Jess glanced back at Vi; the girl didn't make any response. Reluctantly Jess shook her head. "No police. We need to lay low for a while until we can get our bearings. And Aran's hurt; we need to look after him." Once out of the hotel, as it became evident they would not be confronted or chased, it had not taken many steps before the boy's many hurts became evident to them; his injured foot, his bleeding hand, his many new bruises to layer atop the old. Now he slumped against the seatbelts in the rear of Mark's car, almost dozing, as always unable to understand the conversation in English in the front seat.

"You're not looking crash hot yourself," Mark said. "I mean, you're always hot. But frankly, you're a mess."

Jess had to agree. Her back was a hundred little agonies against the upholstery, her throat was sore and hot, her hands stung in her lap where she held them. Her whole body ached. "I don't have any money," she said reluctantly. "You'll have to pay for a motel."

"I can do better than that," said Mark.

IV

Night had been banished from the Hotel Ulupna. Flooded with brilliant white from floodlights set up in the circular drive, the hotel was an island of white in a sea of blue and red.

Burgess stood on the edge of the lake of light and scratched at his head as he surveyed the chaotic movements of the crowd of officers. The triple-zero call had brought the locals on site before the professionals were even aware of the incursion. Now police thronged the concrete field in front of the hotel, barred from the building by the forensics teams who were already inside. A particularly dense knot of law enforcement clustered around the point where a victim had landed, although after a fall from twelve stories up the description of 'body' might have been optimistic.

This was an almighty balls-up and cleaning it all up was going to be a royal headache.

Williams approached from the left of the plaza. Burgess turned to meet him. "So?"

"The local in charge is Superintendent Kelly May. She's agreed to do what she can to keep her men back and pull forensics out as soon as they've finished. But that's going to take a while, there's incidents on at least three different floors."

"At least that's something," said Burgess. "We need to clear some of these guys out. Too many eyes. I've called for a team." Williams nodded; this mess was way too big for two men to sanitise. "They should be here in five."

Williams turned to stare at the hotel. "At least a dozen casualties. Do you think they've gone hot? What do you reckon this was about?"

Burgess shook his head. "Has to be something internal. The family in P-A were nobodies — in the wrong place at the wrong time. This must be the same perps. What we have here is a hit team."

"Yeah, but are they after one of theirs, or one of ours?"

"I'll give you two guesses."

"Fugitive situation?"

"Could be. I'd love to know who they're chasing."

"It's looking like a couple of the vics might be ours," said Williams. "Whoever they're chasing might have given them a bloody nose. Do you reckon they got them or is it still on?"

"Not going to speculate," said Burgess. "Here's the team."

They arrived in two civilian cars, both blue Toyota Priuses, gliding almost silently to a halt on the edge of the floodlit area. They parked to block off the driveway into the hotel. Any visitors unlucky enough to be returning to the hotel in the early hours of Tuesday morning were going to require negotiation skills.

The five men gathered around Burgess and Williams, standing with an easy freedom that could instantly turn into action. Burgess addressed them. "Sorry to drag you out at this hour," he said. "But we have to move fast. There's been a major incursion here. As you can see, the locals got here first; we're working with them and they'll get out of our way. Details still unclear, but it looks like at least a half dozen intruders went into the hotel and only three or four came out. It was all late at night and they didn't leave any witnesses." Which made his job easier, but wasn't so lucky for the civilian bystanders.

"It's a mess inside. Property damage, civilian victims, multiple EM discharges. I want everything catalogued and cleaned. I want all witnesses collared — that means knocking on doors, gentlemen. It's the middle of the night so they'll be off balance, don't go soft on them. I want IDs on all the vics. We're going to check off every name on the register until we can place every person on the list. That's a lot of work and I want it all done and dusted, and the site cleared, before dawn. That's at five-forty this morning, which gives us less than five hours. Let's get to it, gentlemen."

Moving in a ragged chevron, the seven of them advanced on the command post that Superintendent May had set up. The Super was alert, her uniform immaculate despite the hour; the men around her were dishevelled and frayed and clearly unhappy to be working, but Kelly May exuded an air of control and when the police moved into her radius they moved with new purpose and energy. Important to get her on side; if she chose to become obstructive she could be a real hassle. Burgess plastered a fake smile on his face as he approached, his hand extended.

"Superintendent May? I'm Brad Burgess. You've met my colleague."

"You're the feds," said Superintendent May. "You want to take over?"

"We want to work with you," said Burgess, stressing the preposition. "You've done a lot of good work very quickly and we don't want to step on your toes. We do need to go in and start doing our thing as quickly as possible. How are forensics going?"

"We could be here a week," said May. "Although somehow I don't think you're going to give us that long."

"My people have some special skills that may assist," said Burgess. "You get to keep all your data, we just want to share." Someone else would have to face her wrath when they confiscated the evidence later, but for now he was empowered to promise whatever he needed to secure her cooperation. "We'd like to clear some of these guys from the courtyard. I'm sure your men won't be unhappy to be sent home. Keep a dozen at most, to control the media when they get wind, to control the site." Frankly he was surprised the media weren't already all over it. A lot of investigative reporters were on holiday in early January; thank God for small mercies.

"I guess you're the boss," said May.

They organised lanyards with special badges for the team so the forensics guys inside would know to cooperate. As the men entered the hotel Burgess and Williams retreated to the side of the courtyard.

"A giant pile of trouble, the Director said." Williams lit up a foul-smelling cigarette. "He wasn't wrong."

"Trouble? This is a huge cluster-fuck. You know what this means, of course."

"Going to be hard to keep this one quiet," Williams said. "I understand there was a complete blackout in Port Augusta; no press at all."

"Amazing, it all worked for once," Burgess agreed. "But there'll be reporting here. So far we're pretty sure they're not aware we're watching. That might have to change."

"Too many people. They're bound to talk."

"I think our little cold war just went hot," said Burgess. Then he grinned, patting the holster at his side; the service pistol there gave him a feeling of security. "Thank God. I was getting tired of all this covert bullshit."

V

An hour out of Melbourne, they reached the outlying suburb of Cranbourne: a place where people worked hard and dreamed big. Stately manors coexisted uneasily with council housing blocks, the streets dotted with luxury BMWs and VW Kombi vans.

Their destination was a palatial mansion, modernist in style with glass and silver in abundance. "Harold spends the better part of the year overseas," Mark explained as they pulled up outside. "Comes back a month a year for tax purposes. We pay him a small retainer and we get to use the place for photoshoots and video — how the rich people live, that kind of thing. Aspirational lifestyle. He's not due back in Melbourne until May."

The entry hall was dressed in marble and dark oak. Jess helped Aran across the floor, leaving a trail of gore. Much of the blood on him was not his own and had dried to a dark crust which flaked as he moved. Mark reassured them about the bloody footprints they were leaving across the marble: "It'll wash off, don't worry about it. I'll take care of it."

Jess herself moved with slow caution to avoid causing her back or her hands to flare up again. Her ribcage had stiffened and was hot to the touch, and she kept herself rigidly straight to hold off the stabbing pain when she twisted.

"The couches are wipe-clean," Mark told them as he settled them. Even the short journey from the car had drained the last of Jess's strength; too little rest and too much fear had driven her to the edge of exhaustion and all she wanted to do now was sleep. She thought about this for a second and reconsidered: a bath and *then* sleep.

Mark fussed around, trying to settle Aran comfortably with his swollen foot elevated, helping Vi find the kitchen for water. Jess slumped bonelessly in the couch, eyelids drooping, and watched. This side of Mark — the shining knight, riding to the rescue — had been in hibernation for what felt like a long time.

Eventually Mark came across to her. "You can take the master bedroom." He hooked an elbow under her arm to help her to stand. "It's this way."

As he helped her stumble along wide corridors and up a half-flight of stairs, Jess wondered if he had thoughts of joining her, if he might try to ignore their recent history, but to her dull surprise he ushered her in the door to the bedroom and helped her to the bed, then made his excuses. "I'd better look at the boy's foot," he said. "It didn't look good. He might need an ambulance."

"No ambulance," said Jess, but it came out as "N'ammlance". For some reason she found this funny and had to choke back a giggle.

Mark glanced at her with concern from the doorway. "I'll check on you soon." The door swung gently closed as he departed.

The master bedroom was large enough for a dinner party, Egyptian cotton coverings in geometric patterns on the bed, walk-in robes almost big enough to park a motorbike. To one side, Jess found with delight, was an ensuite complete with a small spa tub. The thought of a hot bath was overwhelming. In deliberate slow motion, wincing with every movement, she managed to take off her shirt, her shoulder-blades sending spikes of pain with every flex of her muscles. Eventually the shirt came off, and she examined it briefly; a hundred rents in the fabric. It might have been stylish in another decade, but Jess had never been hot for the look of ripped denim and it was unlikely she'd wear this again.

She caught sight of herself in the vanity mirror. The face she saw there she barely recognised. The slick of blood from the cut across her forehead had dried, and she blotted at it with a towel; it left behind a ragged line down her cheek, scabbed and sore. Her side was mottled purple and brown, too painful to touch, but somehow Utara's kicks had not managed to break the skin. Her hair was matted and tangled from neglect. How long since she'd last showered? It felt like weeks.

She turned to the bath. Bending to reach the taps, Jess nearly overbalanced, and was barely able to lower herself to sit on the tile floor, arms and forehead resting on the edge of the tub. The open air was delightfully cool against her back, and she rested for a moment.

She was still resting like that fifteen minutes later when Mark came back into the room: sitting in her bra on the tile floor, halfway to sleep.

She was almost dead-weight as he helped her out of the bathroom and back to the bed. "You're not safe to bathe," he told her, his voice not unkind. "You'll go to sleep and drown yourself." She didn't have the energy to protest. Moments later, a flash of anger when he reached for the strap to her bra gave her enough strength to try to bat his hands away.

"Don't be stupid," he said. "I'm not making a move. You've got glass in your cuts and you can't sleep like that." Her resistance leaked away as quickly as it had arrived, and Mark's hands were gentle as he unhooked the bra and put it aside.

Sitting cross-legged on the bed with Mark behind her, carefully pulling shards of glass from her skin and dabbing away crusted scabs with a warm moist towel, she could almost forget that, only days ago, she had left him. His warmth, the sound of his breathing, the strength of his hands reminded her of times past, pleasanter times, and she found herself hazily daydreaming until the hurts at her back faded.

"Remember the time we flew to Los Angeles?" Mark asked, and Jess nodded, her head moving more slowly than seemed normal; it was an effort to raise it again. "We took a Friday night flight, and you couldn't sleep on the plane."

"You snored all the way," Jess murmured, remembering that endless night and morning. An endless hell of sleeplessness, but it had also seemed romantic to watch her husband sleep.

"We were meant to visit Hollywood," Mark said. "But you were so tired you couldn't stay on your feet, so we just spent the first day in the hotel."

"Don't talk to me about hotels," Jess said. "Don't want to think about hotels now."

"Hotels aren't always bad," said Mark. He put aside the towel and the dish of glass slivers, and then Jess felt him rubbing a cream into her shoulders, analgesic and antiseptic. She relaxed into him, enjoying the massage. "I seem to remember giving you a massage that time, too."

"Did we have a spa bath in that hotel?" Jess asked, finding herself unable to remember; somehow it seemed crucially important.

"I was a junior, I'd been working less than a year. You'd only just started as an assistant. How were we going to afford a spa room?"

"Look at us now," said Jess.

"Look at us now," Mark agreed. Plastering a final band-aid across the last of the deeper cuts, he sat back on his heels, the mattress settling under his weight. "That'll do for now. We'll have to keep an eye on it to make

279

sure you don't get an infection."

"Thank you," said Jess, carefully turning to face him.

"For pulling shattered glass out of your skin? Don't mention it."

"For saving my life," she said. "For coming after me."

For a moment silence stood between them, stormclouds of recrimination hanging in the air. Mark took a breath, his face serious. He was going to say something and she'd be reminded of how horrible the last years had been and she'd end up hating him again and she didn't have the energy for that. No energy for arguments, no time for thought.

So she didn't think. She leaned forward and kissed him.

She had been threatened, attacked, injured; she had been afraid and lost and dispossessed. She hadn't slept properly in what felt like forever, and she just needed some kindness, some human contact. She needed love; failing that, sex would do. The man before her was her husband; he was her rescuer, and her healer, and her support when she most needed it. It had been a long time since she had *wanted* him.

Her lips on his. Mark almost pulled back in surprise, in defence, an automatic response to what felt like overreach. But it was *her* coming to him. So he let it happen — more than that, he welcomed it. He'd hoped for this. A reconciliation, a recovery of the love they shared, the love that he still felt for her.

For all his infidelities, all his petty betrayals, all the one-night stands trying not to visualise her face beneath him, it was still her that he wanted. He returned her kiss at first tentatively and then with more fervour, and she didn't pull away. His hand found her bare breast, the nipple stiffening under his palm, and he put his other hand behind her neck and started to lower her to the bed.

At the touch of the mattress on her injured back, she bucked under him, and using a strength he hadn't known she possessed, she turned him over until she was above him. He smiled as he felt her hands at his belt buckle, breaking the kiss only to lower his lips to her breasts. Then her weight was gone, as she stood aside to take off her trousers. She moved now with urgency, the pains of the past hour forgotten, as she helped him remove his shoes, his trousers, as she put a palm on his chest and pushed him down on the bed again.

She straddled him, and he reached out to wrap his hands around her back, to pull her to him. He felt band-aids under his fingers and hesitated, until she reached down to his hands and forcefully removed them. As she started to move above him, he reached instead for her breasts and caressed.

Tension rising. He wasn't used to being the one pursued; he was always the one in control, the one to dictate the pace. She was moving slowly, small motions, and he was deep inside her and the sensations were unfamiliar but so luscious. He caught his lower lip between his teeth and bit gently, forcing himself to hold back. He would not... *would not!...* disappoint her now.

And then she shuddered in release and slumped forwards into his arms, and he was kissing her forehead, her eyes, her nose, his hands avoiding her back by stroking her hair. He whispered her name and waited for her to catch her breath; his own pent-up urgency almost too great to ignore.

But her weight shifted as she rolled off him. He paused for a moment, feeling confused and betrayed, upright and quivering. But she was halfway to sleep already, curling on her side, her back to him, and he realised that for the first time in many years he was not going to be satisfied tonight.

He considered the possibility of taking care of it himself — it wouldn't take more than a moment. But his arm was under Jess, and he didn't want to jeopardise this unexpected reconciliation. Instead he gathered himself closer to his wife, awkwardly pulling a blanket over them, and tried to ignore the overhead light.

Sleep was a long time coming.

Monsoon

I

Jess woke alone, the sun high and the morning well under way. She lay motionless for a few minutes, staring at an unfamiliar ceiling, taking the time to put her thoughts in order; to make sense of the last twelve hours.

There would have to be a reckoning.

The crushing fatigue of last night was gone, vigour returning to her limbs. Her back hurt when she stretched, and her hands were checkered with narrow cuts that stung under hot water. Her neck was sore to the touch and her throat raw. The cut on her forehead and cheek was no longer angry but had scabbed to a dark crust that hurt when she smiled. But she was alive, and in the broad daylight through wide panels of glass yesterday's violence felt distant.

Seeking the kitchen, she came across Aran in an expansive gym. Weight equipment lined the walls and crash mats carpeted the floor, and Aran stood in the open space practising his sword drill. His back was to the door and Jess watched him unobserved, as he flowed from movement to movement, the sword tracing intricate and blur-fast patterns through the air. His short and slim frame moved gracefully, displaying a mastery Jess had not yet seen first-hand; he faltered whenever his weight fell onto his left foot, but whatever injury he had suffered did not stop his exercise. He had been unable to stand on that foot just last night. *Oh, to be young again.* He was shirtless, slim muscles bunching under the young skin, and for the first time Jess could see traces of the man he would grow into. That man might be considered attractive, but recent experience had taught her that all attractive men were violent narcissists and she didn't want to deal with thoughts of Mark right now.

The kitchen, when she found it, turned out to be large and airy - plenty of space to put in cameras for images of smiling women cooking pasta. She passed grey marble bench tops and chrome sinks as she located the refrigerator. Mark must have been shopping: she found fresh milk and bread, butter and jam. Mark had been busy during the morning and had cooked breakfast while she slept. Scrambled eggs, one of the few dishes her husband was capable of cooking without committing crimes against Jamie Oliver. The eggs had congealed in the fridge; she took one look at the lumpy mass and her stomach turned.

She was ravenous enough to suppress her qualms about raiding a stranger's fridge. Making herself a quick and rough sandwich, she spent more time locating the makings for a large, strong coffee.

She carried her coffee with her as she continued her investigation of the house. Beyond a large open lounge, glass doors opened onto a patio overlooking a swimming pool, and beyond this she found a home cinema: a darkened room with a television that seemed to take up most of a wall.

Vi sat in a recliner chair facing the screen and watched a cable news channel. Reflected light from a conflict in the Sudan poured across the young Empress's face.

It took a few moments for Vi to find the mute button on the remote control. She considered Jess seriously. "You look terrible."

"I feel much better," Jess said as she took a seat. "How are you?"

Vi held up a hand and flexed her fingers. "Just bruising. They came after me, but you and Aran are the ones who got hurt."

"Professor Reed," Jess said. "The lad in the foyer. At least Aran and I are still alive." She paused before continuing gently. "I'm sorry about Reed."

"So am I," Vi replied. "If we had not gone looking for him he'd still be alive. He wasn't even able to help us in the end."

"You do realise..." Jess had to clear her throat before she could go on. "You realise he was probably your father."

Vi surprised her with an unconcerned shrug. "Perhaps. I was never his daughter. I never met him. My mother always had plenty of suitors. I had all the father figures I could have needed."

"He came here for your sake. You might never have become Empress."

"Not for my sake," Vi answered. "He was in love with my mother. And he was afraid of my grandmother." Her lips twitched a smile. "Everybody was terrified of my grandmother."

They fell into silence for a while and watched the flickering images on the television screen. The news had moved from Africa to Afghanistan. Another dusty wasteland, more men with guns: without volume, only the subtitles made the distinction. "If this is the only kind of information we had from this planet," Vi said, "it is not surprising I was led to expect a warlike world."

Jess considered. "Some parts of the world are still violent. But here in Australia — most of the world, actually — we've had enough of war. We're finding other ways to keep order. Even with a few hundred countries rather than one world government."

"And yet, you still fight." Vi nodded towards the screen.

Jess shook her head. "That's different. That's not a war of expansion... we're not trying to capture a new country. We barely know what to do with our own, we don't need another stretch of desert." She shrugged. "The last time one country tried to annex another, it led to one of our biggest wars. We're doing okay without a world government. We prefer councils, where governments come together to cooperate."

"We tried something similar. Long before the line of Empresses began," Vi said. "It didn't work. The self-interest of countries will always take precedence over cooperation."

Jess didn't feel like arguing with her. The girl was avoiding thoughts of last night. She would have to face that discussion, but Jess wasn't in a hurry to do so either. "It seems to work for us. Maybe we haven't been at peace for five hundred years, but we haven't been at war for almost seventy. That's a good start."

Vi gestured at the television. "Perhaps *you* have had peace. They have not."

They sat in silence while the news moved on, the muted presenters mouthing earnest and serious silence. Eventually the scene changed, politicians in suits playing political games replaced with men in lycra playing sports.

"I don't know what to do." Vi's voice was soft, almost inaudible. "I don't even know who I am, anymore. The course of our lives is shaped by our memories. By what they make of us. I have so many memories I don't know what they will make of me.

"I was told to find Hareth Rede; that he could help us. Now he is dead. I don't have a goal. You asked me what kind of a life we could have here. I have no idea." She turned her eyes on Jess and they were wide and frightened. "We're never going home, are we?"

Jess sighed. She didn't have any answers to offer. "No, honey," she said. "I don't think you are."

II

Better than anyone could have expected.

Aran practiced his sword drill until his muscles burned, until the darkness behind his eyelids was filled with visions of precise and ordered movements, until his hands cramped around the grip of the sword; and then he practiced some more.

From time to time, during the long hours of the day, the Empress summoned him for continued lessons. As was required of him, he turned his full attention to the strange slow language they used here; to discussions of this world's society. As if they were going to be here a long time. They did not discuss plans or where they might go next. And when the Empress tired of teaching him, he returned to his sword.

Sometimes the man — Mark — attended the gym room. Aran tried to suppress his jealousy; Mark's rippling muscles stood in stark contrast to his own inadequate, scrawny frame.

Sometimes for variety he moved into the house's enclosed courtyard, his sword carving the air into intricate, invisible sculptures as he rehearsed the movements. *High thrust. Low parry. Turn, riposte. Orino pose — lunge.* The moves were familiar, the sword an extension of his own arm, the attacks and retreats burned into his muscle memory. The ritual gave his mind space to tally his performance.

His victories and his mistakes. Over and again; and again and again, the mistakes. *Blood sheets over his hand; the knife slips from his slicked fingers as Heth falls.* No amount of combat training and training duels had prepared him for that. *He takes the sword from the Captain's resisting fingers and exults in victory, but too soon: he is unable to avoid the man's fist.* Every victory, marred with failure. They were free, safe from pursuit, but his mind kept picking at the scabs. *Obi grunts as the sword slides through him, as easily as through the straw dummies the first-years duel; but even in death he mocks Aran, taking the sword with him as he tumbles into the stairs.*

"Don't fret," the Empress told him, early on their first day in the borrowed house. "You did well. Better than anyone could have expected of you. When we get home... *if* we get home... I'll ensure that Captain Gabe knows of your valour."

She could hardly have been more hurtful if she had tried.

He frankly doubted that they ever *would* get home. Hareth Rede had been their best chance. He had been disappointing, and now he was dead. So now they were marooned on an alien world, with no resources and no direction. He was the Empress's sworn servant, the only Imperial Guard who counted, and when she ignored his counsel it was not because she disagreed with him; it was because she disrespected him.

Whatever she might say, '*Captain Gabe*' told him all he needed to know.

Was this all he would ever achieve? Would he forever be a pale substitute for his own father?

Time to face facts. There was no use in holding false hope. With the rebels encircling the Capital, with the Barrier down and the palace itself under bombardment, the likelihood of Empress Jede and Captain Gabe escaping was remote. He had known it at the time. Gabe had known it. His father was dead. Best to accept it.

When Gabe placed the band, signifying acceptance into the Guard, around Aran's arm, there had been an unspoken communication. *The last faithful defender*. It had been a passing of the flag. He had been trusted with the highest of responsibilities, and he had stayed true to that calling. And yet the Empress did not recognise him, did not value his true worth. He would never be good enough. His responsibility bound him; his vows were fetters; he was sworn to her protection and he would stay with her as long as they both lived. But he would never be *her* Guard.

So he trained. He practiced until the pain in his muscles almost drowned out the disappointment, until the sweat running down his face felt like tears, but no amount of pain and sweat could wash away the realisation that he would never earn her respect.

III

Mark returned during the early afternoon with his arms full of groceries. He smiled when he saw that Jess was up. "You're looking better. How are you feeling?"

"I'm fine," Jess replied. "You've been busy." She nodded at the shopping bags, but Mark didn't ask for help as he wrangled them into the kitchen.

"Vi told me you guys haven't eaten properly in days. I've no idea how much kids eat so I thought it was better to over-cater."

Jess eyed the groceries as he unpacked them. The morning had left her useless and bored. "Would you mind if I cooked tonight?"

"I don't mind. You know how I cook." He paused. "Actually, I'd kind of hoped you'd ask. *I* know how I cook."

"Thanks." She helped him find places to store the vegetables. Thinking about recipes was a prosaic task that helped her keep her mind off the strangeness of the situation, but as usual Mark didn't read her mood.

"So what's the plan?" Mark's voice was serious. "We can stay here a while, but we can't look after these kids forever."

Jess noted the *we* but didn't challenge him on it. "I don't know. Maybe rest a bit longer. Aran's foot needs time to heal. After that... Elliot said he'd organise some resources for them. Maybe he'll be willing to help out."

"I've taken a week of leave," Mark said. "Hopefully that will be long enough."

"I need to think," Jess said as they packed the last of the cans into the cupboard. "I'm going for a walk."

"Sure. I'll show you around. Don't expect too much: it's not Hollywood."

"No," Jess said. "I need... some space. I just need to be alone for a while, okay?"

"No problem," said her husband, but she could tell from his eyes that he didn't understand as she left him standing there.

She did walk, but her walk took her only as far as the master bedroom. She wedged a chair under the door handle to keep it closed as she finally ran herself the long-overdue bath. She hadn't bathed since Friday and she felt tacky, coated with a layer of grime.

It was an unaccustomed luxury to soak in a tub. Lowering herself into water as hot as she could stand, she felt like a marshmallow dissolving into chocolate. She let the heat soothe away the aches at her back as she allowed her mind to drift.

She left the bathroom with no more answers than she had started with. There was only one hope for Vi. Elliot had to provide more than just a full bank account. Two kids alone in the world with no support: they wouldn't last more than a week. If they didn't hear from Elliot soon, they would have to go to him. The thought of another quest — another long journey — repelled her, but she couldn't abandon them now. She would help them that far. Get to Elliot, confront him at home if necessary. Surely once they had his support, with all his resources, when they had papers and money and compatriots around them — surely then, she'd be able to leave them with a clear conscience.

And then? Beyond that point, Jess couldn't see; she had no conception of what would happen next. She supposed she would need to go to the police, clear her name of suspicion over the roadhouse theft, reclaim her car. Take back the remains of her life's possessions and finish the interrupted journey to Perth. Trade interplanetary Empresses and assassins for job seeking and promotions and dating. Plans she knew she would have to make, but right now they didn't seem to apply to her.

The day dragged by with infuriating slowness. She spent time in the home theatre, scanning the news channels for reports of their fight in the hotel.

"A gas leak?" Vi protested after the second such news article ended. "Does your media always lie to the public?" She sounded outraged.

Mark, leaning against the doorjamb, shrugged. "More often than people would like to think. To prevent panic, to keep the terrorists off balance. They don't need much of an excuse. You'd be surprised how easily they can invent a cover story."

"Gas leaks don't blow up hotel rooms or shoot university professors," Jess said.

Mark shrugged. "Block off the damaged rooms for renovations. Get rid of any security camera footage. Can't be that hard. I didn't see anybody about — there probably weren't too many witnesses at one in the morning."

Twelve dead. The number reverberated through Jess's mind as the afternoon wore on. There was the man she had shot; the second man she had thrown out the window. B. Clarence. Professor Reed. Maybe Utara, if Mark had hit him hard enough. Four, that she knew of, perhaps five. Who else?

She found herself glancing sidelong every few minutes at Aran as he practiced his swords and his aerobics, as he worked with Vi on his English, as he obsessively stripped and reassembled the three flingers he had brought with him out of the hotel. *Twelve dead.* How many of them had been his work? How does he live with himself?

Two deaths on her personal conscience had been sufficient to ensure she would never sleep soundly again.

IV

Late afternoon found her working in the kitchen. It was as well-equipped as she expected, and Jess had her pick of knives and pans for cooking. It felt good to be working with her hands, absorbing herself in the details of oil and condiments and spices. Attracted by the aromas of sauteed onion and garlic, Vi leaned against a benchtop to watch. Jess used a short knife to trim an inch of fat off the pork chops as she said, "You'll have to forgive me. I'm making do. It's probably not going to be up to palace standards."

"Some of the Lords are gourmands," Vi said, "but I am used to eating simply. I'm sure it will be fine. It smells more than fine."

As she cooked, Jess told the girl her thoughts. "I don't have any better ideas. If we confront Elliot, perhaps he'll know someone else from Zama who might help you. He said he kept good records."

Vi looked at her seriously. "I already owe you so much. I will never be able to repay you."

"Maybe not," agreed Jess; she then surprised herself by saying, "It's not been exactly *fun* but it has certainly been interesting."

The four of them ate around a dining table made for twenty, a cluster of seats and dishes sitting at the end of the table like an ice cap. Jess had always been a good cook and her hearty, if simple, sweet and sour pork on rice seemed to meet with approval. Vi and Aran had never eaten anything like it but that didn't stop them putting away two helpings each.

They discussed over dinner but there were no new ideas forthcoming. The consensus was that they would stay for a few days — off the radar, away from pursuit — while Aran's bruised foot healed. There was no reason to expect that the police would trace them here. Mark had driven across town during the morning and taken a large amount of cash from a distant auto-teller, and his car was now parked inside the large garage adjoining the house; Jess prevailed on him to turn off his mobile phone. He had spent much of the afternoon working on his laptop, but when he assured Jess that he was using a "remote proxy" to hide his internet address, she had to assume he knew what he was talking about.

"We should be safe enough here, then," she said. "For a few days, at least, we'll wait here."

So they waited.

Their borrowed house had a large and modern dishwasher but Jess wasn't sure how it operated and chose instead to wash the dishes by hand; the hot water stung her hands, but it was another domestic chore to postpone the inevitable confrontation. But in this she was to be disappointed.

"You don't have to do that." Mark entered the kitchen. "They'll wait."

"We're in a borrowed house. Let's do our best to keep it clean?"

He came up behind her and wrapped his hands around her waist. "Then let me do it. You should rest."

She reached down with soapy hands to remove his arms. Freed, she stepped away from the sink, putting some space between them. "Mark. What do you think is happening here?"

He frowned. "I was kind of hoping you'd forgiven me."

"You saved my life. I'm very grateful you turned up when you did. I don't know what we'd do if we didn't have this house. But don't think for a moment that makes everything okay between us."

Mark nodded, leaning against the counter. "Of course it doesn't. It's a journey. Forgiveness is a journey. I want you to come home, take the time you need, let's get back to the way we were."

The way we were. How little self-knowledge did he have? "Have you forgotten? I left you. I packed all my stuff in the car and drove away. I'm not coming back. That's what *leaving you* means."

Mark eased along the bench towards her as if by closing the distance between them he could heal the rift that separated them. "You're being stupid. Look, things are weird... whether or not these kids really are from another world, they need our help. I understand that. Things won't be normal until we've done whatever we need to do with them, get them settled or whatever. But we're going to have to go back to our life eventually. You need to come home and take the time you need to–"

She cut him off. "You don't get it. I don't need *time*. I've given you time. You've had *years*. I've been trying to fix things and you haven't been interested. You only want to fix it now because I'm actually leaving you and you can't bear to lose the things that belong to you!" By the end of this she was shouting.

"I know I haven't been the most supportive–"

"Supportive? You've been sleeping with other women — oh yes, it's been bloody obvious! What's worse is that you haven't even tried very hard to hide it!"

"Okay, yes, it's true! But listen, it's *you* that I'm with. Right now, I'm *here*. It's you that I want. I don't want anyone else, I never have!"

"Yes, *that* was pretty fucking obvious on Friday night."

There wasn't much Mark could say to that. "I don't know why I... really, I don't," Mark said. "I was angry."

"That's your excuse?"

"It's not an excuse!" He paused for a moment, breathing heavily as the flush receded from his cheeks. "Maybe this is the best thing that could have happened to us. Maybe it's exactly what we needed... a chance to forget about our jobs, our responsibilities, a chance just to talk like adults. Can we do that? Can we have a discussion like two grown adults?"

"Adults don't hit each other when an argument isn't going their way."

"I shouldn't have hit you. I'm really sorry. It won't happen again, I promise."

"No, it won't," she agreed, turning her back on him and facing the sink. The last of the bubbles were dissolving like a symbol of their relationship.

He reached out and snared her hand in his. "Don't do this. Don't shut me out. Don't give up on *us*."

She snatched the hand away from him. "Don't touch me," she hissed. "Don't you ever touch me again."

"For god's sake, you're my *wife*!"

She stared at him coldly. "You're not my husband. Husbands don't punch their wives."

"That's it then? We're done?"

"We're done."

"What about last night, then?" His voice was bafflement, anger, confusion and pleading all at once. "What was that?"

How to answer? Last night was a mistake; an error of judgment. Last night was a farewell to times past. Last night was Jess taking control of her life at last; last night was liberation. So many answers, each one only telling a part of the story. She decided on an answer that was at once simple and complicated.

"Last night was goodbye."

V

It was Wednesday afternoon and Jeff Lang was wrapping up his investigation into a blatant case of graffiti when his mobile phone chimed at him.

The grizzled old man who owned the warehouse was in full flow. "...and I can't have this kind of language next to my own logo. It's bad for my reputation." He seemed more concerned about the spray-painted images on the outside of the building than the broken windows and the similar defacement inside.

"I think we have enough to go on," Jeff told him. "You're not the only place they've hit in the last week. We'll let you know as soon as we find anything out."

It took another fifteen minutes to extricate himself and return to his cruiser on the street, the proprietor watching him all the way. Jeff kept his face forward until he was comfortably settled behind the steering wheel. Only then did he pull out his mobile to check the message.

Need to talk. Come see me tonight. A.

Thoughts of graffiti and vandalism fled. The off-the-books investigation he was carrying on with Adele Ferguson was going nowhere but that didn't matter. Spending time with her was forging a friendship which might become more. He grinned as he dropped his phone in the passenger seat.

There was something on the seat that he had not put there.

A large manila envelope rested on the upholstery. Automatically Jeff glanced around the car; all the doors were locked as they should be. The windows were all fully rolled up, in defence against the heat of the day, and there was no sun-roof; nonetheless, somebody had managed to get something into his locked car.

Don't bloody well touch it, he thought, but he was already reaching for it. He knew that he should take it straight back to the station for forensic analysis, but that would have required more self-restraint than he could muster. If somebody is able to get an envelope into the car through a locked door, he reasoned, this was no simple robbery. That was outside the capabilities of a civilian. This came either from another cop, or from somebody with very sophisticated resources.

He donned a pair of latex gloves before he picked up the envelope.

It was thin and light — no bomb. It was not sealed, the protective paper strip still over the adhesive. Inside the envelope were several sheets of paper. Unlikely threats of anthrax in his mind, he held his breath as he carefully lifted the papers out of the envelope.

The top sheet was a blurry photograph from a speed camera. It took him a moment to recognise its significance: the vehicle captured was one he had seen before. And as he saw the contents of the other sheets of paper, he realised that his off-the-books investigation was very much alive.

Adele Ferguson lived in a beaten weatherboard house in a street full of beaten weatherboard houses. It was five minutes past five when Jeff pulled into the driveway and strode to the front door. The grass of the front lawn needed watering; the only other time he had been here had been at night and he hadn't noticed.

Adele met him at the door in shorts and a tank top. Her house was ineffectively cooled by oscillator fans and Jeff found it oppressive as he entered the hallway. He hadn't taken the time to change out of his uniform and the long-sleeved shirt was already damp with sweat.

She led him to the dining room that had served as their centre of operations the last time he was here. The notes and paperwork of their last discussion had been cleared; on the table sat a manila envelope and several sheets of paper. "This arrived today," she said. "Somebody left it on the table while I was in the back yard. All the doors were locked and there's no signs of a break-in. The only open door was the back door and I was right there. Somehow they got into my house to leave this. How did they get into my house, Jeff?"

He held up his own manila folder. "Probably the same way they got into my car."

They took some time to compare the contents of their folders. It felt like Christmas, children opening their Santa stockings. Adele's package contained a copy of her own forensics report on the dress, but beneath this was a photograph. Blurry and distant, it showed three people in a corridor: a woman and two children. One of the children was a girl of about fifteen and somebody had circled her on the photograph in black Texta. "I think this might be the owner of the dress," Adele said.

A woman and two children. Was he looking at the first photograph of the mysterious children from the roadhouse? It seemed likely.

The photograph had identifying marks around the edges that Jeff recognised immediately. "This is from a security camera. Look, here's the camera ID. Taken late Monday night: 231847, that's a time stamp. Give me a moment — I want to try something." It took him five minutes on his laptop, Adele waiting patiently while he hacked into databases, to identify the location of that camera. "That's the Hotel Ulupna, in Melbourne. Victoria."

"That sounds familiar. Didn't they just have some kind of health scare?"

Jeff frowned. "That might be what they're calling it."

Underneath the security photograph was one more sheet of paper. To Jeff it looked like the rendition an artist might make of an alien species after a particularly bad hangover. "Friendly chap," he said carefully.

Adele shook her head. "It's an electron microscope image. I think it's our friend the dust mite. But I'll tell you one thing: this doesn't look like any species I've ever heard of. That's a pretty distinctive proboscis our friend's rocking. If this was a known species that would be an obvious identifying mark, and I've spent the afternoon hitting the books. I think we might have a brand-new species here. But who sent it to me... and why?"

Then it was Jeff's turn. "A speed camera photo," he said. "Recognise the car? The red utility there. That's the Holden we saw two days ago in the car park of the university. That's our thieves."

"Where was this taken?"

"Newell Highway, near Jerilderie." She looked blank, so he added, "New South Wales."

"What the hell are they doing up there?"

"Beats me, but they're travelling north. See, this is northbound."

Next from his folder was a sheaf of paper he quickly identified as a forensics report. "It's from the house. Ballistics. Guesses as to the kind of weapons... doesn't look like they really have any idea." He continued leafing through the stapled pages. "Looks like they tried to burn it. The perps, I mean. The fire didn't take." He shook his head. "There's a lot here. A lot of reading."

He dropped the report back on the table and rolled his shoulders. "Maybe we're meant to read on the way," he said, tossing the final contents of his envelope onto the table. "Somebody obviously wants us on the case."

Two airline tickets fanned across the wooden surface.

Adele reached for them, then hesitated. Instead, she rested her slim hand on his forearm, and even with all the mysteries that surrounded them, the touch felt electric. "Jeff, wait."

"What's the matter?"

"It's clear someone knows about us," Adele said, her voice serious. "Somebody who knows a lot more about what's going on than we do. Somebody with access to resources. Someone who's staying hidden."

"True."

"We're breaking the law," she continued.

"Not really," he said. They'd been careful not to overstep their bounds.

She was undeterred. "We're interfering with a police investigation. We've withheld evidence. And now someone's watching us. Is this really safe?"

He took his time to consider, but his answer was never really in doubt. As a young man, he had gone through a phase of reading science fiction.

He'd read Asimov, Arthur Clarke, Heinlein. But it was one line from a documentary series, name long forgotten, that had carried the most impact and stayed with him even as he outgrew his interest in lasers and spaceships. "The universe probably teems with life," the narrator had said, "but the vast distances between worlds and the impossible amounts of energy required to get there will ensure that we can never meet them." The young Jeff Lang had spent many nights thinking of that image: a universe of worlds, all inhabited by intelligent races shaking their fists impotently at the sky in the certain knowledge that the galaxy is full wonders they will never be able to visit.

He gave his response slowly, choosing his words with care. "I don't know what's going on with these children, with this woman. I'm sure we're barely touching the surface of this case, if we can even call it that. And yes, somebody else knows a lot more than we do. But I can't help feeling that we're on the edge of something wonderful here, something amazing. Can you walk away from that? It might not be safe, it might not be wise, but I can't leave it at that. Can you?"

Her fingers closed over the tickets as she grinned at him. "Hell no. I was just asking."

VI

Vi spent the hours submerged in other women's lives. Since leaving her home, they had been on the run, with barely a chance to take breath. Now, free of pursuit, still and safe at last, she could allow her mind to wander through her inherited memories. No more would she allow herself to be ambushed by surfacing memories. *No more.* So she dimmed the lights, she left the viewscreen — the 'television' — turned on but mute, closed her eyes and let herself drift.

The Empress Ramia seemed a good place to start. The only Empress to be usurped, exiled from the capital with only a few allies, the High Council irretrievably corrupted. For a while, Ramia lived again in her head. A hundred times she had read the chronicles, until she could recite them by heart; now she could watch as each event occurred.

She submerged herself in the history as Ramia travelled the countryside marshalling support, raising an army, spreading the word of the True Empress. Her heart leapt with exultation as she stormed the Capital with her rag-tag army of loyalists, the people rallying behind her in their thousands. She watched, helpless, as Tolo — her guard and husband — duelled Lord Aresto; and her stomach turned as he took a grievous wound, the wound that would eventually kill him. From the extremities of defeat, she witnessed Tolo's last heroic effort, as he struck home a final, fatal blow to end Lord Aresto. Later still, she stood before traitorous Lords and Ladies, subdued by her forces; her heart devoid of pity as she ordered them executed before her. It was Vi's own hand that held the sword as the false Empress was executed.

Come back.

Vi drew in a shaky, ragged breath as she forced her mind back to the present. She glanced down at her hands in the half-light of the television, half expecting to see them black with the usurper's blood, and was almost startled to see them clean. The only blood on her hands was of the civilians in the town behind them, and in the hotel they had fled. Utara might have wielded the weapons, but he was only here because of her. Those deaths were at her door. But the Crown was more important.

Uki stares in horror at the contraption before her. Archivist Malleo regards her with sympathetic eyes. "It won't be as bad as it looks," he says, his voice confident. "It's not terribly different to installing a data point."

"Data points," Uki tells him, "don't look like something that could be used to trap jerra-bears. Does it have to be so... pointy?"

"It's a delicate operation," Malleo says apologetically. "Personally, I would prefer to put my faith into this than the hope that my hands won't tremor at the wrong moment. We've had a one hundred percent success rate in testing."

Recently, at least. For this version of the hardware. Uki doesn't correct him, but she is fully aware of the many — many! — failures and partial successes during initial development and testing. Fortunately, there are always more prisoners. But the Empress is more important than any prisoner. And the Crown is more important, even, than the Empress.

"You're sure this is absolutely necessary?" She already knows the answer. The capacity of the Crystal Crown is nearing its limits. This has been under discussion for many years, and his nod doesn't surprise her. "Then we will proceed. But just in case, we will synchronise my memories in the traditional way before we do. I will not take the chance of losing both the Empress-elect and the Crown in the one ill-omened day. The Crystal Crown will suffice for another generation, if need be."

"We'll be working in the best possible conditions," Malleo reassures her. "We have the very latest facilities at Repose."

"One more thing," says Uki. "Tell nobody of this. There is no need to forewarn the candidates of this change, not until we are certain." Let them know what awaits, and more than one will baulk. Let them see the mechanism that will be used henceforward in passing on the Crown, and she wouldn't be surprised if they all withdrew their candidacy.

Vi's eyes were wide in the dimness. Her recollection of the archivists' tool was clear and fresh; she had seen it herself only days ago. But she had known of it practically her whole life. For her, it had been a necessary hurdle, a trial to pass, one her predecessors had faced before her. Bimini had been presented with it with no warning, no preparation. The young Empress-elect must have been braver than the Lessons recorded.

No, she wasn't. The recollection came back to her and Vi found herself needing to grin. *They had to hold her down.*

VII

It was always possible that Mark would rescind his offer of help. He was just petty enough to do it; even before things went south between them, Jess had understood and tolerated his easy jealousy. Back then she could hold her own, meeting his provocations with gentle passive-aggression.

300

Now, of course, he held the keys to the house; he possessed their transportation. If he took things as badly as she suspected he might, he could pitch them out onto the streets and leave them to their own devices. Jess spent Wednesday in a welter of dread.

But her fears did not immediately come to fruition. Although he avoided being alone in a room with her, and though the air between them bristled with resentment, he did not renege on his promise. Mark spent much of his time, when not buried in his laptop, teaching Vi the technology of the house — the television, the oven and microwave, the air conditioner; and exercising alongside Aran. Jess watched from a careful distance, noticing how Mark helped Aran with his language skills, giving him words like *bicycle* and *window* and *door*. Under the combined tutelage of Mark and Vi, Aran's English improved by the hour.

After the haste of the last few days a heavy inertia had settled and she wandered dully around the big house, aware that they couldn't stay long. She wasn't cut out for a sedentary life and the confines of the plush house quickly became a gilded cage, but the thought of leaving seemed to require more energy than she could bring to bear. She spent time trying to read Professor Reed's book but found it heavy going and she could only handle it in small doses. *Utopia: A thought experiment.* Reed's attempt to combine the best elements of Zaman society with Australian experience; to her it seemed unconvincing.

She cooked a decent lunch on Wednesday, and found a pair of shorts and a t-shirt in her shrinking collection of clothes in which she could make use of the swimming pool.

Despite the size of the house, she and Mark could not entirely avoid each other's company. She was at the sink, cleaning up after dinner, when Mark entered the kitchen behind her. Not meeting her eyes, he deposited his plate on the counter and turned to go without a word.

The old Jess might have let it go. Avoiding conflict had been a primary life skill. But over the last four days a new resolve had grown, springing from her responsibility for others in peril. The new Jess would rather bring risks into the open and understand what she was facing rather than wait for them to fester. "Mark, wait."

He paused in the doorway but did not turn. "Yes?"

She couldn't read the set of his shoulders; either hope or anger. If it was hope, she was sorry she would have to quickly puncture it. "Why are you still helping us?"

"Did you expect me to just leave you behind?" He sounded aggrieved. "Maybe there's no chance left for *us*. But you're in trouble. These kids are in trouble, and if you ask me these kids *are* trouble. Do you *want* me to stop helping you?"

"You can't always save me. It's not your responsibility any more. And I can't afford to rely on you."

He turned to face her, and she saw at once that it was anger simmering in his eyes. "We're still married. Officially if nothing else. Now I don't know what's going on here; I don't know where these kids are really from, but I don't believe for a second that they're from another planet. It has to be some kind of a con. They're playing you."

Shaking her head: "I don't think so."

"It's all some kind of a sick game," Mark insisted.

Jess lifted her fingers to the cut along her face, scarring nicely now. "Does this look like a fucking *game* to you?"

He had the good grace to flinch at the reminder of her injuries. "I haven't got it worked out yet. But I'm not leaving you in their clutches. We have a shared bank account and anything you give them comes from me too. As long as you're here, you're stuck with me."

"I'm not going to spend your damned money," Jess protested.

"No, you bloody won't," he said. With that said, he turned to go; paused in the doorway and his voice was almost too quiet to hear as he added, "And I couldn't bear it if anything happened to you."

VIII

On Thursday the hot weather broke, and the house was lashed throughout the day with squalls of rain driven by gusts of cold wind.

Confined within the house, a kind of cabin fever descended upon them. Aran exercised with the weights and his swords with redoubled ferocity until even Mark had to give up and nurse his sore muscles. Vi retreated to the home theatre and rarely stepped away from the television. Even Jess started itching to get moving, but her restlessness wasn't sufficient to overcome her continued reluctance to commit to another road trip.

Over a lunch of sandwiches, they talked about Utara's squad. They had no way to be sure how many of them had survived the incursion to the hotel. Jess had killed two; Aran three. Utara may have been killed, or not; Mark felt sure that he'd struck hard enough to make sure of it, but Vi was unconvinced. "Even if he wasn't too badly hurt," Jess said, "he still needed to get past the police. With any luck he got arrested. I'd like to see him talk his way out of that one." Utara and Jarem had talked about a whole squad, so the likelihood was that there were another five or more soldiers from the original team out there.

"How much longer should we wait?" Vi asked.

Aran's foot was healing rapidly, and Jess was no longer feeling like a mass of welts every time she sat down, but a glance through the big glass windows at the sleet sapped any motivation to move on. "Friday," Jess said after a moment. "Tomorrow. If we don't hear anything before lunch tomorrow, we'll start out."

The remainder of Thursday passed with a slowness that was both interminable and inexorable. Every second dragged, minutes seemed like hours and hours of inactivity felt like an age. But every moment in that eternity of frozen moments brought them closer to their inevitable departure, and even though the chosen course this time was her own, the choice had been so inevitable that she still felt coerced. Heading home to Perth had been entirely her own decision; since then her every movement had been dictated by necessity and by the will of others.

As Friday morning broke upon them with a light fog, forecast to burn off quickly on the way to another hot day, Jess still didn't really want to go. Nonetheless, the children were anxious to get moving and Jess' self-imposed deadline approached with too much speed. Vi came upon her as she was repacking her backpack in preparation for the lunchtime deadline.

"I promised to let you go when I was settled," Vi said to her, watching as Jess folded clothes and placed them carefully in the bag. "I still mean that. Even if the *dahla* won't — or can't — help us, you should go."

It wasn't that easy, of course. Jess was held lightly by expectation but much more firmly by her sense of responsibility. "Even if you don't have anywhere to go? With no plans and no help?"

Vi stared at her seriously. "I'll *make* him help us."

Jess held off preparing lunch in unconscious procrastination until she could no longer avoid the truth of the noon sun overhead. The four of them gathered in silence to eat a sombre meal. In the hallway near the front door they had gathered their repacked bags; Mark had refuelled the car and they were out of excuses.

Jess took a deep breath, ready to bow to the inevitable when, with timing to prove that fate has a sense of humour, the silence was broken by the warbling of a phone.

It took Jess a moment to realise where the call was coming from and another moment to find where she had left Elliot's phone. It was still ringing as she brought it to her ear.

"Hello... it's Jess, isn't it? You're still with the... the children? I promised you some resources." Elliot's voice sounded strained. "But I've been thinking and— I'd like to do more to help." He paused, as if hesitating over the words. "I want to speak to you some more. I'm inviting you to come up to my offices. I'm sending my private jet and my pilot. Come see me. Come see me today."

Gathering

I

Jacob Elliot's private jet sat on the tarmac waiting for them. White and sleek, it looked too small to carry passengers, more like a toy than a ten-million-dollar aircraft.

They never made it inside the terminal. Elliot's staff met them in the car park and walked them directly to the runway.

The pilot was a short man, tending to wrinkles as if he had been shrinking for years without his skin accommodating the changes. Glancing over their backpacks without offering to help carry, he nodded his approval. "Should be a short trip up," he said, and that appeared to exhaust his store of conversation.

The pilot's companion was a sturdy but handsome woman in a grey suit that hung loose and didn't constrict her movement. Her eyes narrowed as she took in the old bruises and cuts both Jess and Aran sported, but that double-take was the only sign of her surprise. "Alice Farrow," she said. "I'm Mr Elliot's head of security. This way, we're in a hurry." She didn't offer a hand to shake.

Jess hesitated, but Vi was gazing at her, clearly expecting her to take the lead. *Okay then*. "Jess McTi... Cartwright," she said, correcting herself at the last moment. "Jess Cartwright." She could feel Mark's eyes hot on her back but she refused to turn. "These are Vivian and Aaron Roche. And Mark McTiernan."

Farrow nodded at the introductions. "Thank you for coming. Mr Elliot is looking forward to meeting you. Follow me please. We'll get in the air right away; we have a fifteen-minute window before we lose the runways for an hour."

Farrow set off at a rapid pace, not looking back to make sure they followed. Mark stared over his shoulder at his Aston Martin in the open-air lot, surrounded by Holden wagons and Ford SUVs. Watching him, Jess allowed herself a moment of amusement at his discomfort. Abandoning his beloved car might be more of an emotional wrench than learning she had left him.

As they approached the plane, Farrow flipped open a mobile. "Yes, sir... yes, they're here. Four passengers... Yes, four. The girl and boy, and one man and woman." Farrow glanced at them sidelong and Jess wrenched her eyes away, glancing instead at the plane.

The jet looked no longer than a limo, its low-slung body almost touching the tarmac, stubby engines seeming too insubstantial to provide the power of flight. Jess followed the pilot up the steep stairs to enter the plane. The interior was crowded but plush. Jess had never been inside a small jet and only a couple of times in a large commuter plane, but it looked nothing like she had expected. It looked expensive, everything modern in tones of grey and black.

Farrow was tolerating no delays. She made certain they were all settled in their seats; the bucket chair swallowed her in its thick cushioning as she sat. She had barely fastened her belt when the jet began taxiing for position on the runways and Farrow hastened to her own seat. "When we're safely in the air you'll be able to move around, and there'll be refreshments available. We'll be there before you know it."

Then the invisible hand of inertia pushed her back into the upholstery of her seat as the jet accelerated. Jess felt her fingers grabbing too tightly at the armrests but she couldn't make them relax; she didn't like flying. Never had. Mark seemed unperturbed, but he was more experienced at air travel. And Vi and Aran both looked faintly sick — whether at the noise or the G-forces she couldn't guess. *This shouldn't be new to them. They have flying bloody cars where they come from.*

Almost as soon as it had begun their steep climb was over and the jet levelled out. Jess carefully kept her gaze averted from the spacious windows and watched instead as Farrow unshipped bottles, cans and glassware from a narrow cupboard.

Vi had her eyes screwed shut, her face bloodless and pale. Jess leaned across to her. "How are you doing?"

"Our flitters are a lot smoother."

"At least you're used to flying. I like being on the ground."

True to her word, Farrow had refreshments on hand: a selection of red and white wines, three different beers and scotch with ice. Mark accepted the latter, and Aran would have taken one also, had not Jess intervened. "It's an intoxicant," she said. Vi translated for her. "A drug. It will slow you down and take away your reflexes, your balance, your thinking."

"*Gett en-jat'r haak,*" Aran said. "Thank you." His English was slow and faltering, but recognisable. At this rate all they would need would be a few weeks before he could get by. A few weeks and they'd need less help.

A few weeks? Was she considering staying with them that long?

Just days ago she'd been attempting to cross the Nullarbor desert in a car that hadn't been washed for years, for fear of dissolving the dirt that held it together. Now here she was in a private jet flying north to visit the moderately famous and immoderately wealthy Jacob Elliot. Whilst the serendipity of his invitation could not be denied, Jess couldn't suppress a cynical suspicion that things were not as simple as they seemed.

Not really my problem, Elliot had told them a week ago, and sounded like he meant it. Perhaps he really had reconsidered his ability to help. People did have changes of heart. But if there was one thing the last week had taught her, it was that nobody could be trusted; if they helped you, it was because they wanted something.

She glanced across the aisle at Mark, sprawled in his chair with his scotch, gazing through the windows.

Farrow had finished serving her passengers. Jess looked up as the woman slid into a spare seat and swivelled to face her. "Next month marks my twentieth anniversary working for Mr Elliot."

"Okay. Congratulations?" Where was the woman going with this?

"I joined Elliot Industries when he was just starting his business. Had a couple of patents to his name and not much else. Security was simpler then. It didn't sound like a great career move, but once I'd spoken to Mr Elliot I knew he was on his way up.

"Elliot Industries grew quick. I stayed with the company. Didn't take long before I was given a team to look after. Now I'm head of the security team, looking after the labs, the factories, the whole distribution chain."

"I'm sorry," said Jess, "but why are you telling us this?"

Farrow nodded. "Three reasons. One: so you can understand. I'm responsible for the security of this company and its trade secrets, as well as of Mr Elliot himself. But I'm still an employee, and I have to follow orders. I'm to put myself at your disposal. Mr Elliot has authorised me to provide you whatever assurances you feel you need to be comfortable. After I hand you over to the chauffeur, I'm supposed to go home and have a long weekend. I've never been *dismissed* before, and I sure as hell don't like it, so you'll need to excuse me if I sound a bit pissed off."

Assurances. Only people with ulterior motives think in terms of assurances. Jess tried not to let her hardening suspicion reach her eyes.

"Reason two: understand I'm quite serious when I say that if you hurt Mr Elliot — if he's in some kind of trouble because of you — I'll make it a personal mission to come after you. I've been with him a long time. I care about him, I care about his family, and I care about his company. I don't know who you are, and I don't like not knowing."

"And the third reason?" Mark drawled the question from his position a couple of seats back. Jess hadn't been aware he was listening.

"Yes, the third reason," Farrow said. She shifted in her seat to stare directly at Aran. "Unless you're Batman or Sir Edmund Hillary, you've got no excuse for having so much hardware on your belt." Vi's uncomprehending look must have demanded further explanation. "I was a cop for fifteen years. I know a concealed weapon when I see one. The only reason you're on this plane at all is that Mr Elliot told me to expect you to... well, his exact words were "It's not so much that they wouldn't get through security, they wouldn't get into the airport". I was specifically ordered not to search or detain you. That's the only reason I'm not taking those from you, and don't make the mistake of thinking I couldn't. But if you think about using them, you'd better be prepared for me to come after you. Whatever you do to Mr Elliot, I'll give back to you with interest."

Vi shook her head slowly. "We're not here to harm Mr Elliot. We don't want to bring him any trouble. Remember, *he* invited *us*."

Farrow's eyes roamed across the long scar and yellowed bruises on Jess's face and neck, the fading discolouration on Aran's cheek, Vi's bandaged hand. "You may not want to bring him any trouble," she said, "but if you'll forgive me mentioning it, you look very much to me like trouble follows you."

II

McLaren Station had once been a grand estate, centre of a thriving cane sugar plantation. In the early 1860s Brendon McLaren, intrepid colonist, was amongst the first to settle the region, forging the estate that bore his name out of scrub forest by sheer determination and sweat and a lot of blood. Not much of it his own. His extermination of the indigenous aboriginal population was commended for its ruthlessness. A century later, McLaren's estate had been carved up and subdivided, a young couple from Sydney purchasing the remnants in the 1960s with the intent to repurpose it as a hobby farm and bed-n-breakfast. For decades, McLaren Farm provided generations of children a chance to milk cows and collect eggs and ride ponies and step in chicken shit, and not a word was said of the layer of human bone that formed the estate's foundation.

McLaren Farm folded in the 80s and the property fell vacant, untended for years before Jacob Elliot took possession in 2005. This much Jess remembered from the article in the *Monthly*. The journalist had been impressed at the money Elliot was pouring into restoring the estate to its former glory. From the air as they overflew the property, the manor at its centre seemed like a castle.

309

They descended into Jacob Elliot's private airfield through blustery southerly winds, still an hour before dusk, but with night encroaching early under the ominous cloud cover. They were greeted on arrival by a limousine standing empty at the edge of the tarmac. "Hop in," said Farrow. "I'm driving."

It was less than ten minutes' drive to McLaren estate, then another five to wind their way along the estate's interior roadways. They passed through open fields dotted with occasional livestock: a couple of cows, a solitary goat, a rabble of sheep. "We keep the animals to control the grass," Farrow explained. "Nobody tends them. They're pretty much feral by now." Leaving the paddocks behind, they started encountering outlying buildings which in years past may have been shearing sheds and hay barns. Several of these buildings had been recently renovated with tall wire fences and concrete cladding replacing the original timber rails and weatherboard walls. "Various research and development hothouses," Farrow said. "Elliot makes sure that good ideas get the team and resources they need."

Jess wasn't sure what she had expected of Elliot Industries; an industrial block of factories, perhaps, or a gleaming steel skyscraper. She found it a little hard to credit that the world-spanning juggernaut of Elliot was centred on a rural farmstead.

Soon they approached the main estate house itself. A three-storey colonial mansion, meticulously restored, its surrounds dressed with immaculate garden beds, topiary animals and English hedgerows. Scaffolding enfolded one of the mansion's wings, unfinished walls and canvas-sheeted windows. The maintenance of a heritage building never ends.

The driveway ended in a lake of dark gravel, surrounding a grassy central island hosting an impressive bay laurel sculpture in the shape of a rearing horse and rider. Jess raised an eyebrow as they stepped out of the car.

"We have six full time gardeners on staff." Farrow nodded to indicate that Jess should take the lead towards the house.

Gravel crunched underfoot as she led the way, Farrow a step behind on her left, Mark just to her right. The mansion loomed overhead, and Jess suppressed a shiver as they approached; dozens of windows, shielded with heavy curtains, stared down at them. The sense of being watched was almost tangible. After the heat of the past week, the cool wind at her back was chilling.

"Welcome to Elliot Industries." Startled, Jess wrenched her gaze away from the house. Clad in a breezy grey suit, Jacob Elliot had joined them whilst she was staring upwards. His tie whipped over his shoulder to wave in the wind.

The difference in his appearance now compared to when she saw him last could hardly have been starker. Then, despite apparently having flown from Brisbane to Adelaide, then driven through the night to meet them in Port Augusta, he had been immaculate and elegant, a figure from the pages of GQ magazine. The man who stood before them now was neither immaculate nor elegant. His suit was rumpled as if it had been slept in, a dark stain marring the front of his shirt. He hadn't shaved and a rough shadow darkened his cheeks. Dark pouches under his eyes betrayed sleepless nights. When the wind shifted in the wrong direction, a funk of tobacco wafted from him.

The revelations of the war on Zama and the Empress's presence on Earth may have shaken him more than he had let on. Still, Jess's suspicion that there was something insincere in his offer of help hardened towards certainty. "Thank you for the invitation. I have to say it came as a bit of a surprise."

Elliot's eyes ranged over her shoulder to the vehicle sitting abandoned on the drive, then to the side, registering Alice Farrow's presence. "Alice? I thought you were going home."

"I am. I just wanted to make sure they reached you safely, sir."

"But they haven't, have they? My instructions were to bring all of them. Where are the... the children?"

Farrow hesitated. "They wouldn't come."

"We're being cautious," Jess said. "I'm sure you understand. If you knew what we'd been through you wouldn't be surprised when I say we're not taking chances."

Elliot sighed. "I said I'd help you. You know whose side I'm on."

"You made it clear that your involvement went as far as providing some paperwork and no further. *You* changed the rules, not me."

"Fair enough," said Elliot. "A man's allowed to change his mind, but I can't blame the Empress for being suspicious. I need to convince you of my goodwill?"

"Something like that."

Elliot turned from her to face Farrow. "If you're determined to stick around, you can do something else for me. Go back to wherever you left the... the children, make sure they're safe and comfortable, and wait for me to call you. When Miss McTiernan here decides I'm worth trusting, you can bring them in."

It was as good a compromise as Farrow was likely to get, but she didn't look happy about it. "No problem. I'll wait for your call."

Elliot watched as Farrow trudged back to the limousine. With a final reluctant glance back, she slipped into the vehicle, and a moment later gravel crunched under the tyres as she rolled away. Only when the limousine was well clear did Elliot turn his eyes back to his guests. "So. I see you didn't take my advice. You're still tagging along with the Empress."

"For the moment," Jess agreed.

"The plan worked? You escaped whoever was chasing you?"

"For a while," said Jess. She touched her face gingerly. "They caught up."

"Apparently they didn't get what they were after. May I ask what happened? Did your violent young friend... ah... happen?"

"It's a long story," Jess said. "There's still a few of them out there. They won't track us here."

"Well, that's good news. Hopefully I'll be able to add a bit more. Who's your friend?"

"This is Mark," Jess said. "He knows everything. He knows about the Empress. He knows about Zama."

"Oh yes, I know all about Zama," Mark said. He thrust a hand forward. "Mark McTiernan. Very nice to meet you, Mr Elliot."

Elliot stared at the hand until Mark withdrew it. "McTiernan."

"I'm Jess's husband."

"Ex-husband," Jess muttered.

"Not yet."

Elliot took a deep breath. "The reason I invited you here is that I believe I can help the Empress more thoroughly than I originally suggested."

"Frankly, what would help us most at the moment is the money you promised us," Jess said.

"I know what I promised. Money, documents, bank accounts, credit history. All very nice to have but it's missing the most important thing."

"What's it missing?"

"An *identity*," Elliot said. "So she has all the money she could need. What's she going to do with it? How's she going to live her life? She's a sixteen-year-old girl. Being Empress doesn't mean a thing here. She won't last fifteen minutes by herself before someone's asking inconvenient questions. Where are your parents? Where do you live? Oh, and where'd all the money come from?

"Then there's the boy. Maybe, just maybe, she might be able to bluff her way through. But how about *him*? He doesn't speak English. He's all of, what, twelve years old? He has the skills of a SEAL and the impulse control of a chimpanzee. How long before he hurts someone? He'll end up in an orphanage somewhere. If he's *lucky*. I don't think any amount of money is going to help him right now."

Jess quoted his own words back to him. "Not my problem. I'm going back to my own life once she's got what she needs, once she's settled."

"Settled," Elliot snorted. "What does that even mean? You really think that money's going to solve all their problems? Or did you maybe have something else in mind?"

Jess blinked. "What do you mean?"

"Perhaps it's crossed your mind that the Empress needs more than just money. She needs a family, adults who can look after useful things like taxes and property and jobs. And to manage all that money, the credit histories and bank accounts that I promised."

"That's *not* what I was thinking," Jess protested.

"Of course it wasn't," said Elliot. "I've done little *but* think about this for days. You know as well as I do that they can't stay here. This planet wouldn't be good for them, and they certainly wouldn't be good for it." He paused and scratched his neck. "Look. I really do just want to help, but I can do better than help them find a way to live here.

"I can help them *go home*."

III

Elliot led them across the gravel expanse away from the mansion. Their destination was a large building at the side of the complex. It may once have been a barn but had been extensively modified, with steel sheeting and sealed metal doors. "We call this HERS," Elliot said. "High Energy Research Sciences."

"Is there a 'His'?" Mark asked.

It was meant as a joke, but Elliot nodded. "Information Sciences. Over that way. The main building, behind us, is mostly admin offices now."

"You don't live there?" Jess asked.

"God no," said Elliot. "It's big enough for a family of sixteen and a staff of twenty, and my wife didn't like the idea of vacuuming eighty rooms a day. No, we've converted what used to be a groundsman's cottage and we're very comfortable there."

The first drops of rain were falling, heavy droplets splashing across the gravel. Jess blinked as one caught her eyelash.

"Twenty years I've been living a double life," Elliot said, "and for most of that time it's worked. Elliot Industries started strong and has grown, year on year. Turns out I have a good head for business and I've picked the right people. Zama's technology isn't at all like ours. A Zaman paperclip is a technological breakthrough here."

The converted barn loomed over them, and whilst the exterior still showed its heritage, the modern trappings were obvious. The main entrance was a single steel door large enough to drive a tank through; inset was a man-sized door. It required a keycard, a number code *and* a retinal scan to authorise entry.

As the metal door slowly slid aside, Mark said: "That's a lot of security. What have you got in there... a nuclear bomb?"

Elliot played a straight bat. "Our work with radioisotopes is in a different building. In here we do some of our most sensitive, commercially valuable work. We need to keep it safe from competitors. I'm going to show you some of our most valuable projects. You should feel privileged; apart from my employees, there's probably only five people in the world who've seen what I'm going to show you."

Beyond the entry was a large chamber — *hangar* was the word that came to mind — floored in concrete, with metal H-rails overhead and strip lighting on the walls. In the further recesses of the chamber, a row of large cubicles housed what looked like buggies and a tractor. To the side of the door, a security booth housed a guard.

Elliot and the guard exchanged nods. "We need two guest passes."

"Just two? I thought we were expecting three," the man replied in a voice that didn't entirely hide its Russian accent.

"The others will be joining us soon." Elliot led them past the booth.

Further along the wall stood a bank of tall metal lockers. "Leave any smartphones, laptops or tablets here. If you carry them with you, they run the risk of being corrupted. There are strong electromagnetic fields inside. I don't suppose either of you has a pacemaker? Good."

Mark wagged his phone in the air. "Flash memory," he said. "Should be safe against magnets."

"Not against EMPs," said Elliot. "We build EMP-resistant phones for the military and even those sometimes get wiped in here. I wouldn't risk it. If you want to bring it, it's your choice. We had a Suit from Infrastructure here a few weeks ago. His phone burnt through his shirt and gave him second degree burns to the nipple."

They waited while Mark turned his phone off and deposited it in the locker. For a man who'd been known to drive forty kilometres home to pick up a phone accidentally forgotten, this showed his dedication: "I'm not letting you out of my sight," he had told Jess, and so far it had been true.

Elliot led them further into the chamber. "The high-energy labs are underground. We could have built what we needed above ground level but I didn't want to spoil the farmland. Besides, you can never be too careful working with high energy physics."

"I'll bet," said Jess. "Especially if you're reverse-engineering someone else's technology."

"Don't worry, we're very careful, very methodical. I have no intention of setting off a fusion explosion or creating a black hole by accident. We have some of the best and brightest working here. My head of high energy research is... let's just say, uniquely qualified. Zama gave me an alphabet and a glimpse at *See Jack Run*; my own people are writing *War and Peace*.

"Like I say, life here has become very comfortable. I've been very successful, made a lot of money. Most of it gets poured back into Elliot Industries. I'm not exaggerating when I say that we intend to change the world with the work we're doing here."

With that, Elliot brought them to a halt. They had reached a square slab, carved into the floor and bordered in yellow. Elliot drew a remote-control clicker from his pocket and a moment later the platform lurched as machinery under the floor ground into action. A metal railing rose from the floor to surround the platform, and then the chamber was rising around them as the platform lowered them into the earth. "Here we go."

"I take it back," said Mark. "Forget nukes. He's got the Batmobile in here."

"God's sake, Mark," protested Jess.

Elliot affected not to notice the sarcasm. He waved a hand at the wall. "We have a standard lift and stairs, but I find the goods lift gives a better view."

The lift traversed a single level, releasing them into a cavernous chamber. Around the sides of the open space were culverts, several of them occupied with vehicles — at first glance, police cars and army trucks. "It's not research, but adding EMP protection to vehicles is a nice money-spinner," Elliot explained. "Helps pay for some of the more interesting work."

The building was quiet and empty; it felt like night. Like these corridors were just waiting to be thronged with lab-coated scientists with wire-framed glasses and clipboards. Their steps echoed in the open space as they crossed to a door in a side wall. Elliot's swipe card opened the door for them and he led the way into a white corridor lined with glass walls. Behind the glass on both sides of the corridor ranged laboratories of various sizes. Fluorescent white light gave the place a clinical air as they walked. The brilliant lighting bleached the colour from the surroundings and from her skin.

Elliot directed their attention to security cameras dotting the ceilings at regular intervals. "We do a lot of work for Defence. That comes with a variety of security obligations. We get watched pretty closely. Which is why my *second* life is becoming more difficult. Every now and then I have to pack up at short notice and fly to some back-of-beyond location and rescue a Zaman refugee. It's getting harder and harder to keep that side of my life a secret. People recognise me. If the wrong person sees me in Ballarat or Wooloomooloo it could all come down like a house of cards. And I never know when I'm going to be called upon, or where."

"New arrivals don't always appear in the Nullarbor?" Jess asked.

"I wish. No, it's not that predictable. I've had people turn up in the suburbs of Darwin and out in Gippsland. I once had someone appear in the middle of Bass Strait. I never found that poor bugger. Gate technology is finicky; it's sending people billions of miles across the galaxy. Like using a pea shooter to extinguish a cigarette from two miles away. It only takes minute fluctuations in current and voltage and the exit moves across the whole damn country. Think of it like lightning. Never strikes in the same place twice. That's why I've been doing my best to build a lightning rod."

Another lift took them another level down. "Welcome to Level two. This area is highly restricted. Employees and special cases only."

"I feel privileged," Jess said wryly.

"Oh, trust me, you're a special case. The projects under way down here will be the next big things over the next decade. Crystal data storage. Magnetic information retrieval. We're making progress — slow, but real — towards building a sustainable generator that taps into the magnetic field of the planet itself. Do you remember when I told you that your flinger could change the world? If I could reverse-engineer it, we'd have free and inexhaustible energy for the whole planet inside of a year."

Inexhaustible, perhaps. Somehow she doubted Elliot would let it go for free. "I'm an Earthling. If you'd just told me that, I might have given it to you."

"Perhaps, but I don't think young Aran would have been happy about you handing over your only flinger," Elliot said. "It wasn't top of mind. I had a sword at my throat, remember." He brought them directly to a set of steel double doors at the end of the corridor. The doors swung open at a touch.

"Not very secure," said Mark, surprised.

"Actually, it's the most secure part of the building," said Elliot. "I have an RFID chip implanted. These doors only open in my direct presence. This is my laboratory."

More precisely, his lab was still a short distance ahead. As they passed through the doors, lights overhead hummed to life, revealing a gleaming steel staircase stretching downwards. Elliot led them down the stairs with the comfortable ease of familiarity. Jess couldn't help glancing at Mark as they followed; he looked grim and focused, seemingly as uncomfortable as she was.

At the end of the stairs another pair of double doors were closed. Elliot turned to face them. "I told you I was trying to build a focus for the Gateway, something to pull the portal to a set location? Well, in our research we accidentally went one better. There are only three people in the world who know about what I'm about to show you, but behind these doors is the best way that I can help the Empress." He turned to the doors and flung them open, stretching his arms grandiosely wide. "Welcome to my wormhole!"

IV

The limousine followed the gravel drive as it curved around to the east side of the mansion, descending a low ramp into the shadow of an underground garage. The engine purred as the vehicle passed concrete pillars and took its place, coming to rest between a blue sports car and a behemoth Hummer. Then, for a moment, the garage fell back to silence, punctuated by the soft *plink* of the car's cooling engine.

Crouched in the footwell of the rear passenger seat, Aran fought the urge to straighten. For such a large vehicle, the space below the level of the windows was cramped; with his backpack wedged tight between his back and the seat, he felt trapped.

Once he had been stuffed into a ventilation shaft deep in the bowels of the

Guard Academy, and it had been four hours of muscle cramps and airlessness before he was found by maintenance staff and released. The back of Farrow's car was probably not as bad, but it felt worse.

The car rocked as the big woman stepped out of the front seat. It seemed a very long moment before she called softly.

"We're alone," Vi said, rising from her crouch beside him.

It was a graceless process unfolding himself and his tangled backpack from the car. Vi was already several steps away by the time he was free, and he hastened to position himself in front of her. He kept one hand on his belt, flinger to hand; if Farrow was misleading them he wanted to be able to respond instantly.

"Keep your weapons hidden," the Empress had instructed. Easy for her to say; *he* was the one who had to protect her from enemies she hadn't even considered. It pained him like a scratch, that he should be required to protect the Empress while being denied the authority to direct their approach. His solution was necessary but deeply unsatisfactory: he would obey exactly as long as he judged her safe, and not a moment longer.

Gabe had told him once: *Sometimes, protecting somebody means ignoring what they say they want. It's your job to keep them alive and safe, not happy. They'll deal with it, and if they don't, there's always another person who needs protection.*

He turned on a heel, surveying the deserted garage. Concrete pillars were the chief feature, widely spaced down-lights casting dim pools of illumination, reflecting rainbows from oil on the concrete floor.

Farrow directed them to a metal door in the garage's side wall nearby. Her voice was still tight with anger. She might have been instructed to make them happy, but she hadn't taken it well when advised of the Empress's plan. She didn't like misleading her boss, but Vi had been adamant: it was this *assurance* or they would walk. A toothless threat, because where were they going to walk to, now they were at Elliot's private airfield? But Farrow had been instructed to keep them happy, so she had acquiesced. She hadn't been happy about it then, and she still wasn't happy now.

"This is the service wing of the building," Vi translated. "She says it should be deserted; everyone was sent home."

"The woman goes first," Aran said. "I don't want her behind us."

"Don't be so suspicious. We're among friends."

"I'm your Guard." The words were his own but he was echoing his father's voice ringing in his head. "A guard *has* no friends. He suspects everyone. You're the Empress. You decide our direction, but it's my job to be suspicious."

The Empress shook her head. "I'm humbled by your vigilance," she said, and Aran couldn't tell if she was being sarcastic.

The door from the garage opened onto a narrow hallway. An arched doorway to the left gave access to a large kitchen — dark and deserted. Farrow had already explained that the manor was equipped to support conferences; kitchens and a dining hall had been retained from the original design. They passed other menial chambers: laundry, larders and storerooms. Farrow stalked the corridor with determination. Aran didn't drop his guard, keeping his shoulder against the wall and his eyes constantly mobile.

The surroundings were trying to lull him into a false sense of familiarity. The oak panelling, the polished wooden floors and the ornate gold-filigree door handles could have been lifted directly from Harrock Hall. Four years at the Academy had done little to blur memories of his ancestral home.

There were differences. Lighting was provided by overhead incandescent bulbs rather than inset glow-tubes. Rather than data terminals the walls were lined with side tables and niches holding displays of indigenous relics. Framed paintings dotted the walls: landscapes, abstract shapes, portraits. Aran's steps faltered as they passed a familiar face on the wall: Jacob Elliot, immortalised in paint. "One man owns all of this?" Obscene. Even a Guildmaster would blink at this display.

"We need him," the Empress murmured in reply.

Aran glanced at the displays as they passed. Ovoid shapes of animal hide sat alongside long shafts of cured wood sharpened to points. He recognised spears and shields when he saw them. This world might not have been the warring landscape he'd been told to expect, but violence was never far below the surface. Humans are human, whatever planet they're on.

He reached behind his shoulder to open the first couple of inches of the zip that sealed his backpack. When he was able to brush his fingers gently across the pommel of the sword he felt safer. A sword at his back and a flinger at his belt: it might be enough.

Rounding a corner in the corridor, Farrow stopped so abruptly that Aran almost ran into her back. Instantly alert, he demanded: "Why have we stopped?"

Farrow's response was so soft as to be almost a whisper; the Empress's translation was even lower. "The security room ahead. Someone's inside." Farrow was checking the keys, secured by a short chain to her belt. She had not lent her keys to anyone.

Betrayal, then. Or else, an unexpected threat. In either case, *not a moment longer* had just expired. There was no pleasure in being proved right. He drew the flinger from his belt.

Farrow was saying something, her voice cold with anger. Aran waited impatiently while Vi translated. "The door's been opened, not broken. The *dahla* may have let them in." Aran wondered why Farrow would be so dismayed. Perhaps she was unhappy to have her authority usurped. Aran could sympathise.

"Stay behind me," he told the Empress. He would have preferred the Empress wait in the corridor, out of danger, but if there was speaking to be done he would need her to translate.

The security room was spacious and modern, control desks showing camera feeds from locations within the house. A bank of computer equipment filled one wall. The centre of the room was dominated by a table-top touchscreen displaying a schematic of the manor and surrounds. All of this Aran registered in the space of a second. The control desks were serviced by a series of swivel chairs, and two of the chairs were occupied.

Farrow had come to a halt, ramrod-straight just inside the door. She snapped out a question, the unfamiliar syllables sharp to Aran's ear, and whilst the meaning was unknown to him the intent was clear. *Who the hell are you?*

Aran didn't have to wait for a response. He already knew.

The man in the nearer seat was slower to realise. His eyes focussed first on Aran, then over Aran's shoulder to where the Empress was advancing through the door. They came to rest last on Aran's flinger, aimed at his chest. Half out of his chair, he froze, then let himself settle back down. He blinked, twice, and the sudden pallor of his cheeks was the clearest evidence of the man's surprise.

Jarem Co-Telek, previously Master of Services for the Imperial Palace, previously Gatemaster for Zama. Here. Sitting in Jaob Elliot's mansion. There could be only one reason for this.

"You were supposed to be with the *dahla*," Jarem said. Then he grimaced. "You didn't trust him." He was in local garb, a charcoal jacket too large for him over a black t-shirt printed with a rotting skeleton and jagged script. Previously clean-shaven cheeks had given way to ragged stubble after a week without a shaver.

"With good reason," the Empress said.

If the occupant of the second chair required a razor it was hard to tell. He might have been one or two years older than Aran himself, no more. Upon their entry he had turned his chair to face the door but made no attempt to stand.

Aran's stare dared him to reach for his flinger where it rested on the desk. "Keep your hands where I can see them." Aran tightened his finger on the trigger. Safer just to fire now and worry about ramifications later, but the Empress laid a restraining hand on his forearm.

"There's no need for violence," Jarem said. "Utara wants to speak with you, Empress."

Farrow's anger had deepened, finding herself ignored and surrounded by a language she didn't know. Veins stood out on her neck as she snapped out a question in her own.

The Empress answered with a short phrase of English, and Farrow fell silent, her jaw working as if she wanted to protest. The Empress turned to Jarem. "We thought we were done with you. We destroyed your tracer. Did you repair it, or do you have another?"

"Neither," Jarem answered. "We're not here for you. You took our cube reader, and if we're going to get home we need our data. Jacob Elliot and his company is at the forefront of crystal storage." He swallowed. "Imagine our surprise when we found out that Elliot already knew about data cubes. It didn't take long for Utara to get the rest of the truth out of him."

"What have you done to him?" Vi asked.

"Nothing permanent. He's working for us now."

The younger man's eyes were fixed unblinkingly on Aran. His hands were open on the desk — too close to his flinger. Aran's hand ached with the effort of not pressing the fire-stud on his own. He kept his aim steady as he edged his way around the bank of video monitors that stood between them.

Jarem was still talking. "Utara thinks it's fate. He thinks you're *meant* to come back with him."

"Perhaps fate has another purpose in mind for our meeting." The Empress spread her hands. "You came here with a full squad. How many are left?"

Jarem shrugged. "Rather fewer. Captain Aesk is angry about that." The colour was coming back into his face.

Aran was close enough now. Staying out of reach in case of a sudden lunge, without lowering his own weapon, he reached out with his left hand and slid the flinger away along the desk. The younger man's eyes ignored the weapon, ignored the other occupants of the room. His stare was reserved for Aran alone, and Aran had had about enough of it. "Do I know you?"

"No reason you should," the boy growled. "I'm Jad Hec-Voyen. My father wasn't famous. I don't come from a prominent family. We're not nobles."

"Then what are you staring at?"

"A child. A nobody who's only protected by his father."

You're a loser, just a baby. Go on, run home to your daddy. Niosk and his ceaseless needling were years behind him. He'd stopped crying himself to sleep at Yan's scorn a long time back. He refused to let this boy get to him, but his voice was tight as he replied. "I'm not a child. I'm an Imperial Guard."

"Aran. We have no time for this." The Empress's voice was stern, but Jad Hec-Voyen was still staring at him, and Farrow was still talking. The Empress turned away to respond.

"You think you're a Guard," said Jad. "You think you're special. You're wrong. Privilege doesn't make you a fighter."

"I'm *Captain* of the Guard." As the Empress's protector, he had earned that role. *I have supplanted my own father.* That thought unsettled him but he had to put it aside as Jad responded.

"If you're the best the Empress can find, she's in trouble."

"I am the best," said Aran. "The best on this planet. The best back home."

"Not even close. I've been watching you for years on *To the Band*. You're not even half as good as Keres, *and* you're a lot less good looking."

To the Band. It was impossible to spend any time in the Academy without being aware of the ubiquitous cameras, but after a while the trainees forgot they were there. Aran had never met anyone who admitted to watching the show.

"He's bigger," said Aran. "But I'm better." Despite his pounding pulse, Aran was calm. If you'd asked him a week ago he would have had doubts. That had been before the hotel, before Obi and Heth and Rodd.

Jad seemed unimpressed. "Then I'm better than both of you."

"Maybe *you* should have joined the Guard, if you're that good."

"I attempted the Trials," Jad spat. "My father was a cabinet maker. Just to qualify I needed to be top three in my Region. That was easy. But we didn't make the quota, because the Guard roster was full. Because of you and your privilege."

Aran's ears felt hot but he was sure he was calm. "I've worked. I've earned my position. I've never received special treatment."

"As if the son of Captain bloody Gabe was ever going to be turned down. You never even had to qualify. One less place available for people who *do* pass. Because of you, and all the other nobles like you with nothing better to do with your life than to join the Guard and play soldier."

Aran touched his fading bruises. "I'm not *playing*."

Jad ignored that. "When Lord Harke is in charge, there won't be any preference given to applicants because of family. People like *you* can go back to growing turnips or whatever you're actually good at."

Aran's answer was interrupted as the Empress responded. "*Lord* Harke? He is no lord. He doesn't believe in the nobility. How can he expect to take on a title?"

"Lord Harke doesn't believe in *inherited* titles," Jad said, reluctantly turning his attention away from Aran. "He says that anyone should be able to be a Lord."

"So how shall lordship be determined?" Vi asked. "On what merit should people seek preference? By force of arms?"

"Through skill," Jad insisted. "There should be Trials, same as for everything else. Treat the Lords like Guildmasters."

Aran snorted in derision. That was a laughable proposition.

The Empress agreed. "The High Council does not grow. Through the stability of the nobility we ensure the stability of the Empire. Likewise the Guard. There are only so many spaces."

"I'm a better fighter than most of the cadets. The Trials are supposed to find the best. I should be in the Guard."

"And who will you fight, with your superior skills?" The Empress shook her head. "You could have joined the Militias. They can always use good fighters. But you'd know about that."

An unexpected sound in the corner of the room drew Aran's attention. Jarem was laughing. This man, who had thrown in his lot with the enemy. Who betrayed the nobles, the Empress, without apparent remorse. Was he now mocking the Guard? Aran wasn't about to let that pass. "Do you find this amusing?"

"He joined the rebellion because he wants to be a Guard. That's a perverse joke, he just doesn't know it." Jarem turned to face Jad squarely. "I've lived in the palace all my life. I know the Guard. I know how they spend their time. What they don't show on *To the Band*."

Aran stiffened his shoulders and stood a little straighter at the reminder. "We train."

"Yes, they train. They train hard," Jarem said, speaking not to Aran but to Jad. "They fight each other so hard and so long, all of them vying to be the best. But when they're not training? They spend most of their time standing at attention and parading. Hours of it, day after day. Training, and parading. Parading and training. It's a performance art. They're not fighters: they're *athletes*." He snorted. "Or they were, until you came along."

Aran stared, astonished at the sheer effrontery of it. Was *this* what he really thought of the Guard? The Guard protected the nobles, the Empress —

From what?

The last true attempt on the life of a noble was three generations ago. It had been part of a plot in one of the Regions, he seemed to remember, but not the details. Since then?

No. The Guard were the *reason* nobody attempted violence towards the Lords, towards the High Council. Nobody would dare attack, so long as the Guards' vigilance remained.

Nobody — until Harke. And how had the Guard helped against the rebellion? Barely at all.

Why would anybody attack the Lords anyway? The High Council ruled with a soft hand, deferring local matters to the Low Councils. Gabe had told him once, *The High Council is ceremonial. Nice to look at, good to know it's there, but of no real importance to the way people live.*

Ceremonial. Another word for *performance art.*

The engineer's words had fallen on deaf ears and Jad was still arguing. "I'm supposed to build cabinets for the rest of my life? I'm better than that."

The Empress leveled a finger at him. "*Better*? You're too good to build cabinets? Your father was not *too good* to build cabinets. Generations of your ancestors have followed that trade. Who are you to say that it's unworthy of you? For hundreds of generations, sons and daughters have followed in their parents' footsteps. Aran is no different."

Jad's face was contorted with rage. "I don't want to be like my father!"

The Empress sighed. "Then choose another path. Find a new sponsor and take the Trials for any profession you choose. Or – "

"Lord Harke said —"

The Empress ignored his interruption. "Right now I have need of soldiers. Abandon Harke's doomed rebellion. Join with me. Join Aran's command. I will make you a Guard, right here and now."

Aran's command. The idea thrilled him. And it repelled him: offering mercy to one such as this went against Aran's very soul. He was about to say something — although he wasn't yet certain what it would be — when Farrow's patience expired. The woman interrupted with a stream of angry questions, indecipherable English spitting across the floor.

The Empress turned to respond, and the moment was lost. Aran could see it in Jad's eyes, the tightening of the muscles of his cheeks. The boy had been thinking about the offer, but no longer.

You don't want that, and neither do I. Aran suppressed a smile. "You're lucky I don't fight you. You might be the best in your region, but I've been training as a Guard for four years."

Jad sneered. "I know your tricks. I trained under Trig Velesson. He was a Guard for *thirty* years."

Aran didn't know the name. Trig Velesson could hardly have made a name for himself to be so little remembered. Behind him, the Empress was arguing with Jarem, voices rising and falling. Aran tried to ignore them. "I defeated Obi, and Heth, and Rodd. They were bigger than you."

"They were brutes," Jad said dismissively. "I would have beaten them too. I'm better than they ever were and I'm better than you. Take up your sword. Let me prove it."

Tempting, but impossible. "The Empress does not wish it."

The argument was rising to a crescendo, harsh foreign syllables flying. Aran dared them a glance. Jarem was involved now, emphatically pointing a finger at the floor, bristling at the Empress, but she was steady and resolved as she answered. Whatever she said met Farrow's nodding approval, but Jarem's retort sounded scathing. Voices rose until all three were shouting. He wondered if he was going to have to —

Jad lunged. Aran had been waiting for this, expecting it, hoping for it. Nevertheless the sudden movement took Aran by surprise. The young rebel jerked out of his chair, but Aran's reflexes were on a hair trigger, his attention tuned to a fever pitch. Even as Jad moved, Aran was firing.

But Jad wasn't going for the flinger. He moved in the wrong direction, and Aran's disc skipped off the console and buried itself in the concrete wall. The next moment, Jad had lifted his sword from its resting place beside his chair, rolled, came smoothly to his feet. Sword in hand.

Aran's stomach turned. No time to wait for the flinger to recharge; Jad was terribly fast. Jad leapt across the console towards him. It was all Aran could do to get his own sword clear of the backpack and in front of him to deflect the first strike.

This fight was nothing like the duel with Obi. Jad was whip-fast and skilful. Aran ducked and weaved and swayed, parried and blocked and deflected, and despite his best efforts Jad's blade got past his guard to nick his cheek, his shoulder, his shin. In moments, he realised that it was possible that Jad had been telling the truth; Jad was better than him.

The room was too small, too cluttered. Farrow was shepherding the Empress into a corner, out of reach of the flashing swords; Aran could spare her no attention as he concentrated on keeping Jad at bay. He circled, trying to get the central desk between himself and his assailant, but Jad was mere steps behind him.

Whoever Trig Velesson had been, his training had been excellent. No room for showy moves and intricate sword-work; Jad's technique was efficient and murderous, each flash of sharp steel a potential killing blow. It was all Aran could do to find room for his own attacks between fending off Jad's strikes.

"You're slow," said Jad, his breath coming fast and shallow. "You're better than the cameras showed. Not good enough." He feinted left, struck left again, then whipped the sword around in an arc that would have opened Aran's throat if he'd been an instant slower. Aran's counterattack was pedestrian by comparison, but it forced Jad to block and gave Aran a momentary reprieve.

Aran didn't attempt to reply. Sparing his breath for anything other than combat would get him killed. He pressed his attack, trying to take the initiative, but Jad evaded his strikes with apparent ease, then spun inside Aran's guard and struck at him with an elbow, a blow that would have crushed his throat had it landed. Aran retreated as Jad reset his stance.

Combat strategies flashed through his head faster than he could speak them. *Need to control the fight* and *Step outside the beat* and *Turn his own momentum against him.* Useless, all. Jad now had his measure. The older boy now on the offensive, using short slashes and thrusts, and there were no openings for Aran to exploit. He retreated under the remorseless advance. Hooked one foot around a rolling chair, sent it skimming across the floor at Jad, but Jad stepped around it without pause.

"Looks like there's going to be an opening in the Guard," said Jad, suddenly changing his approach and cutting low, but Aran had guessed his intent and was ready. He guessed wrong. Jad reversed his sword instead and struck upwards with the hilt, the blow glancing off Aran's bruised cheek. It wasn't a significant blow but it forced Aran backwards two steps, off balance, and now Jad attacked in earnest, pressing forward and Aran's feet were badly positioned, he'd lost his stance. He stumbled, let his fall turn into a backwards roll, away from his attacker, coming back up to his knees with the sword held high in defence. The bank of video consoles was at his back, and there was nowhere left to retreat. With the advantage of height and mobility, Jad seemed to realise that the fight was all but won, and he shifted from his light strokes to heavier, two-handed attacks. Aran blocked one, ducked under another, brought the sword up for a third, and lost his grip on the weapon as Jad twisted his blade and pivoted. Aran watched as his sword slid away across the floor, and Jad grinned as he started his approach for a final strike against his disarmed opponent.

Then Jarem stepped forward and kicked Jad's feet out from under him.

Jad stumbled and fell, his sword spilling from his grasp. Aran rolled, scooping up Jad's fallen sword as he came back to his feet. Jad was already attempting to rise, one hand braced on the floor and the other clutching at his skull, but Aran rested the tip of the sword on the back of Jad's neck and all the fight went out of him in an instant.

"You're welcome," Jarem said. The technician stared down at Jad, flat on the floor, and shook his head. "The Empress and I have come to an agreement. Just as well Jad doesn't speak English."

Aran stared at Jarem. He owed his life to this traitor. To cover for how that burned he snarled. "You betrayed the Empress, and now you've betrayed Utara. Nobody will ever trust you again."

Jarem sighed. "I was hoping for gratitude."

Gratitude? Aran could think of nothing appropriate to reply.

Jarem shrugged. "Never mind. We need to get moving. Before Utara realises where you are and comes to get you."

"We're not going anywhere," the Empress said.

Utara. Of course, he must be here somewhere. With more men. On ground that they knew, while Aran did not. He kept Jad's sword pointed as he stepped across to retrieve his own. "Jarem —" He swallowed against his nausea. "Jarem is right. We must leave."

"Utara holds the *dahla*'s wife and children," the Empress said. "We know what Utara does to hostages. And we've sent Jess into a trap. We must get them all out."

"That's a *really* bad idea," Jarem said. "Utara has the upper hand here. Come away now, he'll never find you."

Aran had to agree. Utara still had half a dozen men at his disposal. One or two at a time, with the advantage of surprise, Aran could take them. But they wouldn't underestimate him again. "We should get out of the building. We can plan a rescue after we're —"

On the video monitors, the image streaky with spots of rain, a dark figure approached. Crossed swords formed a V above his shoulders, as he took up a position outside the main doors. Other screens showed other figures converging on the manor from different angles.

Too late to run.

"They're here," Aran said. "They know where we are."

Sitting on the floor, Jad was grinning.

V

"Welcome to my wormhole!"

Gigantic pillars lined the sides of the cavernous chamber, each six feet around and ten high, faced in burnished chrome. The pillars were interspersed with banks of floodlights that warmed into gentle life as they entered. "Nice," said Mark, turning on his heel like a tourist in a cathedral as he crossed the threshold. "Russian missile silo chic."

Jess had given up trying to convince her husband to treat the situation with solemnity. The best solution was to ignore him. "What is all this?" she asked.

"Magnetic fields," Elliot said. Behind him the doors glided silently closed. "Zaman technology: the use and manipulation of magnetic fields for energy generation and transfer. These are field generators. With these I can create and shape high-power fields."

"This might be a stupid question," Mark interrupted. "But if you fire up a huge magnetic field to try and catch a Gateway from the Nullarbor, isn't that going to throw off every compass and GPS between Melbourne and Darwin? Might draw some attention, and I thought you wanted to avoid that."

The Fixer essayed a thin smile. He raised a finger above his head and pointed at the ceiling, and for a moment he reminded Jess of John Travolta in that dance movie. "It's a tight field and it's directed that way. I assure you, it's no threat to airliners."

The centre of the chamber held a slightly raised platform like a stage, and as they approached light reflected off a patterned metallic inlay. To the side of the platform stood a console, enough controls evident on its face to rival the space shuttle. "So this is it," said Jess. "You've built your own working Gateway."

Elliot looked abashed. "Not quite. The gateway is stable. But that's not much use if we can't control its exit point."

"Now I'm impressed," said Mark. "This has got to be worth some cash."

"It's not for commercialisation," Elliot said. "This is one technology Earth's not ready for. I'm not stupid; I realise science can't be stopped. Our work gets published. Someone, some time, will develop this application. I reserve the right to 'discover' it first. Until then I'm holding onto it."

"You didn't say anything about this last time we met," Jess accused. "Why not?"

Elliot shrugged. "I didn't trust you. The girl might have been the Empress, but she might not. Even if she was, she might not have appreciated my reverse engineering a Gateway that could send all her undesirables back home to Zama. Besides... it wasn't ready. We've made a lot of headway just in the last few days."

The last few days? Alarm bells jangled in her head. Something wasn't right; it was *too* coincidental. She hazarded a question. "What do you still need? How soon until you're able to send the Empress home?"

"I need more data. Every time Zama opens a Gateway, I get another data point. We're still not close enough."

"It doesn't sound like Zama's going to be opening many more gateways," Jess pointed out. "So how do you proceed from here?"

"We proceed with you."

The reply came from behind them.

Jess turned. The man had been standing in the shadow behind a field pillar and now he stepped forward into the light. The familiar scar stood out pale on his face. That face Jess would never forget; it had burned into her memory as he carved a gash into her skin. Utara was not holding a knife now. Instead he held a flinger at the ready. Jess didn't take her eyes off him as she hissed at Jacob Elliot. "You bastard."

"He has my kids," Elliot said softly. "I'm sorry. I had no choice."

"You were supposed to bring the girl," Utara said. "What do I want with these two?"

"She wouldn't come. I don't know where she is... I did what you asked."
Elliot's haggard face was sketched in an expression of defeat. "I was
working on it. If you'd waited a little longer..."

"She's in the main building. My men spotted them." Utara faced Jess
directly. "You've brought her back to me. Now you can help me finish
this."

"I'm not helping you," Jess said.

He ignored that, running his eyes over Mark. "And are you the hero who
struck me from behind? I won't turn my back on you again."

"I'm *not* helping you," Jess repeated. "No point using me as bait. The
Empress won't hand herself over for me, and even if she would, Aran
won't let her."

"You could convince her," Utara said. "But I expect you won't."

"Why would I do that? After what you've done?"

"If you don't, I'll be forced to give her an ultimatum," Utara said. "And
when that fails, I'll have to kill you."

VI

"Who *are* these people?"

Alice Farrow had demonstrated substantial patience but it had now come
to an end. There were intruders in her security room. Strangers had
conducted a sword fight there. She'd been adrift amongst long
conversations in a foreign language. Of course the woman was angry.

Vi could sympathise. Farrow deserved answers but they didn't have time
for a long discussion. "Those men are soldiers. They are here for me. They
will kill you if you get in their way."

"This isn't the first time you've met them." Farrow nodded at Aran with
his cuts and bruises.

"Your employer — Mr Elliot —helped us escape them once before."

Jarem interrupted. "Utara has Elliot's wife and children under guard in one of the smaller buildings. He's threatened to torture them, and I believe him. I think he enjoys it."

On hearing that, Alice Farrow went white. "When?" she asked, her voice tight.

"Yesterday," Jarem answered.

"*Yesterday*," Farrow repeated. "I should have—" Her voice trailed off as if she wasn't sure exactly what she should have done.

This is probably not the first time your employer has kept secrets from you, Vi thought, but it wouldn't be helpful to voice.

"They're not coming in," Aran observed. The men outside had taken up position in front of each door to the manor.

She slipped smoothly into Zaman to reply. "They underestimated us last time. They won't make that mistake again. I don't think they have many men to spare."

"I'm ready," Aran said. "I'll finish them."

Utara wasn't about to send his forces into the building, but he would surely love to see his enemies come out. "You will not set foot outside this building. They cover all the exits, and they now know you for a threat. They'll shoot the moment they see you."

Farrow pulled a phone from her pocket, but Jarem shook his head urgently.

"They know what police sirens sound like, now," he said. "Utara gave orders. They'll kill the children." His face was bloodless except for high points of colour in his cheeks. "I told him not to hurt the children, but he doesn't listen to me."

Farrow lowered the phone. "Where are they? How many?"

A short exclamation from Aran drew Vi's attention back to the screens. "Something's happening."

The camera was directed across the open drive to a building standing across from the manor. The strengthening rain outside obscured the figures of four — no, five — people exiting the building and crossing the gravel drive.

The lead figure was the *dahla*. Next came a shorter man, with a hand wrapped in the hair of a woman as he dragged her out of the building. Vi's lips tightened at the sight. That had to be Jess. Which made the next figure Mark McTiernan; another soldier she didn't recognise brought up the rear.

Two soldiers at the manor doors. Another two on the screen. Jad and Jarem in here. That left — how many? Perhaps two more?

"Where's Captain Aesk?" She turned to Jarem, but she spoke in English for Farrow's benefit. "Where are the rest of your men?"

"I don't know. Utara doesn't consult me on battle plans."

"What *do* you know? Utara kills children. You have chosen a side. Tell us all you can."

"I don't know anything," Jarem protested. "They left me with a minder. You think young Jad here knows anything about computers?" He squinted at the camera monitors. "That's Illen at the front door. At the rear, I think that's Quain. Yes, definitely; two swords, he thinks he's an expert. Utara you already know. The young man with him is Rigge. I don't see the captain, but his wound is worse. He's probably sitting down somewhere, he can barely walk. I'm telling you everything I know. I'm helping."

Utara's little group had paused under the rearing topiary horseman as if it could offer shelter from the weather. At this closer distance she could make out more detail. Utara's companion had forced Mark to his knees beside Jess, and Utara kept his hand in Jess's hair as he stared directly at the camera. With his other hand he gestured towards the manor, a clear beckoning.

"He knows about the cameras," Farrow said. "He knows we're watching."

"Please tell me you're not going to talk to him," Jarem begged. "This is a big building. There must be other exits, ways out that he can't see. Don't try to meet him on his terms."

"I'm not going to talk to him," Vi said. "You are."

VII

Jess knelt with a gun to the back of her head and wondered what she could have done differently. From the moment Mark walked in the door on Saturday morning, she had been set on a path where every decision and every turn had led her to this point. At first it had been compassion driving her: how could she abandon helpless children who needed her aid? But she could have left them in Port Augusta. Elliot had asked her to. That was when she started making her own decisions. Each one logical, considered, inevitable: one step following another to bring them to this confrontation.

Perhaps she should have been more attentive as they first entered HERS. *I thought we were expecting three*, the guard in the booth had said. That might have been enough to tip her off; the tone, bordering on insolent, far too familiar for an employee. The same guard stood behind them now.

But no. No reason she should have guessed the man was from another planet. She'd pegged his accent as Russian. And all she had at that point were vague suspicions about Elliot's motives.

No, there was not one decision she could have made differently. The Empress, trusting her implicitly, had depended on her understanding of this foreign world, and in that dependence Jess had found something she needed. There had been plenty of opportunities for Jess to betray that trust and bring their run to an end, but after that morning in the cafe she had given up on ideas of leaving.

Now, with rain needling her head and back, streaming down her face and plastering her clothes to her skin, she had nobody to blame but herself.

Utara stood two paces to the front, staring at the mansion beyond the topiary soldier. She had to raise her voice to be heard over the rain. "This is your big plan? You think that the Empress will trade her own freedom for mine? You wish."

"Of course she won't. I'm going to give her the ultimatum anyway." Utara turned to address her directly. "I'm looking forward to killing you, but it will be much more enjoyable if I can make it her fault." Jess wondered if his grin indicated that his last statement was in jest, or if just the thought was turning him on. "As far as the Empress is concerned, I just want to talk. Hush now. We're about to begin."

Across the drive, the door to the manor had cracked open. Through the rain it took Jess a second to recognise the figure who stepped out; too solid for Vi and too tall for Aran. A moment later she remembered the man who had accosted them on the road after Ivan's truck had run them off. *Is he carrying messages for the Empress now?* A second later a more sinister explanation occurred. *She's already captured. Or dead.*

"Who's that?" Mark asked. The guard had forced him to his knees with his hands behind his neck; that was overkill. There was no fight left in Mark McTiernan, not since Utara decided to demonstrate his seriousness. A dark bruise was rising above Mark's eye where Utara had struck him with the butt of the flinger. He was probably fortunate Utara had not decided to use the business end, but apparently there was value to keeping them alive for now.

"He's on their side," Jess hissed. "We met him before."

"Quiet," demanded the guard behind them. Jess complied. She wanted to hear what Utara was saying anyway. But she couldn't understand a word. Utara and Jarem carried out their negotiations — if negotiations they were — in their own language.

Utara did much of the talking, the furry Zaman syllables falling in rapid-fire succession. *Maybe he likes the sound of his own voice.* Jess could only stay quiet and hope that someone would advise her when they reached a decision.

Jacob Elliot, standing to Jess's left, took pity on her. "The Empress is well. Farrow and the boy have control of the manor. After your last encounter, Captain Aesk doesn't want to send his troops inside. Utara's asking her to come out peacefully."

Jess risked a response. "What's he offering in return?"

"He says he'll let you go. But he says that if she *doesn't* give herself up, he's going to kill me. And you." The only sign that Elliot was concerned at the threat to his own life was a brief pause before he continued. "She'll have nowhere to go. No help, no way to live, no allies."

Jarem seemed to have little to say in response to Utara's ultimatum. Once Utara stopped talking Jarem turned and headed back to the building.

Utara switched to English. He sounded confident. "Your girl Empress will give herself up. She doesn't have any choice. She can't survive here without Mr Elliot. If she doesn't come out of her own accord, I'll kill him in front of her. If she *does* come out, I won't hurt her. I'll bring her home like she's made of glass."

"You can't kill me," Elliot said, sounding far from confident. "You need me to open the Gateway back."

"I don't. You said it yourself. You're not the expert. I have Jarem, and you've already built most of the machinery."

"Perhaps the Empress can't survive here without me," said Elliot, "but neither can you. This is *Elliot* Industries. There will be questions asked, if I'm suddenly nowhere to be found."

"Perhaps I'd rather not return at all than come back without her," Utara said. "I keep my promises."

"She'll never trust you," Jess said. "You've given her no reason to believe that you'll treat her properly, that you'll let us go."

"You have my word, if the Empress submits to return with me, you won't be harmed. Neither will she."

"Let me talk to her," Jess said. "Maybe I can convince her."

"I don't think so. Jarem is quite sufficient as a go-between. I'd rather keep you here as another incentive."

"She won't agree. She's too stubborn. You'll have to kill us."

He was facing away from her but his shrug was eloquent. "Won't *that* be devastating."

If the discussion between Utara and Jarem had seemed long, the wait for a response was interminable. There was sharp gravel underneath one knee and the pain there was growing, water soaking into her pants where she knelt. Utara must have been almost as uncomfortable, with the rain steadily beating on them and slicking his hair to his face, but he seemed content to wait.

"Look," said Elliot.

Jarem stepped out of the manor house and stopped on the front verandah under the limited shelter of overhanging eaves. His shouted response gave Jess no clue to Vi's answer, but Elliot again came to the rescue.

"She says yes."

Showdown

I

Calla would not have approved of this plan. Vi could almost hear her voice in her head, taking her to task for *failing to value the Crown*. Famously, unapologetically pragmatic, Calla would not hesitate to follow Jarem's advice and melt away into the night. Despite knowing this for a false economy, Vi couldn't quiet that voice. With Jacob Elliot alive and on her side, she had help, resources, allies. Leaving him behind would leave her marooned and helpless on a foreign world.

Somehow Calla's voice turned that into *Better that than to place yourself into the usurper's clutches.*

Jad's angry stare was distracting. The boy sat trussed to a chair and gagged in the corner of the room, far enough clear of the consoles that he couldn't get up to mischief even were he to get a hand free, but no amount of binding was going to interrupt his glare. The logical approach was to blindfold him, but the sixteen-year-old in her made her hesitate, squeamish to engage in cruelty. Ramia's ruthlessness came to the rescue, and when she finally dropped a canvas bag over Jad's head she found herself comfortable with the decision and much less distracted. With Aran and Farrow gone, she could take some time to think in the quiet.

On the monitors Jarem was bringing Utara her terms. Obscured by rain and distance, she couldn't make out Utara's expression through the camera. A slim man of moderate height that you could pass on the street and not think twice. You might never have known the reptilian heart that lay within. Until you saw his eyes up close. Until he looked at you and considered what he would like to do to you. Vi had experienced that gaze. She would have given anything not to have to put herself back into his grasp.

There was no other way. She had to take the risk.

Everything revolved around Jacob Elliot. If he lived, there was still hope; there was no doubt, though, that Utara would not hesitate to kill him at a moment's provocation. That would be that: the end of Vi Corala, Empress of Zama. Maybe not immediately. She might escape, might survive for now. But live or die, the line of Empire would end with her. The Crystal Crown would be lost forever. *That can't happen. I have to do this.*

A darkening in the doorway announced Jarem's return. The Gatemaster hesitated in the doorway. "He agrees to your terms. Safe passage for Aran, and he'll let your friends go free. You'll be fairly treated. If you *don't* come out, he'll kill the *dahla*. He'll kill the girl. And he'll burn this place to the ground."

Vi took a deep breath. "That's it then. Thank you. For your help."

"When I agreed to help you, this is not what I had in mind," Jarem said. "Are you sure you want to do this?"

"I don't see I have a lot of alternatives."

"You can still get out." Jarem glanced at Jad, gagged and bagged in the corner. "There's no lack of windows you could climb through. Utara will never find you. He'll give up soon, you'll never have to worry about him again."

"Yes, he'll give up," said Vi. "Take the remains of his squad and go back home to Zama. Leaving me here – stranded on a distant planet. Safe, and free to make a new life for myself.

"And then one day, fifty years from now, seventy, I'll come to the end of my life. And on that day, the history of a thousand years will die with me. When I die, there will be no new Empress to receive the Crown. Nobody will even know it exists. I can't let that happen. I must go home. For the sake of the Crown, I must return to Zama, and Jacob Elliot is the only real chance I have of that."

"I could build…" Jarem started, but trailed off even as he was saying it. Vi could guess what he was about to say.

"You can build a Gateway? It's taken the *dahla* half a lifetime and enormous riches to build his. Without him, without his resources, what hope do you have?"

"If you go back with Utara, Harke will never let you return to ruling Zama," Jarem told her.

"Harke will kill me. He wants to destroy the Crown and he can't do that without digging it out of my skull. But what is served by my remaining here? The Crown is kept safe for a few more years before it dies, a thousand light years away from where it belongs? If I return, perhaps it might be preserved. I must at least try."

"You're a brave girl," Jarem said.

"I'm not a girl," Vi replied. "Not any longer. And now we've kept Utara waiting long enough. Time to end this."

II

The rain had steadied and strengthened, now beating out a continuous tattoo on the gravel drive. The last sliver of the sun was hugging the horizon, rays of late afternoon light cutting underneath the cloud and tinting the landscape in amber. The rearing horseman beside them stood silhouetted black against the sky, frozen in the instant of driving its hooves down onto the intruders below.

Jess was saturated, her blouse clinging to her like a second skin. The cold had put her into fits of shivering, but Utara seemed to ignore it, standing two paces to the front as if he was immune to such prosaic discomforts as water.

Utara was talking to the other soldier, voices inaudible under the rain. In her peripheral vision she could see Mark kneeling. The cut on his scalp was bleeding, a slow weep of red that the rain failed to wash away. She murmured to him: "Still think it's a hoax?" Just saying it made her feel mean, but not enough to regret it.

Utara had beaten the scepticism out of him. Mark shook his head. "I'm sorry," he said, leaving her to wonder whether he was apologising for being so easily overcome, for his lack of trust, or perhaps for the punch that had set them all on this journey.

"You might be interested to know," Elliot said quietly. "They're arguing over letting you go. Utara wants to keep his promise but his man disagrees."

"We're no threat. What are we going to do, shout at him?" Jess was too cold and too tired to be diplomatic. "If he decides to kill us, your family is next."

"I know. I really hope that he keeps his promises."

"Promises," Utara interrupted, turning to face them, "are only good until you break one. I'm not going to give you a reason not to trust me. Keep behaving, your family will be unharmed." He settled his eyes on Jess. "As for you two, if the Empress comes quietly as she promised, I'll keep mine. I'll let you go."

Across the gravel, the front door of the manor cracked open. Shadows coalesced into movement as the girl Empress stepped out of the building, hands held open at her sides. Steadily, calmly, she came forward into the rain, her hair immediately plastering down over her forehead. She flinched visibly as the soldier by the door fell in beside her and took her arm in his grip, but she didn't take her eyes off Utara as she approached.

"Brave girl," said Utara, almost admiring. "Your highness. We meet again."

Vi stopped mere paces away. "General Utara. We have an agreement."

"*Lord* Utara. I like the sound of that better."

"You might need to ask your Emperor," Vi said. "Even in his new world of anarchy you don't get titles for free."

"He's not *my* emperor. Besides, you're quite a bargaining chip."

"He certainly does appear intent on recovering me," Vi said. "Willing to send you away with no guarantee you'll be able to get back. He must be aching for your safe return. Well, you have me. What happens now?"

Utara swept his gaze around, staring at the rain. His stare settled for a moment on Jarem, standing under the shelter of the manor doorway, but as quickly dismissed him; he was looking for something else. "Where's the boy?"

"I let him go," Vi said. "I don't trust your men not to hurt him."

"They won't hurt him if I tell them not to," said Utara. "He has a data pad that we need back."

"I have it," called Jarem. Aran's abandoned backpack dangled from his fingers. "It's all here."

"As agreed," said Vi.

Jess couldn't see Utara's smile but his shoulders relaxed visibly in relief. "Good. Then let's get out of this rain. Your highness, it's time to show you the marvellous invention your friend has built. Rigge, bring them." He shouted to Jarem through the rain. "Come along, wizard."

Vi glared at the general. "You promised to let my friends go."

"And I will. But it would be a shame for them to go without seeing you safely returned home. We don't need them talking to anyone until we're gone; we shouldn't need long."

Illen came forward, pulling Vi by the arm; closer to them, Rigge gestured with his weapon that Jess should stand.

Utara touched his ear; Jess caught a glimpse of blue light. He spoke in rapid Zaman. Jess could guess what he was ordering: *Find the boy.* She didn't blame the general. In their position, she wouldn't want Aran out there unwatched either.

"You won't find him," she said. "He's too good."

"If you don't catch him," Elliot said, "I have equipment that can track him." Jess shot him an incensed glare, but he shrugged it off. It shouldn't have surprised her; his family was at risk. It still felt like a betrayal.

The long wait on her knees had turned her muscles to lead and a thousand needles were assailing her toes. Behind her, Mark was having almost as much difficulty. With an effort she made it upright, and then hissed as her back complained. Behind them, Rigge jabbed his flinger into her shoulders as they started moving, stumbling, back towards HERS.

III

Once more Elliot led them into the depths below the laboratories. Each secure door sealing behind them took them another step from rescue. Empty, sterile laboratories watched the little group as they passed. Jess rapidly ran the sums through her head. Friday night now: it would be days before life returned to these halls.

She couldn't blame Elliot. Children change all the rules. Anyone would sacrifice the Empress of a distant world for the sake of their family; even Jess would. If the tension in his shoulders was anything to go by he wasn't happy about it, but he had made his choice and they couldn't count on help from that quarter.

Behind the businessman came Vi and the soldier, Illen, his hand still wrapped around her forearm. Her shoulders were straight, her steps firm. "Do not fear," Vi had whispered to her as they clustered at the door of HERS while Elliot entered the access code.

Jess wished she could share the girl's confidence, but it wasn't even genuine. The girl was trying to reassure *her*; it should have been the other way around. Wasn't comforting your children part of what being a parent was about? *They're not your —*

She recalled her mother's voice, a discussion long ago. *You look happy,* her mother had told her. *But you're not happy. You won't ever* be *happy until you have children.* A long-standing refrain between them: her mother's iron-clad views of how the world should be. There's only so many times you can hear a thought before some part of you believes. A part of her had been waiting for a daughter she could lavish with affection and protection, a daughter who would finally make her happy.

She's not your daughter, she thought again, and that sounded like Mark's voice. It was true enough, but the response that followed on its heels was entirely her own.

She's the closest you will ever have.

A sobering realisation, but the more she pondered the truer it felt. *Too old to start afresh.* She could re-enter the dangerous pool of dating, kiss a thousand frogs in hopes of finding a new prince. She could marry again. She might rediscover trust.

But at slightly-more-than-thirty, she couldn't fool herself. The chance of doing all that in time to have children of her own was... slim. At best.

Best to admit it. She would never have the experience of waking during the night to comfort a crying baby. Not for her to nurse a child from her own body, or smooth a band-aid over a scraped knee. She would never experience the travails and joys of toilet training, of teaching a child about language, about manners, about the world around her.

But then, that had never really been what she wanted from a child. She'd never wanted a baby. She wanted a *child*: a protege, a companion, maybe even a friend.

Vi had only been in her life for a week, but that had been time enough to fit perfectly into the hole in Jess's life. Completely unreasonable, but also undeniable.

They clustered at the secure door above the final flight of stairs for a moment, and she took the chance to edge closer to Vi. "Don't give up," she murmured. "This isn't over yet." Fine words. Now she just had to think of a way to overcome three armed men.

Vi's smile was tight-lipped. "I know."

That was all the time they had, as Rigge nudged his flinger into her back to start her moving.

I know? The words gave her pause. For all that they had thought they were being clever, approaching Elliot separately in case of some expected betrayal, they had not planned for this. Aran was off, who knew where; he wouldn't be able to breach the chamber below. No rescue from that front. So what was Vi planning? *What don't I know?*

She was still wondering as they stepped through the final double doors into Elliot's Gate chamber. The ranks of steel spheres leading down the long room to the control console and the platform seemed to capture Vi's attention and she stumbled slightly, the others jostling her from behind as they entered. *Of course. Nobody's told her yet that Elliot has a Gateway.*

Utara stepped past them into the chamber. He smiled like a bishop and stretched out a hand in the direction of the platform. "Your highness, our way home. As soon as my technician and your *dahla* can set the coordinates, we can leave this world in peace." He waved to attract Jarem's attention from the steel sphere he was examining. "Do you have what you need?"

Jarem nodded. He hefted the backpack. "With my data, it won't take long. This is good work."

"How long? Hours? Days? Weeks?"

The technician shrugged. "Hours," he said. "Maybe a day."

"We'll have you home by morning," Elliot said. "Let my family go."

"In due course," Utara said. "We can wait in here. Girl, make yourself comfortable. Rigge and Illen will take care of your needs." He pointed with a crooked finger. "Find a seat in the corner and stay quiet, and you won't be harmed. If you resist, Illen will break your legs." The two soldiers started to usher them away from the doors, and Jess forced her feet into motion. *More waiting.* The longer the wait, the more chance there would be an opportunity to...

To do what? Escape? There was no escape.

"Not you," said Utara. "You wait right there."

It wasn't until Rigge caught her arm and brought her to a halt that she realised she had been isolated, the other soldier forcing Mark and Vi further into the corner.

Utara faced the Empress. "I'll have my men give the grounds one more sweep for your boy. If we don't find him, he's on his own. I'm bringing everyone in here while we wait for the Gate. If he's outside those doors when we're done, he's on his own, and good luck to him." He waved a hand at the doors. "This is your chance to call him in. Do you wish to?"

"I don't have any way to contact him," Vi said.

"Worse luck for him." Utara raised a hand to his ear and murmured a few words of Zaman. Then he frowned, tapped at his temple again. Twice more. When he spoke again, his voice was dangerous. "Is this some kind of trick?"

Jacob Elliot's smile was frozen. "You won't get a signal out," he said. "The chamber's shielded."

From the side of the chamber Jarem nodded. "Unshielded magnetos this size, induction rings aren't going to work."

Elliot's voice was defensive. "Earth technology doesn't — We never had to think — I'm sorry. I should have realised."

Utara maintained his stare, but the sense of imminent explosion dissipated. "I don't punish honest mistakes. How far will the effect reach?"

"The main garage," Elliot said. "That should be far enough outside the field."

Utara nodded. "Rigge." The soldier listened as the general gave orders. He holstered his weapon and headed back to the doors.

Three left. With Rigge gone, it was just Utara, Illen and Jarem to worry about. There might never be a better time. But her throat ached at the thought of approaching Utara, remembering how easily he'd overpowered her last time. She glanced to the corner, where Illen stood over Mark and Vi, but Mark didn't appear ready to move either.

Utara turned back to face Jess, standing alone in the empty space before the doors and feeling very isolated. And he grinned.

A wave of cold surged up from her stomach into her throat.

Don't be stupid. He'd promised to treat them well. She forced herself to meet his eyes. "So what happens now?"

"Now, Miss McTiernan, we wait for the technicians to complete their work," Utara replied. His eyes flicked to the side; she followed his gaze. Mark and Vi were safely out of the way, seated on the floor in the corner of the chamber, Illen standing over them like a sentry. "Do you know why I brought you down here?"

She had been wondering. He could have put her in with Elliot's family. It would have been more efficient, combining your prisoners in a single group. Utara struck her as a man who valued efficiency. "You don't want us alerting the authorities," she guessed. "You didn't know how long you'd be stuck here."

"True," said Utara. "I don't need you causing me further trouble. But that's not the reason." His teeth glinted, and a moment later she realised that there was a knife in his hands and it was glinting too. He took a long, slow step towards her.

He promised —

Her stomach was an empty pit. She couldn't move her eyes from the blade.

"The last time we met, I had to cut our engagement short. We're going to be here a while. I thought we might spend some quality time together."

Jess raised a hand to her face and her fingers traced the scar down her cheek. "Quality time."

"The scar suits you," said Utara. "But I don't need a slave. Not on this planet."

"You're kidding," Mark McTiernan said, speaking up at last, driven by desperation. "I thought promises were only good until you broke one? If you hurt her, why would Elliot trust you to keep your promise to him? You still need his help."

"That was true at the time," said Utara.

"We weren't in here," Jess whispered. *The most secure part of the building.* "He's got what he wanted from Elliot. He doesn't need him any more."

"I don't need the *dahla*. I don't need his family. And I don't need you. So here we are. No interruptions. No schedule. Nowhere to run. We have all the time we need. Might as well relax and enjoy this." He held the knife up at eye level, another step closer. "Now, where were we?"

IV

Getting onto the roof was easy. The real trick would be staying there.

Driving rain had reduced visibility to a few metres and turned the roofing tiles into slick ramps to oblivion. Runnels of water cascaded across the tiles before joining the torrent overflowing the gutters, a thousand tiny waterfalls threatening to carry Aran with them. Night was encroaching and the tiles were beginning to blur in the shadows; with this cloud cover, it would be a dark night.

Captain Aesk is on the roof with a gun.

Darkness was his friend. In the dark and the rain he could stalk the night, picking off Utara's rebels one by one. Aran had watched from a distance as Utara ushered the Empress into the HERS building, two other soldiers falling in behind. One holding Elliot's family in one of the outlying buildings. Jad subdued in the manor. That couldn't leave many. Aran could make short work of them all.

But not with Aesk on the roof with a watchful eye.

The access door from the stairwell opened onto a small landing on the roof, a plateau surrounded by steep angled drops on all sides. The apex of the roof branched in different directions from the platform, a ridge along each wing of the manor. Through the downpour Aran could make out the next flat platform to his left, a darkened rectangle announcing the cubicle that protected the gears and engines that controlled the lift. Shelter from the rain, but it was too enclosed. Aesk would want to stay in the open. *So where is he?*

The scaffolding. The logical position for a sniper would be where scaffolding enfolded the manor's face. Flat surfaces, partial shelter, footing much more secure than the roof tiles.

Aran crouched low against the skyline and carefully, testing each step, went in search.

Within moments the scaffolding was in view, a grid of metal railings and wooden platforms jutting above the roofline. And within the shadows of the lattice, a darker shape; a man-sized space. Aran froze where he was, ignoring the rain that beat on his back. The shape of the captain was too low, too small, and he realised a moment later that he was sitting. *He's in a chair.*

Getting close would be tricky. He would have to trust his weight to the tiles. But the wind was gusting and biting through his wet clothes; between his shivering and the wind and the rain, he couldn't be certain of a shot from here.

Moving gingerly, testing each footfall carefully for a secure grip, Aran inched down the slope of the tiles towards the guttering. Step by step he moved closer, his target becoming clearer.

The wooden chair was wedged into the space between the guttering and a rail of the scaffolding, and the Captain himself was hunched in the chair, one leg awkwardly stretched out to the side as if in counterbalance. Aesk was staring intently into the night, the rifle laid across his knee. Aran considered that weapon. It might be a good weapon at range, but against that, it would take Aesk time to bring it to bear when he came under attack. Not that he intended to give him that opportunity.

Moving slowly, covered by the constant rain, Aran reached for a flinger from his belt. The wind swirled, slapping water directly into his eyes, and sounded like the whistling flight of a razor disc. The flinger was in his hand —

— *that wasn't the wind.* His footing faltered as he twisted to see behind, tiles shifting underfoot with a muted *chink* of masonry.

There was a man on the roof. Standing at the crest, silhouetted against the night sky, the man had a clear shot with his flinger. Only distance and the gusting wind had saved him from the first shot. The figure on the roof was short, a thick mane of black hair plastered to his neck and shoulders. The name came back to him in a flash. *Quain.* Utara had described him as the clever one.

Below him, Captain Aesk was coming awkwardly to his feet, attention caught by the sound or the movement. "Quain?" Even as he was saying this he caught sight of Aran, his eyes widening.

"He almost had you," Quain shouted. He stalked along the ridge, hunching low to give Aran less of a target. Too small, too distant, firing uphill. It wasn't worth spending a disc. Aran couldn't even crouch, not without losing his footing on the tiles.

How did he get behind me? It didn't matter: it was what it was. Mere seconds until Quain could shoot again, and Aesk below with his own weapon coming to bear. No time for analysis. Aran made his choice and leapt.

The tiles were slick underfoot as he plunged down the roof towards Aesk.

The Captain saw him coming and managed to pull the trigger. The sharp *crack* of the gunshot snapped at his ears. Aran completed the descent still on his feet. Momentum almost carried him over the edge of the roof but his foot caught the scaffolding and brought him to a halt.

Now Quain couldn't shoot without risking his commander. Aran spared an instant to snatch a glance in time to see the soldier reaching instead for his sword. But Aesk was closer, demanding his attention. The big man was turning his weapon, the barrel coming around. Far too slow: like a flinger, not intended for close-quarters combat. Aesk was shouting something, but Aran ignored the words. His right hand, clutching the flinger, was outstretched for counterbalance, so he used his left fist to attack. His punch was uncontrolled and had no weight behind it, bouncing off the taut muscles in the captain's chest. Still, it was enough; Aesk's balance shifted, his weight coming down on his injured leg. It failed to support him, and he fell like a dead tree, the scaffolding shaking under the impact.

Aran couldn't wait to see if the Captain rolled off the roof. Quain was almost upon him, and instead of a flinger he had a sword in each hand. *Seriously?* Guard training covered the techniques of knife-fighting, blades in each hand, but swords were another matter. Twin swords might look impressive but they're too awkward to handle. Aran needed only one. He drew it and flowed to meet the soldier.

Combat is like dance: it has a rhythm. Find the beat. *Then step outside of it*. Aran had learned that lesson the hard way, when Aesk used it against him in the desert. Quain's swords flashed through the air, slashing inches from his face, from his arms, striking sparks off Aran's own sword as he blocked, and he found the rhythm, stepped into the rhythm, synchronised to the beat, and danced. His heart beat with the cadence as he spun and blocked and counterattacked. He spotted a gap in the fence of steel and took advantage of it to deflect both swords and strike past them. Quain was forced to retreat, off balance, or be run through.

Never lose track of your opponents. Aran dared a glance behind. Mere seconds had passed. Aesk lay on his back against the gutter, water rushing around his shoulders and splashing over his legs as he brought his rifle around. But Aran was the Captain of the Guard and the deadliest person on this roof. He kicked the weapon out of the Captain's hands and sent it over the side of the roof into the darkness.

The rhythm was turning him to face Quain again. The soldier was a ball of fury, doubling his efforts. Against a mere militiaman, Quain's two swords would have seemed an impenetrable barrier of sharpened steel, a terrifying force of nature.

To Aran they were merely a fence, and fences can be penetrated. Aran stepped backwards out of the strike, paused a half heartbeat. *Step outside the beat.* Aran chose his own moment and lunged. Quain gasped as Aran's sword sunk through the soft flesh of his shoulder. The soldier reeled backwards, and the water on the tiles did the rest of the work. Quain's feet turned under him and he slid, tumbling uncontrollably, carrying him remorselessly over the edge of the roof.

I don't believe it. Aran stared at his empty hands, his sword wrenched from his grasp by the falling soldier. He'd never lost his grip on a weapon in the Lessons; here, he'd lost count.

He turned just in time to meet Aesk's shoulder as the big man bulled into him. The captain roared in wordless rage as his weight and momentum carried them both down to the roof tiles. A pile-driver fist landed in Aran's midriff, and in an instant the air was gone from his lungs and the training was gone from his thoughts and everything had changed.

It wasn't Aesk atop him, it was Niosk, it was Yan, it was a dozen other bullies who had plagued his life for as long as he could remember. And he was again a scrawny boy with a name that would not protect him. The boy that Aran had been was well practised at this. Curl into a ball, protect yourself, weather the storm and wait for it to be over. He tried to pull his knees up and found the captain in the way.

A fist pounded into his stomach and suddenly his throat was filled with bile. He couldn't draw breath. The big man had him in a bear hug and all Aran's training had deserted him. He flailed ineffectively, trying to strike back, and achieved nothing. "We're offering you safe passage," Aesk shouted, his face inches from Aran's. "Come peacefully and you won't be harmed." The Captain had no intention of allowing Aran to come peacefully; he grabbed Aran's shoulders and plunged him into the gutter.

The water in the gutter was ice cold and six inches deep, and at the first shock of submersion Aran couldn't help but gasp. Suddenly his mouth was full of water. Aesk had a hand on his throat and held him down, head underwater, and Aran was going to die. He wasn't trained for this. He had no strategy for this situation.

But he was *Captain of the Imperial Guard*. Everything he had been taught – every strategy and tactic in even the most advanced learning programs – every move practised until it could be completed without thought, without hesitation. *They were all new once.* And if *he* couldn't improvise a new solution, who better?

With desperation he struck at the Captain's weak points. Groin, armpit, neck. The man was an ox, inhumanly strong, impervious to pain, and Aran was twelve and fragile. He reached for the Captain's legs, for the injury he knew was there, but it was out of reach. Darkness was roaring at the edge of his vision as he clawed for Aesk's eyes. The big man threw his head back and his eyes were beyond his fingertips, so Aran instead drove his fingers into the man's nostrils.

That was more effective than he had anticipated, and for a second the pressure was gone, Aesk recoiling. Aran jacknifed his head above water, gasping great breaths into his lungs, but the reprieve was only momentary and Aesk was coming back for the kill. "We promised the girl not to hurt you," the big man roared, as his fingers reached for Aran's throat.

Aran drummed his heels into the water, scooting backwards, beyond the scaffolding. The gutter groaned under him, but Aesk was remorseless, flinging himself down onto the boy who had killed his men. A fist drove into Aran's face, and only the short range robbed it of the power that would have knocked him unconscious and ended the fight there and then. Aran's head rebounded back into the gutter and water flooded over his face once more.

With a sudden snap, the gutter lurched underneath him. Surprised, Aesk paused for a second, giving Aran another second to snatch a breath, and then the gutter was falling away under him, breaking away from the roof and bending downwards, sudden waterfalls rushing past Aran's ears. Suddenly tilted head downwards, it was instinct, not training, that made Aran lash out his hand and wrap it into Captain Aesk's shirt. The big soldier had no strength in his leg to pry himself loose, and then the gutter

357

was swinging free completely, and underneath Aran was nothing but empty space. Hopelessly overbalanced, Aesk toppled over the top of him, a momentary shadow wrenching the fabric out of Aran's hands, and then he was gone.

Desperately flailing, Aran's fingers brushed against something. With a last frantic effort he threw his weight to the side and his hand latched onto the edge of the guttering, as his body pivoted and slid out of the gutter, wrenching his arm painfully as he arrested his slide, hanging over the edge. The guttering swung and groaned and shook...

And held.

He let the rain run over him as he drew deep, ragged breaths and wondered at the implausibility that he was still alive. Then he started the delicate climb back to the security of the roof.

V

Vi had lived a hundred lives, and each of them was punctuated with betrayal.

The number of times the Empress had experienced treachery was beyond counting. Councillors going back on their vows; conspirators and special interests vying against the Crown; the infidelity of husbands and consorts. All these she had experienced, and more.

Utara reneging on his promise to treat them fairly was no more than a blip. That didn't make it any less disappointing.

Utara was approaching Jess, the knife held at eye level like a hypnotist's pendant.

"How about me?" Vi's voice sounded reedy in her own ears. She put her shoulders back and mined steely resolve from Calla. "Do you still need my cooperation? Hurt her, and you'll lose it."

He paused. "You have a point. I don't need anything else from you. What are you going to do, bite me? If you do, you'll regret it. I didn't promise to bring you back unharmed."

He tilted his head, then barked rapid-fire instructions across the chamber. "Freedman Illen. Disable the man. Don't hurt him too badly, I have plans for him."

The words were in Zaman; Mark was slow to react as Illen swung into motion. "Look out!" Vi cried a warning, but too late: Illen was right there. The soldier stamped a booted foot onto Mark's outstretched ankle.

Mark gasped in agony as Illen ground his heel into his captive's flesh. By the time Illen stood back, the flinger once more steadily trained on them, Mark was white-faced, curling around his pain.

"Just in case," Utara said in English. "You'll have your turn, but you won't interfere. Now, where were we?" He lifted the knife and turned back towards Jess.

"No," said Vi. "The deal's off. I'm not going anywhere with you."

Utara sighed, once more pausing to face her. "I don't think you have a choice anymore, *girl*."

"You're forgetting something."

The voice came from an unexpected direction. Vi and Utara both turned in surprise. Jacob Elliot, standing neglected beside one of the pillars, cradled something small and boxy between his hands. It gave a *snap* as he folded it closed. "Something important."

"Am I?" Utara pointed the knife. "Enlighten me."

The *dahla* dropped the object into a pocket. He didn't answer, but started moving. Within a half dozen steps he was within reach and Vi flinched, but she wasn't his target. Elliot bypassed Utara with barely a glance at the knife, and instead approached Illen, standing over Jess's groaning husband.

The soldier turned his flinger to meet the businessman.

"What am I forgetting?" Utara asked again.

Elliot ignored the flinger. He took a final step, bringing him face to face with Illen, separated by the weapon levelled at his collarbone.

"Actually, I don't care," Utara said. "Illen, shoot him."

Illen took a single, stumbling step backwards, then pressed the trigger on his flinger.

Nothing.

Illen blinked, staring at the inert weapon, and Elliot struck. His punch was so unexpected Illen had no time to react before the fist took him on the bridge of his nose. Illen reeled and the *dahla* kicked him between the legs.

The scarred rebel collapsed, his inert weapon clattering across the concrete. Elliot kicked him in the head, and Illen's eyes fluttered closed and stayed closed.

"Flingers won't work in here either," Elliot said.

Utara turned away from Jess to face the *dahla*. "You've just sealed your family's fate. And your own."

"You were going to kill me anyway," said Elliot. "Maybe you still will. But not my family. They're safe. The boy got to them. Your man is dead." He had Utara's full attention now, and he backed away. Headed further into the chamber, towards Jarem and the central console.

"I don't need them." Utara followed the *dahla*, stalking new prey. "I don't need the boy, I don't need you." He transferred the knife to his left hand and reached with his right for his sword. "Wizard. Can you fix the Gateway without this man's assistance?"

Utara had left Jess untended, but she had no weapons beyond her fists, and she wasn't stupid enough to try sucker-punching Utara. Mark was disabled. And who knew what side Jarem was on? With Illen out of action it was just Utara left. But the *dahla* was unarmed and had seconds before

Utara chopped him to pieces.

It was up to Vi.

"I can," said Jarem. With Elliot coming in his direction, Utara close behind, Jarem was trapped: nowhere further for him to retreat.

"Good. I'm about to kill the *dahla*."

"No." Her voice sounded distant, feeble. Vi swallowed and forced more volume. "You won't kill anyone." She straightened from her crouch and turned to face the General. Illen's sword was an unfamiliar weight in her hand. She gave the air a couple of exploratory cuts, getting the weapon's balance.

"What are you doing?" Jess exclaimed, her words echoed a second later by both the *dahla* and Mark McTiernan.

"You want to *fight* me, girl?" Utara snarled. A slow smile stretched his lips, teeth showing. "This should be *fun*."

"Yes, I'm a girl," Vi said, dropping into a classical fighting pose, the sword held at an angle across her body. Utara was not a bulky man, but she felt frail by comparison. She couldn't let that unnerve her. "I'm young." Her eyebrows drew down as she set her feet. "But I carry the experiences of thirty Empresses, and some of *them* were trained. So if you're coming, then come."

Utara grinned at her, apparently unimpressed. "At your command, *Empress*," he hissed as he leapt forward, and with the chime of steel on steel, combat was joined.

VI

The Empress Jojah studied the open-spear for twenty years, reaching the eighteenth level of mastery before laying it aside.

One off-hand comment in one obscure manuscript. That was the extent of historical record of Jojah's hobby. Jojah, one of the more obscure

Empresses, reigning in a time of peace and plenty, responsible for no great social reorganisations or technological advances, was all but forgotten. And yet, sword in hand, Vi could sense the shape of her. Her expertise and her instinctive understanding of movement in combat.

Utara came forward, sweeping his sword in a blow that would bury the blade deep into her torso, seeking a quick ending. Jojah surged forward in her memories to meet him. He had committed to the strike, sure his opponent was unable to strike back, certain this one blow would end the fight. A presumption, and she punished him for it. She spun aside from the sword, lashing out one-handed, striking the inside of his knee. It struck with the flat of her blade: Jojah wasn't used to edged weapons.

Vi let go, allowed herself to be swept up in the muscle memories of an Empress long dead.

There was danger in this. Submerging herself in memories surrendered herself. I am not them, but they are me. They are a part of me. *I am Vi Corala and I am Empress.* Committing her body to rely on training that she had never personally experienced brought the possibility that she would attempt a reflex response that her untrained muscles and her frail teenage body could not handle. One moment of weakness was all Utara would need.

Her successful strike had given him pause, and now he was more circumspect, moving with deserved caution and a limp. But it was not a mistake he was likely to repeat, and as she circled, reading his moves ready for his next attack, he held the advantage. He was stronger, faster, probably better than she was. He would outlast her. If she fought this to the bitter end, she would lose; she and Utara could both see that.

The Empresses' strength was not in force of arms. It was in accrued knowledge. Her voice was her weapon.

"What do you hope to gain?" she asked. "If you bring me to Harke, what has he promised you? I am Empress. We can make a deal."

"I'm not interested in deals," Utara replied. He struck a tentative blow that she parried with ease. "Your Empire is fallen, *girl.*"

Jess had retreated to the corner where her husband still lay. From there, she called to them. "You don't expect Harke's revolution to succeed, do you? Revolutions rarely do."

Vi nodded. "The Regions will never accept him. The Low Councils will fight him."

Utara's next strike was harder, and blocking it almost knocked her weapon out of her hands, the shock rattling through her arms and into her teeth, forcing her to stumble backwards three steps. Utara grinned. "I'm counting on it. You don't think I wanted to trade an Empress for an Emperor, do you? He won't last a year."

"Then what *do* you want?"

"Athara," the general hissed. "It's time for my homeland to remember its place, to regain its rightful glory. We used to be a nation of warriors, of conquerors. We will be, again. My people are ready to fight."

"With you as ruler, leading them to victory, I suppose?" Vi would have laughed, but she couldn't spare the breath.

"All they require is a leader," Utara exulted. "With me at their head, the people will rise up, reclaim the..."

"Oh, grow up!" Vi parried another strike, spun aside, and flung reality at him. "I remember Athara. Pleasant countryside, very pretty. A hospitable people. Really nice cheese. They're not warriors. They haven't been for a long time."

"I will *make* them remember," Utara shouted.

"Really? You expect them to welcome you back with open arms? I doubt all your countrymen feel the same way. Athara is law-abiding. Peaceful. One of the Council has a holiday house there."

Howling in fury Utara ran at her; spurred into intemperate action at last. Fury gave him speed, and it was all she could do to keep him at bay, retreating further into the chamber. *Don't let him close the distance. If he can seize you, he can kill you.*

363

They were still circling, and her footing was not as expert as it should be. Behind Utara, Jess dashed across the floor, circling them, heading for something behind her. Vi couldn't turn to see what she was up to. *Don't get yourself killed.*

Circling each other, probing for weaknesses. *Whatever you're doing, do it fast.* Her breath was coming in shallow gasps, her vision blurring around the edges. As they turned, the light towers at the sides of the room turned into strobes, the long shadows of Elliot, Mark and Jess falling across her eyes.

"I'm looking forward to cutting off your pretty head," Utara growled. "I'd do it for free, Lord Harke be damned."

"Doesn't leave... room... negotiation." She barely managed to get the last word out, heaving for breath. She was a Noble. She didn't so much as climb stairs. Her lifestyle in the Capitol had not prepared her for this exertion and each deflection was weaker, each dodge was coming more slowly, each step was less sure.

Utara's grin widened as he sensed imminent victory. He increased his pace, putting more power into his strikes. Vi stumbled back before him, the raised platform and its welter of electronics looming up behind her. Jojah's training saw a half dozen openings, spaces through which Utara was vulnerable, but she was spent; she was barely able to keep his sword away from her throat. Her arms were on fire and her fingers ached; the constant shocks into her wrists seemed to have set her whole body quivering. Under another series of withering blows from Utara, she fell back further, the sword vibrating in her hands so strongly she thought she would lose her grasp on it. One more strike like that, two at most, and she would be finished. Utara was still coming, an unstoppable force, and she couldn't do it any more.

She couldn't feel her hands any longer. The sword fell from her nerveless fingers, clattering to the floor. "I yield!" She tried to raise her hands in surrender and couldn't get them above her shoulders.

Utara ignored the surrender. "Too late, girl," he snarled. "Way too late," and the sword was rising high above his head.

"Now!"

The shout was Jess, somewhere behind her, but even as it clashed through the air there was a blur of movement from another direction. A streak of orange: Mark McTiernan, leading with his shoulder as he barrelled into Utara's back. Vi blinked her eyes clear and now Mark McTiernan was grappling for the general's sword.

"You're dead," Utara rasped, fighting back. "You're all dead." He twisted, trying to get his arms free, but Mark was all bulging muscle, and he was overcoming Utara's resistance by sheer force.

Vi rolled to her feet and skittered to the side to stay clear of the wrestling men. She couldn't help. Her hands were empty and the men were too closely intertwined to intervene.

The *dahla* was shouting. "Highness! Over here!" Putting the general behind her she stumbled in his direction, casting her eyes across the floor, looking for her discarded sword. Instead, her eyes alighted on Jess, standing at the central console, punching her fist down at a big red button.

With a deep rumble felt through the floor, the kleig lights around the perimeter of the room dimmed as the chrome cylinders spun into life.

"Take my hand!" Elliot shouted over the rumble. She followed his instruction, his hand warm but clammy as it enfolded her own. Elliot pulled her in close, startling her with the sudden intimacy as he wrapped his arms around her and took a firm grasp on a handle inset into the wall. "Hold tight."

In the centre of the chamber, above the central platform, arcing electricity played across the electronic pillars, seized into a solid bar of brilliant blue lightning between the two posts, and was gone. In its place, with a sound like the tearing of wet silk, a dot, a swirl, a pool of blackness formed. And then the chamber disintegrated into a maelstrom of howling wind and pressure. Her ears popped as the air was sucked out of the room; with a glitter of silver her discarded sword was picked up by the hurricane and swept into the terrible darkness of the portal. Elliot's arms tight against her shoulders kept her in place even as her hair whipped around her head and lashed into his eyes.

"Mark!" Jess screamed, her voice almost lost in the roar. Struggling with Utara in the dead centre of the chamber, directly in front of the gateway, her husband was knocked off his feet and spun in the air, losing contact with the general. Together, as helpless as each other, they fell towards the portal, circling like leaves in a drain. For a second Vi lost sight of them as they were flung around the side of the pillar, but moments later a thrashing shape disappeared into the vortex — which was already collapsing on itself, rapidly shrinking, the hurricane dispersing.

And then it was over. The arc lights returned to full brightness. The gateway fell quiescent.

Elliot relaxed his death grip on the anchor point. He withdrew his arms and almost jumped clear of her. "Sorry. For the familiarity."

The handle recessed into the wall was an inch thick and the same grey as the wall's concrete, and she wouldn't have seen it if not directed to it. Would she have been able to keep her grip on it against that tornado? She flexed her fingers and knew what that answer would have been. "That's quite all right."

"Mark!" Jess's cry was like a wounded beast, but her fears were unfounded. Her husband struggled to stand awkwardly on his uninjured leg, from where he had hooked an elbow around the base of the left pillar. Jess ran across the chamber to him. For a second it appeared she was going to throw herself at him, but then she paused, awkwardly crouched. Brought herself back upright and shook her head instead. "That was bloody stupid, Mark McTiernan."

"Your idea," he said. "That was intense." His first attempt to stand ended with him falling ignominiously onto his backside. Ignoring the damage to his dignity he slowly brushed imagined dust off his sleeves. "He's gone, I hope? I couldn't see."

"I didn't say you should fight him," Jess snapped. "Just push him in."

"Yeah, well, that didn't work. Is he..."

"He's gone," said Jess. "You got him."

Vi studied the gateway pillars, the empty space on the platform where the void had formed. "Where did you send him?"

"I don't know," said Elliot, "but it's unlikely to be improved for his presence."

Aftermath

The storm had blown itself out an hour ago, leaving behind sporadic spatters of rain and a pitch-black night. The temperature outside had dropped precipitously but the manor house was centrally heated and comfortably warm.

Jess sat nursing a coffee in the conference centre's food hall. In his student days Mark had worked in a cafe and operating the coffee machine behind the bar had proved no challenge. Now he sat across the table from Jess in uncomfortable silence, broken only when he rose to refill their cups.

The hall was cavernous and lonely and Jess and Mark sat in stillness. Elliot had hastened off to his liberated family after seeing his guests into the manor, and Vi had reunited with Aran and then taken her leave to look after other business. "Loose ends," she had said. So Jess and Mark were left alone to occupy themselves.

A tolerance for silence wasn't Mark's strongest attribute. Speaking slowly and cautiously, he broke it. "Back there, when you thought that I was going to be sucked through the... the portal, whatever it was. You sounded like you cared."

Jess blinked, her thoughts interrupted. "I want you out of my life." Unconsciously she brought one hand up to rub at the faded bruise on her temple. "I don't want you dead."

"Well, that's progress, I guess."

"No offense. I'll always care about you. I just... don't want to be around you."

"So what happens now?" Mark was staring at her with the puppy-dog eyes that were his secret weapon, but they'd been married long enough that she was immune to their charm.

"Now? I don't know. Eventually, we'll get divorced, I guess."

"No rush," said Mark. "Plenty of time to make up your mind. I meant, though, what happens *now*? You and the girl? Are you done?"

Jess shook her head. Her decision had been made for some time, even if she hadn't admitted it yet. "I don't know."

Real life beckoned to her — and it repelled her. The way forward seemed beset by insurmountable obstacles. Her return to life would require negotiations with the police — to prove she wasn't dead, that she hadn't been responsible for the attack on Bruce and Dot, that the carnage in the hotel in Melbourne hadn't been her fault. Oh god — they probably had camera footage. She tried to think, unsuccessfully, whether there had been cameras on the ceiling in the hallway where she had shot the man running at her. Then there was the man she'd pushed out the window. She didn't have a clue how she would even begin trying to explain all this to the police, but that was a hurdle she would need to get over before she could reclaim her car, her belongings, her life.

And once that was all done — if it ever could be — the real work of rebuilding her life would start. Moving back to Perth. Facing her parents. Finding a new job, making new friends... Once upon a time, she might have found all this an energising challenge, but right now it seemed far too hard, and somehow as alien as a distant planet.

Vi still needed her. What Utara had said was true enough: Vi and Aran couldn't live in this world without assistance. Elliot couldn't be trusted, might not even want to become the children's guardian. "I don't know," she said again. "I can't leave until I'm sure she's going to be looked after."

"Elliot will take care of her," Mark said. "God knows he has the money."

"He also has a life. He might have plans of his own, you know."

"And you don't? You have a life too."

She couldn't meet his eyes. "Right now, I'm in between lives."

"Well, I'm not," said Mark. "*I* still have a job, responsibilities. A mortgage. I'm going home."

"I'll keep paying my share," Jess said. "In case you were worried."

"Yeah, right. You just chucked in your job."

"I'll get another one. *My* problem, not yours." *Paying the mortgage,* she didn't tell him, *is only the start of my problems.*

II

They spent the flight north in comfortable conversation. They talked of childhood dreams and adolescent plans, of family and duty, of their work. Jeff told her of his career plans, his visions of seniority and his commitment to country policing. Adele spoke about her unsatisfying scientific career, her family issues, her move into teaching and the new, gentle pleasure of guiding students to an understanding of the world around them. They spoke of relationships and expectations and the newfound companionship that was forming between them. They steadfastly avoided talking about the one question that needed answering.

It was only in the airport lobby, waiting to collect their luggage from the conveyor belt, that Adele broached the subject.

"So we're here," she said. "Now what?"

Jeff shrugged, checking the locks on his suitcase for signs of tampering. "Now, I guess, I'm going to call on Brisbane HQ."

"You're just going to walk in and ask," Adele said. "You do realise that this investigation is off the books."

"I know that," he responded. "But they don't. Look, we're not going to get anywhere without more information. I'll duck in, get guest access to their databases and find out what we need. If someone's reported the car, that information will be easy to find. It's nine at night; by the time they're able to reach anyone in Port Augusta we'll be long gone."

"What if nobody's reported the car?"

He shrugged. "Let's cross that bridge when we get to it. I have a few ideas. First things first, let's find a hotel and get a couple of rooms."

"A couple of rooms?"

He almost dropped his suitcase. He shot her a sidelong glance. "You had something else in mind?"

"I had a few ideas," she said, and smiled at the goofy grin that spread across Jeff's face.

Jeff's grin lasted all of twenty seconds as Adele hefted her own suitcase and fell in beside him. At this time of night the airport was emptying, the wide terminal making its transition to an empty expanse of concrete and glass. To their left stood a lonely chauffeur, holding up a printed sign, and Jeff's smile fell away as he came close enough to read his own name on it. His hand tightened on Adele's arm, as he directed her attention. "Looks like we're expected," he said quietly.

The chauffeur had seen them and was lowering the sign, and Jeff turned their path to bring them to the man, but there were others aiming for them now: two men in rumpled cream suits marching toward them. Jeff came to a halt and held Adele back, waiting for the men to come to them.

"Good evening, officer Lang," said the first man as he came near. "Doctor Ferguson."

"Good evening," Jeff answered. "And you are?"

"My name's Burgess," the man said, without offering a first name. "My colleague is Mr Williams. Thank you for coming."

"We couldn't very well turn down your invitation. It was... intriguing."

"If you'll come with us, our cars are outside. Don't worry, you're not in trouble," Burgess added. "Quite the opposite, in fact."

"What if we don't want to come with you?" Adele's voice was cool but Jeff fancied he could hear the fear underneath.

It was Williams who answered. "That's up to you," he said. "We're not here to arrest you. If you don't choose to come with us, we'll never bother you again, but you'll never find out what we're offering you, and I promise you'll never find what you came here looking for."

"You've come this far," added Burgess. "You're here because of a dress and a dust mite. We promise, what we have is much more exciting."

Bemused and off balance, Jeff let himself be steered towards the glass doors. Outside, parked in the loading zone, stood two dark cars, nondescript and sleek and screaming *government vehicle* to onlookers. Burgess held the door open for him and placed his suitcases gently into the boot, and it was only as the man was climbing into the seat beside him that he realised Adele had been taken to the other car. He considered making a scene, but it was way too late for that. *In for a penny, in for a pound.*

"Who are you people?" Jeff asked as the car smoothly powered away from the terminal. "Federal police? Military police? CIA?"

"None of the above," said Burgess. "You won't have heard of us. We keep a low profile. And we rarely spirit people off the street."

"I'm a sworn police officer," Jeff said. "If I become aware of a crime, I'm obligated..."

"We're international," Burgess interrupted. "Operating at the highest level of discretion. Obviously, you have to do what you feel is right, but let me show you our authorisation first."

"I'll look at it," Jeff said. "So why did you go to so much trouble to bring us here? I suppose it was you guys who put the tickets in my wagon?"

"It was," said Burgess. "We brought you here to make you an offer. There's something you might be able to help us with."

Jeff blinked. "Why me? There must be a hundred officers right here in

Brisbane with better skills and more experience."

"True enough. But none of them know anything about the Yallara roadhouse robbery. You're already involved, and for what we have in mind, that's important."

"Doctor Ferguson isn't a police officer. She's been helping me in a scientific capacity, that's all."

Burgess raised an eyebrow, half seen in the darkened interior of the car. "We know all about Doctor Ferguson. We don't have a local microbiologist. It's recently come to our attention that we might need one. Don't worry, we're not asking her to do police work and we're not asking you to do science."

"And if we say no?"

Burgess sighed. "We're not the Gestapo. Like any other job offer, if you turn us down you go your own way, no questions asked, no regrets."

Jeff stared out the window at the streets of Brisbane passing by. Out there it was Friday night, and people were strolling, laughing and completely oblivious to a world that included shadowy government agencies and shadier propositions.

"So," Jeff said after a moment, "are you going to tell me about this policing job that's so important that only I can do it? First question, I guess: is it going to be dangerous?"

Burgess smiled, his teeth shining in the dark of the car. "Oh, absolutely," he said.

III

The ceremony was a sombre affair, with celebration thin on the ground. The celebrants and guests were significantly outnumbered by the soldiers on guard around the perimeter and the sweating television crews covering the event. Harke was making very sure that the footage was being streamed live over the datanet. There could be no doubts about this. The Empress of Zama was marrying a commoner. This was setting a new precedent.

By convention, noble marriages were held in the grand cathedral that still stood in the centre of Capital Island. The religion had ceased practice centuries earlier, but the building was still used for some formal ceremonies; the rest of the time it was a tourist attraction and entertainment venue. It had survived the shelling of the city, five of the six stained-glass windows with their depictions of the Six Holy Fathers intact.

Emperor Harke stood before the High Altar in his new formal robes. He'd designed them himself, a combination of the ostentatious pomp of the Lords with a more practical, everyday touch. The robes fell from his shoulders and collected into baggy trousers rather than swirling around his ankles, the cape was shortened to not impede movement, and he'd done away with the flared collar and the winged shoulders entirely. In his new regime, he was unambiguously in charge, but it was important to him that he show that he was of the people. *Anyone* could aspire to his place. In the fullness of time, obviously. Aspirations were fine, but not while he was in the chair.

The Empress was in full finery. The public would expect it. Her flowing white dress billowed behind her as she walked down the aisle towards him, supported at her elbow by a handmaiden. For a moment Harke regretted the mistreatment she had required; most of the signs of her physical depredations were hidden safely away under the layers of cloth, but her unsteady gait and her wandering eyes betrayed her infirmity.

Then she was at his side and he took her arm firmly in his own. Close to, her eyes were unfocused and her lips slack. Her stretches of alertness were becoming rarer, and this was not one of her good days. He glanced, concerned, across the altar to where Joteun stood. *Will she remember the words?* The heavyset man nodded slightly in reassurance, but Harke wasn't going to rest easily until this was done. For the first time he wondered if a live broadcast might not have been a bad idea.

Lord Fenwyth was the celebrant. The old man had put up very little fight upon his capture. Harke had not had the heart to strip him of his title; enough that the man no longer had any official role or status. Besides, it was useful to be able to occasionally trundle him out to officiate at meaningless ceremonial occasions, at least until Harke could get around to appointing another Archivist.

His forbearance did not stretch so far as to allow Fenwyth to retain his formal robes. Now he was wearing a grey jumpsuit suitable to any trades worker. Without the bulk of his silks and the ostentation of cape and wings, the old man's age was clear; his head rested atop a scrawny neck, giving him the appearance of an elderly turtle, and his hands shook as they lowered the ribbon of unity over the loving couple's wrists.

Harke barely paid attention as he repeated the oaths of marriage after the Archivist, his mind wandering. "I take this woman to hold to my heart, as long as we live," he said, and took solace in the knowledge that this wasn't likely to bind him for very long. Jede had been a strong, still relatively young Empress when she gave up the Crown, so she might survive it for a while, but according to the records and his own physicians she was unlikely to make it much past a year. Still, a year would be sufficient. He would require less time than that to secure his own legitimacy as Emperor.

When it came time for Jede's contribution to the service there was a fraught moment, her lips moving soundlessly as the cathedral stood in silence, waiting for her oaths; but then the moment passed and she was speaking the words as she had been taught, as they had been drilled into her mercilessly for days, and while her voice mumbled and her words slurred, they were clear enough.

Then it was done. With a thumb seal from Fenwyth to complete the records, the marriage was official under law. Harke shot a glance at Joteun. They'd planned this moment, rehearsed for it. While the cameras still rolled, there was still one unavoidable risk. By rights, an Empress marrying a commoner should immediately abdicate, and that was just the kind of trick that Jede might try to pull. Joteun was signalling to the media that it was over, that they should cease their broadcasts; guards, looking uncomfortable in formal robes, were hastening forward to take charge of Jede and bundle her out of the building. Harke held his breath as his new wife looked about herself in sudden confusion and fear; threatened by the rapid movement she seemed on the verge of bolting for cover, but Harke laid a steady hand on her forearm and she settled. She put her other hand over his, clinging on like a little girl to her father, and Harke allowed his smile of relief free reign.

That was the picture that would accompany the story for the next week: Consort Harke smiling beatifically as Empress Jede clung lovingly to his arm.

There was still a long road ahead. He had won the Capitol by force of arms and violence, but what he had accomplished here today was the first step to winning the people, and he could tell as he stood arm in arm with his new wife that the process had begun, as around him the cathedral broke into spontaneous applause and cheers. And for the first time, he felt like an Emperor.

IV

"You're not going to let me kill them," Aran said.

He hadn't intended it as a question but the Empress seemed to take it as such. "Hasn't there been enough killing already?"

In the corner of the room the subjects of their discussion sat waiting. No doubt they were paying avid attention despite the bags over their heads. Illen had come around as they were dragging him back to the manor house, but he had not put up a fight as they seated him beside their other captive. He and Jad made a fine pair, trussed and bagged.

It would be safest to take care of them and throw their bodies in with the rest. It was going to be a busy night. Aesk and the rest of his men would need to be collected and disposed of as well. It wouldn't do to leave corpses lying in the open in broad daylight. But corpses were easier than prisoners.

"I don't trust them," Aran insisted.

The Empress sighed. "I said nothing about trust. You're the Captain of the Imperial Guard. Prisoners are your responsibility. I would prefer you not to kill them, but the choice is yours."

Which was no choice at all when her wishes were so clear. She already had a low opinion of him, defying her would not help. The prisoners would live. Unless, or until, they did something to force his hand.

Jad in particular concerned him. The young man had no respect, and Aran's performance during their duel wouldn't improve matters. It might be best all-round if Jad was killed while trying to escape. All it would take would be a well-judged lapse in his attention for the rebel to make the attempt... a dishonourable thought, and one that Aran would have to give due consideration.

"They're trapped here with us now," the Empress continued. "I don't think they'll give us any more trouble."

Two captives to watch and no prison to put them in. *Three* enemies, when you counted Jarem. The rest of their enemies dead or subdued. He should feel proud. Instead he was unsettled.

Gabe's voice in his head: *Never take someone else's word for it. Always see a body. Check it yourself if you can.* Sensible advice that he had never heard from his trainers.

The Empress assured him that the Utara was dead and gone, but Aran could still feel his presence. Without seeing him fall, without seeing a body, he suspected that he would always carry a distant suspicion that Utara would leap from the shadows at any moment.

Worse, that Rigge had disappeared into the night. The man wasn't likely to go far. He could be out there in the darkness even now, plotting any kind of mischief.

He wasn't about to voice his concerns aloud. "We can lock them up somewhere," he said. "We don't need the technician either. The *dahla* will help us."

"Let's wait and see what he has to say," the Empress answered.

Silence hung in the air after this, as Aran paused, waiting for... what? What was he expecting? Praise? Respect?

He didn't need reassurance; he wasn't looking for respect. All he really wanted now was approval. All he'd *ever* wanted, in truth. His father, with advice offered freely and endlessly; Drillmaster Warren, battle-hardened, drilling the lessons into the young man's head until he could hear that gruff voice in the midst of battle.

Not once had either of them told him he had done well, and now the voices were silent.

What good is victory without an audience?

"I want to go home," Aran said.

"We will," said the Empress. "Soon."

V

The night was close to pitch black, a solid cover of cloud shrouding the moon and stars, as Jess walked to clear her thoughts. After the drenching earlier the night had turned to crystal and she dressed warmly before stepping outside the manor. She had a moment of doubt as she fished her last pullover out of her backpack. The last remnant of her old life, the rest abandoned in the desert with her car. Hard to imagine that was less than a week ago, but she hadn't been preparing for a long time on the road.

Her breath frosted as she walked, circling the big building. The chill air was less oppressive than her future.

If she walked into a local Brisbane police station tomorrow: first, a short-lived relief. People solicitous of her needs and comfort. That wouldn't last. Soon the questions would start, and they would never end. Why was she in the roadhouse that day? Why help the children escape? Her heedless use of credit cards would place her in Port Augusta; it wouldn't take too much of a leap to identify the bus they had travelled on. Tracing her tickets would lead back to her mother.

Or they might skip all the preliminaries, go straight to the good stuff. How would she explain her face on security cameras in Melbourne, or in the hotel? Did they have her fingerprints on door handles, on her coffee cup? On the skin of the man she had thrown out the window? Who was Professor Gareth Reed, exactly, and what had they wanted with him?

The trail would lead them to Jacob Elliot. It would destroy his life, the lives of his family — his wife and children, whom Jess had not met. If they started investigating Elliot, would they also find records of other refugees from Zama?

There was no way out. No way to clear her name. No story she could concoct that would satisfy them. Not until they had Vi and Aran in hand. Not until they unravelled the entire complicated mess. Who knew how many lives that would destroy?

She was on the edge of a precipice, a house of cards that could all come crashing down. Had Vi considered all of this? Had Elliot?

They couldn't afford to let her go.

That was a sobering thought. If it had not occurred to them yet, it surely would soon. She didn't think Vi would consider hurting her, but she couldn't say the same for Elliot. He had a lot at stake: his riches, his family, his freedom. How far would he go to protect himself?

She considered walking away into the night, but they'd flown over miles of open fields to get here. Even if she were able to keep a straight line towards Brisbane, it would take days of marching, and if Elliot came looking he would catch her for sure. No, she needed a vehicle. Perhaps — the Jeeps parked on the first lower level of HERS. She could bide her time, wait for an opportunity.

She had walked all the way around the building now, and as her steps led her back towards the manor's front doors, a small figure crossed the gravel to meet her. Jess paused under the rearing hedge horseman to wait for her. Even the girl's walk had changed; her stance was somehow indefinably stronger than it had been when they first met.

"It's cold out here," said Vi as she approached. "Are you alright?"

Jess nodded at the girl. "Are you?" The Empress was bundled into a thick, padded raincoat that gave her the stature of a sumo wrestler.

Vi ignored the question. "Utara and his men are gone," she said instead. "Aran and I can take care of the rest. Jad and Illen won't cause us any trouble."

"Jad?"

"One of Utara's men," she explained. "He's not happy but he's not a fool. For the moment, Jarem's decided he's on our side as well."

"For the moment."

"With Jarem, who knows how long that will last. We'll watch him."

"Don't forget the gateway," Jess said.

"Yes, the gateway. I don't want to... there's a saying. Something about hatching?"

It took a moment. "Don't count your chickens before they hatch."

"Yes, that. Until we are sure that we can use it safely, we are trapped here. But Jarem will be helpful. His knowledge is irreplaceable."

"*That's* convenient," said Jess, her voice only mildly cynical.

"A good outcome. I wanted to thank you for your help. And to say that it's time I kept my promise. You don't have to stay."

Jess picked her next words carefully. "It might not be as simple as that. The police will be looking for me. The moment I pop my head up, there will be questions. Questions I won't be able to answer."

"I know," Vi replied. "But I made you a promise. When they ask you questions, tell them the truth."

"They'll come looking for you."

"Then that will be my problem."

Jess hesitated. "So what are you going to do now?"

"That depends on what the *dahla* can offer," the Empress replied. "Perhaps we really can go home to Zama. Much will depend on the status of the Gateway."

In the time they'd been standing, Jess had begun shivering. "Let's get inside. It's freezing out here."

VI

They met Jacob Elliot at the doorway as they re-entered the building, the older man materialising out of the darkness without warning. He gestured them inside as if chivalry were still alive.

"Are your family well?" Vi asked him.

He turned from fastening the front doors closed and locking out the chill. "They're shaken. They don't know what's going on and I didn't know what to tell them. I'll have a lot of explaining to do. But they're okay now. Your boy rescued them." He paused before continuing. "Farrow says she's never seen anybody so fast. Or so dangerous."

"It's a good thing he's on our side, then," Jess said, rubbing her arms vigorously.

The heating was on and the house manor was comfortably warm; Vi unfastened the parka she'd borrowed. She nodded at Jess but didn't let herself be diverted. "Where is Farrow now?"

"She's keeping my wife company," Elliot said. "After what they've been through I didn't want to leave them alone. But there's still some cleaning up to do. I'm not expecting staff here until Monday but I wouldn't want one of my employees to come in over the weekend to find corpses on the lawn."

Vi nodded. "That would lead to inconvenient questions."

"If Aran is up to a bit more work tonight, we'll look after things."

"We have already talked. He is at your disposal."

Elliot tilted his head at her. "So... your Highness. What do you require of me?"

Jess stared at the man with narrowed eyes, but Vi couldn't detect any irony in the man's voice. "I'm hoping to accept your offer. I want to go home to Zama."

The *dahla*'s eyes shied away from hers. "The Gateway works. But I don't know where it opens. It might take some time before we can use it safely to get you back to Zama."

"Jarem said a day," Vi pointed out. "He has data from the Gate on Zama."

"He overestimates his abilities. It's going to take some time."

She shrugged in the way she'd seen him do it. It felt strange on her shoulders but seemed to get the message across. "There are questions I must address before I can return. I doubt 'Emperor' Harke will send anybody else after me quickly. He'll wait to hear from Utara."

"I can set you up with somewhere to live," Elliot said. "For a short while, at least. I'd offer you space here on site but I don't have anywhere people wouldn't see you."

"I'm grateful for any help."

"You're the Empress. More to the point, you saved my wife and children. Whatever you need, you'll have it."

"If we had not come here," Vi said mildly, "your family would never have been in danger."

"You didn't have a choice about coming here," Jess said sharply.

Elliot inclined his head. "But you did have a choice about saving my family. I won't forget that." He smiled at her. "Don't forget, I have all the money and resources we could need. I'm happy to give you anything you ask for."

"What I would really like," she said, "is access to your records."

"My records? For what purpose?"

"You told us that you have helped settle hundreds of exiles from Zama," Vi said. "It is my intention to find them and ask them how, and why, they were sent."

"They might not be safe to meet. If your mother exiled them."

"I do not believe she did." *I would have known. Jede would have told me.* "I wish to know who did send them. Perhaps an imperial pardon might help sway their opinion."

"I can't help you directly. I'm watched too closely. But you'll have resources, somewhere to live, access to my records. Perhaps, Farrow..."

The future stretched in front of her. With Elliot helping, finally she could stop running. Vi smiled. "I recommend not. Best to limit the number of people who know about me."

"I'll stay," said Jess. "I already know you. I'll stay, for a while at least. Just until things settle."

The promise gave her a flush of pleasure, and not just because she needed Jess's help. "We would not have made it without you."

Jess returned a smile warmer than it had any right to be. It gave Vi pause. Aran was her dutiful subordinate; Elliot owed her gratitude. But Jess was the closest thing she had to a friend.

For the first time in what felt like forever, they were safe. Plenty of loose ends, but they had time to tie them. She had support and a mission. A mystery to keep her involved while Elliot and Jarem worked on the Gateway.

There were no guarantees. A long road ahead, and even if they did manage to return home, there was a world to win back; a usurper in command and an army at his fingers. But she was the Empress. She had led armies into battle, had fought against vicious enemies in single combat, and she had prevailed against far greater odds.

She didn't know how or when, but of one thing she was certain. She was going home, and she wasn't going alone.

THE END

ABOUT THE AUTHOR

Dan Payne

Dan Payne has qualifications in science, communications and information management. He has worked as a science communicator, a web programmer, a market research engineer and a librarian. Currently he works in software engineering and support. He writes works of magic realism in the genres of science fiction and fantasy with a distinctly Australian edge.

Dan lives in eastern Australia with his daughter, who is in charge, his wife, who is definitely in charge, and his two cats, who think they are in charge.

When he's not writing, Dan enjoys performing and composing music on piano and Hammond organ, oil painting and playing tennis.

If you have enjoyed *The Crystal Crown*, please leave a review on Amazon or wherever you purchased this book.

Look out for **Army of Exiles: War of the Exiles Book 2**. Coming in 2024.

danpayne.com.au

Dan blogs at:

ozfenric.wordpress.com (Politics / Philosophy)
tfaof.wordpress.com (Short fiction, craft of writing)

www.ingramcontent.com/pod-product-compliance
Lightning Source LLC
Chambersburg PA
CBHW020251120726
47904CB00001B/163